ONE PARIS SUMMER

Denise Grover Swank

BLINK

BLINK

One Paris Summer
Copyright © 2016 by Denise Grover Swank

This title is also available as a Blink ebook. Visit www.zondervan.com/ebooks.

Requests for information should be addressed to:
Blink, 3900 *Sparks Drive SE, Grand Rapids, Michigan* 49546

ISBN 978-0-310-75516-6

Any Internet addresses (websites, blogs, etc.) and telephone numbers in this book are offered as a resource. They are not intended in any way to be or imply an endorsement by the publisher, nor does the publisher vouch for the content of these sites and numbers for the life of this book.

This book is a work of fiction. Any character resemblances to persons living or dead are coincidental.

Cover design: *Brand Navigation*
Interior design: *Denise Froehlich*
Interior illustration: © *PaNaStudio/www.istock.com*

Printed in the United States of America

16 17 18 19 20 21 /DCI/ 20 19 18 17 16 15 14 13 12 11 10 9 8 7 6 5 4 3 2 1

*To my daughter Julia—her
obsession with Paris inspired Sophie
and Mathieu's story.*

CHAPTER *One*

"WE ARE NOW making our final descent into Charles de Gaulle. Please make sure your seat belts are fastened, your seat is in an upright position, and tray tables are stowed away."

Paris, France.

My stomach twisted into knots. This city was one of the most desirable vacation spots in the world, but I didn't want to be here.

Sighing, I shook my sleeping brother. "Eric. Wake up."

He lifted his eye mask and took out an earplug, his eyes barely open slits. "Have we landed?"

"Not yet."

"Then leave me alone."

I had no idea how he could still be sleeping. I was so freaked out, I hadn't slept at all.

We were about to see our father for the first time in ten months.

But Eric could sleep through anything. Fireworks. Mom's yelling. Alarm clocks. Mom claimed it was because he was a seventeen-year-old guy. I decided it was because he was lazy. The fact that he had excellent grades was pure luck and charm.

I leaned over Eric and lifted the window shade, taking in the sight below the plane. Densely packed, grungy-looking buildings covered the landscape.

He groaned and blindly shoved my arm from the window. "I swear, Sophie . . ." But rather than finish the sentence, he turned away from me.

"You have to put your seat up, Eric. The flight attendant is coming down the aisle."

He turned back around and slid his mask to the top of his head. "What's she gonna do? Arrest me?"

He shot me a sardonic grin. My brother was such an idiot. But he was older than me by fifteen months and twice as popular at our private high school. Girls found his idiocy charming. I had no idea why.

"They *might* arrest you. You hear about people being taken off planes all the time."

He snorted. "Good thing they're taking me off the plane in the city I want to be in."

"You don't want to be here any more than I do."

His eyebrows lifted. "Good point. Maybe if I put up enough of a fight, they'll send me back to the good ol' USA and you can spend eight weeks in Paris with Dad on your own."

Panic rose in my chest. "You wouldn't."

His lips twisted in disgust. "I couldn't get so lucky. Dad would probably bribe some official to make me stay." But he still hadn't raised his seat.

The flight attendant was two rows ahead, gathering trash. "Eric."

"*Relax*, Sophie. It's no wonder you don't have a boyfriend. You're too uptight."

"Some of us like to follow the rules."

"No kidding, Soph. Live a little."

The flight attendant stopped next to our row and looked at Eric's reclined seat. "Sir, would you please return your seat to the upright position?"

"Of course," he said, flashing her his flashy smile. "Be happy to."

"*Merci.*"

She moved past us, and a smug grin lit up his face. "See, Chicken Little. The sky didn't fall on your head."

"Shut up." My tone was harsher than intended. "I can't believe Mom trusted you enough to send us alone to Paris together."

"She couldn't exactly ship us in a box from Charleston, could she?"

I couldn't believe she was sending us at all.

"Be a good girl or Dad might not let you be in his wedding."

"Good." I crossed my arms and flopped back in my seat. "I have no *intention* of being in his wedding."

"You may not have a choice." He didn't sound happy about this, and I was sure it had more to do with concern for his own fate.

"He can make me give up my summer—the one summer I actually had plans—but he can*not* make me be in his wedding." I shuddered. I couldn't even imagine my father with another woman.

"*Please.* I had to quit my job at the golf course. My girlfriend broke up with me because she didn't want to hang out alone all summer. I gave up a whole lot more than you did."

That was debatable. My piano teacher had set up lessons for me to take with a local college professor to prepare for a scholarship competition in the fall. Now I worried I wouldn't be ready. The colleges I wanted to go to were expensive. "At least Dane is coming on Sunday."

A mere six days ago, Dad had called to drop his double bombshell—one, he was marrying a woman he barely knew, and two, he insisted we come to the wedding and spend the entire summer with him, his new wife, and her daughter. No discussion. No concern about whether his plans fit into our lives, only a sheepish *I'm sorry.*

Eric had been even more vocal in his refusal, but Mom had surprised us by insisting we didn't have a choice. In fact, she seemed downright happy about Dad's remarriage, but then she'd handled his departure better than any of us. In an effort to appease us, she'd talked Dad into letting each of us have a friend stay for a few weeks. Eric's friend first, then mine.

I'd considered losing my passport, but my friend Jenna—who was supposed to come after Eric's friend Dane—had a conniption. "That's just so wrong," she'd said as she sat on my bed, painting my toenails. "Who turns down Paris?"

"I'm not rejecting the entire city of Paris. Only my father."

"So tolerate your father and enjoy Paris! Surely there's something you want to do there."

I thought for a moment. "I want to see the Eiffel Tower. I hope I'm not too scared to go up."

She nudged my shoulder with hers. "Maybe you can get Dane to take you up. Just think, you'll get almost four entire weeks with Dane Wallace." She gave me a goofy look. "You and Dane. In Paris. Alone." Dane got to stay longer because Jenna couldn't come until the end of July. Not that I was complaining *too* much. I'd been lucky because Dane hadn't been Eric's first choice. His best friend, Dylan, couldn't afford to leave his job all summer.

I rolled my eyes. "We won't be alone. Remember *Eric*, aka the reason for Dane being there? And don't forget my new stepsister, Camille." Only her name wasn't pronounced the normal way. Dad said it *Cam-ee*.

"Whatever." She shifted on my bed. "Look. You've crushed on the guy for over two years. This is your chance. It's destiny."

I gave her a serious look. "You mean it's *your* destiny to come to Paris the day after Dane leaves . . . aka the reason *you're* pushing this whole thing."

"Soph! It's a trip to Paris!"

In the end it didn't matter what I wanted. My mother was so adamant, she very well might have shipped us in boxes.

The plane's nose dipped forward, and I gripped the armrests, sucking in a breath.

"The plane isn't crashing, you idiot," Eric groaned. "It's called landing."

"I know," I said through gritted teeth. Like it was natural for a hulking metal object to coast thousands of feet into the air and back down. Forcing my grip to loosen, I closed my eyes and imagined I was sitting at my piano at home, my hands poised over the cool, smooth keys. My fingers started to involuntarily play the B-flat minor scale.

I opened my eyes when I felt the wheels touch down on the runway. Eric was giving me his trademark look of disgust. "I'm not sure if you noticed, but that's an armrest. Not a piano."

"It calms me down. Would you rather I freak out?"

His expression suggested that neither was his preferred option.

The prospect of eight weeks of separation from my piano almost freaked me out more than the fact that my father was getting remarried. While I would have loved to go to Julliard, my real dream was to study in Europe. No matter where I studied, scholarships were essential. Mom was a nurse raising two kids on her own now. And although my father's job *sounded* fancy—architectural restorationist—he didn't make much money. His career had also required us to move around a lot, but Dad had assured us we could finally grow roots in Charleston, where we'd moved in my sixth-grade year. There were plenty of old buildings there to keep him busy until we graduated.

It had been a great plan. At least until last August.

Eric gave me a look of mock pity. "You really think Dad's going to come through on his promise to get you a piano in his apartment?" He shook his head. "Then you probably believe Mom wanted us to come to France because she wants us to get reacquainted with dear ol' Dad."

My mouth dropped open, but nothing came out. What was he talking about?

He leaned closer, his eyes narrowing with contempt. "Grow up, Soph. Mom wants to go to the beach with her new boyfriend in July. Why do you think she wanted us to come to Paris so bad?" He paused, his silence daring me to answer. "We're too old for a babysitter, but what kind of mother would she be if she left two teenagers alone for a week? Dad only wanted us for a few weeks, but *she* insisted on the entire summer so she could spend more time with her boyfriend guilt-free."

"What?" I asked in disbelief. "No."

He shrugged. "Believe what you want."

I stared at him for several seconds before deciding he was full of crap. "Why do you always have to be such a jerk?"

Leave it to my brother to make a difficult situation even worse.

CHAPTER *Two*

I WAS IN no hurry to get off the plane, but Eric shoved me into the aisle. I was exhausted and unprepared for the long walk to the immigration lines.

Mom had warned us we'd have to talk to a customs agent before we could leave the airport. Since I was the one who had filled out the immigration card for our family, I handed it to the bored-looking man behind the counter, along with our passports. He riffled through the blank pages of our booklets, then examined the front page with all my information. "What is the purpose of your visit?" he asked, still studying the book.

"Uh . . . we're seeing our dad."

"Is he a French citizen?"

I shot a glance toward Eric, who rolled his eyes, apparently thinking I didn't know the answer to the question. "No. He's American."

"Where will you be staying?"

"At his apartment."

"How long will you be staying in Paris?"

"Too long," I grumbled. When he looked up at me with a blank expression, I said, "Eight weeks."

After a few more questions, he stamped a page in the middle of our passport books and handed them back. "Welcome to France."

He might as well have said *Welcome to your summer of hell.*

Eric took over and led the way to baggage claim. After instructing me to stay with the carry-on bags like it was an important job, he proceeded to wrestle our three massive suitcases off the carousel.

"I'm not a kindergartner, Eric," I said in a dry tone.

He scowled. "I never said you were, *Sophie*." He pulled the second bag off the conveyor belt and shoved it toward me. "You wanna trade places?"

I caught it as it rolled to my side but didn't say anything, tired of keeping up with him. He gave me an odd look, as though confused by my lack of reply, then grabbed the last of the suitcases.

We rolled our bags toward the exit in silence. Irritation rolled off Eric in waves. That, along with our bickering, made me realize he was nervous about seeing Dad too.

I wanted to turn around and beg my way back onto the plane for the return flight to New York. I'd never get away with it, which meant I had no choice, and that made me angrier than anything. It wasn't my fault our father had run off and left us. Why should we have to change our lives to fit *his* schedule?

As I followed Eric, I took several deep breaths in a feeble attempt to keep myself together. It didn't help that I was working on approximately two hours of sleep. I figured we had a several-minute walk, enough time for me to calm down, so I wasn't prepared to turn a corner and find a crowd of people waiting behind a metal railing, many of them holding signs scrawled with passenger names. My eyes were drawn to the left, and I found him, peering over the head of a woman in front of him.

Dad.

The joy I felt at the sight of him caught me off guard, but it quickly slipped away, leaving fear in its wake. I wasn't ready for this.

"Eric! Sophie!" he called.

Eric looked over his shoulder, making sure I was still behind him, then made a beeline for our father.

Dad closed the distance and engulfed Eric in his arms, holding him for longer than I would have expected. I watched them, realizing with sadness that Eric was now nearly as tall as our father. Then my gaze shifted to the black-haired woman next to them, who was studying me with open curiosity. Her scrutiny made me uncomfortable, but I felt compelled to return it.

She wore a royal blue skirt and a silky cream blouse. I wasn't a shoe expert, but the cream leather pumps on her feet looked like they had cost a fortune. Her makeup was perfect, and her hair hung in loose curls that brushed her shoulders. But it was her face that captivated me the most. Her dark chocolate eyes were soft and kind, and her mouth tipped up into a warm smile.

I still stood on the secured side of the imaginary line, my feet anchored so that I blocked the traffic flow behind me. A middle-aged man bumped into my shoulder and broke loose into an angry tirade I didn't understand, but I barely noticed. My breath was stuck in my chest.

I couldn't move.

"William," the woman next to my father murmured in a musical accent.

Dad set loose my embarrassed-looking brother and turned his attention to me, eyeing me as though I were a skittish wild animal. "Sophie."

Less than a year had passed, but he looked older. New wrinkles were etched around his eyes and there was gray scattered throughout his dark hair, but his eyes had changed the most. I always remembered them filled with laugher and love; now they held only profound sadness.

I remained frozen, waiting on him. He was the one who had left *me*, and I'd waited ten months and six days for him to come back, growing angrier each day. Now I was facing him on unfamiliar turf. The unknowns of this trip scared me to death, and all I wanted was for my dad to tell me everything was going to be okay—though *he* was the one who had done this to me.

I wasn't about to make the first move.

Tears filled his eyes, although I was unsure why. Was it because I wasn't running to him like I used to every night when I was little, greeting him with a squeal of delight when he came home from work, smelling of sweat and marble dust? Or was it because I'd grown an inch taller and my hair was three inches longer, and he now realized everything he'd missed? Had it hurt him to miss the father-daughter dance at my school? Did he long for our Sunday night ice cream dates at Cold Stone? Or the spring nights we'd sit together on the back porch, watching thunderstorms roll in? He'd stolen nearly a year of our lives together and I couldn't forgive him for that, no matter how much my mother insisted I should.

But I loved him too. Still. In spite of all the pain he continued to cause me, and that pissed me off even more.

He took two steps toward me, crossing the line that separated my life from his, grabbing my arms and pulling me to him. I stiffened, then sank into his chest and fought the tears burning my eyes. My face pressed against his shirt and I breathed him in, taking in his changed scent. He had switched his usual musky shampoo for something lighter, and while I could still detect the crushed stone embedded in the fiber of his clothes, that was different too. And that was what broke loose my tears. His new smell. This man was no longer the Daddy I knew. He was gone from me forever.

"I've missed you, Sophie." He clung to me, whispering in my ear as he smoothed the hair on the back of my head. "I'm so sorry."

I could barely hear him through my sobs. He pulled me away from the crowd, still holding me close, and led me over to Eric and the black-haired woman. I cried for nearly a minute before I settled down, now humiliated because everyone was staring at me . . . and because I had shown my father more emotion than he deserved.

Eric stood to the side, grimacing with irritation. I'd probably embarrassed him for life, but I didn't miss the concerned lines around his mouth. When one of us was in trouble, we had the other's back.

The black-haired woman held a tissue in her hand, but I could tell she wasn't sure if she should offer it.

Eric took the tissue from her and held it out to me, searching my eyes for confirmation that I wasn't about to fall into additional pieces. God forbid I should cause any more of a scene at Charles De Gaulle airport. He already had enough fodder for his "What I Did over Summer Vacation" essay without his irrational sister adding any more drama.

I snatched the tissue from his hand and swiped at my face, hoping I hadn't smeared mascara everywhere.

Dad stood awkwardly at my side, as though unsure how to proceed. The woman gave him a pointed look, then her eyes darted to me and back to him.

He got the not-so-subtle cue and cleared his throat. "Sophie, Eric, I'd like you to meet my fiancée, Eva Mercier."

Eric stared at her for a moment, then blushed and held out his hand. *"Bonjour, Madame Mercier. Enchanté. Merci pour m'accueillir en ta maison."*

Traitor.

Her eyes widened in surprise as she smiled and shook his hand, breaking into a musical burst of French.

Eric laughed and answered in her language, stumbling over several words, but she chuckled, and then said in English, "Your French is quite good."

"Thanks. I'm hoping this summer will help me get an A in my AP French class next year."

"AP French?" Dad asked, clearly impressed.

Eva cleared her throat, a delicate sound, but it stopped my father in his tracks. A warm smile lit up her face. "I'd like to say hello to Sophie. We don't want her to feel left out."

Dad's face reddened, and he offered me an apologetic smile. "You're right. This is my beautiful Sophie."

I bristled. My father used to call me *my beautiful Sophie* all the time. He had no right to lay claim to me now. He'd relinquished that right the day he left.

Eva took a step toward me, and to my surprise she wrapped her arms around my shoulders and pulled me close. She gave me a tight squeeze and then leaned back, still holding my upper arms. "Sophie." My name sounded sophisticated in her accent. "You're just as lovely as your father said."

My tongue lay in the bottom of my mouth like a slug.

She kissed both of my cheeks and then dropped her hold. "I'm so happy you're here and so grateful to spend the summer with you."

"Thank you." I knew I should offer more—tell her I was excited to be here or I couldn't wait to get to know her, but I couldn't summon the energy to lie.

Eva seemed undeterred by my lack of enthusiasm. "Are you two hungry? Thirsty? You must be exhausted."

Eric glanced to me and then back at Eva before taking over as the Brooks siblings' spokesman. "We're fine. I don't know how much Sophie slept, but I had a long nap on the plane, so I'm good."

Eva gave us a motherly smile, full of tenderness, and something prickled in my heart. I wanted to hate this woman who was stealing my father from me. She was supposed to be the wicked stepmother from fairy tales. Of course, Dad hadn't married her yet, so maybe the welcoming act was just that—an act. She didn't want to give him a reason to back out of the wedding.

But even I doubted that possibility. Something about her seemed genuine.

"Why don't we head back to the apartment," she said in flawless English. "Your father and I have the morning off, so we'll get some lunch with you before we head off"—she paused, then added—"to work."

He was going to work? He hadn't seen us for nearly a year, and he was leaving us already?

He must have read my thoughts, because he grimaced as he took the handle of one of my suitcases. "I don't have enough vacation time built up yet, and we're in a critical phase of the restoration of one the gargoyles on the south side of the church. I just need to drop by for a few hours and then I'll be home."

Home? Home was four thousand miles away.

But if he sensed *that* sentiment, he ignored it. He and Eric led the way to the parking garage—both of them tugging a suitcase. I trailed behind with Eva. She was probably worried I would have another mental breakdown and try to run away.

"May I take your suitcase, Sophie?" she asked sweetly, giving me her full attention.

My grip tightened. "No thanks. I've got it."

I knew I was being a brat—but my entire life was in utter chaos, and the only thing I had control over was the stupid suitcase my mother had lent me for the trip. I hated the ugly brown-and-green print, which made my attachment to it even stranger, but it contained half of the personal belongings I'd packed for the next eight weeks.

As we walked into the parking garage, my father broke into a mini-lecture about the best way to overcome jet lag. He stopped at the back of a black sedan that was sleek and shiny and totally unlike anything my father had ever driven. He and Eric wrestled the luggage into the trunk. After he closed the lid, he seemed to notice my confusion. "It's Eva's brother's car. We don't need a car in the city."

My eyebrows lifted in surprise. He'd mentioned that he took the Metro to work, but it had never occurred to me that he didn't also have a car.

My father opened the back passenger door and ushered me in. I glanced up at him, but he was looking over the top of the car at Eva. I immediately slid into the backseat, smashing up against the lone suitcase that didn't fit in the trunk. My brother got in next to me and shut the door.

A few minutes later, Eva guided the car out of the parking garage and into the gray morning, all of us mired in silence. Eva was the first to come to her senses, and she started to ply us with questions about our flight, our schoolwork, and our friends. Our lives. Eric, the traitor, gave her detailed answers and added information in response to Dad's follow-up questions. He seemed suddenly accepting of our incarceration. My answers were short and concise, and despite how it probably looked, I *was* trying to be as polite as possible. It was hard being civil when my father kept staring at the woman he was marrying the next day like he couldn't wait for his wedding night. It made me want to barf. Once I got the nausea part under control, tears began to burn my eyes again.

One year ago, my father would have been sitting at our kitchen table, eating the scrambled eggs and bacon I'd made for him before he went to work. One year ago, I would have been laughing at his goofy jokes at the dinner table. One year ago, he brought me to Cold Stone because he knew Jenna and I were fighting over a boy we both liked. As we sat across from each other, enjoying our ice cream, he promised me he would always be there when I had a broken heart.

Liar.

And now he was staring at this woman—this stranger—and the look he gave her told me she was now his everything.

He'd replaced his family. He'd replaced me.

I blinked and forced myself to get control. Grow up, Eric had said. He was right. Parents got divorced and remarried all the time. And I got that. I did. But why did my dad have to leave me behind in the process? Why was it an all-or-nothing deal?

Eva drove down the Parisian highway, and I studied my surroundings, my heart growing heavier with each mile. The sky had turned a dark gray, making the clouds look heavy. The concrete buildings lining the road were gray too. Everything was dreary and depressing. Back home, I would fall into a deep funk when we had more than two days of clouds and rain. I needed sunshine and blue skies.

When I was little, my third-grade Sunday school teacher told us hell was full of fire and brimstone. I had no idea what brimstone was at the time, but I knew she couldn't be right. I raised my hand, and when she called on me, I said that if hell was a land of punishment, I didn't think it would be hot and full of fire. It would be a world without color and music. Without dancing and laughing. Without sunshine and flowers. My teacher, an elderly woman, chuckled and rubbed my head, announcing that I had an overactive imagination. But when I explained my theory to my father later that night, he pondered it for several seconds before a warm smile lit up his face.

"You know, Sophie, I dare say you're right," said the man who found happiness restoring the beauty of the past.

Now, as I opened my eyes and found him looking over his shoulder, staring at me with profound sadness in his eyes, I knew he was probably the one person who truly understood me.

Somehow that only made it worse.

CHAPTER *Three*

"HERE IT IS," Dad said as Eva pushed open the heavy wooden door to her apartment. "Home sweet home."

I didn't respond, not that I *could* respond after carrying my fifty-pound suitcase up three flights of stairs. Leaning against the handle, I sucked in deep breaths.

"Sophie," Dad said, shoving my other suitcase through the door as he stayed on the landing, "I told you I would get it."

While part of me had wanted to jump at the offer, another— louder—part had wanted to prove to him I didn't need him anymore.

Eva grabbed my suitcase and rolled it into the apartment. I followed her inside, Dad and Eric close behind.

I expected to walk into a living room, but instead we were in a long hallway with white walls, lots of molding, and multiple sets of doors. The walls were at least nine feet tall with more heavy white molding on the ceiling. The wood parquet floor looked freshly polished, but it was the purple upholstered bench against one wall that caught my eye. The deep plum velvet was framed by scrolling, painted white wood.

It was totally something I would have picked out.

But I didn't have time to dwell on it. Eva pushed open the second set of tall French doors on the right and I followed her into the living room. The walls were painted white like the hall. On the opposite side were two sets of large windows that overlooked the street below. On the wall to the left was a small fireplace with ornate, carved trim—all in white. A large mirror

23

with a gold gilt frame hung over the mantel. Two red sofas faced each other with a rustic-looking coffee table between them. Two upholstered chairs in cream with red flowers flanked the fireplace. A small ornately carved desk was in the corner.

I walked into the middle of the room, astounded. I had thought places like this only existed in magazines and on Pinterest.

"Feel free to look around," Eva said, smiling when she realized I was interested in the décor. "Consider this your home now."

Eric was checking out the flat screen TV in the corner and looked up at Dad. "An Xbox?"

I rolled my eyes. Leave it to him to get excited over a game system.

"Sophie, would you like to see your room?" Eva asked.

"Yeah."

I followed her back into the hallway and she pointed to an open door on the opposite wall. "This is the kitchen. The washer and dryer are in there as well."

White cabinets lined two of the walls, and there was a small refrigerator, stove, and dishwasher. A table with three chairs was pushed against the wall.

"There's food in the cabinets and refrigerator, and there's a small grocery store down the street," Eva said. "Of course, you're welcome to anything we have."

"Thank you," I mumbled.

She continued on down the hall and I followed her to another door on the left. "This is where Eric will sleep. And this is my room." She gave me a quick glance as she pointed to the door on the right. "And your father's, of course."

I sucked in a breath suddenly, remembering why I was here.

She waved to the last door on the left. "And this is your room."

I walked through the now open door to find two twin beds, both covered with white duvets and teal throw pillows. A large window framed by silky, matching drapes overlooked the street. I walked over and looked out, gasping at the sight of the Eiffel Tower off to the left, not a half mile away, looming gracefully over the buildings around it.

"You'll share this room with Camille," Eva said.

My eyes widened, and I turned around to face her.

"My daughter."

"Oh." So I would be sharing a room for the next two months with someone I hadn't even met and hardly knew anything about. Dad had told us little about Eva—let alone her daughter—over the last four months, but I'd refused to talk to him after the Paris call last week.

"She's a year older than you, seventeen." She smiled softly and picked up a framed photo from a bedside table, glancing at it before turning it around to show me. "She's at school taking her final exams. She'll be home around six."

The girl in the photo looked a lot like Eva, and the smile on her face made her look just as sweet. Maybe sharing a room with her wouldn't be so bad after all.

Dad appeared in the doorway with my suitcases. He set them against the wall and stared at me for several seconds before he turned to Eva. "We need to hurry if we want to eat lunch."

She nodded and murmured something in French. He answered and gave her a bright smile that stabbed me in the heart. She edged past him into the hallway, but he hesitated, looking like he wanted to say something. Finally his mouth tilted up in a soft smile. "I'm glad you're here, Sophie."

A lump filled my throat. I forced out, "So I'll be here for *your wedding?*"

His smile fell. "Look, Sophie, I know I haven't handled things well . . ."

I put a hand on my hip. "You *think*?"

"Being hostile isn't going to help."

"And what exactly *is* going to help? You ran off last August, and the only reason we're seeing you now is because it's suddenly convenient for *you*. You didn't even come home for Christmas!"

He cringed. "I wanted to."

"Don't. Just don't." I tried to swallow my grief. "You might think you've fooled us, but it's pretty obvious the only reason you invited us is to look good in front of your *new* family."

He took a step toward me. "It's not like that, Sophie," he said softly. "I promise."

"You *promise*," I spat out in disgust. "You promised a lot of things, Dad. How many have you broken this past year?" Christmas was just the first on a long list.

"*Sophie.*" His voice broke.

I shook my head. "We better go or you're going to be late going back to *work*. I'd hate to screw up your *priorities*."

He started to say something, but I brushed past him.

Eric and Eva were waiting by the front door. The guilty look on Eva's face told me she'd heard everything. And the way Eric refused to look me in the eye told me he'd heard too, and was embarrassed again, although I wasn't sure why. I was only repeating everything he'd already said at home.

As I walked toward them, something stopped me in my tracks. "Where's the piano?"

Dad was behind me and cleared his throat. "We haven't had a chance to get it yet, Soph. We'll get one in the next day or two. I promise."

I couldn't take any more broken promises.

We walked to a café down the street, tension thick between the four of us. The sky was even darker than before, and now it was sprinkling.

Dad grabbed a table inside, and we all sat in silence for several awkward moments before Eva started talking again, first in English, then in French with Eric. My father added to the conversation every so often, but I kept silent, watching the passersby through the windows.

After our food came, Eva switched back to English and filled us in on their work schedules. Eva worked at a bank, so her schedule was often the same as Dad's. Today was the last day of classes for Camille, so she would play tour guide while the two of them were at work during the day.

"The church wedding is tomorrow afternoon," Eva said, taking a sip of her wine and watching me closely. "It's a small ceremony. We'll have photos taken, and then we'll go to a restaurant to celebrate over dinner."

Neither Eric nor I said anything.

"Did you bring something to wear?" Dad asked.

I looked down at my open-face grilled ham and cheese sandwich—Eva had called it *croque monsieur*—trying to think of a snappy retort, but my sleep-deprived brain refused to cooperate.

Eric gave me a strange look before turning back to Dad. "Mom bought us new clothes."

Dad picked at his salad, then lifted his head and studied my face for several seconds. "Sophie, I know you're upset about the piano, but I've been thinking . . ." He shot a glance to Eva before turning back to face me. "Maybe this would be a good opportunity for you to focus on something else for a couple of months. You tend to lose yourself when you spend hours at the keyboard." He stabbed lettuce onto his fork. "It might be a chance for you to reevaluate what you want to do with your life."

My mouth dropped open in shock. My father had always encouraged my music. Where was *this* coming from?

Encouraged by my silence, he continued. "You're young and in Paris. Camille and her friends are going to show you around." He leaned closer. "Maybe you should take a break from piano. Relax."

Eric shot me a glare that said *don't do this here.*

I took a breath, then said in a firm voice, "You promised Mom I would have access to a piano. You told her you would get me one. That was part of the deal."

Eva patted my hand. "And we'll get you one, Sophie." She cast an irritated glance at my father, but her expression faded to tenderness when she turned back to me. "If your father promised, then we'll make sure you get one."

We finished lunch, and after Dad paid the bill, we walked out into the misty drizzle.

Eva handed a lanyard with a key to Eric. "This is your key to the apartment. The fob will get you through the electric entrance doors. You and Sophie are free to wander around and investigate, but I wouldn't go too far today with your jet lag."

"I don't have jet lag," Eric protested.

Dad cast a quick glance at me, then released a short laugh. "Maybe *you* don't, but Sophie looks like she's about to pass out."

I shivered, feeling damp from the drizzle. "I'm fine."

"If you can make it for a few more hours, you can go to sleep tonight and most likely be on Parisian time tomorrow."

"William." My father's name rolled off Eva's tongue. "We need to go." Eva grabbed my arms and pulled me close, kissing my cheeks. When she leaned back, she smiled softly. "Sophie, I really am happy you are here. I hope you give me a chance."

I didn't answer. Part of me wanted to give her a chance. But I couldn't say the words. Maybe later, but not now.

She released my arms with a sigh, turning her attention to Eric. After she hugged my brother, Dad gave him a handful of money. "We won't be home until after six. You have my cell number if you need me."

Eva grabbed a taxi, and we stood there on the sidewalk and watched them drive away.

Eric stuffed the money into his front pocket. "Let's walk over to the Eiffel Tower. He pointed to my left. "That way."

I froze on the sidewalk. "We can't walk around Paris on our own! Are you crazy?"

He rolled his eyes. "Sophie, we're not five years old. Besides, Eva gave us her blessing." He used air quotes to emphasize *blessing*.

I could see the entrance to Eva's apartment building several doors down, and even though I didn't really want to go back up there, the thought of wandering around a city where I couldn't even speak the language with no working cell phone of my own—Eric was the only one who got international minutes—freaked me out. "No way."

Eric pointed to the Eiffel Tower. "It's only a few blocks away. We're both capable of reading street signs and I can speak a little French."

Maybe so, but I'd seen the movie *Taken*, and while Eric wasn't a shrimp, I was 99 percent certain he couldn't single-handedly take on a human trafficking ring. "I don't want to walk around," I said. "I just want to go to bed."

"Dad said to stay up."

At the moment, Dad was the last person I wanted to listen to. "If I try to go on a walk, I'll pass out on the street, and you'll have to carry me back and up three flights of stairs."

"That's what you think," Eric said, laughing, but then rolled his eyes. "Who lives on the fourth floor with no elevator?"

"Crazy people," I grumbled as I wrapped my arms around myself to keep from shivering. "I don't want to walk because it's wet and cold." My short-sleeved T-shirt was already damp.

"You're full of excuses." People were walking past us on the sidewalk and giving us strange looks. "Look. Let's use the money burning a hole in my pocket to get you a jacket and umbrella." When I shot him a questioning look, he shrugged and grinned. "Hey. He never said what to spend it on."

I snorted. "You think you've got enough there to buy a piano?"

He laughed again. "You sure gave Dad crap today."

My eyebrows lifted. "You don't think he deserved it?"

"Oh, I think he deserved it. It's the fact that you were the one doing it that caught me off guard. Back home you barely ever fought with him. Of course, you were always his favorite."

Anger burned in my gut. "No. I wasn't." When he started to protest, I interrupted him. "Yeah, I thought we were close. But he shot that out of the water the day he drove away." I shook my head in disgust. "He obviously doesn't love either of us very much. He hasn't come back *once*, not even for your big basket-ball game."

That struck him silent. "Fair enough," he finally said, looking into my eyes.

"Why do you want to hang out with me, anyway? Back home you can't ditch me fast enough."

His grin returned. "I guess we'll be forced to spend a lot of time together this summer if Camille really is our tour guide."

"So is this like conditioning for all the hours you'll be forced to spend with me over the next few weeks?"

"Sure. Consider it that." He laughed again, and I suddenly real-ized we hadn't felt this easy together for a long time. It was kind of nice. "But I don't plan to hang out with you girls all summer. After we get the lay of the land, Dane and I will do our own thing."

Dane. With everything else going on, I'd almost forgotten he was joining us in two days. At least I had *something* to look forward to.

We stopped at a store with women's clothing in the front window. I found a sweater I liked, but nearly fell over in shock after we figured out the euro-to-dollar conversion.

"That's probably worth more than half of my Paris wardrobe," I whispered to him. "I'll just go back to the apartment and get one out of my suitcase."

"No you won't." Eric pulled it off the rack and handed it to a sales clerk. "I'm not going back and climbing those stairs. Dad owes us."

He paid for the sweater and an umbrella, nearly wiping out his supply of money. He grinned when he handed me the sweater.

"This feels like I'm saying 'In your face,'" I said as I shoved my arms into the sleeves. I gave him an evil smirk. "Now I really love it."

He opened the door to the shop, smiling and shaking his head. "Maybe there's hope for you yet."

The rain had stopped by the time we started walking again. I had to admit that Paris was charming. It was like historic Charleston in some ways—full of older, well-maintained buildings. But here, there were so many more of them.

Eva had told us Paris was laid out in twenty numbered sections called arrondissements. The first was in the middle of the city on the Right Bank—the north side of the Seine River—and the other sections spiraled out clockwise. Eva lived in the 7th Arrondissement, which was on the Left Bank, or south of the Seine, right near the part where the river curved around. She said her apartment had been in her family for three generations. As we walked, we noticed that most of the buildings were five or six stories tall with shops at the bottom and apartments on top. The streets were narrow, and while there were cars, most of the people who were out and about seemed to be on foot. Eva had warned us that everything was more expensive in the 7th, especially clothes and anything we might want for souvenirs. Cheaper items could be found in the Latin Quarter. Which made my stomach flutter with anxiety when I thought about what Dad would say when he found out how much money Eric had spent on my sweater.

Now that I thought about it, it was even more shocking that Eric had spent the money on *me*.

We trudged along in silence for several minutes until Eric pointed up at the ornate trim and balconies on the buildings. "Dane is going to freak out."

"Why?"

"He wants to be an architect. He can't wait to get here and check out the buildings."

"Really?"

"Yeah, I think Dad's going to let him come spend a day at *Sainte-Chapelle*."

"Isn't that awesome," I grumbled. Dad had abandoned us hours after picking us up from the airport, but he already had plans with Eric's friend. I knew my jealousy was stupid, but it burned in my gut anyway. "Why do you think Dad made us come this summer?" I asked.

Eric seemed to consider my question. "Because it would be weird if his kids weren't at his wedding." He paused. "And maybe he really *does* want to spend time with us."

"Well, I don't want to spend time with *him*." At least not when it was only on his terms.

"Then don't. Hang out in Paris all summer." I heard an excitement in his voice I hadn't heard before.

"That's what Jenna said."

"Wow. Jenna and I have something in common." His words were clipped, my cue that he was done with my complaints.

It wasn't long before we reached the edge of a park, the Eiffel Tower jutting up into the sky above us.

"It's bigger than I thought," Eric said with something like awe.

"Yeah . . ." The excitement I felt caught me by surprise.

The tower had always looked impressive in movies and pictures, but it felt so different to be here, standing at the base of something so monumental. There was a huge crowd gathered beneath it, and people strolled on sidewalks surrounding huge patches of grass. The rain clouds had become a lighter gray, and a few rays of sunlight broke through.

And in that perfect moment, I wondered if things might turn out all right after all.

CHAPTER *Four*

I WAS SO, so wrong.

Since we'd spent so much money on my sweater and the umbrella, we didn't have enough money to buy tickets to go up the Eiffel Tower, causing me a moment of regret for the extravagant purchase. It was the one thing I really wanted to do while I was in Paris.

Eric and I walked back to the apartment, stopping by a coffee shop for a caffeine boost to help keep us awake for several more hours. By the time we climbed the stairs to the apartment, I was exhausted.

Eric said he was going to play Dad's Xbox, so I decided to check out my temporary room. Considering my soon-to-be stepsister already lived in it, it was surprisingly impersonal. There was a dresser between the two beds, and I picked up one of two photos perched on top. Eva and a man were sitting in the picture, his arm draped around a young teen girl. Her black hair and dark eyes were so similar to Eva's, I would have recognized her as Camille even if Eva hadn't shown me a different picture of her. Based on the background, the photo could have been taken anywhere. Who was the man? Eva's previous husband? I knew she had been widowed a couple of years ago, but not much else.

The other photo was of a young girl with an older woman, standing in a vineyard. The girl looked like a preteen Camille and bore a resemblance to the woman. Was she Camille's grandmother? I set the frame on the dresser and looked around. Other than the photos and several textbooks stacked up next to the bed on the left, there was nothing else that told me anything about my new roommate. Only that her room was very different from my warm, cozy room full of throw pillows back home—it made me wonder how different she was from me.

Camille's clothes filled the dresser and the cabinets that lined the wall next to the door. The cabinets reminded me of something I'd seen in the demo apartments at Ikea. Finally, I turned my attention to the closet. I learned two things from riffling through the hanging clothes—one, Camille's clothes were much more sophisticated than my own, and two, judging from the lack of storage space, I might be spending the next two months living out of suitcases. I pulled out a dark gray dress that looked like it belonged to a businesswoman, not a seventeen-year-old girl, and held it up in front of me, wishing I had a mirror to see how it would look on me. I hung the dress on the closet door, then turned my attention back to the closet. Nope, no space.

After hugging me good-bye at the airport, my mother had whispered in my ear that there was a present tucked into my suitcase to remind me of home. Suddenly I needed that piece of home. I lay one of my bags on the floor and unzipped it, digging through my clothes. After flinging a small heap of belongings onto the floor, I finally found it: a jar of peanut butter. I smiled even though tears burned my eyes.

I missed my mom. If one good thing came out of my father's abandonment, it was that we'd gotten closer.

A sudden wave of exhaustion hit me, and I lay down on the bed, still cradling the plastic jar. I closed my eyes, telling myself that I'd rest for just a moment. But when I opened them, I found myself staring into the face of the girl in the photos. Only now she looked several years older and not nearly as friendly.

She broke into a string of French, and although I didn't know what she was saying, it was pretty clear she wasn't happy.

I sat up and blinked. "I don't understand you." Why had I never considered the fact that Camille might not speak English?

She stopped ranting and put one hand on her hip. She narrowed her eyes and pointed a long finger at me. "Stay out of my things."

"You speak English," I said in surprise.

"And I take it you speak no French at all."

"No."

She released another angry tirade I couldn't understand, then took a deep breath and switched to English. "You Americans are all alike—you think the world revolves around your pathetic country, and it shows in how you behave." She pointed to the open closet door with her dress still hanging on it. "That is mine. Stay out."

I crossed my legs on the mattress and shook my head in confusion. "I was only looking. I didn't do anything to your stuff."

"You touched my dress!" she shouted, pulling the dress off the door.

"It's a *dress*, for cripes' sake. Calm down!"

"Did you try it on?"

This girl was unbelievable. I jumped to my feet, getting angrier by the minute. "Yes. I put it on naked and rolled around in it. And I haven't showered for days."

"Heathen!" she screeched.

Eva appeared in the doorway, her eyes wild with worry. Turning to Camille, she spoke in French accentuated with angry gestures. Camille answered back, flinging her hand toward me as she spoke.

"I'm standing right here!" I shouted.

Camille spoke in her native tongue, but Eva held up her hand. "Camille, speak in English. And we don't have time for this. Dinner is ready."

36

Camille balled her hands into fists and released a cry of frustration, then stomped out of the room.

Eva gave me an apologetic look. "I see you met Camille."

"Yeah . . ."

She was silent for a moment and then sighed. "My daughter is taking this situation just as badly as you are." She offered me a soft smile. "I apologize for her behavior."

I wanted to argue that Camille appeared to be taking it worse, but opted to keep my mouth shut.

Camille shouted something in French and the front door slammed.

Eva put her hands on her hips and looked up at the ceiling before lowering her gaze to mine. "She's going to spend the night with her friend Marine."

I supposed it was wrong to let Eva see how relieved I was to hear that.

"Camille is having trouble adjusting to all of this. Give her some time to get used to you being here," Eva said, giving me a reassuring smile. "I'm sure you two will become friends by the end of your holiday."

I wasn't holding my breath.

CHAPTER *Five*

THE WEDDING OF Eva Mercier to William Brooks was a small, quiet affair. Thankfully, only eighteen guests were present, three of which were the children of the bride and groom. An hour and a half before the wedding there was some question as to whether there would only be two, but Camille stormed through the apartment door fifty minutes before we needed to leave for the church.

I was in the bathroom finishing my makeup when she threw the door open and glared at my reflection in the mirror. We might have had a communication barrier, but I had no problem interpreting her intent.

I made one last swipe with my mascara wand and—heaving a heavy sigh—grabbed my cosmetic bag and started to leave the room. When I reached the opening, she blocked my path, her eyes burning with hatred.

I forced a smile. "If you want me to leave so you can use the bathroom"—I slowed my speech and enunciated every word—"you need to get out of the *way.*"

"I think we need to make some things clear," she said in her perfect English. She had even less of an accent than her mother.

This girl pissed me off, but I wasn't about to let her see that. I put a hand on my hip, jutting it out for effect. "Yes, I agree." I lifted my eyebrows in an exaggerated manner, then said sweetly, "Since I seem to be the only one with manners, why don't you go first, Camille?"

Anger flickered in her eyes before her expression settled into simple disdain. "This is my home. You are a guest here."

"I couldn't agree with you more."

"I may have to share a room with you, but it's *my* room. You're only *borrowing* a bed."

"How gracious of you."

"And you will not touch my things again."

I held up my free hand, clutching my cosmetic bag against my stomach with the other. "I wouldn't dream of it."

"Good," she said in a hateful tone. "Then *maybe* you will survive the summer."

"Thanks for the vote of confidence." I pulled back my shoulders so I could look into her dark brown eyes. Thankfully, she was only a couple inches taller than me. "I don't want to be here any more than you want me here. So we only have to endure the summer, then we can both go back to our regular lives."

She didn't answer. Instead, she stayed in the doorway, looking like she was about to throttle me. Perhaps she expected me to cower in fear, but I wasn't going to give her the satisfaction.

"Are you going to stand there all day, or are you going to let me out?" I tilted my head and gave her a blank look that was intended to convey indifference.

She backed out of my way, then brushed her shoulder into mine as I walked past. She slammed the door behind her, and I stood in the hall for a moment, wondering why this girl hated me so much.

My father, dressed in his wedding finery, was standing in the open doorway to his bedroom.

I ignored the worried look on his face and marched into my—correction, *Camille's*—room and dug a dress out of my suitcase. Of course it was wrinkled. After I put it on, I went into Eric's room and found him with an open book.

I stood in the doorway, my eyes widening in surprise. "Are you actually reading?"

He shrugged and put it down. "I found it in the bookcase. It's a Tom Clancy novel. In French."

"You don't even read Tom Clancy novels in English."

He shrugged again. "I was bored. What do you want?"

"Our evil stepsister won't let me unpack my clothes. Can I hang some things in your closet later?" At least then I wouldn't feel like a hobo.

"Sure. Whatever," he said, picking the book back up.

I gaped at him for several seconds. It would seem I had not only landed in a foreign country, but an alternate universe.

Camille finished getting ready moments before it was time to go, easing her mother's anxiety slightly. Eva looked radiant in her short white dress, perfectly offset by her bouquet of red roses and white lilies. Dressed in the sophisticated gray dress I'd pulled out of the closet, Camille looked just as beautiful as her mother. Then there was me, little Sophie Brooks from Charleston, South Carolina, representing her southern roots in a pink sundress and white sandals—and feeling inadequate in so many ways compared to the two women in front of me.

Wearing gray dress slacks, Eric fidgeted with the red tie knotted at the collar of his long-sleeved white shirt. I almost mentioned that he and Camille seemed to have color coordinated their outfits, but bit my tongue. Eric had lost his apathetic mood from earlier, and the dark gleam in his eye and his clenched jaw suggested he was slightly volatile. I knew it wasn't directed toward me, but I didn't want to be the one to set him off.

I didn't have time to dwell on my insecurities or the fact that everyone seemed to match but me, because we were hustled out the door and down to two waiting taxis. Eva and Camille got into the first one, and we piled into the second—Dad in the front passenger seat and Eric and me in the back.

We rode in silence, my father's leg bouncing slightly—a tell-tale sign of nerves. If he was so anxious, why was he doing this? I wanted to ask him, but I didn't want to fight. We'd spoken barely twenty words to each other the night before—and that word count was generous—making it apparent he was already tired of dealing with my attitude.

The service was held in the chapel of a centuries-old Catholic church. Eric stood in as my father's best man, and Camille was her mother's maid of honor. I sat on a hard wooden pew, bored and . . . hurt. My father hadn't even found a role for me in the wedding. I wasn't sure why I cared. Hadn't I told Eric I wouldn't do it even if he made me?

A photographer took photos afterward, and I learned that Eva's sister and brother were in attendance with their spouses and children. My father worked with one of the other guests, but it seemed like most of them were Eva's friends. It suddenly occurred to me that we were the only ones from home here for Dad. The sadness I felt for him caught me by surprise before I quickly tapped it down. There were several children ranging from preschool age to preteen, but I had trouble putting together who belonged to whom.

Since the wedding party was so small, the photos didn't take long, and before I knew it we were being taxied off to a restaurant. I ended up in a cab with Eric and one of Eva's friends. Dad had gone with Eva and Camille after someone reassured him my brother and I would be right behind him. Eric spent most of the ten-minute ride conversing with the woman in his broken French while I leaned my forehead against the window, staring out at the Parisian streets.

I'd never felt more alone in my life.

After we pulled up to the restaurant, I made a quick visit to the restroom. I stared at my reflection in the mirror, fighting the tears building behind my eyes.

"You will not cry over that jerk who calls himself your father," I ordered.

But tears swam in the eyes of the girl in the mirror anyway.

I spent several minutes thinking of things that would dry my eyes, potential methods of torturing Camille Mercier ranking high on the list. When I finally got my emotions in check, I found the small private room for the dinner. What I saw there made me blink back new tears. Dad and Eva were seated together on one side of the table, and Eric and Camille were right beside them, but the lone empty chair at the table was down by Eva's nieces and nephews at the opposite end.

My father glanced up when I walked into the room, and his eyes filled with guilt and horror when he realized where the seating arrangement had left me. He leaned close to Eva's ear, presumably filling her in on the situation. Panic flashed in her eyes as she scanned the seats around the table.

"Sophie," she said, standing. "We'll move you closer."

My father had arrived in the first taxi, and I'd arrived in the last and proceeded to spend several minutes in the restroom. In all that time, it hadn't occurred to him to save me a seat.

I stared into his face. "I'd rather sit down here."

He started to say something, his guilt obvious, but I ignored him and sat by the preschool-aged girl who was playing with a small doll. She spoke to me in French as I scooted in my chair, and I repeated the phrase Jenna had taught me before I left: *"Je ne parle pas français."*

She looked slightly confused by this and quickly forgot about me, but the preteen boy next to me said, "I speak English."

I offered him a smile.

He grinned, his cheeks tingeing pink. "I'm Michel. I can translate if you'd like. I need the practice."

I didn't really care what anyone had to say, but it beat doing nothing for the next hour or so. "Okay," I whispered. "But I'm most interested in anything that's said about my father or my brother and me."

A sly grin spread across his boyish face and he winked at me conspiratorially. "So I'm James Bond," he said in a thick French accent.

I lifted my eyebrows at the comparison. "Yeah. Exactly like that."

Michel helped me order from the menu and then told me about the new bike he'd recently gotten for his birthday. I nodded and tried to look interested, especially since it was obvious he had a small crush on me. I wasn't a complete ogre. Talking to Michel was better than sitting there in silent despair. Besides, he was sweet and easy to talk to.

I studied Camille out of the corner of my eye. After our encounters, I suspected she probably flew a broom all over the city instead of taking the subway, so her behavior surprised me. She spent most of her time talking to her aunt and uncle, smiling sweetly and speaking without the sharpness that edged her voice whenever she spoke to me. One of her cousins got up and wandered around the table, stopping next to Camille's chair and asking her something I obviously didn't understand. Camille laughed and touched her fingertip to the little girl's nose, then pulled her onto her lap.

Maybe Eva was right. Maybe Camille and I could become friends after all. We both just needed some time to get used to all the changes.

Camille turned to face her aunt halfway down the table, and her gaze landed on mine. Her soft smile fell and her eyes turned hard as they pierced mine, making it very clear that she wasn't having the same charitable thoughts.

Whatever. I found myself okay with that, which was unchar-acteristic. I usually wanted everyone to like me.

After we ate, the waitstaff brought out a small two-tiered cake and bottles of champagne. Only the two youngest children were deemed too young to be served champagne flutes. The rest of us lifted our glasses to toast the bride and groom. I had to admit my father looked happy when he stared at his new wife. I honestly couldn't remember him ever looking at my mother that way. That knowledge hurt worse than anything else.

"What was the toast?" I asked Michel, my curiosity getting the better of me, especially since Eva and her sister had teared up and Camille's scowl was deeper than ever.

"My father said he hoped Aunt Eva and Camille will find the happiness they once knew."

"Before Camille's father died?" I asked. As ticked as I was at my dad, I couldn't imagine how I'd handle it if I lost him forever. Sure, he lived thousands of miles away now, but at least we could talk.

"Yes. They were very happy before—*oh!*" Michel said, licking frosting off his fork. "Uncle Thomas is now talking about your father's civil service yesterday."

I turned to the boy in confusion. "What civil service?"

"The marriage service."

I shook my head, wondering what had gotten lost in transla-tion. "But we just went to their marriage service."

Michel's mouth puckered. "No. In France, the church ser-vice is"—he struggled to find a word—"extra. Here, you must get married in the court. My uncle said it was a lucky thing the mag-istrate relaxed the four week bans rule."

I took a deep breath. "Wait. One thing at a time. What are bans?"

"When a duo applies for a wedding, they post the ban. It must post four weeks before the duo can get married."

"Four weeks? But your uncle said they relaxed the bans. So was it shorter?"

He listened for a moment and shook his head. "No. It was four weeks, but since your father is American, it should have been posted longer."

I grabbed his arm, desperation washing over me. "You're telling me they applied for the license *four weeks* ago?"

"Yes." He nodded with earnest eyes, oblivious to my inner turmoil.

"And they were really married yesterday afternoon." I swallowed, trying to dislodge the lump in my throat. "Everything today was superfluous."

"Sur-per-flus?" he asked in confusion.

"*Unnecessary.*"

His confusion remained, but he finally seemed to understand that I was unhappy.

"Not needed," I supplied.

"I . . ." Uncertainty wavered on his face. "No. Many Catholics do it this way."

The walls were suddenly closing in around me. "I need to go to the restroom." I scooted my chair out and glanced down at my father, who was deep in conversation with someone at the end of the table, but Eric's gaze lifted to mine with a questioning look.

I shook my head and left the room, heading for the front door. I walked several feet down the sidewalk and rested my butt against the building.

He'd lied to us.

My tears broke loose, silently streaming down my face. If the bans were posted four weeks ago, that meant he'd asked Eva to marry him over a month ago. But when he called a week ago, he said he'd *just* proposed. Why hadn't he told us earlier? And why hadn't he taken us to his real wedding yesterday? We were here, so he'd willfully dis-included us.

I leaned the back of my head against the building, wondering what had happened to my previously perfect life.

"Vous allez bien?"

I turned to face a guy close to my age, standing to my right. He was a good six inches taller than my five four. He had dark, wavy hair and deep blue eyes that were filled with concern.

I wiped my face with the back of my hand, released a tiny sob, and said, "I don't know what you said. I don't know what anyone is saying here." I started to cry again.

He slipped off his backpack, unzipped it, and started to dig around inside. "Are you lost?" he asked, looking into my eyes.

The kindness and worry in his voice caught me by surprise.

He handed me a tissue, and I reluctantly took it.

"It's clean," he said, and a smile spread across his face, lighting up his spectacular eyes.

I dabbed my face, realizing two things. One, this French guy was impossibly cute, and two, I was an ugly crier.

It really wasn't my day.

"Define lost," I said, then realized the context was probably lost on him. "No, I'm not lost. My father and brother are inside."

He closed his backpack and slipped it back over his shoulder. "But you are outside crying."

"Yeah. I'm having a bad day." I shook my head and laughed. "Make that a bad year."

"Then let us hope your year gets better after now."

I looked into his eyes and smiled at his slightly twisted English. For the first time since I'd gotten off the plane, I felt like I might not hate *everything* about this trip. "Yeah. Let's hope so."

His smile seemed to set loose a swarm of butterflies in my stomach. There was no better way to describe it.

"Are you here on holiday?"

Even the reminder of why I was really here couldn't steal my sudden joy. "Kind of."

A phone dinged, and he pulled his out of his front jeans pocket to check the screen. His grin faded. "I must go."

"Oh."

His phone rang this time and he answered, irritation wrinkling his forehead. He responded to the person on the other line in terse French. After he hung up, he gave me an apologetic look and started to speak, but the restaurant door flew open and Eric stomped out.

Why did Paris seem to breed so much irritation? Maybe it was something in the water, like fluoride.

"Dad's flipping out," Eric moaned. "He thought you took off." He grabbed my arm and tugged.

I jerked loose. "Like I could. I don't have any money, and I don't even freaking know where he lives."

The French guy backed up several feet, looking torn.

I turned to Eric as he said, "You need to come back inside *now*."

"I will in a minute. First I need to talk to—" But when I glanced to the spot where the French guy had been standing, he was gone.

Leave it to my dad to steal this too.

CHAPTER *Six*

DAD APOLOGIZED FOR my having to sit at the opposite end of the table. Camille had taken my sudden departure as her own cue to bolt, so Eva insisted I sit by them for the rest of the night. Probably to make sure I didn't escape again.

We went back to Eva's apartment, but all four of us were subdued. It had to suck for Dad and Eva to spend their wedding night with two unhappy teenagers—and a third who had run off to heaven knew where. But they were the ones who had chosen to have a rush wedding.

I had a hard time falling asleep in my new bed, but was selfishly thankful Camille never came home. With any luck at all, she'd be gone the rest of the summer.

But I should have known luck wouldn't be on my side. She was back the next morning, as sullen as ever. And I thought *I* was being dramatic. Which I was by lunchtime. Whenever I was stressed, I played the piano. In some ways, my father could be credited for the tremendous progress I'd made over the last year. But I was more stressed than ever, and now I had no outlet.

My not-so-gentle request slipped out minutes after we sat down for lunch in the dining room. "When will I be able to play a piano?"

"*Piano?*" Camille spat out like she'd eaten a rotten potato, dropping her fork with a clang.

Eva murmured something in French—her tone suggested it was a warning. My new stepmother turned to me with a soft but tired smile. "Your father says you are quite good and want to study music at uni." She cast a pointed glance at Camille.

I nodded. "Yes."

"Then we must get you a piano to practice. We will see to it tomorrow."

Camille bolted to a standing position, her chair screeching across the parquet floor, speaking in a stream of rapid French.

Eva's eyes narrowed, and her responses sounded just as angry.

My gaze shot to Eric, who was watching the entire scene in wide-eyed silence as Camille turned and left the room and then the apartment, slamming the front door on her way out.

My new stepsister had a love of slamming doors.

Eva took a deep breath, but her eyes were filled with tears. "I apologize for my daughter's behavior." She forced a soft smile and focused on her plate. Then she rose from her seat. "The car will arrive soon to take us to the airport to pick up Eric's friend."

My father stood and took her into his arms. She rested her cheek on his shoulder, her eyes closed. "Eric and I can do it. You stay and get some rest."

"Merci," she whispered, a tear falling down her cheek.

Guilt oozed in, catching me by surprise. Despite everything, I didn't want to upset Eva. If she had been a friend's mother, I would have instantly loved her. But it wasn't like I was some spoiled kid insisting on a pony. I couldn't go all summer without practice if I wanted to get that scholarship.

Confused by my conflicting emotions, I picked up my plate and Camille's and took them to the kitchen. I had just turned on the sink to rinse them when Eric came in with the rest of the dishes. Neither of us said anything, but I could tell he was unsettled too. He never volunteered to help clean up at home.

After Dad and Eric left, I swallowed my rising excitement and nervousness about Dane's impending arrival and hid in my room. I tried to Skype my mom on my laptop, but my timing was off and she was on her way to work. We talked for a few minutes, and I lied through my teeth and told her everything was great. I wanted to tell her the truth—I'd intended to—but the worry in her eyes stopped me. She'd been happy, especially over the last six months, then even more so when she started dating Mark back in April. She'd moved on, and obviously so had Dad. So why couldn't I?

The night before I'd left to come to Paris, she'd come into my room and told me I didn't have to be mad at my dad on her account. That she liked her new life. I had planned to ask her if Eric was right and she really had sent us here so she could go to the beach with her boyfriend, but I chickened out. I couldn't deal with any more drama.

A couple hours later, I heard voices in the hallway and left my room to investigate. Dane was sitting on one sofa with Eric, and Dad and Eva sat on the one across from it.

Dane's face popped up when I entered the room, and a smile spread across his face. "Hey, Sophie."

My insides did a little dance. Maybe Jenna was right. Maybe I stood a shot with him after all. Back home he never would have smiled at me like that, let alone said hello.

I sat in one of the armchairs in front of the fireplace and watched him as he answered Eva's questions. The way his Adam's apple bobbed when he talked. The cowlick on the right side of his forehead that pushed his dark blond hair away from his face while the rest fell forward. How his gray eyes brightened when my father started talking about his job and what he was doing.

Eric caught me staring at his friend, and his eyes narrowed in warning. He knew about my secret crush, but Dane barely gave me the time of day at home.

Camille came home well after dinner, when I was getting ready to go to bed. I heard her and her mother murmuring in

French before she came into our room. I was already in bed, strategically facing the wall so I wouldn't have to look at her. It was nearly ten o'clock—early for me. I was still jet lagged, but the sun hadn't set, which felt weird.

"I know you're awake," Camille said in a low tone that held no friendliness. "My mother can insist you share this room with me, but you are *not* my sister. I don't even *like* you."

I rolled over and sat up, pulling my knees to my chest. "I never claimed to be your sister." And I was fairly certain liking your sibling wasn't a requirement. At home, Eric and I were often proof enough of that.

She tilted her head, her dark eyes blazing. "If I could figure out a way to make you go away, I'd do it."

I didn't expect her to be my new best friend, particularly after her not-so-welcoming greeting the other day, but I couldn't understand her hostility. I hadn't asked for this either. "I'm sure it's not that easy to dispose of a body when you don't have a car." My voice dripped with sarcasm.

She looked puzzled for a moment, then she scowled and turned away from me.

I was a little afraid to go to sleep. While I doubted she'd murder me in cold blood, I could think of a whole list of other possible offenses. I finally drifted off, only to be roused by Eric's irritated voice.

"Are you coming or not?" Eric stood in the doorway, leaning his shoulder into the frame.

I sat up, still groggy. "What?"

"Notre Dame. Remember?"

Now I was awake. Eric, Dane, and I had made plans to see the Notre Dame cathedral today, and I was actually excited to see a little more of Paris. Oh, and my wicked stepsister was coming too. "You said you would wake me an hour before it was time to go!"

"Camille said she woke you. Did you go back to sleep? We're leaving in ten minutes."

That witch.

I jumped out of bed. "Give me fifteen."

"Camille says you only have ten. We're meeting her friends."

Crap. "Fine." How was I supposed to dress to impress Dane in only ten minutes? But that was probably her plan. Maybe she was hoping for an excuse to leave me behind. Not a chance.

I was ready in nine minutes, and I looked surprisingly good given my stingy time allotment. My long dark hair was pulled back into a neat ponytail, and I was wearing a pair of white capris, a pale blue cotton blouse, and white sandals. I stuffed a hundred American dollars into my pocket, hoping we could stop by a bank and exchange it. I also took my phone. I couldn't use it to text or call, but the camera still worked.

Camille and the guys were waiting in the entryway.

"Finally," Eric grunted.

Dane gave me a teasing smile. "Soph was just getting her beauty sleep."

To my utter embarrassment, my face warmed, and I looked away from him. Thankfully, he didn't seem to notice, but of course Camille did.

She broke out into a smile, her eyebrows lifting. "Let's go see Paris. I'm ready to have a wonderful day."

Somehow it sounded like a warning.

CHAPTER *Seven*

I LOST INTEREST in Notre Dame after about ten minutes. I had never been in a seven-hundred-year-old church before, and it was certainly impressive. But it wasn't too different from many of the projects my father had worked on—only on a larger scale. Maybe I would have loved it more if it hadn't been so crowded. The throngs of people made it difficult to see anything.

But to be fair, Notre Dame didn't stand a chance against the beauty of Dane Wallace. I seriously could not believe my luck. Like me, Eric was only mildly interested in the cathedral, and I was sure Camille had seen it a million times before. Poor Dane needed someone to share his excitement, so I gave him my full attention, not necessarily a difficult task.

"Did you know Notre Dame was the first building to use flying buttresses?" he asked, looking at the stone structures over our heads.

"Really?" Dad had told us that once, back when I was in grade school and he was working on some church in Virginia. I was still Daddy's little girl back then, scooping up his every word and committing it to memory.

I couldn't believe Dane was actually talking to me—Sophie Brooks, Eric's little sister. But Camille soon took over the conversation, pointing out little details Dane didn't know, like the fact that French revolutionaries had replaced a statue of the Virgin Mary with Lady Liberty and beheaded the statues of biblical kings after mistakenly assuming they were statues of the kings of France.

Soon he was hanging on her every word. We squeezed between a family with three young children, and Camille glanced over her shoulder to give me a triumphant smile. She wasn't even interested in Dane. But she knew *I* was.

"The inside is impressive," she said as we stopped in front of yet *another* statue of some saint. "But the real view is from the top."

"The top of what?" I asked.

She rolled her eyes like I was an imbecile. "The cathedral."

I swung my head around, taking in the massive room. "We've almost made it completely around this place and I never once saw any stairs."

"They are on the outside." She gave me a condescending look. "Of course."

Of course. I wanted to roll my own eyes but wouldn't give her the pleasure.

She lightly set her hand on top of Dane's. "But there is usually a wait and we are to meet my friends at *Jardin du Luxembourg* in an hour and a half. So we must get in the queue."

I'd forgotten we were going to be meeting her friends. More snotty French kids. *Great.*

Dane's face lit up, but I couldn't tell if it was because of the location of her hand or her suggestion. "Will I be able to see the gargoyles up close?"

Camille gave him the sweetest of smiles. "*Very* close."

Dane cast a questioning glance at Eric, who shrugged. "Why not? Let's do it."

I followed them through the crowd and out the door into the sunshine. While the last few days had been cool, today was warmer and more like home. But Camille was right about the line. There was a forty-minute wait.

"We could try to come back another day," she said, scanning the people hugging the side of the cathedral as they waited to turn a corner and go inside a door. "If we were to get here earlier in the morning, the wait would probably be about twenty minutes. But today is sunny and the view will be better."

Dane shook his head. "I'm only here for four weeks. Let's go up today. I want to see a ton of other places while I'm here. We might not make it back."

We moved to the back of the line, and I was grateful we were in the shade. Dane read a sign in one of the shop windows across the street in French, then said in English, "Only paying customers may use the restroom."

Camille turned to him in surprise. *"Parlez-vous français?"*

A grin spread across his face. *"Oui. Un peu."*

Eric said something in broken French, and before I knew it, the three of them were having their own conversation.

The guys seemed oblivious to my exclusion, but after several minutes Camille's eyebrows lifted. *"Parlez-vous français, Sophie?"*

My eyes narrowed. "No."

"Sophie struggles to master *English*," Eric said with a teasing grin.

Dane broke into laughter, although I probably had better English grades than both of them. I rolled my eyes to show my indifference, but inside I was fuming. Camille was ruining everything.

"We should switch to English since poor little Sophie doesn't understand," Camille said with a pout. It was so obviously fake, but my brother and Dane seemed clueless.

"Nah, she'll be fine," Eric insisted. "I'm taking AP French next year. I need the practice."

Thirty minutes later we finally made it inside. I knew this was a disastrous idea the moment I saw the narrow circular stone staircase leading to the gift shop. But it was too late to back out now, and besides, I didn't want Dane and Camille to know I was a baby. Eric purchased all our tickets to go to the top of the cathedral while Camille took a phone call, sending glances toward me that made it clear she was discussing her annoying American stepsister. Since Dane and Eric were poring over some book about the cathedral, I wandered around to look at the crappy tourist knickknacks, wondering who actually bought cheap snow globes with plastic replicas of Notre Dame and the Eiffel Tower. Thankfully, they called for our group to line up.

Eric and Dane were first in the line, and I fell in behind them. Camille ended her call with a chorus of laughter and joined us, smirking when she stood next to me. The look in her eyes told me she was up to something, but I was clueless as to what.

The line started moving as our guide led us through a hallway, then started up a tighter spiral staircase than the one leading to the store. My heart began to race, but I urged myself to calm down. It might be a confined space, but common sense dictated that nothing was going to happen to me. Still, I'd seen the outside of the building. There were a lot more stairs to climb.

I shot a look up to Eric, but he seemed oblivious to my rising panic. I was claustrophobic, a fact of which he was well aware. He had loved playing hide-and-seek with me when we were kids because I was always ridiculously easy to find.

Overcome your fear, Sophie. Taking a deep breath, I decided I could do this. For once, I could conquer what I knew was an unrealistic anxiety. And I did okay for about fifteen steps . . . until I couldn't see the entrance behind me and there was no visible doorway above me. I stopped in my tracks in the middle of the spiral staircase.

Eric sensed my abrupt halt and turned around. "Sophie?"

I struggled to catch my breath.

"Mademoiselle," the guide said none too gently. "You must continue up."

I wondered how he knew I understood English, but the thought barely registered because the rest of my body was in full protest.

"Oh crap," Eric groaned. "I forgot."

I shook my head, tears filling my eyes. "I can't do it." The mass of irritated people behind me only drove that point home. Even if I tried to keep going, there'd be no turning back if I changed my mind. Given my current luck, I'd spend the rest of the summer on top of Notre Dame Cathedral.

"What's wrong?" Dane asked, sounding confused.

"Sophie hates small spaces."

"What does she think is going to happen?" Dane asked him— not me.

Camille's upper lip curled. "Don't be such a child."

Eric started down the few steps he'd climbed. "You guys go on ahead." Resignation was heavy in his voice. "I'll wait with Sophie."

The protests from the crowd behind me grew louder, and the man at my back gave me a small shove.

"*Mademoiselle*," the tour guide said, more insistent. "You are blocking the guests."

I turned to Eric, who now stood in front of me. "I'm sorry."

He looked into my face, and to my surprise his eyes softened. At home, he would have been irritated. "I know. Let's just go wait out front."

"No, I can wait by myself."

"I can't let you go down there alone," he said. "Dad would kill me if you got lost."

He didn't really want to stay with me, and I couldn't say I blamed him. He wanted to go up there with his friend. "I'm not stupid," I said, feeling irritated, but mostly with myself. "I'm sure I can find the front of the church even with my supposedly subpar English and non-existent French skills. You go up with Dane and I'll wait for you." I purposely left Camille out of the sentence, daring to hope they might forget her up at the top.

"Soph," he pleaded.

I shoved his arm. "I'm fine. *Go.*"

Conflict waged on his face, so I made the decision for him. I spun around and pushed my way through the cranky crowd. They had to go back down the stairs to let me past, and several people broke into applause when I reached the bottom, only adding to my humiliation.

Thankfully, Eric didn't follow me. I had no desire to ruin the experience for him. Plus, I needed a few minutes to get a grip. This day wasn't turning out as I had hoped, and it was only eleven thirty.

I exited where the line went in, and it wasn't hard to find the front of the church—a four-year-old could have done it. A huge paver stone square extended from the entrance, crowded with people speaking several languages, none of which I understood except for a British family and a smattering of German from a young couple who were having an argument. I had a feeling some of the words they were slinging around weren't in Ms. Maloney's German II lesson plans.

A group of people seemed to be centered in a specific area, about thirty feet from the carved front doors, and I decided to head in that direction. Now that I was alone, separated from the drama of Dane and Camille, I had to admit that the cathedral spoke to me. It wasn't just like any other old building. I craned my neck to look up at the carved figures over the doors, breathtaking on their own. Maybe I would actually enjoy coming here with Jenna.

Boys and stepsisters ruined everything.

When I heard cheering, I turned my attention back to the loose circle of what looked like a group of college students. A couple stood in the center, their arms around each other's necks as they stared into each other's eyes.

Curious, I moved toward the circle as the couple moved to the side. A woman with two blonde braids grabbed the hand of the guy next to her. His face turned beet red as she stopped in the center and planted a kiss on his lips. The other students went wild.

"That's the way to show him, Karina!" a girl next to me shouted in an English accent. Her short black bob bounced as she shot her fist into the air.

As soon as the blonde woman broke the kiss, a big grin spread across her face. "Who's next?"

Several people laughed. Their happiness was contagious, and I couldn't stop myself from asking the girl next to me, "What's going on?"

She cast a glance at me and broke into a wide grin. "They're kissing on Point Zero."

"What? Why?"

She pointed to the couple's feet. A bronze star was embedded into the ground with four stones around it to form a circle. "That's Point Zero. It used to literally be the center of Paris. There are lots of superstitions about it. Some say you can stand on it and make a wish, and it will come true. Others say it will bring you good luck if you kiss your true love while standing on it."

The blonde woman started to walk back to the side of the group, but the guy pulled her back and kissed her again. The students cheered them on, several of the guys letting out a loud "Woot!"

The girl next to me leaned closer. "Chris has had a crush on Karina for eons, but he's shy. So she decided to take matters into her own hands."

"Are you on a school trip from England?" I asked.

She laughed. "No. I'm an Aussie. Australian," she added when she saw my blank look. "We're here at uni for a winter seminar."

I squinted in confusion. "But it's summer."

She laughed. "It's winter for us. The whole bottom of the world thing."

"Oh."

The guy put his arm around Karina and led her off to the side, leaving the center empty.

"Who's next?" someone shouted.

The girl with the black bob shoved me into the middle of the circle, and my heart caught in my throat. Did they expect me to kiss one of these college students? Jenna would have loved to do it, but I'd never kissed a boy at all. I sure didn't want to do it with some guy I didn't know, let alone surrounded by a group of cheering students.

I shook my head as I stumbled into the center. "I . . . uh . . ."

"Make a wish!" the girl with the bob said. "Close your eyes and make a wish. They say it will come true within the hour!"

I knew that was a lie. It was as superstitious as those stupid chain texts that used to freak Jenna out—forward this to seven friends within the next hour and you'll find your true love, but if you don't, a piano will fall on your head. Still, their excitement was contagious and I wanted to play along. At least these people wanted to include me. But what on earth should I wish for?

"Sophie!" I heard my name shouted from above my head, and I glanced up to see Eric and Dane waving to me. Camille was leaning her head against Dane's shoulder. Their faces were too far away for me to see her expression, but I knew it had to be smug.

I ignored them and closed my eyes, now even more confused about what to wish for. I thought I'd wanted Dane, but that dream was unlikely since my beautiful stepsister had staked her claim. Maybe Eric had been right on the plane. Maybe I was too uptight to have a boyfriend.

I heard the students around me getting restless. Jeez, I was so anal I couldn't even get making a freaking wish right. Without thinking, I mumbled under my breath the first thing that popped into my head. "I want a boyfriend."

My eyes opened, and the group cheered. I couldn't stop myself from smiling. These Aussies were a happy bunch. I was half-tempted to beg my way into their group for the rest of the summer.

They started walking away from the medallion, and the girl with the bob waved. "Have a wonderful holiday."

"You too."

I watched them wander off, wondering why I'd wasted my wish. I should have wished for the piano scholarship, reconciliation with my dad, or a whole list of other more important things. Then I reminded myself it wasn't real. It wasn't worth kicking myself over.

Twenty minutes later, the others joined me in the square.

"You should have gone up," Eric said as he walked over, looking relieved to see me still there and in one piece. "The view was awesome."

"Were you frightened, Sophie?" Camille asked, her voice overly filled with concern. "When I was in primary school, I had a friend who was frightened to go to the top as well."

I opened my mouth to argue, then shut it just as quickly. Anything I said would be defensive.

Disappointment and surprise flickered in her eyes, but it quickly faded.

"I'm starving," Dane said as he glanced around the square. "I say we eat now."

Camille dug her phone out of her pocket and sent a text. After several seconds, she looked up at the boys. "My friends have found a place at *le Jardin* and they have food. We'll take the Metro and be there in about fifteen minutes."

"The Metro?" I asked. I hated the Metro. It was underground, and although it was much larger than the staircase in the cathedral, it still made me uncomfortable. We'd taken one train to the station across the street from the cathedral, but I had a feeling I'd gotten off easy with that trip.

Camille looked at me like I was an idiot. "The Metro is how we get around. We take it everywhere. Get used to it. Now let's go." She spun around and started walking toward the corner.

Eric and Dane took off after her, leaving me straggling behind. They were waiting for me at the entrance to the station, and Camille shot me a look of impatience before addressing all three of us. "It's lunchtime and the station will be busier than this morning. We are taking the B train to the Luxembourg exit. Stay together so you don't get lost." She looked into my terrified face. "If you get separated, stop and stay exactly where you are, and I'll come get you."

Eric shot me a scowl. "Relax, Sophie. People ride the Metro every day. You'll be fine."

I knew he was right, but anxiety still prickled the hair on my arms. Camille led the way down the stairs and through the turnstiles, and soon we were weaving our way through tunnels and descending more stairs. Sure enough, the platform was much more crowded than it had been a couple of hours ago, and a train was already rolling in as we approached it.

Camille looked back to see if we were still following, then stepped to the side and pushed the boys in front of her. "Take that one," she said, pointing to an open car.

People were spilling off it, but the guys plowed ahead. Camille slowed down and turned toward a group of young men. She pushed through a small opening between two guys, but before I could follow her, they moved closer together and closed the gap.

I nudged their shoulders tentatively. "Excuse me." Panic descended as I watched Camille board the train.

But they ignored me until someone pushed me from behind. I stumbled into one of the guys, who gave me a dirty look.

"I have to catch that train!" I said, telling myself to calm down. But then I saw the doors close and the train started to pull away. My worst nightmare had come true.

I was lost in Paris.

CHAPTER *Eight*

I STOOD IN place, forcing myself to take several breaths. Eric would just get off at the next station and come get me. I stepped backward until my back was pressed against the tile wall and waited, my fear rising with every passing second.

About ten minutes later, I was still waiting, proud of myself for holding it together for so long, but the tears burning my eyes were winning over my determination to be brave. I had no idea how to get back to Dad's apartment building. I didn't even have his phone number, not that my phone would work here anyway. I reached my hand into my pocket to see if I had a tissue and realized my money was gone. Panicked anew, I checked both pockets in my capris, only finding some lint. I'd been pickpocketed.

My terror ramped up about two hundred degrees and my imagination kicked into overdrive as to what could happen to me in the seedy underbelly of Paris. They never showed this part in their guidebooks.

After ten more minutes, people were openly staring. I would stop crying just to get scared all over again and start anew. One woman stopped to check on me, speaking in rapid French, but since her train was approaching and I couldn't understand her, I waved her off.

"Do you make a habit of crying in public places?" a deep voice asked, and I turned to see the guy who had talked to me outside the restaurant after my father's wedding.

My mouth dropped open in surprise. I had thought I'd never see him again. Maybe fate was on my side after all.

He was just as handsome as I remembered. Today he had on a gray T-shirt and dark jeans, both of which he filled out to perfection. His black hair was a little less unruly, but his blue eyes were just as bright and appealing.

"Not usually." And that was all it took for me to start crying again. *Great*. I knew I had to look a hot mess, given the fact I'd been sobbing on and off for twenty minutes. There likely weren't enough tissues in the world to fix my face. Not that I *had* tissues.

"Are you lost?"

"In a way." I looked around. "My wicked stepsister ditched me here. Just moments after telling me I should stay where I was if I got separated from them, so call *that* a coincidence." I couldn't help adding the sarcasm. "I suspect she's not coming back. She's going to leave me down here to be eaten by rats."

I took a deep breath, feeling less panicked now that he was here, although I wasn't sure why. Even though my brother was right—I was overly cautious, and I knew it—being friendly with strangers still fell into the risky category. But for some reason, I didn't feel my usual anxiety while talking to this guy. Maybe it was because he was my only lifeline at this moment.

His mouth quirked into an amused grin. "I think you are safe from the rats. I've never seen more than two at a time, and I think it would take more than that to eat you."

I gasped. "Are there really rats down here?"

He didn't answer, just slid off his backpack and dug out a napkin to hand to me.

I took it and blew my nose, none too ladylike.

He walked over and leaned against the wall next to me. "Do you intend to live down here now?"

I smiled despite myself. "Yes. I've already picked out that corner over there." I pointed over my shoulder.

"Maybe instead of just standing around we should find some cardboard boxes for your bed."

I laughed with him and then we fell silent for several seconds. Instead of acting rationally and asking him to help me figure out how to get to my dad's apartment building, I racked my brain, trying to come up with something clever to say. *Think, Sophie. Think.*

He tilted his head toward me, still smiling. "I'm hungry. Maybe we should get something to eat."

Why did I have to travel to Paris, France, to meet a guy who was interested in me? The thought of going to lunch with him made me more excited than I expected. But as much as I wanted to go with him, I had to stay here. "I can't. Surely my wicked stepsister won't leave me here forever."

"Maybe she won't be back at all."

Fear seized my breath. I had joked about it, sure, but Eric wouldn't leave me here.

He saw my terror, then added softly, "Maybe she sent someone else to retrieve you."

I squinted. "Who?" He gave me a patient look, and realization hit me like a freight train. "You."

"Camille asked me to find you in the station and bring you to *Jardin du Luxembourg.*"

Anger superseded disappointment. The one good thing I'd found on my own in Paris had been tainted by evil Camille.

"What is this?" I stepped backward and gestured toward him. "She sent you here to humiliate me?"

"What?" His eyes widened in surprise.

"You didn't tell me who you were at first because you wanted to see if I'd talk bad about her." It was perfect. I had.

"Sophie, I—"

"You know my *name?*"

"I . . . Camille told me . . ." He groaned in frustration, then held out his hand and took a step toward me. "Camille knew I was changing trains here at *Saint-Michel*, so she asked me to find you. That's all there is to it."

I put my hands on my hips. "Did you know who I was that day?"

"At the restaurant?"

"Of course at the restaurant. Have you seen me anywhere else?"

"Sophie . . ." He swallowed, glancing at the train pulling up to the platform on the other side, then back at me, his face more serious. "I had no idea you were *le diable*"—he cringed—"Camille's stepsister when I met you on Saturday."

Great, she had a name for me. One that even I could translate. "Then how did you find me?"

The corners of his mouth lifted slightly. "You were the only girl crying on the B-train platform."

"She told you I'd be *crying?*"

"Sophie." He ran his hand through his hair.

"Did she?"

He shrugged, then looked down. "Yes."

Fury boiled my blood. She had told me she'd do anything to make me leave. She'd left me here knowing how upset I'd be. And this guy—this beautiful, tempting guy—was a part of it. Sorrow oozed in, but anger chased it away. "Who *are* you?"

He gave me a tentative smile. "Mathieu Rousseau."

That smile asked me to trust him, but how could I trust the friend of a girl who so openly hated me? Her friends would be loyal to *her.* I clung to one last bit of hope. "Her *good* friend or an acquaintance?"

His brow wrinkled with confusion.

"You know . . ." I shook my head and waved my hands in frustration. "You only know her a little bit."

He grinned at my gestures, and I dropped my hands to my sides.

"We have gone to school together since we were six. I know her very well."

I pushed out a breath of disappointment.

"Can you continue questioning me on the train?" he asked, pointing to the arriving cars. "I'm hungry."

I put my hands on my hips. "I never said I was going with you."

He lifted his eyebrows. "So you're staying here on the platform?" He tilted his head toward the staircase. "Maybe you can make the rats your pets and train them to do circus acts to make food money."

I shuddered. "Fine. I'll go with you. But for all I know this is some elaborate ruse to kidnap me for human trafficking."

He gave me a curious glance that seemed to say *What the heck is she talking about?* but he wisely kept his mouth shut. I followed him onto the train. If I was sold into a harem somewhere, I hoped Eric would be eaten up with guilt for leaving me in the hands of a stranger. It would serve him right.

Mathieu found two empty seats that faced each other. He sat in one of them and I sat in the other, crossing my arms over my chest and looking out the window at the platform.

"I'm sure Camille didn't mean to leave you there," he finally said after the train started moving.

So he was one of *those* boys. The ones who were easily snowed into believing anything a pretty girl told him. That made it even worse.

"Sometimes she comes across . . ." He seemed to grope for the right word.

"Like a witch?" I asked. "She did this on purpose. She hates my guts. Deny it."

He sighed and leaned back, stretching his arm along the back of his seat. "Camille is . . . complicated."

"She doesn't want me here, and it's her mission to make my life miserable until I leave. There's nothing complicated about that."

"Maybe if you understood her better—"

I shook my head. "I don't want to talk about it."

He was silent for the rest of the short ride, just two more stops. We rose as the doors opened, and he stood behind me. He was tall enough that his mouth reached the top of my ear, and my hair blew gently against my neck, sending shivers down my spine as he teased, "Maybe I should hold your hand so you don't get lost again."

Then he grabbed my hand, wrapping his fingers around the side of my palm. I wanted to jerk free, but when I saw the crowd waiting to get on, I clung tight. Protecting my pride wasn't worth getting lost again.

He grinned at me, his eyes twinkling. I looked for a sign that he was making fun of me and found none. If I hadn't known better, I would have thought he really *did* want to hold my hand.

I didn't have much time to think about it, though, because he quickly exited the train and pulled me with him. His grip tightened as we pushed through the crowd, several people bumping into me in their hurry to board. After we made it through, he led me up a flight of stairs and out onto a busy street, then dropped his hold.

We walked side by side past a huge garden complete with a massive house. A large round lawn encircled a pointed statue. "Isn't that it?" I asked.

"We're going to the opposite end." We were silent for several moments as we walked beside the gold and wrought iron fence, then he asked, "Where in the States are you from?"

I stopped on the sidewalk. "Look, while I appreciate you coming to get me, I don't trust you."

Surprise covered his face. "Why?"

"You're her friend. She'll do anything she can to hurt me. She's already proven that by stealing my brother's friend when she knows I like him, and . . . well, leaving me at the subway station."

His smile fell. "She tried to take your boyfriend?"

"He's not my boyfriend. I only want him to be." I nearly groaned. Why had I told him that? What if he told Dane? "Look, bottom line, I really want to trust you, but I can't." Which broke my heart. What little interaction we'd had only made me want to spend more time with him, making me regret telling him about my interest in Dane even more.

His face hardened. "You think I would be part of some plan to hurt you?"

"Weren't you?"

Resignation filled his eyes and he continued walking, leaving me on the sidewalk. I hurried to catch up. The garden was huge, so huge it took nearly five minutes before we got to the end of the block. Large rectangular patches of grass filled the space on this end of the lot, and there were several statues spaced every fifty feet or so. Multiple groups of what looked like high school-ers were spread in groups over the lawn, sitting on the bare grass or on towels or standing.

When we came to the end of the longest block I'd ever walked, Mathieu turned the corner, continuing until we reached an open wrought iron gate. We followed the crowd inside, but he didn't stop to make sure I was still with him.

I was beginning to have second thoughts about how I'd treated him. Granted, he was Camille's friend, but he'd been nothing but nice. Sure, my stepsister might have left me behind on purpose, but he probably hadn't been in on the plot.

He walked purposefully toward a group of about a dozen teens, Dane and Eric included. Camille reigned over her group of friends, sitting in the exact middle, and Dane was right beside her. Her dark wavy hair hung loose and she looked absolutely gorgeous.

I had to apologize before he reached his friends. "Mathieu, I want to—"

He made a direct approach to Camille, pointing his finger angrily toward me before he spewed rapid-fire French. I was pretty sure I heard the word *diable* as he gave an extra jab.

Dane laughed as he glanced up at me. "Good job, Soph. You're pissing the Parisians off right and left."

I gasped in surprise.

Eric got to his feet. "Sophie. What happened?" He now looked almost as furious as Mathieu did.

"Thanks for coming to get me," I sneered.

"I can't help it if you got lost like you're a kindergartner. Why didn't you stay with Camille?"

Camille had been having an intense conversation with Mathieu, but she looked up at me and laughed, only making Mathieu look angrier.

I pointed toward her, seething. "She lost me on *purpose*."

Eric groaned. "Sophie, come on. Why would she do that?"

Camille batted her eyes. "Eric, poor little Sophie has suffered a trauma. You shouldn't be so hard on someone so weak and defenseless." She put her hand on top of Dane's and continued to smile, her eyes locked on mine.

"I don't need you to defend me, *Camille*." I took a step closer. "I just want you to *leave me alone*."

Mathieu's gaze darted to me, his face red with anger, and he spit out more French.

Ignoring him, Camille leaned back and smiled. "I can't do that, *baby sister*. My mother told me to show you an *interesting* summer."

While some of the people in the group appeared stunned by the commotion playing out before them, several, including the blonde girl next to Camille, laughed as if they had been part of a conspiracy. In fact, I was sure they had, which only confirmed my decision not to trust Mathieu.

Mathieu's tirade continued, and she turned to him as he gestured wildly between the two of us.

"What's he saying?" I whispered to Eric.

He kept his gaze on my rescuer. "He's so pissed he's talking too fast for me to understand. I think he called you 'annoying and self-centered.'"

My face burned with embarrassment. Now I was glad I hadn't tried to apologize.

When Mathieu stopped, Camille replied in an icy tone. He glared at her for several moments before he turned around and stomped out of the park, leaving his friends in silence.

"Way to ruin the afternoon, Sophie," Dane mumbled, but Camille's smirk wavered a little. When she saw me looking, it quickly transformed into a look of triumph.

Not only was Dane giving all his attention to my witch of a stepsister, but he was turning out to be a first-class jerk. This summer was getting worse and worse. I would have gone back to the apartment, but I didn't know how to get there. So I sank to the ground, sitting cross-legged, and suffered the snotty looks Camille's friends were giving me.

As I took the sandwich my brother offered, I wondered if maybe I should have stayed in the subway and started training rats after all.

CHAPTER *Nine*

WE ONLY STAYED at the park for a half hour. Eric's anger softened, and it dawned on me that he'd gotten so upset because losing me had freaked him out. Dane soon forgot about me in an apparent quest to fit in with Camille and her friends.

Fine by me.

Eric stood and brushed off the back of his jeans. "Sophie and I are heading back."

Camille looked over at me with a pouty face. "Is it Sophie's nap time?"

My brother's eyes darkened and he sucked in a breath. "I'm tired. Jet lag."

Dane looked incredulous. "What are you talking about?"

Eric shook his head. "We'll see you guys back at the apartment."

"Do you know where you are going?" Camille's blonde friend asked. I was pretty sure her name was Marine. There was a little wistfulness in her expression as she studied Eric.

"Yeah," he mumbled, then looked down at me. "Come on."

I scrambled to my feet and followed him, only we didn't leave the garden the way I'd entered it. We headed through it, walking toward the giant fountain.

When were about fifty feet away from the others, Eric slowed down and waited for me to catch up.

"Soph . . ." His voice trailed off, and he rubbed the back of his neck. "I'm sorry."

I nearly stopped in my tracks, but he kept going, as though he were on a mission.

"I'm not sure if Camille lost you on purpose, but she's been a total witch to you since you got back. I'm your brother, and it's my job to make sure you're okay."

I nearly gasped. Never in our sixteen years as siblings had he ever made this kind of pronouncement. But up until this summer—unless we were doing things with our parents—we had lived completely separate lives.

"And I'm sorry I yelled when Camille's friend brought you back. I was so freaked out that something had happened to you. I wanted to go find you, but Camille assured me Mathieu was on it."

I finally found my tongue. "Thanks. I didn't mean to scare you."

"All I could think about was what Dad would say if I showed up without you. He would freaking kill me. Can we keep this to ourselves?"

For one angry moment, I thought he was more worried about getting in trouble than my safety, but one look at him convinced me that wasn't true. "Sure."

Still, part of me wanted to tell my father exactly the kind of witch he'd inherited as a stepdaughter, but I suspected he wouldn't believe me. What difference did it make if he knew? I'd rather keep peace with my brother. I suspected I would need an ally this summer.

He shot me a look of relief. "Camille said there was a *crêpe* restaurant between here and the Pantheon. Do you want to check it out?"

I shook my head. "I can't pay for it. I was pickpocketed in the subway."

His eyes flew open in alarm. "Sophie, I'm sorry."

I shrugged, pretending I hadn't been terrified, but he knew it was a ruse.

He put his arm around my shoulder. "I'll buy to make up for ditching you."

"Thanks."

The *crêpe* shop was a short walk from the gardens. We got a table on the sidewalk and I stared at our view in awe. The *Jardin de Luxembourg* palace was on one side, and the Pantheon was on the other.

After we ordered, Eric seemed lost in thought, staring at the Pantheon, which loomed a block away. He caught me watching him and offered me an apologetic grin. "I bet Dad's in heaven here."

"Yeah." I didn't need the reminder that he'd rather be here living with his new wife and stepdaughter than back home with us. "I know you didn't just want to leave for my sake. What's wrong? No one believed your jet lag story."

He frowned and dropped his gaze to his fork. "Dane seemed preoccupied."

"Oh." It hadn't occurred to me that it would bother Eric to see Dane lavishing all his attention on our stepsister. Would I feel the same way if Jenna only had eyes for Mathieu when she came to visit?

I wasn't prepared for the weird feeling in the pit of my stomach that accompanied the thought. I didn't have time to consider it, though, because Eric changed the topic.

"You have to get more street-smart, Soph."

I gave him a teasing grin. "You want me to join a gang?"

He laughed. "No. But you need to figure out where we live and how to ride the subway by yourself." A sheepish look washed over his face. "In case you get lost again."

I had to admit he was right. So after we finished, we walked the short distance to the subway station. We each took a few minutes to figure out how to buy tickets and how to interpret the train map.

75

"*Pont de l'Alma*," Eric said, pointing to the dot next to the Seine. "That's home base. The RER C. Can you remember that?"

The remembering part wasn't difficult. It was the execution I was worried about.

He made me repeat the directions from the station to Dad's apartment building on *Rue Dupont des Loges*—three blocks south, then three west.

When we reached Dad's building and started the three-flight hike to the apartment, Eric said, "I'm going to ask Dad to get you a phone." I hated him a little, since he was barely out of breath. I was sure all his sports activities helped.

"Why?" I asked in surprise.

"In case you get lost again. Even if you come back home, you can call me and let me know you're safe."

Home. That was the second time he'd used that word. I wondered how he threw it around so easily so quickly. This place definitely didn't feel like home to me.

I started to say something, but the open front door to the apartment caught my attention. That was weird.

Eric pushed past me, but one step inside the apartment told me why the door was open. Eva stood in the hallway, overseeing two men who were attaching metal legs to a brown rectangular box.

Eva looked up, her eyes lighting up when she saw me. "Sophie! You're home. I was hoping to have your surprise ready before you came back."

It was then I realized that the mystery item on the floor of the apartment's hallway was an electronic keyboard.

I took several tentative steps toward it, and Eric shot me a warning glare. An electronic keyboard wasn't even close to the same as a piano.

Eva waved toward the electronic piece. "You'll have some privacy here, and the man at the shop said when you wear the headphones, it will tune everyone out as well as quiet the noise."

I fought a tidal wave of disappointment. Eva didn't know any better, even if my father did. But I wasn't completely self-centered, and the fact that Eva had been the one to purchase the piano wasn't lost on me. "It's wonderful, Eva. Thank you."

Eric's shoulders relaxed.

She moved toward me and pulled me into a loose hug. "I want you to be happy here, Sophie. I want you to think of this as your home."

There was that word again, but even if I had been open to the possibility, the fact that Camille lived here pretty much squelched any hope of that happening.

I gave her a squeeze. "Thank you, Eva. That means a lot to me." And it did. At least *she* was making an effort.

As the men set the keyboard upright, Eva went into the dining room and began to drag a chair into the hall. When Eric realized what she was doing, he grabbed it from her and set it in front of the piano.

"I thought you could use an upholstered chair instead of one of those stiff benches," Eva said softly.

I smiled. "Thank you." I wasn't about to tell her an upholstered chair would be terrible for my posture. My piano teacher would be horrified.

One of the men plugged in the keyboard and showed Eva the power button and all the special features. She tried to explain it to me, but I waved her off. "I don't need them. Just the piano."

"Try it," Eva said, gesturing toward the chair.

My music was still in my suitcase, but I didn't need it. I had countless pieces memorized. I sat down on the chair and curled my fingers over the keys, trying to decide what to play. I settled on *Clair de Lune*. I'd played it in a state competition only a few months ago, so it was still fresh in my memory. Eva was sure to know it, and I had a sudden desire to make her happy. The correlation to my own life wasn't lost on me. Debussy had written the piece while living in Paris in the early twentieth century. It was his attempt to keep the old style of music alive in the ever-changing modern age.

I knew after the first few notes that the keyboard was never going to work. The keys were too easy to press and nothing like the feel of a real keyboard. It might suffice for a week or two, but not the entire summer. Not if I wanted a chance at winning the scholarship competition.

But it was better than no piano at all.

My teacher, Miss Lori, was strict on technical detail, but she also encouraged her students to feel an emotional connection to the piece. Part of learning a new song was studying the composer and the stories behind the piece, all of which made it more than just a few squiggles on a page. Up until last fall, I'd enjoyed playing and excelled at it, but I hadn't felt that connection.

After my father left, Miss Lori told me my pain could bring my music to a deeper level. "Music is more than notes and tones strung together in rhythm and meters, Sophie. You can be the most technically proficient pianist in the world, but unless you make the audience feel something deep in their soul, you are just another musician. Be an artist. Draw from your well of sorrow." She cupped my cheek and stared into my eyes. "Make me *feel* your pain."

Then she handed me the sheet music to Henry Purcell's *Dido's Lament*. "It's a quiet piece from the opera *Dido and Aeneas*, but I think you will feel a kinship to it."

Technically, it was an extremely easy piece to play, but it had been written with the intent to be sung. Without the aria, it wasn't much, yet a haunting sadness remained. And Miss Lori was right: I felt an eerie connection to it. Dido, the queen of Carthage, was wooed by the soldier Aeneas, who swore to love her and then promptly abandoned her.

Miss Lori had known exactly which piece to pick.

My mother and brother became sick to death of the song, but I memorized it and started to feel the intent of the notes.

When I played it for Miss Lori, she was quiet for a good ten seconds, tears in her eyes. "That was beautiful, Sophie. I could feel the sadness in your soul."

And while that sounded incredibly depressing, I was thankful to find a way to purge my sorrow.

My music changed after that. Most of the compositions Miss Lori gave me were centuries old, yet the men, long since dead, could make me feel the emotions they had infused into their compositions—anger, sorrow, loneliness—and all of it poured from my fingers onto the keys. Over the last year, music had become interwoven with the threads of my soul.

So as I played *Clair de Lune* now, I let my distress and sense of betrayal over my father's marriage flow through my fingers onto the plastic keys. The keyboard was so light to the touch that I made errors, but to the unpracticed ear they were minor. Besides, this session wasn't about being technically proficient. It was about exorcising my demons.

When I finished, I set my hands on my lap, then looked up at my new stepmother, surprised by the tears in her eyes. "Sophie, that was beautiful."

I gave her a soft smile. "Thank you, Eva . . . for everything." I knew she was going out of her way to make me feel welcome, and it made me appreciate her, even if I was still furious about the circumstances that had brought us together. The conflicting emotions were unsettling.

She leaned over and gave me a tight hug, and for a brief moment, I thought maybe this summer wouldn't be so bad after all.

And then Camille came home.

"You really got her a piano?" my stepsister asked in disgust. She stood in the doorway, shaking her head. Dane was behind her, looking over her shoulder.

Eva turned to face her daughter. "Camille. Sophie is very talented. She needs to practice."

"I'm very good with dogs, yet you've never let me get one."

Eva sighed. "I have to get back to the office. We'll discuss this more tonight." She went into the kitchen, grabbed her leather purse from the table, and placed a lingering kiss on her daughter's cheek when she came back into the hall. Then she spoke softly in French.

Whatever she said upset Camille so much her eyes filled with tears. Then she immediately headed into her room and shut the door behind her, this time without a slam. I cast an anxious look toward it, wishing I'd thought to grab my sheet music. But I hadn't played for nearly a week. I wasn't looking to practice. I needed to *play*.

Eric handed me the headphones with a wry grin. "I think we need a pair of these at home."

I hoped he didn't get too used to it.

CHAPTER *Ten*

MY MOTHER AND I had been emailing daily, and she kept asking if my father had followed through with getting me a piano. I'd dodged her questions so far, although I wasn't sure why. I used to take my dad's side in everything, but why was I covering for him now? Maybe some habits were hard to break. I finally told her that Eva had gotten me a keyboard, and on Wednesday afternoon—her Wednesday morning, her day off—she video-called me.

"Making sure you had access to a real piano was part of the agreement," she said, her voice shaking with anger. "Your father assured me that would happen, but apparently he's too busy living his new life to concern himself with it."

She was saying everything I'd already thought, yet I still found myself defending him. "Eva went out of her way to get me a keyboard," I assured her. "I'm making do."

She shook her head, her lips pursed in irritation. "That's so typical of him—letting someone else clean up his mess. I'm calling him."

"Mom, please don't. I'll work it out."

She finally agreed, but only because her new boyfriend showed up to take her out to breakfast at the end of her call. I was usually irritated by how quickly she could forget us when he was around, but this time it worked to my advantage.

I hung up and took a deep breath. This was my second day alone in the apartment. Camille and the guys had gone off to meet her friends, but I'd insisted on staying behind, telling them

I needed the practice. Miss Lori had given me several new pieces to work on over the summer.

I also had no desire to spend any more time with my stepsister than necessary.

So I'd spent two full days practicing. After my call with my mother, I pounded on the keyboard in frustration. I tried to play a cadenza, but my fingers slipped over the too-loose keys.

My mother was right. This was never going to work. While I was grateful for Eva's thoughtfulness, I was frustrated with the limitations. I needed a bench to fully slide from one end of the keyboard to the other, and if I had to play on these weak keys all summer, the muscle tone in my fingers was going to suffer. But if I let my mother intervene, it would only make a difficult situation worse.

What I really needed was to talk to Jenna. I risked video-calling her even though it was eight thirty in the morning in Charleston. To my surprise, she was already dressed and standing in her bathroom when she picked up the call.

"I have to multitask, Soph. I'm babysitting the Meriden twins and I'm leaving in twenty minutes."

"The Meriden twins? You must be desperate."

She turned toward her cell phone, her mascara wand in her hand. "Hello! I'm coming to Paris in almost four weeks! I need money. Now tell me everything! The wedding. Your new mom. You and Dane."

I made a face. "It's like I'm in *Cinderella* with a genuine evil stepsister."

Jenna's mouth twisted. "Figures. And your new mom?"

"*Step*mom." I shrugged. "She's nice. It's complicated."

"That's fair. And Dane?"

"He's part of the reason Camille got her evil status."

Her eyes flew open. "She *stole* him? Already?"

"You don't understand, Jen. She's beautiful."

"And so are you. Don't sell yourself short. Plus, you and Dane have history."

"But not the kind I want."

She shook her head. "Where is he right now?"

I shrugged. "Dane and Eric went somewhere with Camille and a few of her friends. I think the *Grand Palais*."

"Wait." She blinked and held up her hands. "Why aren't you with them?"

"Eva got me a keyboard, so I stayed here to play."

"You gave up spending personal time with Dane Wallace so you can stay in an apartment and play a piano?"

I wasn't sure why I didn't just tell her what a jerk he was being. There had been hints of it at home, but I'd chalked it up to teenage boy behavior. Living with him 24/7 had been eye-opening. "I know it sounds ridiculous when you put it like that . . ."

"*Sounds* ridiculous? Soph, that's like rolling over and playing dead. You're just giving her a chance to sink her claws in even more."

"Yeah . . ."

"Wait. I know that look." She grabbed the cell phone off the bathroom counter and it looked like she was walking into her bedroom. "Is there someone else?"

My cheeks grew hot. "No." I shook my head. "I mean, I thought there might be, but it turned out he was just doing Camille's dirty work."

"Start from the beginning. Don't leave out any details."

So I told her about meeting Mathieu outside the restaurant, his subway station rescue, and his argument with Camille in the park.

When I finished, Jenna studied me for a moment. "It's a tough call. Just remember that Dane is coming home and Mathieu is staying in Paris. Dane could be your date to Homecoming while Mathieu will be making French bread."

I rolled eyes. "I seriously doubt he'll be baking bread."

She lifted her eyebrows in mock exaggeration. "But you don't know that, do you?"

I shook my head, grinning. "No. I suppose not."

She lifted her chin with a smug smile. "I rest my case."

"I miss you, Jen."

"I miss you too. Don't stay home tomorrow. Go with them and show Dane that he'll be much happier with you."

"And how do I do that?"

"You'll figure it out. Flirt."

I wasn't so sure. The mere fact that I'd never had a boyfriend was proof of my inability to flirt with boys. And I wasn't even sure I wanted to flirt with *him*.

At dinner that night, I told Eric and Dane I was going out with them the next day. Dad looked ecstatic, and even Eva looked relieved to hear I would be leaving the apartment. But Camille looked like she'd swallowed a pumpkin.

"Where are you kids headed tomorrow?" Dad asked.

"The *Musée d'Orsay*," Eric said, stuffing a piece of chicken in his mouth.

A museum. That was doable. Besides, I actually wanted to go.

I set my own alarm for the next day, making sure I was up in time to get ready. Today we took one subway to get there, the train stopping right outside the museum. Only three of Camille's friends joined us this time—Marine, the blonde, aka Camille's partner in crime; Marine's brother, Julien, who looked a year or two younger than me; and Sarah, who seemed pretty quiet, even in French. I kept waiting for more of Camille's friends to show up, and if we'd spoken a single civil word since we met, I might have asked her. Instead I kept looking over my shoulder to see if anyone else was coming.

Okay, so maybe I was looking for a dark-haired guy with mesmerizing blue eyes.

We spent several hours touring the museum, and I couldn't help thinking that when I was in grade school, we had enjoyed field trips to the art museum for the simple fact that we got out of school. Now we were purposely here, staring at oil paintings of Greek gods and goddesses; who of course were naked. Dane kept laughing and making snide comments about the women's physical features in the paintings. Eric was going along with it, although not as wholeheartedly as his friend.

I shook my head. "You two are disgusting. Grow up."

Jenna may have wanted me to flirt with Dane, but if he didn't think Greek goddesses were up to his standards, I had nothing to offer him. And I was starting to think he had little to offer me. Camille, on the other hand, smirked at their antics like they were naughty schoolboys.

She could have him.

Since the museum went relatively well, I decided to risk another excursion. The next day we met Camille's friends at the *Jardin du Luxembourg* again. I brought a book this time so I had something to do while everyone ignored me. Dane sat next to Camille again, and I noticed that Marine and Sarah seemed to be giving Eric a lot of attention. Mathieu was conspicuously absent, or at least his absence was noticed by me. I wasn't sure why I wanted to see him—to apologize? But I couldn't ignore the fact that part of me liked him. How stupid was that? He was on the enemy side. In the end, I decided it was better he wasn't there. My life was confusing enough as it was without adding Mathieu Rousseau into the mix.

I was lying on my stomach reading when I heard someone call out his name. I turned my head to see him walking toward us, his backpack slung over one shoulder. My heart fluttered, and I tried to contain the happiness bubbling up inside me.

He sauntered over to our group with a big grin on his face, but his smile dimmed in wattage when his gaze landed on me.

Not only did he not like me, he was annoyed by my presence. Great.

Dane leaned toward me. "Hey, Sophie. There's the guy you pissed off."

"Don't remind me," I groaned, but even though I turned back to my book, I watched him out of the corner of my eye. I was on the periphery of the group, and he sat on the side opposite of me with several guys, one of whom was Julien.

They left me alone for the next half hour, but then Dane snatched my book out of my hands.

"Whatcha reading, Sophie?"

I sat upright in disbelief. "None of your business! Give that back!"

Wearing a stupid grin, he started to flip through pages, losing my spot. "It must be really good. A nuclear bomb could have gone off and you wouldn't have noticed."

"Give it back, Dane!"

"No. I want to know what's got you so interested." He stopped turning pages and started to read. *"He pulled me close, his mouth nibbling my ear."* Dane looked at me with a grin. "I didn't know you liked to read porn, Sophie."

Camille and her friends began to laugh.

My face burned as I jumped to my feet. It wasn't porn. It was a PG-13 YA romance, but that didn't make it less embarrassing.

Dane flipped through several more pages and began to read. *"He took off his shirt and I couldn't avert my eyes."* He laughed. "Would you like me to take off my shirt? I'll let you look."

I was going to kill him. He'd teased me before, sure, but this felt malicious.

"Give my *baby sister* her book." Camille's smile was gone. Her tone let me know she wasn't trying to protect me, and I already knew she didn't consider me her sister.

"Why?" Dane asked, leaning back on an elbow. "I'm just getting into this."

I lunged for him, but he rolled onto his stomach. "I'm not done reading."

"Give it back to her." Eric's voice was cold and serious, but Dane's smile only grew wider.

Camille snatched the book from Dane's grip. She slowly began to flip through the pages, then glanced up at me. "Really, Sophie. You read this nonsense?"

"Give. It. Back." I walked toward her, but Marine stuck out her foot just enough to catch mine as I passed. I fell face-first onto the grass, Camille's friends scooting backward out of my way. Mathieu remained still, watching as I hit the ground, my flailing hand knocking over a paper cup of coffee. The lid flew off, and the drink splattered all over Mathieu's white T-shirt and jeans.

Everyone gasped, and I stared up at him in horror.

"M-Mathieu . . ." I stammered as I got to my hands and knees. "I'm so sorry."

Camille began to laugh, which finally worked loose Mathieu's tongue. I had no idea what he was saying, but I knew he was pissed. Not that I blamed him. I heard both my name and Camille's as he pointed at us, spitting out his French vitriol.

I sat up and pleaded, "Mathieu. I'm sorry."

He stopped talking and turned to me. He heaved out a sigh, then stood and walked away.

"Sophie," Marine said sweetly. "Are you okay?"

I considered responding the way she deserved, but I'd already made a spectacle of myself.

Camille tossed the book, and it landed in the grass beside me. "Sharing is learned in primary school here, Sophie. Did you fail that subject in school?"

"Enough," Eric said, his tone letting Camille know he was done. I was grateful for his help, but it was obvious that he resented the need to offer it. Eric was used to being popular. He was finding his place in Camille's hierarchy of friends, and every time he was forced to defend me, his ranking dropped lower.

Camille groaned and got to her feet, speaking to her friends in French. Marine rolled her eyes, and a couple of her friends protested whatever she said to them, but the others sent me looks of sympathy.

"Come along," Camille said. "Let's go."

I stuffed my book into my purse and stood, eager to get back to the apartment and my keyboard.

At least I wouldn't be able to hear Camille's taunts when I was wearing the earphones.

CHAPTER *Eleven*

WE SPENT THE weekend as a family with Eva and Dad. I kind of felt sorry for them—dealing with four sullen teens couldn't be fun. Eric was pissed at Dane and Camille was pissed at all of us, giving everyone the silent treatment. When Eva demanded to know what happened, none of us spilled.

Dad made an effort to talk to me, but I didn't make it easy. I hated pretty much everything about my summer so far—my new stepsister and her stupid friends, the cramped apartment, the frustrating keyboard, and most of all I hated my father for forcing all of this on me. I was supposed to be at home, hanging out with Jenna by the pool, getting a boyfriend who wasn't a total jerk. I was supposed to be having fun and preparing for my piano competition.

"I know about the bans." The two of us were sitting at the kitchen table while I ate a piece of toast slathered in peanut butter.

His face paled.

"And I know your real wedding was the afternoon we came. Instead of taking us with you, you left Eric and me wandering around Paris trying to stay awake."

He cleared his throat and looked down at the table. "Camille couldn't come because of her finals. It seemed more fair that way."

A lump filled my throat. "Fair," I choked out. "Why in the world would you try to start being fair now?"

His gaze jerked up. "Sophie, I know I've hurt you, but I'm trying."

"Hurt me? Talk about the understatement of the year." I stood, staring down at his pleading face. *"You're* the one who left *me.* Forgive me if I don't consider it fair that you didn't see fit to invite us to your real wedding."

I put my plate in the sink and stomped over to the keyboard, where I spent most of the weekend when Eva and Dad weren't making us hang out as a family. My frustration grew with every session. Part of playing was hearing the music, and the keyboard's electronic sound was throwing me off. But I only had seven more weeks. Just seven more weeks before I could return to my real life.

Eric and Dane were back to normal by Sunday night, and Camille and Dane seemed to have made up too, but Eric still seemed wary of her. Camille and me? There was no love lost there. It was hard enough sleeping in the same room with her. Thankfully, she barely spoke to me.

On Monday, I planned to stay in the apartment, but Eva—who was fully aware of the tension between us—left me with no choice. She ordered me to go with them.

As Eva headed for the door, she looked back at her daughter, who was sitting at the kitchen table eating a croissant. "Tell Mathieu I have his form ready. I enjoyed seeing him on Friday morning at my office."

A fire raged in Camille's eyes. "Must we always speak English in our own home?"

Eva gave her a look of challenge. "Yes."

Camille got up and stomped over to the sink with her plate. She shot me a glare as she passed.

I had no idea where we were going. I could have asked, but it was obvious Camille was purposely keeping it from me.

That should have been my first clue.

As soon as we were on the subway, Dane started talking to Camille in French. Eric joined the conversation, leaving me to my own devices.

We changed trains at the same station I'd gotten lost at before, but I was learning the tunnels and felt more comfortable by the time we got onto the next train.

When we got off the train at *Denfert-Rochereau*, the first thing I saw was a line circling a building across the street. The sky was overcast and a gloom hung in the air. The building was so small I had no idea how many people could fit inside.

"Marine and Julien are already here," Camille told Dane. "So we won't have to wait for more than an hour."

By now I'd learned that lines were expected in Paris, but I still had no idea what we were even seeing.

"What is that place?" I finally asked.

Eric shot me a look that said I was crazy. "The catacombs."

My eyes flew open. "The what?"

"Catacombs," Dane said. Then a grin spread across his face. "Oh, that's right. Dark tunnels and tight spaces . . . and then there's the bones. Are you scared, Sophie?"

I knew about the catacombs in Rome. They were the places where Christians were buried in early Roman times. I figured Dane was trying to freak me out about the bones. It was probably full of a bunch of sealed tombs like the mausoleum where my grandfather was buried.

As we stood in line, it began to drizzle. Only a handful of Camille's friends were there—Marine, Julien, Sarah, and a new boy named Thomas. They all gave me a look of disdain before turning their attention to Camille and the boys. Part of me was disappointed Mathieu wasn't there, and part of me was relieved. Every encounter I'd had with him had ended in disaster, and the last two had ended with Mathieu furious. He had to hate my guts, not that I blamed him. Yet I couldn't help remembering that afternoon outside the restaurant and the connection I'd felt with him on the subway platform. Would I see *that* guy again?

Then, just when we were a few feet from the entrance, Mathieu approached us with a wary look in his eyes. Thomas greeted him in French and Mathieu smiled, although he seemed to go out of his way to ignore Camille and Marine.

Camille said something to him, and he turned to look at her before nodding and turning back to his friend. I couldn't help wondering if she'd given him her mother's message.

We entered the building and Eric paid our entrance fee at the counter. After we went through a turnstile, we began to descend a spiral staircase. I assured myself that this would be better than Notre Dame. Still, I briefly considered turning around and leaving, but the family with three little kids in front of us shamed me into staying. The grade school and preschool-aged children didn't look scared. I needed to suck it up. Besides, these stairs were wider and not as steep as the ones at Notre Dame. I could handle it.

When we reached the bottom, I was ridiculously proud of myself. I was still feeling pretty good as we started through the tunnels, but then Dane and Eric started talking about how deep underground we were.

Dane's face lit up. "I read about the Parisian catacombs before I came. The ceiling's curved to help hold the weight. Before, the tunnels used to collapse." He said it like it was no big deal. "Entire buildings would just disappear into the holes."

That caught my attention.

"See the black line at the top of the ceiling?" He pointed above our heads. "There wasn't electricity down here until about thirty years ago, so they used torches to find their way around. Especially when people used to sneak in here at night to party."

Camille shivered. "I can't imagine being down here in the dark. What if there was a power outage?"

Dane grinned and wrapped an arm around her back, pulling her against his side. "Don't worry. I'll protect you in the dark."

She giggled, and her friends groaned at his cheesiness. While part of me wanted to gag, the rest of me was preoccupied with the thought of the ceiling crashing down or the power going out. Trapped inside tunnels deep in the ground.

I will not panic. I assured myself neither was going to happen, otherwise they wouldn't let thousands of people traipse around down here.

"You wouldn't be in the dark."

I turned around, surprised to realize Thomas was the one who had spoken. This was the first time I'd heard him speak English, although he had a heavy accent that made him a little hard to understand. "You could use the light from your phone." He held up the lit screen to demonstrate, then he winked.

I nearly gasped. Was he making fun of me or actually being nice?

"I didn't know you could speak English," I murmured as I turned around. Dane still hadn't dropped his hold on Camille.

"Of course he knows English," Mathieu grumbled, crossing his arms over his chest as he shot a glare at Thomas. "Everyone here knows English. You're the only one who doesn't speak French."

I narrowed my eyes as I glanced up at him. While his statement was true, he didn't have to be so rude about it.

The group trudged through for what seemed like miles of tunnels, probably because I kept thinking about the lights blinking off and the ceiling caving in. The places where water dripped from the ceiling and the slippery floor didn't help. I had to admit I was impressed when we stopped to look at a carving in the rock. One of the builders had created a miniature replica of an ancient building. Other than that, the rest of our trek was just a long walk through a stone passageway. After a half hour, I was feeling proud of myself for making it so far without freaking out.

And then we hit the *real* catacombs.

We came to a larger room with pillars that led to a doorway. Black rectangles with large white diamonds framed the sides. Above the doorway, the rock had been smoothed and engraved with a French phrase.

Eric came to a halt and translated out loud, "Stop! This is the empire of death."

Dane laughed and looked back at me. "Spooky enough for you yet?"

"Duh. It's an underground graveyard," I said, trying to sound unimpressed. I knew what catacombs meant, or at least I thought I did. This was a place where people were buried.

We passed through the opening. Eric, Dane, and the girls were in the front; Thomas, Julien, and Mathieu were behind me. I'd barely made it through the doorway when I realized my error.

The walls were literally stacked with bones.

"How cool is this?" Dane asked, his eyes wide in wonder.

My eyes were wide too, but not with wonder.

Panic washed through me. I was surrounded by hundreds—no *thousands*—of dead people.

I stopped in my tracks, trying to catch my breath.

These weren't just pieces of plaster you could buy at a store for Halloween. These had been real, previously living and breathing people, and now they were just bones in an underground crypt. The empty eye sockets of hundreds of stacked skulls stared at me, taunting me with my own mortality.

One day *I* would be one of those dried-up skulls.

I felt an arm around my back and shrieked.

"Relax, Sophie," Thomas said softly. "It's okay."

I jerked my gaze up to his, expecting to see him gloating. I saw only sympathy.

"They freaked me out the first time I saw them too," he whispered in my ear.

Camille stood next to Dane, her eyes narrowing as she glared at Thomas.

They had a stare-off for a few moments before Thomas took a step away from me. She gave me a triumphant smile.

She'd told her friends to stay away from me. It didn't require much of a mental leap to figure out that she'd told them to be mean to me too.

I'd had my share of encounters with bullies, and I'd never had a problem standing up for myself. But no one had ever hated me this much—and for no real reason. It made it worse that there was nothing I could do to escape her. At least not for the next seven weeks.

I was living in hell.

We continued on. If I thought the previous tunnels were long, these seemed to stretch on for an eternity. How many different ways could you stack bones? *Human* bones. It seemed disrespectful and morbid. Yet we kept trudging onward, passing through tunnel after tunnel until the tunnel we were in bended and doubled back.

We came to an altar built into the wall at a turn in the path, and the group stopped to read the words.

"This isn't French," Eric said. "I think it's Latin."

Eric and Dane had taken two years of Latin in our private school, so our little group waited—surrounded by bones—as they tried to read the inscription. Camille and Marine had wandered around the corner, out of view, and I breathed a sigh of relief.

Apparently I wasn't the only one eager for her to leave us. After the reprimand Thomas had received from her earlier, I was shocked to see him make a beeline for me, leaving a grumpy-looking Mathieu with Julien.

"Are you feeling better about this place?"

I studied his face, sure he was up to some kind of trick, but I only saw friendliness. Still, I wasn't taking any chances. "Won't you get into trouble for talking to me?"

A sheepish look washed over his face. "Camille . . ."

"Yeah. *Camille.*"

Her gaze lasered in on me as she rounded the corner. "Did you call me, *baby sister*?"

Why had I forgotten that stone echoed? I hadn't exactly been whispering.

"I was just mentioning to Thomas that I saw an amazing resemblance between you and this face right here." I pointed to a random skull behind me. "Vacant stare, hollow cheeks. Empty head. It's like the spitting image of you." The southern drawl I'd picked up in Charleston grew thicker with my insult. Then, like the good Southern girl I'd become, I couldn't help adding, "Bless your heart."

Eric stared at me in surprise, but Dane laughed. "Good one, Soph."

I ignored both of them and walked past her. As soon as I got out of this literal tomb, I wanted to get as far away from Camille and Dane as possible. Camille for obvious reasons and Dane because the guy I'd gotten to know over the last few days was not someone who interested me. The crash and burn of that dream was almost too much to bear when heaped onto the pile of everything else.

The group caught up to me. I caught a glimpse of Thomas, and he gave me a grin of approval. At least someone was on my side. The scowl Mathieu was giving him implied that *he* certainly wasn't. And that disappointed me more than I wanted it to.

Julien moved in front of me and turned around, walking backward. "I dare you to touch one of the bones."

His challenge shocked me. He'd rarely talked to me at all, so where had this come from? But then I caught Camille and Marine out of the corner of my eye, giggling.

I shook my head in disbelief. "No. Why would I touch the bones?"

"To prove you're not scared."

"What are we, preschoolers? They're the bones of *dead people.* Why would I want to touch them?"

Marine laughed and said something in French to Camille. Sarah looked slightly horrified.

Julien shot a glance to his sister, then back at me. "Touch one, Sophie." He reached his hand to the top of the dry-stacked heap, his hand hovering over a pile of what looked like arm bones.

Dane laughed. "Do it, Sophie."

Eric's hands fisted at his side. "Cut it out, Dane."

Dane turned to my brother. "What? You yourself said she's scared of everything. This is her chance to prove herself."

I turned to stare at Eric in disbelief.

His eyes widened. "Sophie, I didn't mean it like that. I—"

"Catch!" Julien shouted.

I shrieked in horror. An arm bone was flying in the air, coming straight for me.

CHAPTER *Twelve*

I BACKED UP, screaming, then bumped into the wall of bones behind me. The bone hit me in the chest, and I screamed again.

"Sophie!" Eric shouted and lunged for me.

A security guard rounded the corner and skidded to a halt, his gaze dropping to the bone at my feet. Then he started a scary tirade.

I watched him in horror, tears prickling my eyes. "What's he saying?" I asked Eric, trying to keep my rising terror at bay.

"I don't know. He's talking too fast." He sounded worried, and for some reason I felt better knowing he was just as scared as I was.

Camille moved toward the guard, pointing back at me.

"What's *she* saying?"

His jaw set. "Nothing good."

They continued the exchange before Camille spun around and addressed me with the fakest nice smile I'd ever seen. "I explained to the guard that you didn't realize you couldn't touch the bones. You picked up one and then dropped it at your feet and screamed. He's agreed to let you go, but you have to leave right now." Her smile widened. "He'll escort you out."

Eric was furious. "That's not what hap—"

"This was an *accident*," Camille stressed. "They have punishments for intentional misuse of the bones."

Eric and Camille glared at each other for several seconds, a stepsibling stare-down. Eric backed down first, but he did so with a loud grunt.

"Fine," he said, grabbing my arm. "Let's go, Sophie."

"Hey," Dane said. "We're not done yet, and you have to take me to see your dad. He's giving me a tour of his church."

Eric's scowl darkened.

"You stay," I said. "I'm not going to Sainte-Chapelle." All I wanted was to go back home . . . but I had no home. There was no place I could go in this unfamiliar city that would feel like a refuge.

Eric's face hardened. "You can't go on your own."

His statement only reminded me of what he'd said to Dane, about me being afraid of everything. And while there was undeniably some truth to what he'd said, his words still hurt. "You showed me how to take the train. I can find my way home."

"Sophie."

"I don't *want* you to come, Eric." I sounded hateful, but I was still pissed. "Give me the key."

The guard spoke again, sounding angry.

"Mathieu can go with her," Camille said, turning her attention toward him. "The paperwork *Maman* signed is on her desk in an envelope with your name on it. You can pick it up while you're there."

Mathieu's startled gaze landed on me.

"Fine," I said, reaching my hand out to my brother. "The key. Now."

Marine snickered as Eric pulled the lanyard over his head and handed it to me. "Sophie, let me come—"

I turned my back and walked toward the guard.

"You better take care of my sister," Eric sneered, presumably to Mathieu.

But Mathieu didn't answer. He fell into step behind me as the guard walked in front of us, sending us occasional looks of disapproval. Perhaps he wanted me to look more contrite, but that wasn't going to happen.

Once he led us to the surface—up a million and a half circular stairs—he lectured both of us in French, then turned around and left.

I pushed out a breath. For someone who rarely got into trouble, I seemed to be finding a lot of it in this city. "Do I want to know what he said?"

His brow lowered. "I hope you hadn't planned on the catacombs again soon."

"Not a chance." I spun around, ready to cross the street to the train station, only to realize we were someplace other than where we went in. I sucked in a breath, trying not to panic.

I had a map.

On one of the days I'd stayed in the apartment, Eric had brought me a paper map with the streets and subway stations. "In case you decide to go somewhere around here while we're gone. Then you can find your way back." He'd put a star on the map to pinpoint the location of our apartment.

I dug it out of my bag and opened it up, groaning when I realized it wasn't going to be as easy as I'd hoped. I had to know where I was to figure out how to get back.

"I can find the nearest Metro stop," Mathieu said, grimacing at the large map I had unfolded. The middle kept sagging, but I tried to flick it back open.

"You go ahead," I said in a snotty tone. His attitude in the catacombs had made it very clear what he thought of me. "I want to find my own way."

He sucked in a breath and forced patience covered his face. "*You* have the key, and I have no desire to wait outside of Camille's apartment building for the two hours it will take you to get back. If you're even back by then. I'll just stay with you."

"Suit yourself."

Confusion wavered in his eyes and he looked down at his jeans and T-shirt. "Why do I need a suit?"

If I hadn't been so pissed, I would have laughed. "It's an American thing. It means do whatever you want."

"If I was doing whatever I wanted, I wouldn't be here right now."

"That makes two of us." He'd made it pretty clear he didn't like me, so I was surprised that his words hurt so much. Maybe it was because I was still hanging on to the memory of our first two meetings. But that boy no longer existed for me. Camille had made sure of that.

"I just need to figure out where I am," I muttered to myself. I'd noticed that most of the buildings on street corners were embedded with blue signs indicating the street name and the arrondissement number. The best way to figure this out would be to make my way to a corner.

Mathieu glanced around and took a few steps to the right. Was that supposed to be some kind of hint? I considered going the opposite direction, but why go out of the way just to prove a point? Besides, the direction he was heading in was obviously busier. The sign on the side of the building read *Avenue du General Leclerc*. I knew the entrance to the catacombs was on *General Leclerc*. Now, which way did I turn?

Mathieu leaned his shoulder against the building and released an exaggerated sigh.

I looked up the street on the map, then searched for the street—*Rue Remy Dumoncel*—feeling both shocked and victorious when I found it. Then I looked for the circled M. "Mouton Douvernet," I said, proud of myself. It was on the 4 line, which was the line we'd taken to get to the entrance of the catacombs. I just had to take it to Saint-Michel station and get on the RER C.

I hated that station.

Mathieu grimaced at my pronunciation. "It's *Moo-tahn Do-ver-nay*," he said. "The *T* is silent."

"That's stupid," I said, folding my map and stuffing it back into my bag. "Just about every freaking letter at the end of a word is silent here."

"And yet millions of French-speaking people have no problem with it. English is full of nonsense words. Why does the word *colonel* contain no *R*s?"

I ignored him and took off in the direction of the Metro station. He fell in step beside me. We walked in silence, and I would have walked past the station if Mathieu hadn't stopped at a street corner, waiting for the light to change so he could cross to the other side of the street. I tried to make it look like I'd meant to walk a few steps past him before I spun around and stood next to him. A slight grin tugged on the corners of his lips, and my irritation grew.

Butthead.

Thankfully I had my own tickets, so I descended the stairs ahead of him, put my ticket in the machine, grabbed it on the other side, and pushed through the turnstiles. My smugness quickly evaporated. The train went two different ways. Was I going toward *Porte de Clignancourt* or *Marie De Montrouge*?

Mathieu started to say something, but I held up my hand. "Stop!" I was set on doing this myself.

His groan didn't sway me. I studied the map on the wall and determined I needed to go to the *Porte de Clignancourt* platform. When Mathieu followed, I felt ridiculously proud of myself. Unless he was purposely following me the wrong way to gloat. I considered asking him if I'd been correct, but I decided to just commit to my decision. I didn't want to give him the satisfaction of my doubt.

The train was crowded when we got on, but I found a seat. Mathieu stood, holding the center pole. Once the train started,

I was gratified to see it was going toward *Saint-Michel.* Now I just had to find the right platform for the RER C.

I went the wrong way once we got off the train, and sure enough, Mathieu didn't say a word.

"Why didn't you tell me I was walking in the wrong direction?" I asked as soon as I realized my mistake.

"You insisted you knew where to go."

I was feeling confident again until we got off the train and emerged onto the street. The Seine was on one side, the hourly cruise ships docked below. A busy street ran parallel to the sidewalk where I stood. I racked my brain, trying to remember the specific instructions to get to the apartment building, wishing I'd written them down. I was terrible with directions at home. Here, I was ten times worse.

Mathieu groaned and muttered something in French before heading toward the intersection to cross the street away from the river. Deciding to call it a win that I'd made it this far, I followed. Once he realized I'd let him take over, he wasted no time in walking the several blocks toward the apartment building, turning down a different street than the one Eric had told me to use.

"Are you sure this is the right way?"

He stopped dead in his tracks and spun around to face me. "I've known Camille since we were small children. I live six blocks from her. I know where I'm going."

I supposed I deserved his snotty reply, but that didn't mean I had to like it. "It was just a question."

He shook his head, muttering in French as he turned around and continued walking. He stopped outside the front door of the apartment building and waited for me to pull the key out from under my shirt.

I opened both front doors, then led the way upstairs. When I had a little trouble with the lock on the apartment door, Mathieu said, "May I?" sounding irritated.

"Be my guest." I stepped aside and made a wide sweep with my arm.

He pulled the handle and put his weight into turning the key before he pushed the door open.

Thank God. I wasn't sure I could spend another minute with him.

I walked past him and tossed my bag onto the floor next to the keyboard, plopping down in the hard-surfaced kitchen chair I'd swapped days ago for the dining room one.

Mathieu's look of surprise when he saw the keyboard confirmed he was acquainted with the apartment, which meant he knew where to find his mysterious envelope better than I did.

I ripped the headphone jack out of the side, relieved that I didn't have to wear the headphones. I needed to hear the music, even if the electronic sounds weren't the same.

I was pissed at Camille. Mathieu. Dane. My brother. But most of all my father. *He* was the reason I was here. *He* was the reason I had to play on this stupid keyboard.

I'd spent the last several days working on *Warsaw Concerto*. I still hadn't figured out why Miss Lori had given it to me. It had been written by Richard Addinsell for a 1941 movie, *Dangerous Moonlight*. I liked it because there were parts I could pour my anger into. It wasn't a terribly difficult piece, but it was tricky, especially with the plastic keyboard. I was only about halfway through with marking all the fingering.

I started to play, making multiple mistakes, but I forged on anyway, needing to exercise my demons rather than focus on technical proficiency. I'd screwed up an arpeggio section and pushed on to the trills, which in fairness I'd only marked the fingering on the night before. But my fingers kept slipping off the slick keys and my irritation grew until I smashed my palms into the keys.

It was only then that I realized Mathieu stood in the living room doorway, holding an envelope. His eyes locked with mine, and my face burned with embarrassment.

"You play," he said, stating the obvious.

"Yes, although that was *quite* bad." It wasn't a ploy for a compliment. I knew it wasn't anywhere close to good. I was still working on muscle memory.

"How long have you been working on it?"

"Four days."

His mouth dropped. "You've learned that much of it in four days?'

I blinked in surprise and shrugged. "I've been working on it here for the last several days—like hours and hours—and a couple of days at home before I left. But this stupid keyboard." I slammed my fingers onto the keys to play a string of arpeggios, then rested my hands in my lap. "My father promised to make sure I had a piano to play if I came here for the summer. This is what I got."

"The *Warsaw Concerto* has its difficult parts." It looked like it pained him to admit it.

My mouth dropped open. "You know it?"

"My mother teaches piano."

"Oh." That was surprising. "Do you play?"

"Not well." A wry grin spread across his face. "Much to her disappointment."

I looked at the sheet music, trying to focus on the numbers I'd written over the notes to tell me which fingers to play. I wasn't sure how to handle a non-hostile Mathieu. I liked him a little too much for my own good. "I have a competition in the fall I am supposed to be preparing for. It's for a scholarship. But now I'm at a disadvantage." I was rambling, yet I couldn't seem to make myself stop. "So the only thing I can really do is learn the fingering and hope the rest falls into place after I get home."

He sucked in a breath and pushed it out as though he were about to perform some Herculean task. "I'm probably going to regret this, but I think I can help you."

I tensed. Was this some kind of trick? "How?"

He grimaced. "I have a piano. A nice one. You can play it."

I narrowed my eyes.

"You can come tomorrow morning after my mother leaves. My younger brother will be gone until late morning at swim practice, but if you're still there, he won't care. You can play for a few hours and be back before Camille and your brother leave for whatever they have planned for the day."

I gawked at him in disbelief. "What's the catch?" The thought of hours alone in Mathieu's apartment made my pulse race a little, and it wasn't entirely because of his piano.

"No catch, other than you can't tell Camille."

That was no surprise. "I can live with that."

"Tomorrow, meet me outside at eight and I'll take you to my apartment." Then he walked out the front door without a backward glance.

I couldn't help wondering if I'd made a deal with the devil.

CHAPTER *Thirteen*

THE NEXT MORNING Mathieu was waiting for me on the sidewalk outside the front door. His back was against the building and he was staring at a *pâtisserie* across the street.

He turned to me, his face guarded. "Have you eaten?"

"What?" I shook my head. "No."

Without a word, he jaywalked across the street and went into the bakery. I followed.

"What do you like here?" he asked, looking in the glass case.

"I don't know. I haven't eaten here."

His eyes widened. "You're kidding. It's one of the best in the city. What about when you stayed home the last few days?"

"I just stayed in the apartment and practiced."

He said something in French, then pointed to the case. "What would you like?"

"I didn't bring any money."

"I didn't ask if you had money. I asked what you wanted."

"I don't—"

"I'm getting something, and it would be rude to eat something delicious in front of you, so what would you like?"

I considered arguing, but I was hungry. I'd left before I had a chance to eat. Besides, I was in a pastry shop with a cute French boy who wanted to buy my breakfast. I couldn't turn that down.

The case was filled with delicious-looking confections, but I decided to go with something that looked familiar even if it had a name I didn't recognize. What if I ended up with something stuffed with snails? They ate those here, right? But how could

I go wrong with a croissant stuffed with chocolate? "I'll take a pain au chocolat." I pronounced it phonetically.

He grinned. "It's *pan oh choc-o-lat.*" The baker approached us and asked something in French, and Mathieu turned to me with a grin. "Now order it in French."

"I don't know French."

He laughed. "I just told you how to say it. Try it."

I repeated what Mathieu had said, and the woman pulled the pastry out of the case and put it into a bag before handing it to me. I didn't catch the name of the round flaky pastry Mathieu ordered, but I did recognize what he ordered next. Cappuccino.

She made two and put them on the counter as Mathieu handed her money.

"How did you know I'd want a cappuccino?" I asked.

He grinned. "You can't have *une pâtisserie sans café.*"

I stared at him for a moment, dazzled by his smile. I hadn't seen it much since he'd found me on the subway platform. He truly was a gorgeous guy. The sunlight was behind him, making a shiny glow around his dark wavy hair. The blue in his shirt made his eyes more cerulean than usual. I forced myself to look away, confused by his actions as well as my own. I added a sugar packet to my cup, pretending it was fascinating to hide my embarrassment.

We walked in silence as we ate our pastries and sipped our drinks. I was surprised the cappuccino was better than any coffee I'd had back home.

Mathieu was leading me in the opposite direction from the Eiffel Tower.

"Where did you tell your brother you were going?" he asked.

"I told him I was going for a walk."

"And if you're gone for a couple of hours?"

The thought of playing a real piano for a couple of hours made me giddy. "I told him I wanted to explore. As long as I'm back by ten thirty, he won't worry."

"I'm surprised he let you go."

I turned to look at him, wondering why he had that impression. Was it because of what happened the day before? "He doesn't care what I do. Besides, he and Dane are pissed at each other right now. That has him preoccupied." They had hardly spoken since they'd come home yesterday afternoon, but Dane was so besotted with Camille, he didn't seem to notice.

Mathieu unlocked the front doors of his building and led me to an elevator. "We are on the fourth floor. You can take the small elevator or the stairs."

"Which one are *you* taking?"

He grinned. "The stairs."

"Lead the way." I figured I could at least try to work off the pastry.

I was out of breath when we reached his landing, but less so than I would have been a week ago. Turned out Paris was full of stairs.

Mathieu handed me his now empty cup and unlocked the door. He took both empty cups from me as he pushed the door open. We entered a small entry hall, and then he led me through a door into a large room with a black grand piano.

I gasped and stopped in my tracks. "It's a Steinway. How'd you get it up here?"

"It's my mother's. And they pulled it through the window. Go on," he said, closing the door behind him and tossing the cups somewhere.

A wall of windows overlooked the building across the street. The bright morning sun filled the room, making the black gloss on the piano shine. I had never seen anything so beautiful. "She won't mind?" I whispered.

His eyes twinkled. "No."

"Then why are we keeping it a secret from her?"

He scowled. "Camille."

The mention of my stepsister almost destroyed my good mood. Almost. How could I be anything but happy when I was about to play a Steinway? I pulled my sheet music out of my bag and moved closer to the piano. This was too good to be true.

Mathieu propped open the lid.

"Won't it be too loud?" The lid would muffle the sound a little bit, but my playing would likely be heard in all the apartments around us.

"They are used to it. Besides, they are all at work. Sit."

I sat down on the bench and opened the fall—keyboard lid—then trailed my finger down the ivory keys. I glanced up at Mathieu, who stood to the side watching me. He nodded, the solemn look on his face indicating that he understood how special this was to me, and walked away.

I started with scales, letting my fingers warm up, reveling in the sound, marveling at the responsiveness of the keys. Steinways are one of the best for a reason, and I had never hoped to play one anywhere outside of a piano showroom. Once my fingers were loosened, I lost myself in the rich, powerful sound, ignoring the sheet music in front of me. I didn't want to think about what I was playing—I only wanted to feel the music.

I'd made it through countless pieces before I glanced up and saw Mathieu standing at the piano's side. I stopped and he said, "We need to leave if we're going to be back by ten thirty."

"But I thought I had almost two hours," I asked, puzzled.

He smiled. "You've been playing that long."

I'd been playing for almost *two hours*? I reverently closed the fall as Mathieu lowered the lid. I stood and grabbed the sheet music I'd never played, then stuck it in my bag. "Mathieu . . . this was . . . I don't know how I can repay you. Thank you."

He smiled softly. "Would you like to play again tomorrow?"

I sucked in a breath. "Are you serious?"

"You're very good, Sophie. You need to play on a real piano."

Tears filled my eyes. "I don't know what to say."

"Say you'll play again tomorrow."

How could I say no to that? "Okay."

He led me back down the stairs and out the front door. I looked up at him with surprise. "You don't have to walk me back, Mathieu."

He grinned. "Your brother told me I had to watch out for you. I wouldn't want to face him if something happened to you."

"He doesn't even know you're with me."

"All the more reason for me to make sure you get back safely. No one but me knows where you are."

The scaredy-cat part of me had to agree with him, even though I felt confident I could make it back okay. But I liked spending time with him, not that I'd admit it. I wasn't going to argue with him.

"How long have you played?" he asked once we were on the sidewalk, headed back to my father's apartment building.

"Since I was in kindergarten. My grandmother played. I used to listen to her when I was little, so unlike most kids, I couldn't wait to take lessons. I have an upright at home. Nothing like yours." I turned to look at him. "Does your mother play much?"

"Not as much as she used to. But when she does . . ." His soft smile lifted the corners of his lips. "It's beautiful."

"And you don't want to play?"

His grin turned playful. "We all have a unique set of strengths and weaknesses. After several years, it became apparent to me that playing the piano wasn't one of my gifts. My last recital ended in disaster. I forgot all the music and started playing 'Twinkle, Twinkle Little Star.'" He laughed. "My mother was horrified."

"How old were you?"

His eyebrows lifted, and he gave me a mischievous look. "Thirteen."

"*What?*" I couldn't help giggling.

He gave me an ornery grin. "It was an effective way to stop taking piano."

My eyes widened. "You did it on purpose."

"I'll never confess." His shoulder lifted into a lazy shrug. "Do you plan to study music at uni?"

"Yes."

"Since your father lives here now, do you plan to study in Paris?"

That nearly stopped me in my tracks. I'd never *seriously* considered the possibility—daydreamed, sure, but not as a serious goal. "That would be amazing, but no. I'm not that good."

"You should consider it. You're better than you think you are."

I was sure he was just being kind. But then his mother was a piano teacher, so he was used to hearing the good, the bad, and the ugly. Still, only the best of the best could study in Paris.

The rest of the way we swapped tales about our years of lessons and the songs we'd played. After Mathieu admitted he'd been learning the *Warsaw Concerto* before he quit, I called him on his earlier statement about not being good.

He paused for a moment. "Music is art. I was technically proficient, yet something was missing. I didn't enjoy it, and you could hear it in the music. But you . . ." An embarrassed look crossed his face. "My mother gets the same expression when she plays."

We had reached my front door and both stopped, standing there in silence. I wasn't sure how to respond to his statement, but I wasn't ready to say good-bye yet. There was a tenuous connection growing between us again. His arm softly brushed mine and my skin tingled.

Without Camille in the equation, Mathieu was the kind of guy I'd kill to date—cute, funny, and thoughtful. But my stepsister was very much a part of the equation. And that ruined everything. Still, I couldn't make myself go inside.

Finally, he asked, "What will you tell your brother tomorrow?"

"The same thing I told him today."

"And he'll believe you?"

It was my turn to shrug. "I guess we'll find out." When he looked worried, I added, "I won't tell them what you did, Mathieu. I'll make him believe me."

He frowned, looking down at his feet. "I'm sorry . . . Camille . . ."

I sighed. "Yeah. Camille."

The mention of her was enough to break the spell. I said good-bye and went upstairs, fully expecting Eric to give me the third degree. But he was absorbed in playing a video game with Dane. Apparently they'd made up. Camille was sitting on the sofa, reading a book. She looked up at me with a gleam in her eyes. "What have *you* been up to?"

"Just walking around. I figure I should see as much as I can." Then I added, "Who knows when I'll ever be back?" I figured she'd like that.

She smiled, then looked over her shoulder and asked the boys something in French.

I went back into the hall and snuck my sheet music out of the bag and onto the piano. Could I get away with this again tomorrow? If their disinterest today was any indication, it might work.

Eric walked out of the living room and cast a glance toward me. "You don't have time to practice. We're meeting Camille's friends at the Rodin museum."

"Do French teenagers *really* spend this much time at museums? Don't they ever hang out at the pool?"

"Have you seen any pools around here?"

I hadn't, but I almost said that there had to be one somewhere because Mathieu's brother swam in the mornings. But I bit my tongue. I wouldn't betray his confidence.

"When are we going to see the Eiffel Tower?"

Camille walked up behind Eric, grimacing as if she'd taken a bite from a sour apple. "Going to museums is bad enough. There's no way we're doing something as touristy as the Eiffel Tower." She released an exaggerated sigh. "But my mother says I must play tour guide, so my friends feel sorry for me and come."

Eric gave her an exasperated look. "We don't need a babysitter or a tour guide. I don't expect you to take me anywhere."

I didn't hide my surprise. So Eric was tired of her crap too.

"Speak for yourself," Dane said. "I like it when she plays tour guide."

Camille gave him a sweet smile, and I noticed Eric gave them a glare before he headed to his room.

I followed and stood in his doorway. "I think I'm going to stay here for the afternoon."

He picked up his backpack and slung it over his shoulder. "No. You're going."

"Since when do you care what I do?"

"You're my little sister. Of course I care."

I released a short laugh. "Try again."

He looked up and his jaw tightened. "What happened yesterday was messed up. I told Julien if he ever tried anything like that again, I'd beat the crap out of him."

I couldn't believe my ears. "You don't have to do that on my account."

"Yes. *I do.*"

"Well . . . thanks. But I think it's our new sister we have to worry about."

He frowned. "I know. But I talked to her too. She says she'll leave you alone."

That surprised me. On both counts. "And you believe her?"

"I'd like to."

"Since when did you become so optimistic?"

"Since when did you start wandering off on your own?"

Instead of answering, I went into Camille's room and pulled some money out of my suitcase. Camille hovered in the doorway, but I ignored her.

When I stood to leave, she blocked my exit.

"What do you want, Camille? Normal people just spit it out."

A strange look crossed her face—a combination of worry and fear. "Why didn't you tell my mother about the catacombs? Or what happened in the subway?"

I lifted an eyebrow. "Are you admitting guilt?"

"No, I'm just asking why you didn't mention it."

I put my hand on my hip. "Look, I've said this once and I'll say it again. I don't want to be here. I'm no threat to you. As soon as this summer is over, I hope we don't see each other again for a very long time. I just want you to leave me alone."

Something wavered in her eyes. "Fine." Then she turned around and left.

I still didn't trust her, but I was going to hope for the best.

CHAPTER *Fourteen*

CAMILLE'S FRIENDS MET us at the museum—Marine, Julien, Thomas, and Mathieu. It felt odd seeing Mathieu after our morning together. Part of me wanted to talk to him, but doing so might draw Camille's attention. So I respected the ten feet of personal space he seemed to be maintaining.

Julien swallowed and took a step toward me. "Sophie . . ." He gave Eric a quick glance, then looked back at me. "I am sorry for throwing that bone at you and getting you in trouble."

"I . . ." For some reason I cast a glance to Mathieu, who was looking out at the street with a grim expression, before looking back at Julien. "Thank you."

Everyone seemed to relax after that.

Musée Rodin was full of sculptures, many of which were naked women, but today Dane behaved himself. Perhaps it was because Camille stuck to his side as if their clothes were attached together by Velcro. Marine looked a little lost without her bestie, but she started to follow Eric around like a lost puppy. And Eric didn't seem to mind one bit.

Thomas and Mathieu hung together, and to my surprise, they seemed to be ignoring Julien.

After we made our way through the inside exhibit, we headed outside, on a path that led to a bronze statue I actually recognized from last year's art class. The statue of a man sitting with his elbow on his knee, his chin on his hand, was surrounded by about fifteen people.

"It's *The Thinker*," I said. "It's famous."

"Which explains the crowd," Eric said behind me.

Thomas and Mathieu walked around me to get closer to the statue. Several of the people who had been surrounding it took photos and then moved on. Thomas looked over his shoulder and handed me his phone. "Sophie, take a photo of me in front of it."

I took it, shocked that he was talking to me in front of Camille. I glanced at her to see if Thomas had risked it because she was distracted, but she was not only watching, she was actually smiling. Of course, that could have been because Dane was now holding her hand.

Thomas stood in front of the statue and assumed *The Thinker*'s pose. He squatted and tried to recreate the statue's position, giving a mock pensive look. I snapped several photos, then he stood and grinned. "Your turn."

I looked around at Camille's friends, wondering if they were setting me up for some kind of prank. But Dane and Camille had walked several feet away and were deep in a private conversation. Eric and Marine were chatting, and my brother seemed pleased with his new shadow. I couldn't say I blamed him. She was pretty. She just wasn't good at choosing her friends. Then again, perhaps they had that in common.

Mathieu stood to the side, watching. He wasn't frowning like he had been yesterday, but he wasn't happy either.

Thomas grabbed my wrist and pulled me closer, moving me to the side of the pedestal. "Now sit," he said, smiling when I did just that.

I adopted the statue's position as best I could, thankful I'd worn capris instead of a skirt. Thomas held up his phone and took several photos. Then he handed the phone to Mathieu and said something to him in French.

Mathieu took the phone with the hint of a scowl. "If you don't want to be rude to Sophie, then you need to speak in English."

Thomas didn't look happy with the reprimand, but murmured, "I'm sorry."

"It's fine. I understand." And I did. It would be like someone expecting me to speak German all the time when I could barely ask how to find a bathroom.

I squatted again, and Thomas squatted next to me, both of us resting our chins on our hands. Mathieu held up the phone for barely a moment before holding it out to his friend.

"Your turn, Mathieu," I said, reaching for him and pulling him down next to me. "Would you take our photo, Thomas?"

Thomas's smile wavered, but then he arranged us into matching poses and took our photo.

We wandered through the garden, stopping at *Les Trois Ombres* next. The title meant the three shades, and it featured three figures in a huddle, hunched over and reaching their hands together. Thomas, Mathieu, and I recreated it, with me in the middle, all three of us laughing. Eric took the photos, watching both boys as though he didn't quite trust them.

I was thankful Mathieu seemed more relaxed, but he was still ignoring me for the most part, which hurt my feelings more than I cared to admit. I had thought we were at least becoming friends. Given Camille's previous disapproval, I could understand his reticence, but now I wasn't sure what to think.

Next we reenacted *The Burghers of Calais*, which included six men in a group, all with attitudes that made it look like they'd had a disagreement. I made Eric and Marine join us this time. Marine's face lit up with excitement, but then she glanced at Camille for permission.

Camille gave her a slight nod and Marine grabbed Julien. "We need one more," she said in English.

Dane took the photos this time, but we had a hard time setting it up because we kept breaking into laughter when we tried to hold the statues' facial expressions of outrage and disdain.

When we continued down the path, Eric gave me a huge smile, which I returned. This was the most fun I'd had all summer.

We came to the Gates of Hell next—not the literal gates, but bronze gates with bas relief figures in contorted poses, some of which were very suggestive. As if in unison, we moved on.

Next was a statue of a man and woman, both naked and in an embrace. The man had his hand around the woman's back and was bending the woman backward, his mouth nuzzling her ear. Thomas shot me a grin. "Sophie?"

Eric stepped between us. "Don't even think about going near my sister."

Thomas laughed, and he and Mathieu reenacted it instead, arguing over which one of them was the woman. They finally agreed to take turns, and we all burst into laughter when Thomas licked Mathieu's ear. Mathieu jerked out of his hold and fell on his butt as he scrubbed his earlobe with the palm of his hand.

After I took photos, Dane called out, "Our turn."

We all gaped at him in surprise. While he and Camille had followed us through the garden, they hadn't shown any interest in what we were doing. Camille didn't protest when Dane pulled her forward, wrapped his arm around her back, and held her hand out to the side. Then he leaned her backward and nuzzled her neck as she clung to him.

None of us laughed. I expected to feel some lingering tinge of jealousy, but I mostly felt weird, like I was a voyeur to some intimate moment I had no business watching.

The joyful mood dampened, and the power shifted in that moment. I wasn't sure how, but it was obvious Camille was no longer in charge, although I couldn't figure out who had replaced her.

"*J'ai faim*," Thomas said. "*Nous allons manger des crêpes*." He turned to me. "Have you had *crêpes* from a street vendor yet?"

"Eric and I had some at a restaurant by the Pantheon."

Thomas shook his head in exaggerated disapproval. "*Mais non!* To experience *Paris*, you must have *crêpes* from a street vendor."

Everyone was in agreement, so we left the museum and found a vendor. I ordered a Nutella *crêpe*, excited to watch the vendor make it fresh. When he handed me the parchment-wrapped dessert, I started to hand him a five euro bill, but Thomas intercepted and paid for it instead.

"I am privileged to buy your first street vendor *crêpes*," he said with a bright smile.

I watched Camille out of the corner of my eye, worried she'd try to reinforce her Sophie ban, but she was totally engrossed with Dane.

Thank God for small favors.

After we all had our crêpes, we walked to *Esplanade Jacques Chaban-Delmas*, a nearby park, and sat in the grass. Thomas jostled Mathieu out of the way to sit by me. A dark look crossed over Mathieu's face.

But Thomas looked pleased with himself when he turned and nudged my arm with his elbow. "You must try it."

I took a bite and practically moaned. "Mmm. It's very good."

"See?" he said. "I am brilliant."

I watched Thomas dig into his with gusto, finishing off his Nutella and banana *crêpe* in only a couple of minutes. He began to list the best *crêperies* in the city.

I was amazed at how different today was from yesterday. It was almost too good to be true. I was certain Thomas, Julien, Mathieu, and the others had been following Camille's decree.

For the moment she had decided to be half human and let them interact with me. But I didn't trust my stepsister. What would happen when she changed her mind again?

I decided to enjoy the moment and bask in the knowledge that a guy—a cute *Parisian* guy—was interested in *me*. Thomas was nice and thoughtful, and his light brown hair and hazel eyes were definitely appealing. I should have been interested, but I was hung up on someone else.

Someone who didn't seem the slightest bit interested in me.

I cast a glance at Mathieu, but he was deep in conversation with Eric and Marine. Did I feel this way about him because of our first two encounters, or was it because he had let me use his mother's piano? In the end, it didn't matter. He didn't seem interested.

When we finished, we were close enough to walk back to our apartment. Thomas lived in the 1st Arrondissement, so he took the subway with Marine and her brother, who lived in the 16th.

Dane and Camille were still holding hands, but they trailed behind us so we weren't forced to watch them fawn all over each other. Mathieu remained silent for several blocks before he said, "This is where I turn." Then he waved and headed down the side street.

"See you tomorrow," I said, but he was walking so fast he was already out of earshot.

"You have plans with Mathieu tomorrow?" Camille asked in surprise.

"Uh . . ." Oh jeez. I'd already screwed up. "I just figured he'd join us for whatever we end up doing tomorrow."

"I have a dentist appointment tomorrow," Camille said. "So we won't be meeting them."

"Oh."

"That comic store looks cool," Eric said, pointing across the street. "Did you see this store when you were exploring?"

"Uh . . . no. I headed the other way."

I was worried he'd ask me more questions, but he lost interest, especially when Dane asked him something about taking their senior pictures when we got back home.

I had several hours before dinner, so I spent most of it working on the fingering for the *Warsaw Concerto*. I had gotten to the movement that contained a lot of crossover trills, so I spent a lot of time writing it down and then re-fingering it and making changes. I hoped to play the new parts at Mathieu's the next morning.

Dad got home from work before Eva. She must have told him she'd be late because he was carrying a bag of groceries, with two loaves of French bread sticking out of the top. I looked up from the keyboard, and he caught my gaze.

"Did you have a good day?" he asked.

"Yeah."

He moved closer, standing next to me with a hopeful expression. "What did you do today?"

"We went to the Musée Rodin."

"And . . ." he prompted.

"It was fun."

He frowned, and I knew he was frustrated. Back home I would have told him all about it, but this uneasiness between us wasn't going to change overnight. He was crazy if he thought it would.

A hopeful smile lit up his face. "I was thinking you and I could go out for ice cream after dinner. There's a shop down the street that caters to tourists. It's even better than Cold Stone."

Part of my heart ached to spend time with him, but I wasn't sure I was ready to let him back in. After we went home at the end of the summer, I had no idea when we would see him again. But part of me ached to regain what we'd once had. I missed him.

"Okay," I said with a soft smile. "I'd like that."

It turned out we didn't go anyway. Eva was late getting home from work, and it had been a bad, stressful day. Dad said he needed to stay with her, and it was obvious she needed him more than I did.

While I felt bad for Eva—some kind of international banking deal had fallen through—this was only further proof that I was not his priority.

I decided to go to bed around ten since I needed to get up early. Mathieu hadn't set a specific time to meet in the morning, but I figured it wouldn't change from today.

Camille came in soon after. I had purposely rolled onto my side, facing the wall. I'd spent the last week pretending I was asleep when she came into the room. It was better than having to deal with her. Most nights she fell for it, but tonight she climbed under the covers and waited a few moments before saying, "I'm being nice to you for *the moment*."

The word *moment* hung out there like a big smelly turd I couldn't ignore. I rolled onto my back, staring up at the ceiling. "What exactly are you saying, Camille?"

"I'm saying that for now it serves my purpose to treat you well. But the moment that stops, it will all change."

I had no doubt that it would all change sooner rather than later.

CHAPTER *Fifteen*

THE NEXT MORNING, Mathieu was waiting for me. His backpack was hanging open on his left shoulder, and he held a cup of coffee in each hand. He gave me a warm smile and handed me one of the cups.

My brows lifted in surprise. "Thank you."

"Did you eat?"

I gave him a sheepish grin. "No, but—"

He pulled a pastry bag out of his backpack and handed it to me. "Try this."

I opened it and peered inside. It was the pastry he'd had the day before, and a heavenly smell wafted up to my nose. "Mmm . . . what is it?"

"It's a *Paris-Brest*."

I laughed. *"Excuse me?"*

His face turned an adorable shade of pink. "Brest is the name of a French city."

"Oh . . ." That made sense, although it *was* round and shaped like a . . . I chose to ignore that part. "It looks delicious." I took a bite of the flaky pastry and cream filling and nearly groaned. "Are you trying to get me fat?" Each bite had to be packed with several hundred calories.

He looked confused. "You don't like it?"

I laughed and took another bite. "I love it. Thank you."

He pulled out one for himself and we walked for a block in silence, both of us concentrating on our breakfast.

"So your mother teaches piano," I said. "What does your father do?"

"My father drives a taxi."

I stared at him in shock. "They can afford that apartment on the salaries of a teacher and a cab driver?" As soon as the words flew out, I slapped my hand over my mouth. "I'm so sorry. Can you please forget I asked that?" I considered running back to my apartment and hiding under my pillow.

He grinned. "It's a fair question. But my father doesn't live in the apartment. It's my stepfather's."

"Oh."

His smile softened to understanding. "So I kind of know what you're going through."

"Oh," I said again. Could I get any more brilliant? "I'm sorry."

"I'm not." Then he shrugged. "Well, I kind of am." He turned to look at me. "My parents, they fought all the time. It was bad." He paused. "They married too young, before my mother . . ."

Before his mother *what*?

But he didn't finish the thought. "My mother is better with my stepfather. But me, not so much."

I cringed. "How long have they been married?"

"Ten years."

I studied his face. "And you don't get along?"

"No." He took a bite of his pastry. I suspected it was a ploy to keep from answering more questions, so he surprised me when he said, "But I was an only child, and now I have a brother. A stepbrother. That is good."

"So you two get along?"

"We do now." He grinned. "But not at first. He's two years younger than me. To him, it was *his* house and I just moved in." He shrugged. "It was rough, but now we're friends."

"Is this your not-so-subtle attempt to make me think Camille and I will be good friends someday? If so, sell it somewhere else."

Confusion clouded his eyes. "Sell what?"

I laughed. "Never mind. It's never going to happen. Camille and I will *never* be friends."

"Maybe. Maybe not. But I've been in your situation. I know how you feel. And now I understand how Etienne felt. Maybe you should try to understand Camille's feelings."

I stopped walking. He took several steps before turning around to see why I'd stopped.

I gaped at him. "She put you up to this."

"What?" he asked, bewildered.

"She told you to say that."

His eyes widened. "Why would she do that?"

"Last night she told me she'd be nice as long as it served a purpose for her. Maybe this is part of it."

"She said that?"

I nodded, lowering my coffee cup to my side.

He seemed to think about it for a few seconds before he said, "Camille did not tell me to say anything."

"Are you sure about that? She told all of you to ignore me and be mean to me, didn't she?"

He didn't answer, which was answer enough.

I sighed. "I'd love to give Camille a chance, but she's bound and determined to make my life as difficult as possible. It goes both ways, Mathieu."

We continued on to his apartment, but our good mood was ruined.

As soon as he brought me to the piano, I pulled my sheet music out of my bag. I was determined to play the *Warsaw Concerto* today. Mathieu lifted the lid, so I sat on the bench, lifted the fall, and began my scales. I lost myself in the piano again, working my way entirely through the piece multiple times, even if I had to stop and slowly work out more sections than I would have liked.

Just like the day before, it didn't seem like any time had passed at all when Mathieu appeared at the piano. I stopped playing. "Has it been two hours already?"

He nodded, his face expressionless. "You seemed focused again."

I needed to bring my phone and set an alarm. "Thanks." I lowered the fall and looked down at my lap. "I'm sorry about earlier. I shouldn't have assumed the worst."

He started to say something, then reconsidered. "I understand why you would feel that way."

That was it. No explanation. But I reminded myself that Camille was his friend first. I'd be leaving in little more than six weeks and she'd still be here. It was selfish and unfair for me to ask him to choose between us.

I stood, and he grabbed his backpack.

"You don't have to walk with me, Mathieu."

"I'm headed that way anyway."

We started our walk in silence, but it started to bother me by the end of the first block. "Have you always lived in Paris?" I asked.

His lips tipped up in a grin and he cast a glance in my direction. "*Oui*. Where do you live?"

"Charleston, South Carolina, but I haven't always lived there. We lived in Virginia first, and before that in the Northeast. In Boston. I don't remember living up there much. Only that it was cold and snowy in the winter. I like the South much better." I pressed my lips closed. I tended to ramble when I was nervous.

His grin spread. "You like living in Charleston?"

"Yeah. It's a beautiful city. I like that it all looks so old. And my best friend lives there. Jenna." I glanced at him. "Is Thomas your closest friend?"

His smile faded. "Yeah."

His reaction was odd, but he was sullen enough I didn't want to press for more.

"So what do you do for fun in Charleston?"

I laughed. "We don't go to museums."

He laughed too. "We don't either. Although I am not complaining."

The look he gave me suggested I might be part of the reason he wasn't complaining, but his behavior the day before seemed to contradict that. Maybe I was imagining things. "So what do you do?" he repeated.

"Jenna has a swimming pool, so we hang out there a lot. I was supposed to babysit for my neighbor's kids this summer, but I had to give it up to come here. Eric had to give up his job at the golf course too."

He looked at me in wonder. "You have jobs?"

"Most teenagers do. It's how we pay for our cars and gas and for things like going to the movies and out to dinner. You don't have a job?"

"It's not allowed. There aren't enough jobs, so they can't give them to teenagers. And we can't drive until we're eighteen, either, not that most people in Paris have cars."

He asked more questions about my life in Charleston, and before I knew it, we were standing in front of my dad's apartment building.

He paused and looked at me. "Do you want to play tomorrow?"

I stared up into his deep blue eyes. "Why are you doing this? It's a huge inconvenience for you, and Camille will be pissed if she finds out. Why are you risking it?"

His chest rose as he took a deep breath. "Because it makes you happy." Then he walked away.

What did *that* mean?

I spent the rest of the day obsessing over it. Why would Mathieu care about me being happy? Could he feel the same way about me that I felt about him? Shoot, I didn't even understand how I felt about him.

Only one person could help me sort this out.

I sent Jenna a message asking if she had time to talk to me after Camille left for her dentist appointment at two fifteen. I didn't dare risk discussing it while she was home. It was enough of a risk that Dane or Eric might hear me.

She messaged me back close to two—eight a.m. her time—saying she could talk for about ten minutes at two thirty.

That would have to do.

"Spill it!" Jenna said as soon I answered the video-call. She was sitting cross-legged on her bed. Her laptop must have been propped up on her pillow, because it was level with her chest and not her waist. "Is this about Dane? Did he finally come to his senses?"

"No. Someone else."

"Mathew?"

"Not Mathew. Matt–yue."

She giggled. "Is it a name or a sneeze?"

I rolled my eyes. "It's French," I said, as if that explained everything.

She nodded. "So you like him?"

"Yes. No." I shook my head. "I don't know. He has a piano and he's been letting me play it. Jen—it's a Steinway!"

"So he's started off by giving you expensive gifts. Check."

I laughed. "He didn't give it to me. He's just letting me play it."

"Same thing. So he likes you." An excited gleam filled her eyes.

"I don't know. That's the confusing part. He shows up outside my apartment building and walks me the six blocks to his place. Then he walks me home after I finish. Both mornings he's even gotten me breakfast from the *pâtisserie* across the street—cappuccino and a pastry—but once we're in his apartment, he walks away and leaves me alone."

She gave me a reprimanding look. "Have you ever seen yourself when you're practicing? You have a distinct *leave me alone* vibe." I started to say something, but she just laughed. "Don't even deny it. I've seen it a million times. Sounds like he's smart. So he's cute, smart, and he gives you things." A huge grin spread across her face. "He likes you."

"Don't get too excited," I grumbled. "We talk all the way back to my apartment building, but he practically ignores me whenever we're in a group with my stepsister. And he doesn't want me to tell her I'm going to his apartment."

"Oh." She looked taken aback. "So he's asking you to lie."

My stomach began to churn. "I hadn't thought of it that way."

She leaned forward, resting her forearms on her knees, and began to rub a section of her comforter between her thumb and index finger. "So maybe . . ." I could practically see the wheels spinning in her head. She obviously wasn't ready to give up on Mathieu yet. "You said Camille's friends haven't been nice. Maybe he's testing the waters. He's seeing if there's some spark or chemistry between you two before he risks getting into trouble with Camille."

I shook my head. "I don't know. Camille seems to have lifted her Sophie ban. Their friend Thomas was really nice to me when I got freaked out in the catacombs. Then he hung out with me at the museum and park yesterday. He even bought me a *crêpe* when he found out I hadn't had one from a street vendor yet."

"You better be working out," she teased. "With all these boys buying you pastries, you're gonna put on five pounds. So tell me about Thomas."

My face began to burn. "He's cute."

"And he's obviously nice if he bought you a *crêpe*."

"And he's fun." I told her about posing for the silly photos at Musée Rodin. "And Mathieu joined in, but only after Thomas convinced him."

"And how did Her Majesty react to that?"

I released an exaggerated sigh. "She hardly noticed. She was too busy holding Dane's hand and then mimicking the statue of two lovers in a passionate embrace."

Her eyes flew open, and she screamed, "*What?*" I heard a mumble off-screen, and then Jenna grimaced and called over the laptop screen, "Sorry, Mom!" She immediately returned her attention back to me. "You're just now getting to this part? Spill!"

It was time to dash her illusions. "Dane's a total jerk, Jenna. Like monumental. Even Eric seems fed up with him."

"What happened? Tell me everything."

I told her about how Dane had teamed up with my stepsister to torment me.

She shook her head, and her eyes glazed over. "I don't believe it. I mean . . . I knew he had his moments, but let's be honest, most teenage guys do."

"I know."

"Well, it's obvious Thomas likes you."

"You think so?" I kind of hoped so, which was so many ways of wrong. Especially when I preferred Mathieu.

"So, Thomas . . ." she said, her eyes twinkling. "What do you think about him?"

I grinned. "I'm impressed you got the pronunciation right so quickly. *Two-ma.* They pronounce names so differently here."

"I only know what you tell me. And besides, if French is like Spanish, I suspect it's spelled the same way Thomas is."

That blew my mind. How was I ever going to figure out how to say anything here?

I settled back on the pillows on my bed and put my laptop on my stomach. "I wish you were here."

"Only three more weeks."

"As a token of how much I love you, I haven't started shopping yet."

"What?"

"I'm waiting to go with you."

She tilted her head and gave me a sweet smile. "Aw . . . but that still doesn't distract me from asking about Thomas."

I laughed and sat up straighter. "He's really nice. And funny."

"I think we've established that."

"I like him . . . but . . ."

A sad look filled her eyes. "But you like Mathieu more."

"I don't know . . . maybe."

"Oh, Soph, have you noticed that over the last year you always pick the guys who aren't available?"

My breath caught in my chest. "What does that mean?"

"It means," she said softly, "that you crush on guys who are with another girl or ones who don't even know you exist. Maybe it's like that with Mathieu. It's safer that way. Nothing to risk, which seems to be your M.O."

Part of me wanted to argue with her, but I couldn't help wondering if she had a point.

"I can make a list of examples if you'd like. Austin Carmichael had a girlfriend. Trevor Honeywell is a football player only interested in cheerleaders. Even Dane . . ."

I groaned and then laughed. "Stop. I get it."

"All I'm saying is maybe you should give the guys who *do* want to get to know you a chance."

"Okay. I'll give it some thought." I grinned. "Now hurry up and get here. Then you can see it all for yourself."

She released an exaggerated groan. "Speaking of which, I'm babysitting the terror twins again today, which means I've gotta go." She grinned. "The things I do so I can go to Paris . . ."

"Thanks, Jenna."

"Anytime. That's what besties are for."

CHAPTER *Sixteen*

"THAT'S NOT FAIR!" Camille shouted in English later that night, jumping out of her chair at the dining room table, which surprised me. The English part, not the jumping out of the chair part. She was just as fond of jumping out of chairs as she was of slamming doors. She and Eva had been waging an argument in French, so obviously she wanted to inform the rest of us that her life had been ruined. Which meant it had something to do with me.

Eva gave her daughter a not-so-patient look. "It's my final decision."

Camille shot me a sneer. "She probably doesn't have anything to wear."

I set down my fork. "I have no idea what you two are talking about, but leave me out of it."

My father gave me a pained look. "Camille wants to go to a club with her friends tonight."

Eva started to speak in French, then switched to English. "You know the evenings are family time, Camille."

"We've had almost two weeks of family time. You can't force us to like each other."

I snuck a glance to Eric, relieved to see he was just as confused as I was. "Wait," I said. "What is she talking about?"

Eva grimaced. "Your father and I thought it would be best if all of us spent our evenings and weekends together while you and Eric are here." She looked up at Dad, who nodded in agreement.

"We want all of us to become a family," he said.

All the forced family fun over the previous weekend made sense now, and several other pieces fell into place too. Dad had balked at Mom's insistence that Eric and I should both be able to bring a friend. He'd known it would interfere.

"I will still be here after they leave," Camille said, pointing across the table at Eric and me. "And I spend all day with them. I just want *one night*."

"Let her go," I said, my back stiff. "I don't want to go."

Camille's eyes widened.

"I don't want to go either," Eric said. Narrowing his eyes at Dane, he said, "You two go without us."

Dad studied us for a moment and then turned to Eva. "Let Camille go out with her friends. I'll spend the evening with Eric and Sophie."

Eva's gaze lowered to her plate and she said something in French. Eric's head jerked up to look at her, but he didn't say anything.

We cleared the table, and Camille bolted for her room as Eric and I began to load dishes into the dishwasher.

"What did Eva say?" I asked, handing him a plate after I rinsed it.

"I don't think things are all rainbows and sunshine with Dad and Eva."

My heart skipped a beat. "Why?"

"Eva said a French phrase that means unity is strength."

"Oh." While the prospect of them fighting—and possibly splitting up—might have overjoyed me a few weeks ago, I couldn't deny that I really liked Eva.

No one was more surprised by that than I was.

We made plans to go see an American action film that was playing at a movie theater by the Louvre. We left the apartment and walked for a block in silence on our way to the subway station before Dad asked, "How's it going with Dane here?"

"Oh . . ." Eric hedged, looking down at his feet. "Pretty good. He likes seeing all the architecture."

"Is it weird knowing he's so interested in your stepsister?" Eric shot Dad a surprised look and Dad laughed. "Eva and I aren't blind. It's obvious they like each other."

Eric rubbed the back of his neck. "Not as much as if he were dating Sophie."

"What?" I asked, walking behind them. "Why would that be weird?"

"Because he's my friend. There's no way I could think about him . . . *dating* you without beating the crap out of him."

My mouth dropped open in shock. I'd never considered the possibility that Eric might care one way or another. But then again, I'd never dated before, so I had nothing to compare it to.

"And how are things going with Camille and her friends?" Dad had asked before, but always in front of Eva and Camille. Polite conversation that required a polite answer. But now it seemed like he really wanted to know.

Eric shot a determined look at me over his shoulder. "Honestly, Dad. Camille hasn't been very—"

"She's been amazing," I interrupted. "An amazing tour guide."

Dad slowed down to fall in step beside me. "Really? I've sensed a hostility between you two."

"Hostility? Nope." I forced a grin. "Just a bit of healthy girl competition."

He looked surprised. "Eva said Camille was having a hard time accepting you here."

I shook my head. "Nope. We're not BFFs, but we're good."

Eric shot me an exasperated glance.

I know he was surprised at my response, and honestly, part of me was too. But if Eva and Dad weren't getting along, a feud between Camille and me was only going to make things worse.

I could suck it up and deal with it. Besides, Camille had called a truce, even if it was temporary.

"You have to understand how hard it is for Camille. After her father's death, she—"

I shook my head. "We're good." I had no desire to hear my father plead Camille's case.

Dad looked relieved. "Eva will be glad to hear it. She's been concerned." We stopped at a street corner, waiting for the light to change. "Speaking of Eva, what do you guys think of her?"

Eric seemed to be searching for an answer, so I said, "She's really nice. I like her."

"You do?" Dad asked.

"Yeah. She's trying to make us feel at home, and I know she was the one who bought the keyboard." Maybe Dad couldn't afford to pay for a piano on his own. It wasn't a secret that his career path had been chosen for passion, not prosperity, and now he had to make child support payments. It still pissed me off that he would shrug off my need to practice—even more so because he hadn't once listened to me play on the keyboard. He had no idea how good I'd gotten, but I was too prideful to beg him to listen.

Still, there was no need to go into that now. It was just Eric, Dad, and me—and it almost felt like we were a family again. I wanted to enjoy tonight. Even if it wasn't real.

"Eric?" Dad asked, sounding hopeful. "Do you like Eva?"

"Yeah. She's great."

"I know things happened so fast . . ." He cast a quick glance at me. "And I know I've handled things badly. But I hope you can learn to love her like I do."

Eric and I mumbled our agreement, but it wasn't difficult for me. Mom seemed happier after the divorce too, so it would be easy to love Eva.

Her daughter was a different story.

It took two trains to get to the movie theater, and I was surprised to see it was right outside the station.

"You haven't been to the Louvre yet, have you?" Dad asked as we passed a sign pointing toward the entrance. "Be careful when you go. It's known for pickpockets."

Little did he know I'd already had a firsthand experience with one of them. Eric shot me a glance, hinting this was the perfect opportunity for me to tell Dad about that encounter.

"We'll keep that in mind," I said as we walked up to the ticket counter.

I had to admit that I was getting a better attitude about being in Paris. I'd actually begun to have fun. And not that I'd ever admit it to Dad, but I found some of the architecture amazing. I'd reached a point where I was curious about how things were different here. Turned out movies were a perfect example. Popcorn was salty or sweet and already scooped into small boxes that were sitting on a shelf. Soft drinks—like most soft drinks in Paris—were served in small bottles and not very cold.

The seats were similar to the ones at home, and while Dad had assured us we'd be able to understand the movie, I was relieved when the actors spoke English words as French subtitles flashed across the bottom.

We stayed through the credits, waiting to see if there was a bonus scene tacked on at the end. Our wait paid off—there was a snippet teasing the next movie in the franchise. We stood to leave, and Dad said, "I've really missed hanging out with you guys."

"Then maybe you shouldn't have moved to Paris," I said without thinking. My heart ached so much from missing him it was hard to breathe. I knew I'd caught him off guard—especially since I'd been so agreeable earlier. But all of this real family togetherness was a sharp reminder of what he'd thrown away.

Me. Eric. *Us*.

"Sophie!" Eric spat out.

"It's okay," Dad said softly. "How about we get some ice cream? I think it's time we talked about it."

We found an ice cream shop down the block, then took our cones outside and sat on a low concrete wall overlooking the street.

I took a bite of my raspberry sorbet, surprised by how much I liked it. Especially since my stomach felt so unsettled.

"This is better than at home," Eric said between licks.

Dad gave me a soft smile. "I swear Paris has the best ice cream in the world. From now on everything else will be a poor imitation."

For once I had to agree with him.

We ate in silence for several minutes. I was ready for Dad to tell us what happened, but part of me was scared. Even though both of our parents had said his decision to leave home had nothing to do with us kids, part of me couldn't help but wonder if I could have stopped it from happening.

"I want to tell you more about why I left," he said, keeping his gaze on the street.

"I'm sure you had your reasons," Eric mumbled around his coffee ice cream.

"I do . . . I did . . . Your mother and I thought perhaps it would be better if we kept you away from all of it, but now I think that was a mistake."

"So you wouldn't look like a deadbeat dad?" Eric said, breaking his usual distance from the situation. "I'm not sure how you could spin abandoning your family to make it look good."

"We *both* had our reasons."

"You mean *you* had your reasons," I blurted. "Mom was forced to go along with it."

Dad's mouth dropped open as he turned to look at me. "Is that what she told you?"

His reaction caught me off guard. "No. She refuses to say anything about it at all."

He sighed. "We agreed to keep it to ourselves. I'm breaking that agreement now." He sounded solemn and sad.

I suddenly felt a strange sense of guilt for making him spill, but my brother and I were owed an explanation.

He hesitated, then said, "The fact is that I should have left years ago."

I gasped, and tears stung my eyes. "How can you say that?" It was akin to saying he regretted the last few years—all our talks on the porch and ice cream runs, everything we'd done together. Was I *that* disposable?

But he turned to me and grabbed my free hand, searching my eyes. "I only stayed as long as I did for you, because of you and your brother. It killed me to leave you two." His voice broke.

Eric's gaze sought mine—his eyes full of fury. I was glad to know we were together in this.

"Your mother and I hadn't gotten along for quite some time. The fact is we got married too young and for the wrong reasons."

Reason was more like it. Eric and I had long ago figured out that Mom had been pregnant with him when they married.

I took a breath. "So you're saying your entire marriage was a mistake."

"No, Sophie. We had some really great times. Especially when you and Eric were little. But we never discussed the important things before we got married, like kids or long-term plans. We just figured it would all sort itself out, but it didn't." He swallowed, looking away. "I have always wanted to work in Paris. In fact, right after the wedding, I did an internship here at Notre Dame, and I knew *this* was where I wanted to be. But your mother hates Paris.

140

I figured I could be happy working in the US. There are plenty of old buildings on the east coast. But then your mother wanted more kids, and I was happy with you two. So we compromised. I stayed in the US and she agreed to two kids, but neither of us was happy. She hated that we'd moved around. She'd make friends, only to have to leave them and start over."

"That still doesn't explain why you left," I insisted. "We'd been in Charleston longer than anywhere."

He sighed, a forlorn look on his face. "Sometimes things happen too late. The damage was already done."

"Couldn't you at least have waited until I graduated?"

He hesitated, pushing out a heavy breath. "Your mother and I decided it was time."

"That's a crap answer," Eric finally said, a hard edge in his voice. "We deserve better than that."

Dad was silent again, then said quietly, "Not all of this is my story to tell. Your mother needs to tell you her part."

"But you've hardly told us anything at all," Eric countered. "You must have applied for this job months before you left, but we only heard about it the day you left. Literally a few hours before the taxi showed up to get you. You never even gave Mom or us the option to come with you!"

He shook his head, sadness filling his eyes. "I never expected your mother to come."

Then a thought hit me. In the past, changing jobs had taken him months. "When did you apply?"

"Your mother sent them my résumé in April."

"*Mom* sent your résumé?" I asked in shock. "Why would she do that?"

"I'd heard about the position, so I brought her roses and ribs from her favorite barbecue place to try to warm her up to the idea."

I remembered that night. She'd been pissed, which had seemed uncalled for given the sweet gesture. "She wasn't very happy."

"That's an understatement. She saw right through my ploy." A wry grin twisted his lips. "It went worse than I could have imagined."

"If she said no, then why would she send in your résumé?" Eric asked.

"Because she never intended to come."

I could hear my pulse pounding in my head. Our mother had sent him away.

"Imagine my surprise when I received an email with an invitation to interview."

I shook my head. "But I don't remember you going on any trips. How did you interview?"

"Video conference call."

"And they hired you," Eric said, then added, "obviously."

"Yeah." I had never heard so much defeat and sadness in a single word.

"When did you find out you got the job?" I asked.

"The end of July."

"But you left in the middle of August." I jumped to my feet, feeling betrayed all over again. "You waited two weeks to tell us!"

He sat on the wall and looked up at me. "It wasn't like that, Sophie," he said quietly. "I was going to turn it down. But when I told your mother, she insisted that I had to be out of the house by the end of August one way or the other."

"What?" Eric got to his feet too.

"Why?" I demanded.

Dad was silent for several seconds. There were tears in his eyes as his gaze moved back and forth between us. "She wanted a fresh start."

"But you didn't *have* to leave." I shook my head. "I mean, maybe you had to leave the *house*, but you didn't have to leave *Charleston*. You could have gotten an apartment. I could have come to live with you!"

Fresh pain washed over his face. "It was my dream, Sophie. The job I'd wanted more than anything was right there in front of me."

"*I'm* supposed to be one of the two things you want more than anything. *Me and Eric*."

"You are, Sophie."

Realization filled my head, and I struggled to breathe. "But we weren't enough."

"It wasn't like that, Soph. I promise." His voice rose as he stood, pleading with us to understand. "I was upset and hurt and very angry with your mother. I told her I'd fight for you two, that I'd try to get full custody, but she said she'd use all my travel from when you were younger against me in a custody battle. I lost my marriage, my house, and I was losing you two. I had nothing, so I left."

"You left *us*," Eric said bluntly.

"And it was the hardest thing I've ever done."

His answer was nowhere good enough for me. "You didn't even call! You didn't call for a whole freaking *month*!"

"I know." His voice broke. "It hurt too much to hear your voices."

Eric clenched his fists at his side. His voice had a rough edge. "That's a cop-out and you know it."

We were loud enough that people walking on the sidewalk were openly staring, not that any of us seemed to care.

"I have no excuse. I was wrong."

"So you kept the fact you were leaving to yourself for two weeks, then told us the day you left the country," Eric said. "And

143

then you posted bans for your wedding for at least three weeks before you told us you were getting married and wanted us to come visit. You didn't even take us to your real wedding!"

Dad searched my face, looking for any sign of gloating.

Eric groaned in disgust. "What? Sophie figured it out? Camille told me. How did you find out?"

My gaze met his. "At the wedding dinner. From her cousin."

Understanding flashed in his eyes. "That's why you ran out."

I nodded, fighting back tears. "I loved you, Daddy. I *loved you* and you left me. You have no idea what this last year has been like. I'm happy you love your new job and your perfect new wife and your perfect new daughter, but it's obvious there's no room for Eric and me here."

My father's eyes hardened. "That's not true. We've gone out of our way to make you feel welcome. Camille gave up her room and everything in it to move to the room you two share."

And suddenly I understood why she hated me. Mathieu had been trying to tell me.

"But it's not home," Eric countered. "It's your home, not ours."

Dad took several breaths, his shoulders tight. "I'm not sure what to do about that," he finally said. "But I don't want to send you home early. Please don't ask."

"Fine, we'll stay, but things are changing," Eric said. "First of all, no more forced family time. It's obvious Camille hates it. Second, stop making her take us places. If she wants to go with her friends, let her. Sophie and I will be fine on our own. I know the city now, plus I have the map on my phone."

Dad studied him. "Okay," he said softly.

"We're here to see you, not Eva and Camille. We want to spend time with Eva, but we need alone time with you too."

Our father sighed. "We were trying to bond as a family. You're here for such a short time. But I'll make more time for you. That seems like a fair compromise."

"Fine," Eric said, then added, "And Sophie needs a piano."

"What?" my father and I said in unison.

"Sophie's good, like *really* good. She's so much better than before you left, and she needs to play on a real piano, not the toy keyboard in the hallway."

My mouth fell open in shock. Eric was not only defending me, but complimenting me as well.

My brother turned to me. "I can hear you play, doofus. I'm not deaf."

So much for our moment.

While I would love a real piano, the thought of never seeing Mathieu again filled me with panic. And I knew that was a possibility if I no longer needed to use his piano and Camille was no longer our forced tour guide. I told myself it was the Steinway that interested me, not the guy, but I didn't believe it for a minute.

"We can't get her another piano. They could never get it up the stairs. That was part of the reason Eva got the keyboard."

I considered telling them it wasn't an issue, but I couldn't betray Mathieu.

"She needs to practice," Eric insisted.

Dad ran a hand through his hair. "I'll talk to Eva and see what we can do."

"Thanks," I said, but I held Eric's gaze.

My brother nodded briskly. "I'm ready to go."

My father grabbed us both, pulling us into a hug. "Leaving you was the hardest thing I've ever done. I love you, whether you believe it or not. I'm not perfect, not even close, but I'm trying. Just try to be patient and don't shut me out completely."

Eric said, "Okay," but I refused to answer, although I was questioning my judgment of him. Still, the fact remained that he'd left us. Once this summer was over, I had no idea when I'd see him again. I wasn't ready to hand the power back to him to hurt me again.

I wasn't sure I'd ever be.

CHAPTER *Seventeen*

THE NEXT MORNING I stopped and knocked at Eric's partially open bedroom door. He'd had the apartment key last, and I couldn't get back in if I didn't have the fob for the electronic lock on the front door. I could have pressed the buzzer outside, but with my luck, Eric wouldn't hear it and Camille and Dane would leave me out on the street.

But Dane opened the door, wearing a pair of shorts, no shirt, and a big grin, which fell slightly when he saw it was me. "I'm taken."

I blinked, sure I'd misunderstood. "Well, good for you," I finally said. "I hope you two are happy together. Lord knows it's a match made in heaven."

"Because we're both so good-looking?"

Oh my God! How had I ever liked this fool? "Yeah. That. Tell Eric I need the key."

"Why?"

"Because you're blocking the doorway."

"No. Why do you need it?"

"That's none of your business. Now tell Eric I need the key."

Dane came out of the room, closing the door behind him. "You're practically scared of your own shadow. I can't believe you're leaving the apartment all by yourself. Where are you going every day for *hours*?"

"I said it's none of your business."

I tried to push around him, but he grabbed my wrists and pulled me against his chest. "I want to make it my business."

I gaped at him.

"I know you like me, Sophie," he said, grinning, "and I might be with Camille now, but you and me can hook up when we get back home."

Before I could react, an outburst of French broke out behind me. I took advantage of Dane's surprise to pull loose.

"What are you doing with my boyfriend?" Camille demanded.

I spun around to face her. "Are you *kidding me*? He was the one manhandling me!" I shook my head in frustration. My truce with Camille had been fragile to begin with, but this was sure to smash it to bits. "As Dane pointed out, you two are perfect for each other. You can *have* him."

As I stomped toward the piano, I realized I had another issue. I couldn't take my music without both of them noticing. Great. Now it would be a wasted morning of practice. Especially since I was letting the *Warsaw Concerto* sit while I was learning the much more difficult Rachmaninoff Prelude in B Minor Op. 32 No. 10. I'd barely played it all the way through a few times—and quite badly at that. I certainly hadn't had time to memorize more than a few stanzas here and there.

So now I didn't have a key and I didn't have my music, and I was also running late. I opened the front door and started to stomp out when I heard Eric shout, "What is going on out there?"

"Nothing." I slammed the door shut behind me and suddenly appreciated why it was one of Camille's favorite activities.

I'd made it down one flight of stairs when I heard Eric's voice over my head. "Sophie! Where are you going?"

"Out!"

"Wait up and I'll come with you!"

I stopped and looked up at him. "I'm fine," I said quickly. "I don't need you to come." If he found out the truth, Mathieu might cancel our arrangement.

"At least take the key." He dropped the lanyard through the opening in the spiral staircase, and I was proud of myself for catching it.

"Thanks." I started back down.

"Soph." I stopped and looked up at him. "I'm sorry about Dane."

I nodded and gave him a tight smile. "Thanks for that too."

Mathieu was waiting outside the front door. He took one look at me and his eyes widened. "Are you okay?"

"No." I shook my head. "Yes, I'm fine. Just a bad morning." I started to rub my burning right wrist, which still hurt from Dane's grasp.

Mathieu's eyes darkened. He grabbed my arm and looked at the red marks. Then he grabbed my left hand and found lighter pink finger marks there. "Who did this?"

His fingers were gentle even if he looked angry, and something fluttered through me, catching my breath in my throat. But if I told him it was Dane, what would he do? Would he confront him? Then Camille would find out about our secret meetings, and I might not be able to practice at his apartment anymore. It wasn't worth the risk. Besides, I suspected Dane was about to get an earful from my brother.

"Sophie." His eyes lifted to mine, and I lost my breath for an entirely new reason. He was probably the most gorgeous guy I'd ever seen. His cerulean blue eyes darkened with anger and concern for me, his mouth pinched tight. I felt a sudden urge to pull my hand loose from his hold and smooth the worry lines on his forehead. It occurred to me that my wrists had been firmly held by two different guys in a matter of minutes, but the experiences were so vastly different, I could only marvel at it.

"Who hurt you?"

I blinked, coming out of my stupor. "It's nothing."

"It is not nothing. This is going to leave a mark."

"It was a misunderstanding." I gave a soft tug and he dropped his hold, making me sorry I'd pulled free. I looked around and forced a grin. "No breakfast today?"

He watched me, probably trying to decide if he was going to pursue the issue. Finally, his shoulders relaxed. "No. I thought we could try a different *pâtisserie* today."

"Okay." I started walking down the sidewalk. "Did you go out with Camille last night?" I'd spent the last hour debating whether to ask him. I hated to bring up my stepsister, but I was curious if he went to clubs, if he danced, if . . . Okay, I was curious to know *anything* I could find out about him.

"Yes."

Seriously? Was that all he planned on giving me?

He looked down at me, his expression neutral. "Camille said you and Eric were spending time with your father."

"I'm surprised she volunteered the information."

He frowned. "Thomas asked."

Thomas? It was nice to know that a cute guy was interested in me, but despite what Jenna had said, he just didn't give me any butterflies. Deciding to throw caution to the wind, I playfully grinned up at Mathieu. "You didn't ask?"

His gaze held mine. "Thomas beat me to it."

Oh . . . *there* were the butterflies, a thousand of them flapping around in my stomach, jostling for space.

I broke his gaze and looked straight ahead. "Do you like to go to clubs?"

"It depends on my mood."

"You felt like going last night?" I snuck a glance up at him.

"Only because I hoped you would be there."

I forced myself to breathe normally.

"Here it is." He pointed to a shop across the street from the corner where we usually turned.

We crossed the street and stood at the end of a small line. I tried to peer around the people to look at the counter. "What do you suggest?"

He gave me a blank look.

"Here." I pointed my thumb inside. "What do you like here?"

Understanding washed over his face, and his cheeks turned a light pink. "I love their *croissants*."

I grinned up at him. "*Croissants?*" I pronounced it the French way, trying to roll the R like he did and leaving off the T and the S.

His face lit up. "Your French is good when you try."

"Really? I feel ridiculous."

"You don't sound ridiculous. Would you like to learn more?"

I narrowed my eyes. "Is this some kind of trick?" I teased. "Are you going to teach me how to say *I smell like farts* or something disgusting like that?"

He burst into laughter. "No," he said. "Not unless you want me to."

"I know the names of three French pastries now. At least I won't starve."

His smile lit up his eyes. "Then you can learn more useful things, although it is pretty useful to know the names of pastries."

I sucked in an exaggerated breath and pushed it out. "Okay. I'm ready."

"*J'ai faim.*"

I repeated the phrase. "What did I just say?"

"I am hungry."

"*J'ai faim,*" I said again, then turned to the woman in front of me in line. "*J'ai faim.*"

She gave me a strange look, then mumbled something in French and turned her back to me.

"What did *she* say?"

"She said she thinks you must be so hungry that you have lost your mind."

I grinned, shocked I wasn't embarrassed. I would have been at home, but for some reason, here with Mathieu, I felt lighter and less anxious.

"That was very good." He smiled his approval as we moved closer to the counter. "Try this one: *Où sont les toilettes?*"

I repeated the phrase, then asked, "Did I just ask where the bathroom is?"

"*Très bien.* You can translate as well. Now repeat it."

"*Où sont les toilettes?* You know the trick is remembering it, right?"

"*Pratique-tu.*" His gaze held mine. "Now say, *Je suis très jolie.*"

"*Je suis très jolie.* What did I just say?"

He smiled, and there was a teasing glint in his eyes. "You spoke the truth."

"You aren't going to tell me, are you?"

"You figured out *Où sont les toilettes.* You can figure out the other."

Jolie sounded like jolly. Had he just told me I was happy?

We stepped up to the counter, and he leaned into my ear. "You are going to order."

I looked up at him. "A *croissant?*"

"Yes, but no pointing at all. You will say it all in French."

"I can't do that."

"Yes. You *can.*"

The employee approached us, and my heart thudded against my ribs. I tried to figure out why I was so nervous. I talked to the woman in line. Why was this so hard? But I wanted to order in French. I *needed* to do it. "Okay."

"*Est-ce que je peux avoir deux croissant, s'il vous plaît?*" he murmured in my ear. When I hesitated, he said, "You can do it."

I took a deep breath, then tried to repeat the phrase. I mangled the first part, but managed *je peux avoir deux croissant, s'il vous plaît*.

The woman nodded and tucked two croissants inside a pastry bag. "Did I order two?" I asked him, worried I'd gotten it wrong.

"Yes. *Deux* is two," he said as she put the bag on the counter. "Now say *Est-ce que je peux avoir deux cappuccino, s'il vous plaît.*"

I repeated the phrase, saying the first part better this time. Another employee started to make the drinks, and I was fairly sure she also told me the price because I heard the word *euro* and Mathieu handed her a ten euro bill.

When we took the bags and our coffees and left the shop, Mathieu said, "*Très bien*, Sophie. Very good."

"*Merci.*"

His eyebrows rose.

"I knew that one already." Then a huge smile spread across my face. I had ordered in French!

"You'll be fluent in no time."

My new teacher was definitely a motivating factor.

CHAPTER *Eighteen*

I PULLED OUT my croissant before I handed the bag to Mathieu. "So what's so special about this pastry?"

"Try it."

I took a bite and moaned. "Oh my," I mumbled with my mouth full. "This is the most amazing croissant I've ever had in my life."

"It's a *kraw-san*," he said, clipping the *n* and making the *aw* sound nasal. "It's French, and you're speaking French now."

I laughed. "I've already failed my first lesson."

"We'll just have to keep practicing."

He taught me new words all the way to his apartment—*door, street, dog, baby, man, woman, boy, girl. Stairs*, as we climbed the five flights to his apartment—considered to be on the fourth floor, Mathieu pointed out, because the French considered the street-level floor as ground and the second as first. I learned how to say *I hate to exercise. I play the piano very well.* And *Mathieu is a wonderful teacher.* (I asked how to say that one.)

My smile fell as an unwelcome memory clicked into place. "I forgot. I don't have my music."

He shut the apartment door and walked up behind me. "I think I might still have the *Warsaw Concerto* somewhere around here from when I played it."

"Really?" I asked. "But I started working on something new yesterday."

"What is it?"

"Rachmaninoff Prelude in B Minor Op. 32 No. 10." With any-one else, I would have felt pretentious. But it seemed as normal as asking him *Où sont les toilettes?* "But you don't have to look, Mathieu. I can play my memorized pieces."

"You warm up, and I'll see what I can do."

I ran my fingertips across the smooth finish on the fallboard as I lifted it. I was still amazed I was here—with Mathieu—playing a Steinway. Both things seemed too good to be true.

I'd played through multiple sets of scales and arpeggios when Mathieu set a small booklet next to me, along with a notebook and pencil, then lifted the lid.

I stopped playing and picked up the music. "You found it."

"Yes. My mother has a lot of music here. I brought the paper in case you want to write down your finger placement."

"Thank you." I picked up the sheet music, which looked new. "I'll be careful with it."

He grinned. "I know."

He left me then, so it was just me, the piano, and the music. Rachmaninoff was notoriously hard, partially because he wrote his pieces for himself and he was known for his large hands. From my practice the previous afternoon, I realized I was going to have to stretch my reach or come up with some creative fingering.

I started to play slowly, picking my way through the notes, trying to ignore the many, many mistakes. I was usually self-conscious of other people hearing my mistakes, but I forgot Mathieu was there as I played a section again and again, slowing it down and working on the timing. Mathieu appeared next to the piano again much too soon.

"Is it time already?"

"Sorry."

"No! Don't say you're sorry. I'm so grateful to have these couple of hours." I closed the booklet and handed it to him. "And thank you for digging this out. I was hoping to work on this here. I hope it wasn't too much trouble."

"No. None at all." Then he smiled, that dazzling smile that filled me with warm giddiness, and all I could do was smile back. All too quickly, he broke eye contact and disappeared with the music through a set of glass doors to the left of the living room.

I waited for him by the front door, both nervous and excited to walk the six blocks home together. But then I realized how much time I was stealing from his day, and it felt incredibly selfish. "Mathieu."

He looked down at me, his eyes searching mine.

I swallowed, then forced myself to say, "You don't have to go back with me."

He smiled again, this time softer and shyer. "I'm going that way anyway. I would like to."

Once we were outside he turned to me. "Did you have a good time with your father last night?"

I sighed. "Yes and no."

He watched me expectantly, waiting for me to elaborate.

"It was great being with him, but it was also a reminder of what we used to have." I paused. "The two of us were really close before he left. One day he was there and the next he was gone. It came out of nowhere, or at least that's how it seemed to Eric and me."

"Your parents didn't fight?"

"No. I wish they would have. I might have understood it more if they had."

He shook his head. "*Non.* Before my father left, my parents fought all the time. I felt caught between them. Part of me was sad when they divorced, but part of me was relieved."

"I guess looking back, I can see there were signs my parents weren't happy. I just didn't notice them." I'd lain awake half the night, reliving the last five or six years, looking for the cracks in my parents' marriage. It was funny that I could see them now when I couldn't before. "He told us why he left, and while I understand it now, he still didn't handle it very well. He should have told us the truth. Instead he ran away."

"He left you to work on *Sainte-Chapelle*?"

I looked up at him in surprise.

He shrugged. "We all knew about Camille's new stepfather. Everyone was surprised. Camille's family was very happy before the accident. We were curious."

He had to be talking about the accident that killed Camille's father. I wondered what Camille's life had been like before he died. It was hard to imagine her as anything but the harpy who was bent on ruining me.

"When did you find out he was leaving?"

"We found out he was moving to Paris the day he left."

Mathieu's eyes widened.

"But what I didn't know was that my mother apparently sent in the application for him. When he got the job, she told him he could either leave for Paris or move out of the house."

He was silent for a moment. "And you blame him for leaving?"

"At the time, all I knew was that he left us abruptly and then rarely called. What else was I supposed to think?"

"And now?"

We walked several steps before I answered. "I'm not ready to forgive and forget just yet. He should have told us the truth about his job and why he left. And while I realize he was upset last August, it doesn't explain why he didn't tell us he was getting married until after he posted his bans. Or why he didn't take us to his civil ceremony."

157

"Maybe he was worried his new marriage would upset you, so he kept it to himself as long as he could."

I lifted my eyebrows. "By hiding it from us? It hurt worse when we found out the truth."

"I know he loves you. Camille said she got sick of hearing about you and your brother and how perfect you two are." He grinned. "She hated you before you ever landed in Paris."

"So that's why she hates me?" Somehow that actually made me feel better.

"That and lots of other things. She and her mother became very close after her father died. Then her mother started seeing your father, and the next thing Camille knew they were getting married. She was very upset. She felt like she gave up everything—her mother, her room, her life."

I started walking again, letting this information soak in. It gave me a new understanding of Camille's bitterness and hostility.

We walked in silence for a block. "Would you like to come play tomorrow?" he finally asked, shaking me out of my thoughts.

I smiled up at him. This whole trip had made me feel like I was rafting on a turbulent river of emotions, but with him, I just felt happy. He even made me feel better about the situation with my dad. "I don't want to get you into trouble."

"Do you like coming over?"

My smile turned shyer. "It's the best part of my day."

He grinned, that warm happy grin that twisted my insides into knots.

"What do you do while I play?" I asked. "I get so lost in what I'm doing, I tend to forget you're there."

He tilted his head and his smile switched to mock-insulted. "Wow. Thanks . . ."

Horrified, I grabbed his forearm with both my hands. "That wasn't what I meant! Your piano isn't the only reason I want

158

to go to your apartment." But then the realization that I was touching him washed through my head, and I jerked back self-consciously, immediately missing the warmth and strength of his arms between my fingers.

He stopped and backed up, pressing his spine into the building. His warm grin was gone, replaced with an emotion I couldn't name. "What *do* you mean, Sophie?" His voice was low, and there was a hitch in it I wasn't used to hearing.

"Honestly?" I asked. Should I really tell him how I felt? At home I would never have been so bold, but it was almost easy to say the words when he looked at me like that.

He swallowed. "May I share something with you?"

I was a little afraid to hear what he had to say. Conversations rarely went well after an opening like that. But he had said he wanted honesty from me, and I wanted it from him as well. Especially after everything that had happened with my father. *"Oui. S'il vous plaît."*

He smiled at that, the corners of his mouth twisting up ever so slightly. *"Très bien,"* he said softly, studying my face. "You are a very good *étudiante*, not only with *le piano* but *le français* as well."

I grinned. "I see what you're doing there. Now you're slipping in random French words hoping I'll pick them up."

His eyes danced with mischief. "Is it working?"

"Mathieu est un merveilleux professeur," I parroted back the phrase I'd insisted he teach me at the top of the stairs in his apartment building. He *was* a wonderful teacher.

"Oh, Sophie." He sighed, looking less happy. *"Pourquoi dois-tu d'être si parfaite?"*

I wasn't sure what that meant, but it didn't sound good. "You were going to tell me something." I nudged his arm, eager to get this over with. He liked me—that much was obvious. Yet there was a giant *but* hanging in the air. At least we hadn't crossed any weird boundaries that would make it impossible for us to be friends, because even if I didn't get the chance to play his piano, I wanted to be his friend. I liked being with him.

"Camille and me . . . she was *ma copine*."

I squinted, then shook my head. *"Ma co-peen.* What is that?"

He sighed and scrubbed his palm over his eyes. "My girlfriend."

We stood in such perfect silence for the next few seconds, I could have sworn I heard his heart beating.

"She *was* your girlfriend or she *is* your girlfriend." Then something ugly rose up inside of me—jealousy, plain and simple. "See what *I* did there?" I asked. "That's English verb tense, and the correct usage is *very* important at the moment."

He grimaced. "Was . . . but *c'est très compliqué.*"

Thankfully for me, the translation of "complicated" in French was obvious enough for me to figure out on my own. Crap. My life was chock-full of other people's complicated love lives.

I was still trying to salvage this. "Was it serious?"

"Non."

"Did you end it or did she?"

He rubbed his eyes again, then lowered his hand. "We were only together a couple of weeks. We work better as friends."

"And how's *that* working out?" I asked, trying not to sound angry. I'd seen them together, and they definitely weren't friendly.

He shrugged.

"So what's so complicated? You were together a couple of weeks before you broke up. Camille has moved on, in case you missed the display at Musée Rodin a couple of days ago."

"And last night at the club."

Oh, mercy. I could only imagine what she and Dane had done at the club, making me even more grateful I hadn't gone. "When did you break up?"

"In May."

It was the beginning of July, so barely a month ago. I couldn't stop the groan that rose in my throat. "Did you break it off or did she?" I asked again.

"Why does it matter?"

"Why won't you answer the question?"

He studied me, his eyes full of sadness. "Me. I was the one who broke up with her."

"She still wants you back?" I whispered.

He pushed out a heavy breath. "*Non. C'est compliqué,*" he repeated.

He was right. This *was* complicated. "Mathieu, if you only dated a few weeks and both decided it wouldn't work, what's the big deal? I don't care if she's pissed off at me for seeing you. I don't care what she thinks."

"But *I* do."

"That's really sweet," I said, "But I can handle her."

"*Non,*" he said, getting frustrated. "I care about what she thinks about *me.*"

"Why? Do you love her?" I asked in horror.

"*Non!*" He sputtered out some French, and while the words were unrecognizable, the tone was not. He was slightly angry and very frustrated.

"Then what's so complicated, Mathieu?"

"Her mother . . . she's a banker. I need her."

He needed Eva? "Why? Do you have a lot of money you need to invest?"

"*Non.* Her bank has *le stage en entreprise.* I need Eva's recommendation to get it."

I shook my head. "What's a *stage entre-preeze?*"

He flung his hand to his side in frustration. "When you work at a place before you graduate . . . I don't know the word!"

"An internship?"

"Yes! I want to study international banking, and Eva's bank has a program for students the summer before they go to university. I need her recommendation to get in for next summer."

"Didn't she already give it to you? Wasn't it in the envelope you picked up?"

"*Non*, it was only the approval to apply."

"Surely Eva would give it to you. I know she loves Camille, but I don't think she'd let her daughter sway her like that."

"Camille could tell Eva something that would make her refuse to sign the recommendation."

"You mean like blackmail?"

He shook his head in confusion.

"She'll tell her mother something bad about you if you make her mad?"

"*Oui.*"

I wanted to ask what she had on him, but it wasn't any of my business. Besides, I wasn't ready to lose the illusion that he was the perfect guy. "Just to get this straight: You need Eva to recommend you. Which means you can't piss off Camille and have her tell Eva the big bad thing."

"*Oui.*"

"And because Camille hates *me* so much, she will run and tell Eva the big bad thing if she finds out you and I are friends."

"*Oui.*" I had never heard a word sound so sad.

Trying to push my frustration aside, I gave him a sympathetic smile. "I understand."

He looked like he thought I might be playing a trick on him.

"No, I do. This is your life. Your future. You need this. I'm only here for the summer. You can't throw that away for me." A selfish part of me wanted him to want me more than his future, but I also knew that wasn't realistic. Or fair. He barely knew me.

"Sophie."

I forced a warm smile. "Mathieu, I still want to be your friend, whether you let me play your piano or not."

"I want to be your friend too . . ."

"And I agree to keep it a secret. I would never want to hurt your chance at the internship."

"*Merci.*"

We looked at each other for several seconds, and I wondered how I could have gone from feeling so fizzy with hope to utter devastation in a matter of minutes. "I need to go." I turned and started walking, hoping he hadn't heard the quaver in my voice.

When we got to the corner of my dad's street, I stopped. "I think it's too risky for you to come to the door. Eric was following me down the stairs this morning, and he almost saw you."

He nodded, but looked reluctant. "Are you going out with Camille today?"

"I don't know." I grimaced. "Eric and I told our dad that we don't want Camille to be forced to take us around the city. So I don't know if I'll be invited on any more outings. Which is sad since I had fun at Musée Rodin . . . when everyone started being nicer to me."

His face darkened. "When Thomas started talking to you."

Ah, so that explained his behavior with Thomas. He was jealous, but he had no right to be. Not anymore. He had made his choice, and while I understood it, I didn't have to be held hostage to it. "I guess he's not being blackmailed like you are."

His eyes darkened even more.

"When we're with your friends, I promise to pretend like we hardly know each other. That's all you can ask of me."

"I know." Then he said something in French and walked away.

CHAPTER *Nineteen*

"*WHERE HAVE YOU been?*" Eric shouted as soon as I walked through the front door.

My mouth dropped open.

"Sophie!"

"I . . ." Why was he so furious? "Last time I checked, you aren't my father or even my babysitter."

"No, I'm your brother!"

"He's been freaking out for the last hour," Dane said, walking out of the kitchen. "He even walked around the block looking for you."

Eric shot him a glare before turning his attention back to me. "Where have you been?"

"Out."

"That's not an answer!"

"I thought you wanted me to see Paris!"

"I was worried something might have happened to you! Especially after the way you left. Dad would have flipped out if you had gotten lost while I was in charge."

"In charge? Are you kidding me? I'm not five years old, Eric. I'm sixteen. You're not in charge of me."

He scowled at that, and I stomped off to Camille's room, only to stop in the doorway when I saw her lounging on her bed, flipping through a French gossip magazine. Her upper lip curled as she glanced up at me. "Oh. You're back."

I studied her with my new knowledge rolling around in my head. I knew the apartment had been in Eva's family for generations. Had Camille lived here before the accident? Dad and Mathieu said she'd been forced to change bedrooms because she had to share her space with me. This room was bigger than the one Eric and Dane were staying in, but maybe she had some special attachment to it. Or maybe it was the principle. I wondered how I'd feel if Mom married her boyfriend and he had a daughter who invaded *my* room.

I must have stood there long enough to annoy her. The magazine lowered and her eyes narrowed. "Do you find me so fascinating that you want to watch me all day?"

And just like that, my guard was back up. Camille may have experienced pain in her life, but she didn't make it easy to be understanding. Without saying a word, I grabbed my laptop and started to leave the room, unsure of where to go. I couldn't stay in here, and Eric and Dane were in the living room.

"Where were you this morning?" she asked.

Something in her voice caught my attention. Did she know? "I was out."

She scowled, then looked down at the magazine. "My friends are going to see a movie later. Thomas has asked if you are coming."

I stopped. "Are you inviting me to go?"

"No. I'm telling you that I'm seeing a movie and Thomas will be there. *He* would like you to come."

"What are you seeing?"

She grinned as she continued to study her magazine. "Something French."

I supposed that was a given since we were in Paris. "When are you leaving?"

"In two hours."

"Thanks." It was hard to say it, yet I felt it was warranted. She could have told Thomas I wasn't going and left it at that. But then again, she wanted Dane to go, which meant inviting Eric. Given my brother's recent display, I suspected he wouldn't go without me.

I walked into the hall and sat on the plum-colored bench I'd admired on my first visit to the apartment. I'd sent Mom an email the night before, confronting her with my new insight to their breakup, and I still hadn't heard from her. I also intended to send an email to Jenna, but Eric found me as soon as I opened the lid.

"I'm going to grab a panini from the shop down the street."

"Okay."

"You're coming with me."

I shook my head. "You can't order me around, Eric."

His tone softened "*Please* come get a sandwich with me."

This was the Paris Eric, the one who actually liked to spend time with his little sister. I had to admit he was a curiosity I wanted to study more. I closed the lid to my computer and set it on the seat next to me. "Fine."

He grinned, although it looked more smug than happy.

I grabbed my bag and followed him out the door. "Dane's not coming?"

"No."

We were silent the rest of the way down the stairs, and when we started down the sidewalk, he finally spoke. "I'm sorry about Dane."

"Which part?"

He chuckled. "Yeah, I guess there are multiple things to apologize for." His grin faded. "What happened this morning?"

I shrugged. "He was being a jerk. No different than any other day."

"He has his moments at home, but I've never seen him like *this*."

I believed that. Eric could be a jerk in his own right, but I knew him better than to think he'd knowingly be best buds with a guy who was a jerk 24/7. "I'm sorry that it hasn't worked out for you like you'd hoped," I said. "I know you had plans for the two of you."

He just shrugged, but I knew him well enough to know he was disappointed.

There was a line at the restaurant. As we queued up, Eric said, "I saw you with Mathieu this morning."

All my blood rushed to my toes. *What?*

"I followed you. When I looked out the front door, I saw you two walking down the street."

I waited a beat before I asked, "Are you going to tell Camille?"

"It depends on why you were with him."

"He has a piano."

It was his turn to look surprised. "Oh."

"Yeah . . . the day he came back to the apartment with me from the catacombs, he heard me play on the keyboard. He said he had a piano and offered to let me play at his place. I've gone over there the past few mornings."

"Why didn't you say so?"

"He doesn't want Camille to know."

"Why not?"

I shrugged, feeling defensive. "It's kind of complicated, but the bottom line is that they recently dated for a short bit, although he says it was nothing serious."

"So? She's with Dane now." He didn't sound happy about that either.

"He broke up with her, and I don't think it ended well. Plus, he wants an internship at Eva's office, and Camille has some kind of information she could spill to her mother that would guarantee he loses the position. So, since she doesn't like me . . ."

"He doesn't want her to know he's helping you."

"Exactly."

"What else are you doing at his apartment?"

I gaped at him. "Nothing! I've been playing the piano."

"You didn't take any sheet music today. And you were gone longer than usual."

"What are you insinuating?"

"He's a guy, Sophie. And he's carrying on this secret relationship with you that is supposedly because Camille will get pissed about it."

"He's not like that. And we don't have a *relationship*."

He gave me a look of disbelief.

"*Nothing* has happened between us. Half the time we just argue."

He scowled. "*That* doesn't make me feel any better."

"We usually get some kind of pastry on the way to his apartment, then I play the piano for two hours. He tells me when it's time to go and he walks me back."

"I don't like it."

"I get to play a real piano, Eric. A Steinway."

The line had moved several paces forward and we stepped inside the doorway. "Do you know what you want?" he asked, pointing. The case was full of quiches, sub sandwiches, and personal pizzas.

I asked for a mozzarella, tomato, and basil sandwich on a baguette and Eric got a sandwich with ham. The employee warmed them up, then handed them to us in parchment paper. There were only a few tables, and they were full, so we took our sandwiches outside and ate them while we walked back.

I took a bite of my sandwich and made a sound of contentment. "Why don't we have fast food like this back home?"

"Good question." He took another bite, then said, "We're only here for a few weeks, Soph. Don't get too attached to a guy who lives in Paris."

"I could say the same about you and Marine."

He blushed a little. "There's nothing much there with Marine. I'm smart enough to know not to get too involved when I'm going to leave. But you . . ." He turned to me with worry in his eyes. "You're new to this."

I sighed. "I already told you there's nothing going on. He's not interested in me."

"I don't believe that for a minute. I don't like you being alone with him in his apartment." He paused. "And he's not the only guy I'm worried about."

"Thomas?" At home I couldn't even get one guy interested in me. I couldn't believe I had *two* here.

His eyes darkened. "Just be careful."

"Yeah . . . okay."

He let the subject drop, and we finished our food as we wandered around the neighborhood. I was surprised how comfortable I was becoming here.

Eric stopped outside the apartment building door. "Oh, one more thing. I told Dane to leave you alone. If he doesn't, let me know."

An uncharacteristic rush of affection for my brother washed through me. "Thanks."

He nodded and we went upstairs.

An hour later, we took the subway to the *Opéra* exit. Marine, Julien, Thomas, and Sarah were already waiting for us. I couldn't help noticing that Mathieu wasn't with them, and apparently Camille did as well. I heard her say his name when she addressed them in French.

She didn't like their answer, and neither did Dane.

"What did they say?" I asked Eric.

"I couldn't make it all, but it sounds like Camille specifically asked Mathieu to come and he passed."

"Why would she ask him to come?"

Thomas was edging over to me, and Eric was too busy giving him the stink eye to answer.

"*Bonjour*, Sophie."

I smiled when I heard him pronounce my name with an accent. "*Bonjour*, Thomas."

He looked surprised by my attempt at French.

Eric bought our tickets, and then we went inside, skipping the concessions. I studied the French title, trying to translate it in my head, but one morning of French lessons hadn't helped me master the language.

The theater was mostly empty, so I wasn't surprised when Thomas sat next to me. Eric gave him another dirty look, but he was distracted from his plan of intimidation when Marine sat next to him.

"Have you been studying French, Sophie?" Thomas asked, leaning close to me.

"No," I lied, feeling guilty about it, but I couldn't confess to my lessons with Mathieu.

"I can teach you if you would like."

Part of me rebelled at the idea, and I knew all too well why. Mathieu. Jenna had a point. I tended to pick unavailable guys.

The previews started before I could answer. They were in French—and since I had embarked on this mission to learn more about everything French, I found them fascinating. The movie started soon after, and it turned out to be some kind of rom-com, which surprised me since the guys had willingly attended. I had no idea what anyone was saying, although I listened carefully for the words in my limited vocabulary, catching a few here and there and getting ridiculously excited whenever I did. I found myself wishing Mathieu was there. Thomas was leaning against the armrest next to me, his right knee lightly touching my left one, but I didn't feel a single butterfly.

Eric kept glancing over at us, and I caught his gaze after about the third time, lifting my eyebrows at him in frustration. Marine put her hand on top of his soon after that, and it seemed to make him forget he *had* a sister.

When the movie was over, we left the theater and gathered on the sidewalk. Once again, Camille held court, but with my new knowledge of her past, I saw the group's dynamics in a new light. There was a hint of sympathy in their eyes, and it occurred to me that they tolerated her behavior because they felt sorry for her. I wondered again what she'd been like before, because it was obvious her friends were very loyal.

"Did you enjoy the movie, Sophie?" Thomas asked.

I knew I should give him a chance. He was available. He was interested. But there just wasn't a spark. "Yes, even though I didn't understand most of it."

"I really would be happy to teach you French."

Eric moved closer. "Maybe another time. We're leaving."

I shot my brother a glare as I waved good-bye to Thomas, but I was partially relieved. It bought me more time to work through the jumbled mess of my feelings.

We took the Metro back to the apartment. Camille and Dane sat several rows ahead of us. I studied my new stepsister, wondering how she and her mother could have reacted so differently to their grief and ability to move on. I suddenly had a desire to show Eva how much I appreciated everything she'd done to welcome us into her life.

I had an idea.

After Dad left, I'd started cooking to help Mom. I could make dinner. It seemed like such a small thing, but it was the only thing I could come up with.

When we got to our neighborhood, I convinced Eric to stop at the market with me to pick up the ingredients for spaghetti and meatballs.

He laughed. "You're cooking Italian food in France?"

"You don't complain when I make it at home."

"No complaints. Only an observation."

I ended up substituting sausage for ground beef and getting fresh tomatoes instead of canned since the fresh fruits and vegetables were so good here. Camille seemed surprised when I started cooking dinner, but to my relief she and Dane stayed out of the kitchen. Dinner was almost done when I heard the front door open.

"Oh!" Eva exclaimed front the entryway. "What smells so good?"

"*Bonsoir*, Eva." I smiled at her when she came into the kitchen. "I made dinner." I lifted a wooden spoon filled with sauce.

She closed her eyes and tasted it. "Delicious."

I beamed. "You like it?"

"I can't believe you made dinner," she said, tears filling her eyes.

"It's nothing," I said. "I cook all the time back home. I hope it's okay."

She pulled me into a hug, then murmured something in French before saying, "I am so lucky to have you for a daughter."

"As opposed to having me?" Camille asked, glaring at us from the doorway. "You can have a good daughter now?"

My heart skipped a beat.

"Camille," her mother sighed.

Camille walked away, and Eva turned to me with an apologetic look. "She will grow to accept you."

I wasn't so sure about that. Camille already saw me as a threat, and this was one more strike against me.

"Thank you for making dinner, Sophie," Eva said, struggling not to cry. "This is a very special gift." Then she went into her room and shut the door.

Dad came home soon after that. The guys set the dining room table, and Dad opened a bottle of wine for him and Eva to drink. We all sat down, and it wasn't long before Eva said, "Sophie, I think I have a solution to your piano problem."

I stopped eating, my fork midair. "What piano problem?"

"Your father told me you need to play on a real piano, not just a keyboard."

My face burned with embarrassment. "Eva, I don't want to seem ungrateful. I know you went out of your way to get it for me."

"No." She gave me a reassuring smile. "I understand, and I think I have a solution. At least a partial one."

I waited, a band of anxiety tightening around my chest.

"Camille's friend Mathieu has a piano in his apartment. His mother is an instructor at a *conservatoire*, and I contacted her this afternoon. I asked her if it would be possible for you to use their piano during the day since she and her husband are away at work. She said she would arrange for Mathieu to let you in."

Eric's eyes narrowed, and I could tell he was trying to decide whether or not to say anything.

I wanted to kick him under the table, but my mind was whirling. Mathieu's mother was an instructor at a conservatory? I had assumed she was a teacher like Miss Lori, not an instructor at a music school. But the Steinway and the fact that Mathieu managed to find a spare copy of the Rachmaninoff prelude so easily should have tipped me off.

"Are you open to this idea?" she asked.

I shot a glance to Camille, although I wasn't sure why. If Eva and Mathieu's mother had cooked this up, she couldn't hold it against him. She looked unhappy, but not as furious as I'd expected.

"I don't think it's a good idea," Eric said.

"What?" I squawked.

"I don't think you should be alone with a teenage boy in an apartment for hours at a time." He turned to Dad. "I can't believe you're actually considering this."

Dad looked blindsided. "Uh . . ."

"You would never let me stay home alone with Dori."

He was right. Dad used to insist that Eric and his girlfriend couldn't be home alone together. Which meant I had been stuck playing chaperone more times than I could count. Not that it had stopped them from going into his room and shutting the door.

"Do we really want to talk about how well that rule worked, Eric?" I asked.

His eyes narrowed to pinpricks.

Dad turned to me. "I trust Sophie to make smart choices. I don't see a problem with it."

My mouth parted. Was he saying that because he was trying to earn his way back into my good graces? Or was it time for me to start taking his words at face value?

"I was going to have Camille take Sophie over there tomorrow, but Madeline messaged me later to say Mathieu would come by to show Sophie the way."

"I bet he did," Eric grumbled.

That caught Camille's attention.

But Eva wasn't paying attention to either of them. "Madeline said Mathieu volunteered to pick you up around eight thirty. You can stay until lunch or later."

"Eva . . . thank you. You have no idea how much this means to me!" Not only was I going to get to be more open about practicing—and for longer!—but I would get to see Mathieu every day. I couldn't deny that it made me feel like I was glowing inside.

CHAPTER *Twenty*

ERIC WANTED TO walk me to Mathieu's apartment, a phenomenon that baffled Dane.

"Dude, she's been walking around the city for three days all alone," Dane said, furiously tapping and waving his video game controller, his eyes glued to the TV screen. "Let her go."

I moved closer to Eric, my eyes on his. "You have no say in this. Dad said he trusts me."

"Dad doesn't know all the facts."

"Eric!" I snarled under my breath, my eye on my stepsister, who was watching us from across the room. I put my hands on my hips. "What are you doing up so early anyway?"

Dane groaned. "Your stupid brother woke me up with his alarm, and I couldn't go back to sleep."

I grabbed my sheet music and stuffed it into my bag.

Eric followed. "If you're not back by noon, I'm coming to find you."

I leaned into his face and whispered, "What in the world has you so freaked out?"

His jaw set. "I don't like that he was so secretive. I don't care if he dated Camille or not. He's trying to take advantage of the situation, and it's much easier to do when no one else knows what's going on."

I shook my head in disbelief. "It's not a secret anymore, so calm down." I stomped toward the door and he followed.

"You better be back by noon!" he yelled after me.

"I'll be back by one!" I had no idea if I'd be gone that long. For all I knew, Mathieu liked our current schedule of me leaving after a couple of hours.

He was waiting for me outside the front door. "Since this isn't a secret anymore, I thought I could meet you here," he said, giving me a hesitant smile.

I nodded, suddenly nervous. "Thanks."

We had started to walk the now familiar path when he asked, "Did you ask Eva to talk to my mother?"

I sucked in my breath and came to a halt, horrified he would think that. "No! It was my father's doing. Well . . . and Eva's, I guess. My brother told my dad to get me a real piano to play. Dad must have told Eva, and she remembered your mom."

He nodded, looking like he believed me, thank God. I didn't want him to think I was some manipulative stalker.

"You didn't tell me your mother works at a conservatory."

His eyebrows rose. "I told you she teaches piano."

"That's entirely different than teaching at a conservatory."

He shrugged.

"Does she mind me playing her piano?"

"No. She likes Eva, so she was happy to do it for her."

We started walking again. "Are you okay with this? Everyone knowing that I'm coming over to your house?"

He grinned. "Yes."

"What about Camille?"

"She can't refuse our mothers."

Of course, I had to remember that while we could be open about me going to his house to practice, we still couldn't be together. I had to figure out a way to be okay with that. "Have you had breakfast?"

He beamed at me. "No."

"How do you say 'Are you hungry?'"

An ornery look filled his eyes. "Are you hungry?"

I bumped my arm into his. "In *French*."

"I taught you this yesterday. You've already forgotten?"

"I know how to say *I* am hungry. I want to know how to ask *you*."

"*Est-ce que tu as faim?*"

I repeated the phrase, then laughed. "I really hope I asked you if you were hungry and not if you'd like to buy my goats."

He grinned. "*Tu* is a familiar you. *Vous* is formal. *Faim* is hunger."

I cocked my head and gave him an ornery look. "You taught me *tu*. Does that mean we're past formal status?"

He was still smiling, but his eyes darkened. "Yes." His voice was husky.

I looked away, embarrassed that I'd pushed our boundaries. It was becoming harder and harder not to flirt with him, but there was no point in torturing both of us.

The line was shorter at the new *pâtisserie* today. I fumbled through ordering a croissant, a *Paris-Brest* for Mathieu, and two cappuccinos, then insisted on paying. "You've bought breakfast several days in a row. It's my turn. It's the least I can do after everything you've done for me."

"How long do you plan to play today?" he asked after we'd left the bakery and taken a bite of our food.

"I don't know. At home I just play until I get frustrated or tired. Do you have somewhere to go today?"

"No, but since it is Friday, my friends are going to a club tonight." He turned to me, a wary look in his eyes. "Are you going?"

"Oh . . ." I shrugged. "I'm usually added as an afterthought. You know that Camille would rather not have me there."

"But you went to the cinema yesterday."

My stomach fluttered. He'd asked if I was there. No, maybe not. Thomas or someone could have volunteered the information. "Camille said Thomas asked if I was coming."

"Of course he did."

I wasn't sure how to answer that, so I didn't.

"Where are you going tonight?" I asked.

"I never said I was going." His brow furrowed and he looked utterly unhappy.

I knew the decent thing to do would be to feel sorry for him, but I couldn't. After all, we were both suffering from the same frustration.

If that wasn't messed up, I wasn't sure what was.

When we entered his apartment, I pulled out my Rachmaninoff piece. Mathieu lifted the piano lid for me, and I began to play straightaway. I played the piece slowly, messing up the rhythm and getting frustrated with my fingers.

"Maybe this will help." Mathieu put a metronome by the sheet music, and I glanced up at him in surprise.

"Thank you. It will."

"I hated the stupid thing. You're lucky it's not smashed to bits."

"This is yours?" I was surprised he still had it.

"*Oui*. You may keep it. I noticed you didn't have one on your piano at your father's."

I bit my bottom lip, my heart so full of gratitude it was the only way I knew to contain it. It seemed stupid to be so happy over a metronome—something most piano students hated—but it was more than the object itself. Not only had he been thoughtful enough to realize I needed it, he'd given me the one that belonged to him. Jeez, Mathieu turned me all gushy. "Thank you."

He shrugged. "*De rien.*"

I turned the metronome to a super slow speed, then began to slowly pick through the section I was working on. After a while, the sound of a boy speaking French behind me caught my attention. I turned around to see a boy who looked a year or so younger than me.

"You must be Etienne," I said, turning around on the bench. "I'm Sophie."

He moved closer, studying me like I was an exotic animal plunked down in his apartment. Then he said something in French. Mathieu replied in a short burst of French before he said, "In English."

Etienne grinned. "I've heard a lot about you."

"Oh really?" I cast an amused glance at Mathieu, then back to Etienne. "What have you heard?"

Mathieu's brother seemed to consider his words. "That you are Camille's new sister." Then his smile spread. "And that you are pretty."

I blushed as Mathieu reprimanded him in French.

"Are you staying for lunch?" Etienne asked. "I'm starving."

"Oh . . ." I had no idea what time it was, but it had to be later than usual since I'd always left before Etienne came home from his swimming practice. "I guess I should be going."

"You can eat before you go," Mathieu said.

"Yes," Etienne said, grinning. "Please stay. Eat."

"What time is it?"

"After twelve," Etienne said. He was clearly up to something, but he didn't seem malicious about it. It was like he knew Mathieu liked me and was playing matchmaker.

"Can you call Camille and tell her I'm staying?" I asked. "My brother might come looking for me."

Mathieu's smile fell at the mention of his ex-girlfriend's name.

No, I couldn't ask him to do that. Practicing here was one thing, but eating lunch was going too far. I stood and gathered my music. "On second thought, never mind. I forgot I have something I need to do."

"What is it?" Etienne asked.

"Just a . . . something." *Brilliant, Sophie.*

"Is it with Thomas?" Etienne asked. "Mathieu is angry with him."

I shook my head, feeling a little happier about Mathieu's anger than I should have. "No, it's not with Thomas, not that Mathieu has a right to care." I closed the flap on my bag and gave my attention to Etienne. "It was nice to meet you."

"Maybe you can stay longer and I can ask you questions about *les États Unis.*"

"About what?" I asked in confusion.

"The States," Mathieu said, glaring at his younger brother.

"Maybe next time. Is Monday okay?" I asked as I opened the front door. "You don't have to walk me back, Mathieu. I can find the way."

"I can come—"

I closed the door behind me, torn over my decision. It might be good to put a little distance between us.

It was becoming harder and harder to stay away from him.

CHAPTER *Twenty-One*

JUST AS MATHIEU had said, Camille went to a club again that night. Dane and Eric went with her while I happily stayed at home. She had reluctantly invited me, but I didn't feel like watching Dane and Camille make out all night. And would Thomas expect me to dance with him if he came? I had a feeling it wouldn't be like the dances at my private school in Charleston, which were so lame most people stood around listening to bad music for forty minutes to an hour before leaving early. And if Thomas did want me to dance with him, what would he expect? It was less complicated to just stay home.

Dad and Eva had planned a date night because they'd presumed we would all go out. After Camille and the guys left and they realized I was staying home, they suggested changing their plans and staying home with me.

"Go ahead and go," I said. "I was planning to stay here and play the piano."

Dad frowned. "Have you done anything other than practice the piano today? How long were you are at Camille's friend's house?"

"Several hours, but it wasn't—"

"You spend entirely too much time at that piano."

"What?"

"William," Eva murmured, looking cross.

Dad ignored her. "I told Eva that it would be a bad idea for you to go over to that boy's house to practice. I wanted you to enjoy this summer, not sit at a piano the entire time you're here. You can't hide behind your keyboard and let life pass you by."

"I can't believe you said that! Do you even know me *at all*?"

"I know you better than you think. You're in Paris, Sophie. You need to go out and see the sights. You can play piano in Charleston."

I put my hands on my hips. "I didn't realize I was going to be interrogated for staying at *your* apartment."

"I think you need to be honest about why you sit for hours behind the piano. You're afraid to step outside of your comfort zone."

"Stop," I said, furious now. "Don't you dare presume to know anything about me! I've changed since you left—*a lot*—and you're not even trying to understand me." I grabbed my bag from the piano bench and slung it over my shoulder, then grabbed the key I shared with Eric from on top of my music. "I'm doing what I love. Isn't that why you abandoned us? To do what you love?" I shook my head in disgust. "I'm going out. You have fun coming up with new ways to insult me."

I stomped to the door and slammed it behind me, ignoring my father's protests and Eva's stunned look.

I had no idea where I was going, only that I wanted out, but it wasn't a surprise when I found myself headed toward Mathieu's apartment. I told myself it was out of habit, but I didn't stop walking. When I reached his building, I stopped outside and wondered what to do next. I considered walking past, but I didn't want to be alone. So I took a deep breath and pressed the button next to his apartment number. Seconds later, a man's voice came through the speaker, speaking in garbled French.

"Uh . . . is Mathieu there?"

There was silence for several seconds before I heard a voice I recognized. "Sophie?"

Suddenly tears filled my eyes. I pressed the button, hoping my voice didn't shake. "Mathieu, I'm sorry to drop by, but I really need to talk to someone."

"You can come up."

I hadn't recognized the first man's voice, which meant his stepfather was probably home. I wasn't about to go up to his apartment and embarrass myself any more than I already had. Especially since Eva and Mathieu's mother were friends. "Can you come down?" What was I doing? I was making an utter fool of myself. I pressed the button. "Never mind. I'll just see you on Monday."

"*Non!*" he practically shouted. "Wait there. Don't leave. Please."

I took a deep breath to calm my nerves. "Okay."

I stood to the side of his door, my face pressed to the wall because now that the dam to my tears had broken loose, I couldn't seem to make them stop.

A couple of minutes later, he bolted out the front door of his apartment building. He looked worried, but the worry switched to panic when he saw my tears. "Are you hurt?"

I shook my head. "Just my heart." But that seemed to worry him even more, and I shook my head again and wiped my cheek with the back of my hand. "My father. We had a fight."

Understanding filled his eyes, and he gave me a slight nod.

That made me cry even more, because I knew he empathized.

"Uh . . . would you like to come up?"

"Are your parents home?"

"*Oui.*"

I shook my head several times. "No. This was stupid. I'm sorry. I shouldn't have come at all." I started to walk off, horrified that I'd made such a spectacle of myself, but he grabbed my arm and gently pulled me back.

"Sophie." His voice was soft and understanding. "Just wait here, okay? I have to tell my mother I'm leaving." I hesitated, and he grew more insistent. "Please. I don't have my phone, and she will be worried."

"You're not going to tell her I'm down here crying, are you?"

He looked confused. "No . . . ?"

"She's going to think I'm one of those emotional, drama queen girls. Don't tell her."

"I won't. Come inside the front door." He took my hand and pulled me into the lobby between the double doors. "Wait for me here, okay?"

I nodded, still sniffling. He bolted through the second door and up the stairs, and to my relief, I had myself reasonably together by the time he came back down, a couple of tissues in his hand. He held them out to me, and I turned my back and blew my nose, then stuffed the tissues into my bag.

"This is becoming a bad habit," I said with a small grin. "Next time I cry, I promise to be prepared."

He looked relieved that I'd made a joke. "Where would you like to go?"

My amused look faded. "Do you know that is the first time anyone has asked me that question the entire time I've been here?"

A soft smile lit up his eyes. "I'm happy I'm the first. Where do you want to go?"

"The Eiffel Tower. I can see it out my bedroom window, and Eric and I walked over to it the day we got here, but I've never been back."

"Then we shall go to the Eiffel Tower."

He held the outer door open for me to exit, then fell in step beside me. "You didn't go out with Camille."

"No." I didn't want to admit to my lame reason for not going. "What about you?"

"I was about to leave."

I stopped in my tracks. "Mathieu, I'm so sorry. I didn't mean to keep you—"

"I was going because I hoped to see you." Then he slipped his hand in mine, twining our fingers together.

"Oh." A flutter of anticipation washed through me, stealing my breath.

He looked down at me, then squeezed my hand, his warm and strong against mine. I squeezed back.

"What happened?" he asked.

"My dad just insulted pretty much everything about me."

"What did he say?"

"He thinks I spend too much time at the piano, but he doesn't even know how much time I practice. He doesn't know why I chose not to go to the club, but he thinks I should be there. The only reason he cares is that he'll feel guilty if he goes out."

"I'm sorry."

I teared up again. "How could he forget so much about me in only ten months?"

He didn't answer.

"I used to wonder why he didn't try to take us with him. He says it was because my mother threatened to fight him, but I wish he'd at least *tried*."

"My father didn't fight for me either. I told you they argued, but they were ugly fights. Lots of yelling and throwing things. One day they had a huge fight and my mother kicked him out. I didn't see him for five years."

"Oh, Mathieu. I'm sorry."

He sighed. "He finally came back, and we started having Tuesday night dinners. We still do, and now we're friends."

"Friends? Not a father?"

"*Non.*"

"And you don't get along with your stepfather?"

"No. He's good to my mother, but he'll be glad when I go to university in a year."

My heart hurt to hear him say that. I hardly knew Eva at all, but I knew she'd never so callously dismiss me. "Where do you want to go to university?"

"London, I think. I want to study international banking."

"Like Eva. Which is why you need the internship."

We sidestepped a father who was bending over a stroller, adjusting his baby's straps. Mathieu's hand tightened around mine so we didn't break contact, sending flutters through my stomach.

Get it together, Sophie. Nothing could come from this. We were friends. Friends who held hands. "Your mother is a piano instructor at a conservatory and your dad is a taxi driver. What does your stepfather do?"

"He's also an instructor at the *conservatoire*. He teaches violin."

"Does Etienne play?"

"Not anymore." He grinned. "They stopped giving me a hard time about quitting piano when he quit the cello. What does your mother do?"

"She's a nurse at a local hospital."

"Does she play piano?"

I laughed. "No. Just my grandmother."

"Is your grandmother excited you want to study piano at university?"

I smiled up at him. *"Oui."*

"You should audition for my mother's *conservatoire*."

"What?"

"It's a university, but they have a *lycée* program."

"What's a *lycée?*"

"It's a three-year school, like your high school. Next year I'll be in *terminal*, which is similar to your senior year. You would be in the *première*, or your junior year."

"The university conservatory has a high school? And they study music?" It was tantalizing to think of having my piano lessons during school.

"*Oui*, the program is only a couple of years old. They take a limited number of students, and it's very competitive to enter, but you would have a chance."

I blushed. "You don't know that."

"I've heard my mother's students play. I know." He gave me a smug look. "And I played for eight years myself."

"I want to hear you play."

He shook his head playfully. "No."

I leaned into his arm. "Come on."

"I'll make you a deal. I'll play for you if you agree to audition for the *Conservatoire de Seine*."

"What?" I took a step away from him, but he held on to my hand. "*Your mother teaches at Conservatoire de Seine?*" I'd heard of that school. It was on my dream list. Or more accurately, my daydream list.

"Yes, and you should audition."

"I can't do that!"

"Why not?"

"For one thing, I'd have to live in Paris to go there."

"So?"

I shook my head. "Let's move past the living here part—it's July, Mathieu. When do classes start?"

"The beginning of September."

"Haven't they picked their students already?"

"*Oui*, but sometimes they have dropouts. The school replaces them."

"I *can't* audition. It's crazy."

"Why? Because you've never considered it before? You would get a two-year advance on *conservatoire*."

"But it's in French. I'm not sure asking for a croissant will help me in school."

He chuckled, clearly undaunted by my protests. "They teach the lessons in French and English."

I couldn't believe I was considering it, but it was exciting to pretend I was brave and could take risks. But this was my dream. Only a couple of years early. "It's crazy."

"You already said that."

"And besides, it's too late to audition."

"Lucky for you, I know the director of the program." He winked. "I eat dinner with her almost every night."

"Your mother's the *director*?" Could I really do this? The very thought filled me with anxiety, but I couldn't deny it was appealing. To actually go to school and not only learn from the best, but be surrounded by people who made music their life. It was like a dream come true. "I'll consider it."

His face radiated happiness. "Good."

I couldn't let myself stop and consider that going to school in Paris would mean I could continue to see him after August.

We stopped for ice cream and ate it on the rest of our walk. We'd just finished by the time we reached the *Champs de Mars*, the lawn to the south of the Eiffel Tower. A crowd of rowdy teens had begun to gather even though it wasn't dark yet, and they were jostling for a place to see the Eiffel Tower's light display.

"Do you want to go up?" Mathieu asked.

I clutched my bag to my side. "I'm not sure I have enough money to buy a ticket."

His eyebrows rose. "That's not what I asked."

Did I? My gaze followed the metal structure up into the now pink sky. The thought of going up to the viewing platforms scared me, but I was determined to try. Especially since it was the one thing I wanted to do here. Getting to go up with Mathieu was a bonus. I smiled. "Yeah, I do."

He seemed pleased with my answer. "Then let's go get in line for tickets for the lift."

As we waited, Mathieu told me about life at his lycée, which was located in the 5th Arrondissement—the Latin Quarter. He and his friends had been split up after their version of middle school. Although their high schools were public, they had to apply to enter the good lycées. Their small group had been divided between two schools, both close to the Pantheon, and both very elite. I'd already presumed Mathieu was smart, so this information only confirmed it. Mathieu took the Metro to and from school, as did his friends, and I listened in amazement as he described a life so different from my own I had a hard time imagining it.

Since he shared so much, I told him about my life back in Charleston and my small private high school. He marveled that I lived in a house with a yard (which he called a garden) and that I'd gotten my driver's license the previous spring.

"I can't believe you can't drive until you're eighteen!" I said. "I'd never get anywhere. We don't have a subway and we don't take the bus."

"It's not like many of us drive anyway. Not many people here own a car. Tell me more about your best friend, Jenna."

"She's the best. She's funny and smart, and she always has my back."

Confusion flickered over his face, and I realized I'd lost him with an Americanism.

"If someone is mean to me, she always takes my side. She gives me advice." My face blushed at the thought that I'd sought her advice about him only days ago. "You can meet Jenna in a few weeks. Dane will leave and she'll take his place." I was still looking forward to it, but things would change. For one thing, Mathieu and I wouldn't have any more alone time.

"Are you upset about Dane leaving? Will Eric be sad?"

I heard the hesitation in his voice. "Eric is pretty disgusted with Dane right now." Then I remembered what I'd said about Dane the day Mathieu had found me on the subway platform. Was he worried? "There was never anything between Dane and me. It was just a crush." I grimaced. "And it ended the second I got a good look at his personality."

"Are he and Eric good friends?"

"Dane was one of the first friends he made when we moved to Charleston. We moved a lot when we were kids, so sometimes it was hard to fit in. But Dane isn't his best friend. Dylan couldn't come on such short notice. I think Eric has been just as shocked as I have."

"I've had my friends since primary school, and I've only lived in two apartments," Mathieu said. "Our apartment with my father, and then we moved into Jean Luc's apartment."

Finally, after waiting about an hour in line for tickets, we made it up to the window. For once I didn't mind the Parisian queues.

"It's nearly ten o'clock, and it'll take at least another hour to get up there. Do you have time?" Mathieu asked as I dug out my money.

I knew I should probably check in with someone, but for once I didn't care. "Yes. Let's go up."

It turned out I had just enough euros to buy my own ticket. Mathieu probably didn't have a burning desire to do something so touristy, so I felt bad about making him spend his own money on a ticket. "I haven't been up since I was ten," he said, touching my arm softly to reassure me, the point of contact sending a jolt through me. "And I want to go with you."

Our next line was for the elevator to the viewing platforms. We got off at the second stop, but as soon as we stepped onto the metal floor, I was equal parts excited and terrified.

"Just give me a moment," I said, trying to curtail my embarrassment as I plastered my back against a wall in the middle of the structure.

Mathieu stood next to me with a reassuring smile. "If you can go down into the catacombs, this is nothing. And you did fine there."

I took a breath and reached for his hand. He'd dropped it after we got ice cream. It was perfectly safe to be up here, and I knew it, but I needed to hold on to him now. His belief in me gave me strength.

Mathieu squeezed my hand tight. "Let's see Paris."

I let him lead me out onto the viewing platform, holding his hand in a death grip. The sun had set, and the sky was turning an inky dark blue. Stars were beginning to dot the sky, and the skyline was full of lights. It was magical.

"There is *Arc de Triomphe*," Mathieu said, pointing with his free hand. The white arch was off to the left and illuminated with clear, bright lights. "We should go there too. The view is wonderful."

I looked up at him, trying to figure out if he had suggested we take another excursion together or if it was merely an off-handed remark, but he pulled me to another section. "*Grand Palais*." The interior of the massive arched glass ceiling was lit up, making the building glow from the inside out.

"It's beautiful," I whispered, leaning into his arm as I took in the view.

"*Oui. Très jolie.*"

I shifted my gaze to him, surprised to see him looking at me, his eyes as alight as the building, and it occurred to me that I'd gotten *jolie* all wrong the other day.

I met his gaze without flinching, amazed that I wasn't embarrassed or scared. This was exactly where I was supposed to be. With him.

He slowly leaned forward, and his lips gently pressed against mine. I froze—terrified he would change his mind, or worse yet, think I was a bad kisser. But his lips became bolder, and somehow my body knew what to do. My hands were on his shoulders, pulling him closer, and my lips were moving with his.

It was my first kiss. I'd heard so many disaster stories about first kisses, but this was perfect. My stomach fluttered and the rest of my body flushed. But my heart soared. I'd crushed on several guys, but none of them had made me feel like *this*.

He lifted his head and looked into my eyes, smiling, and in that moment I didn't think my life could be any more perfect.

CHAPTER *Twenty-Two*

"WHY DID YOU come to my apartment to see me?" Mathieu asked as we walked hand in hand back to my apartment.

"I was pissed at my father when I left. I had no idea where I was going, just that I had to get away. Then I realized I was close to your place. I almost didn't stop, but I felt like I really needed to see you."

"Why?"

I looked up at him. "Because you're my only friend in Paris."

He stopped on the sidewalk and kissed me again. This was the fifth time he'd kissed me, and each time was more magical than the last. "I'm happy you stopped."

"Me too. How do you think Camille will take this?"

We turned the corner to my apartment building, and Mathieu tensed. "Sophie, we can't tell her about what happened tonight."

I jerked to a halt, sure I'd heard him wrong. "You're kidding me."

He didn't answer, but the guilt in his eyes was answer enough.

"Are you ashamed to be with me?"

"Ashamed?" he asked, sounding confused.

"I'm a secret you don't want anyone to know about."

We stopped next to the apartment entrance, and his hand lifted up to gently cup my cheek. My knees buckled slightly at the contact. "I want the world to know, but not yet. Let me talk to Camille. If she likes Dane, she might not care that I'm seeing you."

Unfortunately, I wasn't so optimistic. "And if she's not okay with it?"

"We'll figure out what to do if that happens."

What choice did I have? Tell him no and give him up entirely? It really wasn't a choice at all. "Okay."

He kissed me again, his hand still holding the side of my face, tilting my head at an angle as his tongue skimmed my lips. Our previous kisses had been nothing compared to this one. When he lifted his head, the look of wonder on his face took my breath away all over again.

"I'll talk to Camille," he murmured, his gaze on my mouth. "I don't want to hide us."

"Thank you."

"*Bonsoir, ma* Sophie," he said softly, giving me one last kiss.

But our lovely moment ended abruptly when the front door burst open and harsh light flooded my eyes.

"Get your hands off my sister!" Eric bellowed, reaching for Mathieu.

"Eric!" I got between them, pushing him back.

"Eric, I—" Mathieu started to say, but Eric moved past me and grabbed a handful of his shirt.

"Where did you take her?" my brother snarled. "We've been looking for her everywhere!"

"Eric!" I shouted in a panic. "Stop! This isn't his fault. I found him and he agreed to keep me company."

"Oh, I saw how he was keeping you company."

"What we do is none of your business! How did you even know we were out here?"

"I've been watching for you from my bedroom window. I saw you walk past and bolted down the stairs to catch him in the act of molesting you. Sure enough, I was right."

Fury radiated through me. "He wasn't molesting me, you moron. He was kissing me good night. I've seen you do a whole lot worse with your girlfriend back home."

"Ex-girlfriend," he snarled. "And you lied to me."

"How in the world did I lie to you?"

"You told me nothing was going on between you two."

"And nothing was going on between us until tonight."

Eric took several breaths, his chest rising and falling in rapid succession as he tried to figure out what to do next.

Mathieu stood behind me, his hands fisted at his sides.

"Mathieu," I said softly. "Maybe you should go."

He shook his head. "I'm not leaving you alone with *him*."

That set Eric off. "What does *that* mean?" he asked, stalking toward him.

I pushed my brother back. I'd never seen this side of him before, and while it was nice to know he cared about me, I was scared of what he'd do.

Mathieu's voice took on a threatening tone. "I saw what you did to her wrists the other day. I don't think I should leave her alone with you like this."

"Her wrists? What are you talking about?"

All the blood rushed from my head, and I froze in panic. What would Eric do if I told him what Dane had done?

I turned around, my eyes pleading with Mathieu. "He didn't hurt me, Mathieu. I promise. Just go. Camille will find you here."

That was the cold blanket that got his attention. Anger and worry wavered on his face. "Call me if you need help. I will come straight away."

"I'll be fine. I promise. Go!" I shoved his arm, and he reluctantly took a few steps backward. "Go!"

"You better get out of here," Eric snarled, then called Mathieu a string of curse words that made me blush.

"Eric. Stop!"

His anger turned on me. "What the hell, Sophie? When did you start running off with boys?"

"I didn't run off with Mathieu. I ran out on Dad after he told me I should stop playing the piano so much while I'm in Paris."

He shook his head. *"What?"*

I gave him a quick recap of our conversation, which helped refocus his anger. His curse vocabulary was truly impressive.

"So I left. I couldn't stay with him one more minute."

"How'd you end up with Mathieu?" Eric made his name sound like a curse word.

"I just started walking, and before I knew it, I was there. I needed someone to talk to. I didn't have Jenna, which meant I had no one. Even if you'd been here, I wouldn't have talked to you about it."

"Why?"

"Come on," I heaved out. "You barely tolerate me most of the time. Although I have to say this display of brotherly concern has caught me by surprise."

"I'm your brother, Sophie. I care about you. You could've come to me."

"No. I couldn't have. We don't exactly do bonding conversations. But I like how close we've become on this trip, even if it's for no other reason than that we're stuck here together."

"Sophie." His voice softened in dismay.

"It's okay. I'm just telling you I really needed a friend to talk to, and Mathieu was happy to listen."

"Yeah, I saw that," he sneered.

"It wasn't like that, Eric. His parents are divorced and his mother remarried. He understands."

"Oh, I'm sure he understands."

"Stop. I really like him, and you're making what we have sound gross."

"Then why didn't he stick around and apologize for keeping you out so late? Why don't you want Camille to know you two were together?"

I gasped. "Now get this straight. *I* was out late. He was only with me, so don't blame him for that. He asked me where I wanted to go, and I picked the Eiffel Tower. It took hours."

"And Camille?"

"You already know."

His eyes filled with disgust. "So he's keeping you his dirty little secret."

"Stop. Just stop." Tears filled my eyes. I couldn't bring myself to admit he was verbalizing my own concerns. "You can't tell Dad he was with me."

"You want me to lie?"

"I want you to keep it to yourself."

More curse words spewed from his mouth, and then we heard Dad's voice. "Eric?"

Panic rushed through my veins. "Please, Eric. I'm begging you!"

A moment later, Dad pushed open the door to the stairwell.

"Sophie." My father's voice was heavy, and he looked older than I'd ever seen him. Dark hollows underscored his eyes and his face was pale. He rushed forward and pulled me into a tight hug. "I was so worried." His voice broke, and his fingers dug deeper into my back.

I knew I should say I was sorry, but I couldn't bring myself to apologize for telling him off or leaving. Still, I needed to say something. "I'm sorry I worried you."

He pushed me away slightly and looked me over. "We need to get upstairs to tell Eva and Camille you're back safe. They've been worried sick."

I had to hold back my snort. Eva, I believed. Camille . . . please.

The three of us climbed the steps in silence, and I looked over my shoulder at Eric, mouthing, "Thank you." He had kept quiet about Mathieu.

His eyes narrowed.

When Dad opened the apartment door, Eva took one look at me and burst into tears and then a gush of French as she rushed over to me and gathered me into her arms.

"I'm sorry, Eva," I said through my own tears. It only then occurred to me that my absence might have reminded her of the accident that had killed her husband. Now I really did feel terrible. "I didn't mean to scare you."

She pulled back and smoothed my hair out of my face. "You are safe. That is what is important."

I only noticed Camille was there when she spouted off a stream of furious French. Then she switched to English so I could bear the full brunt of her anger. "She ran off for hours, and that's all you have to say?" she asked in disbelief. "You made us come home to help look for her, which was ridiculous. We all just sat here and waited."

Dane gave me a look of disdain.

"Camille," Eva said, sounding weary. "She's home safe."

"After she *ran away* like a baby. She should be punished!"

"Just like you were punished for running away when I first got here?" I asked. "Multiple times?"

Ranting in her native tongue, Camille stomped off to her room.

"Where were you?" my father asked.

"I walked around. Then I went up the Eiffel Tower."

"The Eiffel Tower? Why would you do that tonight?"

"Why not? It's looming outside my window every day, and I wanted to go up inside it."

"You went up in the Eiffel Tower by yourself?" Dane asked in disbelief.

Dad pointed to the hall. "Eric, Dane. Thank you for your help, but go to your room. Eva and I need to talk to Sophie."

Eric still looked furious, and I wondered if he was going to spill everything, but he stomped away, Dane following on his heels.

Dad led Eva and me into the living room. They sat on one sofa and I sat on the other, setting my bag down next to me. My father's gaze was a bit glassy. "You scared us to death tonight, Sophie. We had no idea where you were and had no way of contacting you. You could have been lost or hurt or worse." He stopped and rubbed his mouth before continuing. "I was out of line earlier."

My eyes widened in surprise.

"I still think you could strive for more balance. You're in Paris. You should be out in the city."

"And I was out in it tonight." I took a deep breath and turned to my stepmother. It was time for some honesty. "No offense, Eva, but Camille doesn't like me and she hates it when I trail along. Most of the time I think it would be better for me to leave her and her friends alone."

Eva's mouth pressed into a tight line. "I will speak to her."

"No." I shook my head. "I understand why she resents me. I don't blame her. She has a million reasons to resent me being here. I get that. Maybe things will get better once she's no longer forced to entertain me every day."

Eva nodded, but Dad didn't look convinced.

"And I think more balance would be good. I'll just do things on my own. Or wait until Jenna gets here."

"You can't go wandering around on your own," Dad protested.

The truth was, I hoped I wouldn't be wandering around on my own. I hoped Mathieu would be with me. But there were some serious roadblocks to that plan. For one thing, I wasn't sure Eric would stand for it; more importantly, I realized there was no way my stepsister would ever give Mathieu her blessing. Which meant I was stuck.

"She needs a mobile," Eva said. "Part of the problem was we couldn't get ahold of her, and we knew she had no way of calling us if she ran into trouble. We can get her a mobile so she can check in with us."

"Eric suggested it before, but I didn't think it was necessary . . ." Dad said, rubbing his mouth again.

Now that we had settled the phone question, I needed to make something else clear. "Let's get something straight, Dad." I purposely kept my voice calm. "I love the piano. I'm very good at it, and I plan to major in music in college. But I have to practice. A lot. If I want to win that scholarship, I need to be in top form in October. That's not going to happen if I spend all summer without practicing."

"Sophie, I know you love your music, but what do you realistically hope to do with it? Will you give lessons to kids after they get out of school? Do you want to spend tens or possibly hundreds of thousands of dollars on a degree that will barely make you above minimum wage?"

Eva put her hand on my father's arm, and he stopped and took a deep breath.

"I love you, Sophie. I just don't want you to wake up twenty years from now and look back on your life with regret, wishing you hadn't thrown everything away for your love, only to find out how lonely you really are."

Was he talking about himself?

"But Eva reminds me that you are sixteen and have a mind of your own. You need to make your own choices. I can only give you my opinion."

"Thank you." Tears came to my eyes as I glanced at my stepmother. "Thank you, Eva."

She lifted her knuckles to her lips and nodded.

"So if we get you a cell phone, will you agree to go out and see some part of Paris every day?"

"Yes."

"And you can practice every day, but try to keep it to four hours a day or less."

I started to protest, but I knew it would be difficult to practice that much after Jenna got here. "Okay."

He was silent for several seconds. "You need to call your mother."

My heart skipped a beat. "Why?"

"When we couldn't find you, I called her to see if she'd heard from you. She's pretty upset."

I wondered if she was upset with me, him, or both of us.

"I think she's going to ask you to come home."

His statement hung in the air for several seconds, sending a cascade of thoughts through my head. If I left, Jenna would kill me. She had been looking forward to Paris for weeks. And it also meant I'd probably never see Mathieu again. Sure, the likelihood of us working out wasn't so good, but I wasn't ready to give up on it before we even started. Besides, I still wasn't sure when I'd see my dad next. And while we were clearly still at odds, I wasn't ready to give up on him yet either.

But most importantly, I liked who I was becoming in Paris. I liked the confidence I was gaining, and something had clicked tonight more than ever. While standing on the platform of the Eiffel Tower, looking down at Paris, I had realized I wanted to see more of this beautiful city that filled me with awe. I wasn't ready to give up on it . . . or on me.

"I don't want to go."

Dad's eyes filled with surprise, and his shoulders sagged with what looked like relief. Eva patted his knee.

"She might insist."

I sighed. "I'll tell her going home isn't an option."

"Thank you."

"I'm not just doing this for you," I said. "I'm doing this for a lot of reasons. Besides, I really like Eva. I want to get to know her better."

She smiled, then moved to the sofa and pulled me into a hug. *"Merci,* Sophie."

"If I'm going to call Mom, I'll need a phone."

Dad stood and pulled his from his pocket, then handed it to me. "I love you, Sophie. Even if you have a hard time believing it."

I got up and hugged him, but he was still earning back my trust. It was just one more reason to stay the rest of the summer.

Dad and Eva had started to leave the room when I asked, "Eva, do you think I could sleep out here tonight? I think it might be good to let Camille have some space."

She nodded. "I'll get you a blanket and pillow."

"Thank you."

When they left the room, I walked over to the big windows overlooking the street and called my mother. I hadn't heard her voice in over a week.

"Bill, please tell me you found her," my mother's tearful voice pleaded.

"Mom, it's me."

"Oh, Sophie."

She broke into sobs, and my heart hurt. I did this to her. "I'm sorry, Mom. I didn't mean to scare anyone."

"Did you run off because of the email I sent you this afternoon?"

"What?" Then I realized I'd never checked my email after telling her I'd heard Dad's side of things.

"He broke his promise. I'm sure he told you all kinds of ugly things about me." Then she broke into a several-minute tirade about how irresponsible he was and always had been. As her litany of his misdeeds continued, I listened in amazement. Had she always felt this way? I'd never once heard her complain about him so bitterly.

"Mom," I finally interrupted. "I'm fine. That's not why I left."

"I want you to get on a plane and come home tomorrow."

"No."

"What?"

"No. I'm not coming home yet."

"He's playing Disneyland Dad, isn't he? Taking you to all kinds of places I could never afford. He was like that here . . . never wanting to do the hard stuff. He wanted to be the fun parent."

This was a reminder that all the clues to my parents' discord had been there all along. I'd just chosen to ignore them.

"No, he's not. We do stuff as a family on the weekend, but during the week, he's mostly at work."

"So he's ignoring you."

"No, Mom. We're fine. We do things with Camille and her friends during the day."

"Your stepsister. Do you like her? You never mention her in your emails."

"Yes." I couldn't exactly tell her that we were nearly mortal enemies if I wanted her to let me stay.

"So you like Evangeline too?"

There was a slightly resentful tone in her voice, but I understood. I probably wouldn't be too happy if Mom were bonding with a new daughter back home while I was here. "Mom, I love you. No one could ever replace you."

"But you like her."

"Yeah. I do. She's really sweet, and I'm grateful she's not some fairy tale stepmother."

"Does she cook great French food?"

"No, she barely cooks at all. I miss your shrimp and grits."

"You can have some on Sunday after you get home."

"Mom," I said quietly. "I'm not coming home yet."

"Do you have any idea how terrified I was? No one knew where you were, and I'm stuck here at the hospital completely helpless."

Oh no. She was still at work. "I'm sorry. I really am. If I'd had any clue everyone was so freaked out, I would have come home sooner."

"Home."

Oh crap. I'd never called Dad's apartment *home* before, and it was a bad time to start. "Mom, you will always be my real home. Not Charleston. Not our house. Not this apartment. You."

"I love you so much, Sophie." She started crying again. "I don't know what I'd ever do if anything happened to you."

"I love you too, Mom, but I can't go home yet. I'm not done here yet."

"Okay."

"I think they're getting me a cell phone, so you can call me whenever you're worried." There was a pause on the other end of the line, so I said, "Mom, Eva's incredibly nice, but you are my mom. Nothing is ever going to change that."

"You're growing up and leaving me," she said through tears. "I thought I had two more years, but you're already pulling away."

Guilt washed through me and I wondered if I should tell her I was considering auditioning for *Conservatoire de Seine*. But I'd probably never get an audition, so I didn't see the point of upsetting her.

"Momma, I'll be home in another month and everything will be back to normal." Yet we both knew there was some truth to her words. I was changing, for the better, but I was changing regardless. I wouldn't be the defenseless daughter she'd put on a plane weeks ago.

"So you must be having fun if you want to stay."

"Yeah . . ."

"You met a boy."

I felt myself blushing. "Maybe . . ."

"Tell me about him."

"He's a friend's of Camille's. His mother is a professor at a conservatory. He has a Steinway and he lets me play it."

"Oh . . . so he knows the way to your heart."

My grin spread. "Yeah, I guess so."

"Tell me more about him."

I looked behind me to make sure no one was listening, then opened the massive windows and walked onto the narrow balcony. "His name is Mathieu."

"Oh." I heard the smile in her voice. "Very French."

"He's going to be a senior. He's got very dark hair, almost black, and deep blue eyes. He's about six inches taller than me."

"The perfect height for wearing heels."

I blushed again. "Yes."

"I want to know more."

I told her about him walking me to his apartment and teaching me French, about how he understood what I was going through because his parents were divorced.

"He sounds like a wonderful boy, Sophie. So why do I hear a *but* in there?"

"Camille and Mathieu dated—very briefly—but still . . ."

"Oh."

"He's going to ask Camille for her blessing for us to be together since she's seeing Dane."

"Wait. Dane Wallace?"

I told her about the two of them, Mathieu's internship, and the deep dark secret he feared Camille would reveal.

"I doubt it's as bad as he thinks," she said. "And if Eva is any kind of professional at all, she won't let her daughter influence her decision."

"*Mom.*"

"I only speak the truth."

"Camille will never tell him it's okay, and he won't tell anyone he likes me if she doesn't. But it's his future, Mom. I can't ask him to give that up for me."

"Then don't, Sophie. You're there for another month. Just take what you can have and cherish it forever when you come home. How many sixteen year olds can say they had a summer romance in Paris?"

I gasped. "I can't believe you're saying that. You're telling me to lie?"

"No, of course not, but let me ask you this: if you were back home and your father were here, would you tell him everything that was going on between you and Mathieu?"

"Uh . . . no."

"This is the same. I'm not telling you to sneak around, but if you're going to practice at his house every day, you'll get to see him a lot."

I wasn't sure what to say.

"Your memories will be even more special. Just leave it open and see what happens."

"But . . ."

"It's not like it would ever last. You'll have to say good-bye when you come home anyway. A long-distance relationship when you're sixteen is unrealistic."

My chest constricted at that. She was right. After this summer, I'd probably never see Mathieu again.

"Eric has figured it out. He's gone from ignoring everything about me to becoming obsessed with keeping me away from Mathieu."

She laughed. "He's your older brother. It comes with the job description."

"I miss you, Mom."

"I miss you too. No more scaring me like you did today. I expect that kind of behavior from Eric, not you."

"I'll try."

"Keep sending me email updates. And include Mathieu now."

I grinned. "Okay. I will."

Even from thousands of miles away, Mom knew how to make me feel better. My heart was being pulled in two different directions—back to my mom and what was familiar and to Paris and the possibility of so much more.

If I were totally honest, one person here tugged at me the most. I planned to take my mother's advice and make the most of it.

CHAPTER *Twenty-Three*

DAD AND EVA became even more determined to work on blending our family, despite a collective bad attitude on the part of us teens. Saturday was the Fourth of July and so Dad made barbecue chicken, but Eric complained that it wasn't the Fourth without fireworks. By Sunday night, they'd all but given up, even if our level of animosity toward one another had significantly decreased.

On Monday morning, I woke up with butterflies in my stomach. This would be the first time I'd see Mathieu since Friday night, so I spent more time getting ready and even decided to wear a skirt. Eric was standing in the kitchen doorway in his pajamas and a scowl on his face, nursing a cup of coffee. He watched as I stuffed my music and brand-new cell phone into my bag,

"If you aren't back by noon, I'm coming to his house to get you."

My mouth dropped open. "Dad promised me four hours. It's almost nine now. That's barely three hours."

He shrugged, looking indignant.

"You can't do this, Eric!"

He took a step closer and lowered his voice. "Then maybe I should give Dad a call. I'm sure he'd want to know you're about to spend hours alone with a guy you were making out with while everyone thought you were being murdered in some back alley."

I wanted to kick him. "Twelve thirty. I swear, all I do is practice there. You know how lost I get in the music while I'm playing."

"Fine. But you have to go out with Camille and her friends."

"No!" The mutual desire for me to stay away from future group outings was probably the one thing Camille and I had in common.

"Then let me borrow your new phone to call Dad."

"Fine!" I bolted out the door and down the stairs, pushing all thoughts of my brother out of my head. I ran so fast I was out of breath by the time I reached the bottom of the steps, but the sight of Mathieu waiting outside the front door made me breathless for a different reason.

"*Bonjour*," he murmured, staring into my face, then letting his eyes glance down at my legs and back up.

"*Bonjour*." My stomach was twisted into as many knots as a friendship bracelet. Our kisses Friday night had happened under the cover of darkness. Now it was the light of day, albeit a beautiful sunny day, and I wasn't sure what the rules were.

"Are you okay?" he asked, worry filling his eyes. "Did you get into a lot of trouble?"

"No, strangely enough, I didn't, but it wasn't any less ugly."

He looked confused.

"Eric yelled. Camille yelled. Eva and Dad freaked out. I talked to my mother on the phone and she cried. They worried that I'd been kidnapped or murdered."

He cringed. "I know. I'm sorry."

"How do *you* know?"

"Camille."

"She doesn't know you were with me on Friday night?"

"No. She thought you were wandering around alone. Your brother didn't tell anyone?"

"No. What would you have done if Camille asked you about it?"

"I would have denied it."

"You didn't talk to her about us?"

"Not yet." At least there was an apologetic look on his face when he said it. Part of me was upset, but I reminded myself of what Mom had said. This was temporary at best. I needed to accept it and be happy with what I had right now.

Mathieu tentatively reached for my hand, then interlaced our fingers when I didn't pull away. "Let's go get breakfast."

He seemed just as uncertain about the rules of *us* as I was, which made me feel better. Feeling more confident, I asked him about his weekend.

When we arrived at the *pâtisserie*, he encouraged me to order in French. He paid and grabbed the bags, then surprised me by saying, "Let's sit and eat here."

When I didn't protest, he sat down at a table on the sidewalk, and I sat across from him, suddenly nervous again. Was this a date?

He gave me an apologetic smile. "I know this is stealing part of your practice time . . ."

"No. You know, we've had breakfast together a lot, but this is the first time we've actually sat down to do it." I paused, then said softly, "I like it."

"Your French is getting better. Would you like to learn more?"

I grinned. "*Oui*. But I want to learn useful things."

He took a sip of his coffee. "What could be more useful than learning how to ask for the restroom?"

I tilted my head. "It's hard to imagine anything could be *more* useful, so maybe we could figure out something only slightly *less* useful."

"Do you have anything in mind?" His face lit up. He was wearing a pale blue T-shirt with French writing across the front. The way it stretched across his chest and biceps made me blush a little. This tall, handsome, well-built guy wanted *me*. A warm feeling swelled in my chest.

"Um . . ." I took a bite of my pastry. I'd picked an *éclair* today. "How about *what is your phone number?*"

His eyebrows rose playfully. "Are you asking for my number, Sophie?"

"Maybe."

"Puis-je avoir ton numéro de téléphone?"

I repeated the phrase, then dug out my phone and said, "Well? Are you going to give it to me?"

He leaned over and took it from me, surprise on his face. "You got a phone? When?"

"After Friday night. Eva said they needed a way to make sure I was safe, so they got me one."

He tapped the screen and handed it back to me as his phone began to ring. He dug it out of his pocket. *"Allô."* Then he looked at me. "That is how you answer."

I held the phone up to my ear. *"Allô."*

He spoke French into the phone. I couldn't understand anything past his greeting, but I decided I liked having his voice in my ear. Then he hung up.

I narrowed my eyes and gave him a look of mock reprimand. "I have no idea what you just said."

His blue eyes danced with amusement. "Lucky for me that means I still have a job as your French tutor."

We stayed a little longer to finish our pastry and coffee, then walked to his apartment. "Eric says I have to be home by twelve thirty or he's going to tell Dad you were with me on Friday."

His smile fell. "So I did take away from your practice time."

I squeezed his hand. "No. I loved this morning. Really. And if Camille won't approve . . ."

He stopped and looked down at me. "I'm not ashamed of you."

"I know." But he hadn't even tried.

He leaned down and gave me a gentle kiss, full of adoration and hope, then murmured against my lips, "I really like you, Sophie Brooks."

"I really like you too, Mathieu Rousseau." I always thought of him as Mathieu, not Mathieu Rousseau. "It sounds so French," I thought out loud, then immediately turned beet red.

"You are adorable, Sophie Brooks, even when you state the obvious." Then he began to walk again. "But we must hurry so you'll have enough practice time."

When we entered his apartment, we fell into our usual routine. Mathieu opened the piano, then disappeared; I got out my music and began to play. I was completely lost in a section of Rachmaninoff's Prelude—one I was finally feeling good about—when I noticed him standing next to the piano.

I stopped and groaned, frustrated that I had to stop. "Is it time to go?"

"*Oui et non.*"

I narrowed my eyes in confusion. How could it be both?

"Camille called. She wants me to take you to meet her, your brother, and our friends."

"What? Why?"

"They want to see the *Opéra* and she says it will be faster if I take you."

"They're going to an opera? Is it in French?"

He chuckled. "No. They are touring the building. It's very famous."

"Were you planning to go?"

He grimaced and looked away.

He wasn't. So he was changing his schedule to accommodate my irritating stepsister. "I can just go by myself." I would have put it off altogether, but I'd promised Eric. "Help me figure out which trains to take."

"No. She said you might get lost if I don't take you."

"And I'm sure it wasn't out of concern for me. She's just worried she'll get in trouble somehow. I'll figure out a way to get you out of this."

He didn't answer, so I grabbed my bag off the floor and dug out my phone. I figured I'd send Eric a text begging him to let me cancel, but he'd already beat me to it.

> **You're not going anywhere with that French guy. I'll be outside his apartment at 12:30.**

I wasn't sure whether to be disappointed or relieved. "Don't worry. You don't have to take me at all. Eric's coming to pick me up."

"Sophie," he said, sighing. "It's not that I don't want to go to the *Opéra* with you. I just . . ."

"It's okay." I knew he didn't owe me an explanation, yet I really wanted one anyway. I glanced back at the music, trying to decide what to do. It was 12:20, which meant I had another ten minutes to play, but I wouldn't be able to concentrate. I grabbed the music and tucked it into my bag.

"Sophie."

I forced a grin. "I want to hear *you* play."

A look of surprise filled his eyes, then he laughed. "I told you I would play for you, but you have to audition for my mother's school first."

"That's insane." He gave me a blank stare, and I realized he didn't understand the word. "It's crazy."

He grinned. "Not as crazy as you think." He moved toward me. "But if you aren't going to play, maybe we could do something else before you go."

My stomach did backflips. Did he want to make out? The thought equally terrified and thrilled me.

A blush crept up his face. "I can make you lunch."

I gasped. "Oh. Did I say what I was thinking out loud?"

He laughed but looked away. "No. But I could see it on your face."

Another voice caught me by surprise. "*I* want lunch."

I stood and spun around. "Etienne. I didn't know you were home."

"You're just like *Maman*. Lost in *la musique*. I got home over an hour ago."

"Sorry. Especially if I disturbed you."

He gave me a huge grin. "I have headphones."

I cringed. "Sorry."

"*Maman* said it was only for July, then you would be leaving, *non*?"

"And part of August, but I don't *have* to come here to practice."

Mathieu interrupted. "It won't be a problem, will it, Etienne?"

Mathieu's brother looked back and forth between the both of us, then spoke in French. Mathieu seemed irritated, but he replied with something that made Etienne laugh.

"What did you two just say?" I asked.

"We came to an understanding," Mathieu said. "Etienne will mind his own business."

"And let you play as long as you want," Etienne finished.

"Why do I still think I missed part of this conversation?"

Etienne just shrugged and smiled.

I shook my head, but seeing them together gave me hope. I doubted Camille and I would ever be close, but maybe someday we could have a conversation without wanting to scratch out each other's eyes.

My eyes found the French doors on the opposite wall of the kitchen. I suddenly realized that though I'd been to Mathieu's apartment several times now, I had only seen a tiny piece of it.

"I don't have time for lunch, but I'd love a quick tour of your apartment."

Mathieu's eyes widened. "Oh. Okay." Then he grinned. "This is the living room."

I looked around at the sofa and vintage chairs, the fireplace surrounded by marble and ornate woodwork. "Where's the TV?"

"Our parents don't believe in television," Mathieu said, his tone guarded.

"Which is why we have them in our rooms," Etienne added.

"My mom tried that for about three weeks once. Let's just say it didn't work out." I laughed. "My dad couldn't handle it." But the memory of what used to be still pricked a bit, like a slightly dulled needle. Time to change the subject. "What's in that room?" I asked, pointing to the French doors.

"Father's office," Etienne said. "And it's not allowed."

"We can't go in," Mathieu said. "But *Maman* keeps her music in there."

"Oh." They sounded so adamant I couldn't help wondering how many times that had been pounded into their heads. I wandered over to the room and peered in the glass doors. A large wood desk filled the center of the room, and floor-to-ceiling bookcases lined one wall. Every inch of space on the shelves looked to be filled with music books.

I went into the kitchen next, the two boys watching me like I was an exotic animal set loose in their apartment and they weren't sure what to do. The kitchen was nicer and newer than Eva's, but it had a sterile look. The living room felt much the same way.

"Does your mother cook?" I asked.

"*Oui*," Etienne said. "Madeline cooks very well."

Mathieu's mother's name was Madeline. I filed that piece of information into the folder in my brain titled Facts I Know about Mathieu Rousseau.

"Your brother will be here in a few minutes," Mathieu said. "You probably shouldn't be late."

"Do you have any younger sisters?" Etienne asked. Mathieu playfully smacked him on the head.

"No, I only have one annoying older brother."

Etienne shot Mathieu a look. "Me too."

"I feel your pain." I laughed. "I better go."

"I'll walk you downstairs." Mathieu led me toward the door.

"You can come anytime you want, Sophie," Etienne called out. "Even if you don't have a sister."

I giggled. *"Merci."*

As soon as the door shut behind me, Mathieu pulled me against his chest and kissed me. The abrupt move caught me by surprise, but it only took me half a second to catch up.

"I've wanted to do that all morning," he said, smiling down at me.

I blushed. "But we kissed before we got to your apartment."

"That was hours ago." I studied his face, his grin, trying to commit it to memory. Soon I would have to leave him, and we wouldn't even have *this*.

He cupped my cheek, his hand smooth against my skin. "I'll miss you today."

It was like he'd read my mind. "Me too."

Sighing, he took my hand, and we descended the stairs together in silence. When we reached the bottom, he gave me another kiss, soft this time. "Have a wonderful day, Sophie." Then he opened the door to the small lobby. I expected him to go back upstairs, but he followed me instead, opening the outer door and giving my brother a stare so cold it could freeze the sun.

"Sophie," Eric said, looking me up and down. "It's time to go."

"Thank you, Captain Obvious."

Mathieu watched my brother for several seconds, then turned his back to Eric and lowered his voice. "If you feel unsafe, text or call me. I'll come get you right away."

"Mathieu, Eric would never hurt me."

But I saw him looking down at my wrists before he leaned down and kissed my forehead. "Just remember what I said." Then he walked back inside, shutting the door behind him.

I needed to tell him how I'd really gotten the marks. But would he confront Dane? I didn't want him to get hurt, especially not because of me.

"What was that about?" my brother demanded.

"Nothing." I held on to the strap of my bag. "Where's the nearest Metro station?"

"That wasn't nothing, Sophie."

"It's a misunderstanding that I've tried to clear up, but your hostile attitude isn't helping."

"That's not a misunderstanding. He thinks I'm going to hurt you. *Why?*"

I groaned, trying not to panic. I couldn't tell either one of them about Dane grabbing my wrists. How could I make him drop this? "You have to admit you were pretty aggressive Friday night."

"I would never hurt you." He sounded offended.

"*I* know that, but he barely knows you. And when he sees you with me, you're always threatening him." I took a breath." Have you eaten? Because I'm starving."

He was silent for several seconds. I could see a war waging in his eyes, then his shoulders slumped with defeat. "No, I haven't. We can stop and get something."

It was only a couple of blocks to *La Tour Maubourg* station, which thankfully took us directly to our stop, aptly named *Opéra*. We stopped by a bakery that sold sandwiches and ate them on the way.

Camille and her friends were waiting on the front steps of that impressive gold-domed building I'd noticed from the Eiffel Tower. She and Dane were sitting next to each other, their hips plastered together. Marine and her brother, Thomas, and Sarah were all there.

"*Ou est Mathieu?*" Camille asked, her hands on her hips, as we approached.

"He couldn't come," I said before Eric could respond. "Had other plans."

"You understood me?" she asked in surprise.

She knew we had spent some time together. Should I confess he'd been teaching me French? But Thomas was watching with extreme interest, and I didn't want to hurt his feelings or put any more stress on his friendship with Mathieu. "You asked Mathieu to bring me here, so I figured that's what you were saying. It was, wasn't it?"

Uncertainty wavered in her eyes, then she looked away. "Let's get this over with so we can go shopping."

Dane wrapped an arm around her back. "That's the spirit." Then he plopped a kiss on her lips and started to guide her down the stairs.

The others followed them, but Thomas had found his way to my side.

Eric scowled at him. "I'll be within twenty feet of you, so don't get any ideas."

Good heavens. What had gotten into him? "Eric, give it a rest."

"What's going on with your brother?" Thomas asked as Eric slunk off ahead of us, looking over his shoulder at me.

"I have no idea." I sighed, watching Eric in wonder. For sixteen years, he had acted like he couldn't care less about what I did or who I talked to, and suddenly he was like a wrestler on steroids, ready to beat up any guy who dared to make eye contact with me. "But I plan to ignore him as much as possible. What do you know about the *Opéra*?"

"As little as possible."

We spent about an hour in the building. I got an audio tour for the sole purpose of avoiding conversation with Thomas. I felt guilty, but I didn't want to encourage him.

When we left, Marine said something that got Camille and Sarah excited. The guys didn't seem to balk at the suggestion, so we all headed across the street.

"Where are we going?" I asked my shadow.

"To *Hermé's*. They sell macaroons there."

I'd had macaroons before in Charleston, but I had to admit I was curious. I'd heard French macaroons were worlds better than their American counterparts. So I followed along willingly enough—not that I had a choice.

The macaroons were being sold on the first floor of what looked like a department store. The display case was small, but filled with a wide assortment of choices. The prices were ridiculously expensive.

"Do you want a macaroon?" Thomas asked as we watched the three girls make their choices.

I didn't have any money, and I wasn't about to ask my brother for some.

"I'll pay for them."

I gasped. "Oh, Thomas. I can't let you do that."

"Have you had French macaroons before?"

"No, but . . ."

"What kinds would you like?" When I started to protest, he held up his hand. "I'm buying macaroons, so you might as well tell me what you want. Otherwise, you might end up getting a flavor you don't like."

"You're relentless, aren't you?"

He laughed. "I have no idea what that means."

"It means you won't leave me alone until I say yes."

His grin spread across his face. "Then yes. You will find I am very relentless."

I requested only three flavors—lemon, chocolate, and raspberry. He ordered several for himself and offered me the open box when the clerk handed it to him. I picked the lemon macaroon first and took a small bite, surprised by the delicate texture. The crust crushed in with only a small amount of pressure.

"Do you like it?" he asked.

This macaroon wasn't like any macaroon I'd ever tasted back home. In fact, I decided the imposters from Charleston should be ashamed. "This is delicious." Then I took another small bite, intending to savor every morsel. "Thank you."

"I'm happy to give you your first French macaroons."

Guilt washed over me. I felt like I was two-timing Mathieu, which was ridiculous. I hadn't done anything wrong, and besides, it wasn't like we were boyfriend and girlfriend. But somehow I knew the connection we shared was too special to dismiss. It wasn't right to let Thomas think something could happen between us.

"Thomas," I said, my heart pounding in my chest. The last thing I wanted to do was hurt him. "I feel like I should be honest with you about something."

A strange look crossed his face.

What was I going to tell him? "I really like you, but I have a boyfriend back home," was out of my mouth before I gave it coherent thought. *Oh crap.* Why had I said that? One slip from my brother and Thomas would catch me in a lie. But it was too late now.

"Oh." Disappointment filled his eyes before he looked down. "I hope you'll still want to spend time with me."

He studied me for a moment, then gave me a hesitant smile. "Why wouldn't I spend time with you? We're friends, *non?*"

I pushed out a huge breath. "Yes. I really want to be your friend."

"Then nothing has changed. Now eat another macaroon." He held out the box, and I took the raspberry one, grateful that I now had two friends in Paris. Never in a million years would I have expected that, let alone that both of them would be guys.

I was definitely out of my element.

CHAPTER *Twenty-Four*

THE REST OF the week progressed in much the same way. I spent my mornings with Mathieu and my afternoons with Eric, Dane, Camille, and her friends even though the outings were now optional. It was harder and harder to leave Mathieu when Eric stopped by the apartment to get me. And Thomas and I were becoming better friends now that I'd set up a boundary line between us.

But my evenings were filled with texts—from Jenna and from Mathieu. Jenna's were easy to explain, but Mathieu's were harder to hide. My family wasn't used to me having a phone, so I drew curious looks from them whenever I pulled it out to read my screen. I was terrified I'd get caught.

So I started sleeping on the sofa.

This upset Eva after the first few nights. "You have a perfectly good bed, Sophie. Why would you sleep on the sofa?"

"I'm used to having my own room at home," I said. "I like it out here."

After everyone went to bed, I would lie on the sofa, and Mathieu and I would text until late at night.

We texted about everything and nothing. But the more we texted, the closer we got.

At dinner on the Thursday night of our third week in Paris, Dad looked at Eva and then said, "We've decided to go away on Saturday."

Eric's jaw dropped. "You're leaving us alone?"

Dad blinked and then shook his head. "No. Of course not. We're *all* going away."

"Where?" Camille demanded.

Eva gave her a warning look. "Versailles."

"We won't all fit in a car," Camille said, then narrowed her eyes at me. "I suggest we leave Sophie here."

"Fine with me."

Eva pushed out a heavy sigh. "No one is staying home. We're taking the train."

My stepsister mumbled her protest in French, but our parents didn't change their mind.

When we left Saturday morning, Eva and Dad's chipper attitudes were a sharp contrast to Camille's hostile countenance. Eric and I actually wanted to go, but Dane looked torn between getting excited and trying to placate Camille. I had no idea why she was so angry other than we were actually beginning to look like a family.

Lucky for us, we could catch the train from our Metro station and take it the rest of the way to Versailles, about a forty-five minute trip. From there it was a short walk from the station to the palace. It was ornate and impressive, but the lines were incredibly long. We toured the inside and then walked around the massive gardens, staying until early evening.

On Sunday, Dad surprised us by announcing he had to go to work, and he was taking Eric and me with him.

After breakfast we took the Metro to *Sainte-Chapelle.* The church wasn't easily accessible like Notre Dame. It was behind the walls of several buildings, and the public had to wait in line to get to the outside of the church. Lucky for us, Dad could bypass the line. We went through the employee entrance, which eventually brought us to the courtyard surrounding the church.

While Eric had already been there, this was my first time. Scaffolding was erected next to a section of the exterior on the south side of the medieval Gothic church.

"The stained glass in the chapel has been in the process of renovation for over forty years," Dad said, walking toward the scaffolding. "And that's what's getting the attention from the outside world. But we're hard at work on the structure as well, particularly the gargoyles." He looked down at me. "Do you remember the definition of a gargoyle, Sophie?"

"I'm not seven years old, Dad."

"So you forgot?"

I sighed. "A gargoyle is a drain spout. A chimera is purely decorative."

He grinned. "You remembered."

"More like I couldn't forget it." His happiness faded, and I had to admit it had been a pretty mean response. "Sorry, Dad."

He nodded. "I'm coming late to the project, but there's plenty to do. Weather and pollution haven't been kind to the gargoyles, and quite a few of them need major restoration. The irony is that the gargoyles were designed to drain water away from the building, but water is their biggest source of decay." He looked directly at me. "Sometimes what we see as our purpose hurts us in the end."

Was he not-so-subtly talking about me? "What are you trying to say, Dad? Just spit it out."

"My job is to restore structures from the past. They've been beat up and worn down, and I help bring them back to a state similar to what they were before—similar but not exactly the original." He took a breath. "This is *my* dream. I've wanted to do this since I was a little boy, but look what I've given up to have it. You." He turned to Eric. "And you. I gave up both of you to pursue my dream."

Eric and I remained silent, waiting to see where he would go with this.

"My work here is important, but it's not as important as you." He swallowed. "I didn't think we'd immediately pick up where we left off when you came here this summer, but I had hoped we'd be at a better place than we are now. I underestimated how hurt you would be."

"Are you serious?" I asked, trying to keep my voice down so we wouldn't attract the attention of the tourists around us. "You barely talked to us for almost a year. Did you really think nothing would change while you were gone?"

I expected Eric to tell me to shut up, but he surprised me by nodding in agreement.

"No," Dad said. "Of course not. And while I claim full responsibility for my behavior over the last year, I'm trying to fix it now. I'm trying to fix *us*. Look at this gargoyle." He pointed to a piece of stone sticking out of the building about thirty feet over our heads. "It's broken and worn and neglected. It looks hopeless." He walked down to the end of the building. "But this one looks nearly new." He pointed to a more detailed statue. Its edges were sharp, its curves defined. "This statue was worse than the one over there."

"What's your point, Dad?" Eric demanded.

"My point is that a lot of time and effort went into restoring that gargoyle, and not just from me. Others worked on it as well, and together, we made it nearly as good as new. If I put that much effort into this inanimate object, how much more effort do you think I'm willing to put into my own kids? I was so hurt for six months I couldn't stop and think about how this was affecting you guys, but I know I was selfish and screwed up. I want to fix it."

"You had to drag us all the way down here to tell us that?" Eric asked.

Dad grinned. "No, I brought you all the way down here because there's a place around the corner that makes great *crêpes*. I figured we could stop here on the way."

Eric shook his head, grinning.

"I'm not giving up on you guys. Please don't give up on me."

CHAPTER *Twenty-Five*

AFTER TWO DAYS apart, I was eager to see Mathieu on Monday morning. He seemed to feel the same way, judging from the way he gathered me into his arms as soon as I walked out the door.

"Mathieu," I said, pulling away after several seconds. "What about Eric?"

"I've missed you, Sophie. I don't care about Eric."

I didn't either. But ultimately, Mathieu *did* care. "Let's go around the block. Then you can kiss me again."

He grabbed my hand and tugged me down the street and around the corner. He looked down at me, smiling softly. "I've missed seeing your face."

"I've missed seeing yours more."

He kissed me again, but it was soft and gentle. "Let's get breakfast."

"Okay."

We followed our new routine—sitting outside with our breakfast and talking. Since we hadn't seen each other for two days, we stayed longer than usual. Mathieu seemed on edge, but when I asked him if something was wrong, he just shook his head. "No," he said, looking down at his phone, "but it's already ten o'clock, Sophie. We need to go."

I reluctantly agreed, wondering if I'd done or said something wrong as we walked the rest of the way to his apartment. Once inside, I got to work like I usually did.

My Rachmaninoff piece was almost put together, and I was feeling the pressure to start the next piece Miss Lori had given me.

I was currently stuck on a measure I knew wasn't correct. I'd been listening to a recording of it on my laptop, and though I could tell it was off, I couldn't quite figure out how to fix it. I'd been playing the two tied measures over and over for nearly a half hour. It had to be driving Mathieu and Etienne crazy, but they were too nice to say anything.

"Play that section with a 5/3 time rhythm," a feminine voice said behind me.

I sucked in a breath and spun around to face the woman standing three feet behind me. She wore a gray skirt paired with a pale blue silk blouse. Her dark hair was pulled back into a twist, pinned to the back of her head. She had a kind face, but her eyes were intense as she glanced from me to the sheet music and back again.

"Tie the first note of the right hand sextuplet to the D in the left hand quintuplet."

My heart began to race. This woman was Mathieu's mother. I could see the resemblance.

She made a shooing motion toward the piano. "Go ahead. Try it."

I took her advice and tied the two notes, then played the rest slowly.

"Yes, that's it, but watch the time with that quarter note."

I repeated the measure, then stopped and glanced back at her.

"Don't stop, *mon petit chou. Continuez-vous.*"

I started with the troublesome area, then continued on, trying to forget she was behind me, listening.

When I finished, I put my hands in my lap and waited.

There was the sound of clicking heels, and then she stood beside me at the piano. "Mathieu was correct. You are quite talented."

I blushed. "Thank you."

"As you must have presumed, I'm Mathieu's mother, Madeline Rousseau." She extended her hand, and I stood and shook it.

"Bonjour, Madame Rousseau. Enchanté. Je m'appelle Sophie Brooks."

She laughed, then said in English, "Mathieu said he'd been teaching you *le français. Très bien.*"

"Merci." My face flushed even more. "Thank you for letting me use your piano."

"It's nothing." She waved her hand as if swatting a fly. "I'm sure he's told you, I'm in charge of the *lycée* program at the *Conservatoire de Seine.* We've had two openings come up for the fall semester, which starts the first week of September. We're hosting invitation-only auditions the second week of August. I would be happy to have you audition for our program."

My breath stuck in my chest. "What?" I choked out.

She gave me a warm smile. "You will need a sonata, an etude, and a piece from the romantic period. This Rachmaninoff piece will work for the romantic piece if you can get it cleaned up in time. You're interested, I presume?"

Was I? I was thrilled she'd invited me to audition—Mathieu and I had discussed the possibility, but I'd never once let myself believe it *was* a possibility. Still, I couldn't actually move to Paris, could I? What about my mother? But I found myself nodding. *"Oui. Merci."*

"Très bien. Then I'll send you more information and arrange an audition time for you." She turned, and I realized Mathieu had been standing behind her the whole time. He was smiling, but he looked worried too. He'd already suggested I audition for her program. Had he changed his mind?

Madame Rousseau greeted him in French and then kissed his cheeks.

I glanced down at my phone to check the time. I had forty-five minutes left, but how could I concentrate on my music when

Mathieu's mother was here listening? And my brain was still trying to process the fact that I'd agreed to audition for the *conservatoire*. What other pieces would I play? I only had a month to prepare.

Madame Rousseau took Mathieu into his stepfather's office and shut the door, allaying my concern. She would still be able to hear me play, of course, but at least she wasn't watching me. I set a timer on my phone since Mathieu seemed busy with his mother. To my surprise, they were still in the office when my timer went off. I packed up my music, closed up the piano, and headed for the door, not wanting to disturb them.

But the office door opened, and Mathieu's mother stood in the opening. "Sophie, you'll have to skip practice tomorrow. Our family has plans for Bastille Day."

"Oh." My father hadn't mentioned anything about celebrating. "Thank you for letting me come at all."

"*De rein.*"

Eric was waiting for me on the sidewalk, and he looked confused when he didn't see Mathieu behind me. "Where's your shadow, Mit-shoe?"

I rolled my eyes when I realized he was talking about Mathieu. "His mother's home."

"Really?"

"Yeah. They've spent at least a half hour or so in his stepfather's office."

"So he's in trouble?" He looked entirely too happy about that.

I had to admit I was worried that he might be. But what if his mother had found out his deep, dark secret? Would that make Camille's threat null and void? I decided to tell Eric the exciting news. "His mother is in charge of a special program at the *conservatoire* where she teaches. She walked in and heard me playing." I turned to him and grabbed his arm. "Eric. She invited me to audition."

He came to a halt. "Wait. Slow down. Tell me about this program."

I explained it to him and he watched me with a surprisingly neutral expression. "You hate Paris."

"I don't hate it anymore."

His eyes narrowed. "Because of him."

I shrugged. "I guess he's part of it."

"So you're doing this for *him*? You're going to uproot your entire life to stay here in Paris with him—and he won't even tell his friends about you? Sophie, don't let this guy hurt you like that."

When he put it that way, it sounded so wrong. Was Mathieu really the reason I wanted to audition? I had admitted he was at least part of it. And in a way, Eric was right. The secret had begun to chafe, especially when I was hanging out with Mathieu's friends. My white lie about a boyfriend back home had bit me in the butt. Thomas had begun asking questions, and although I tried to evade most of them, I'd had to tell a few more white lies to cover my first big one.

I didn't want to lie anymore.

My eyes filled with tears. "I think I'm going to stay home this afternoon."

"Soph, I'm sorry. I just don't want him to hurt you."

I tried to hold back my tears. "I know. *Merci.*"

He looked surprised by my accidental slip of French, but he shook it off. "Why don't you and me hang out this afternoon? Just the two of us, like our first day here."

I wiped my cheek with the back of my hand. "Yeah, I'd like that."

"What would you like to do?"

More tears burned my eyes. Mathieu had asked me the same thing before our magical night at the Eiffel Tower. "I don't know."

"Let's start with lunch. I'm starving."

I grinned. "You're always starving."

"Hey! I'm a growing boy. But it's too expensive here. Let's go to the Latin Quarter."

"Sure."

We took the Metro to the Latin Quarter, then found an alley that catered to tourists. The owners and employees stood outside the various open-air restaurants like circus barkers, offering enticements like free drinks and half-price entrees. We picked an Italian restaurant.

"Won't Dane be upset if you don't join them?" I asked after we were seated at a table on the patio.

"Nah." He picked up a breadstick and took a bite, watching the tourists pass with their bags of souvenirs. "He's obsessed with Camille."

"I'm sorry."

He shrugged, pretending indifference, but I could see it bothered him.

"For what it's worth, Marine is totally into you."

His gaze jerked back to me. "What?"

I laughed. "Did you really not know?"

He grimaced. "Are you sure?"

"Yeah. I'm sure. Does that make you sorry you stayed with me?"

"Nah." He took another bite of his breadstick.

"What are they doing today, anyway?"

"They're going to a cemetery outside of town to see Jim Morrison's grave."

"Why would they want to see *his* grave?"

He shook his head. "Duh, because he's a classical legend."

"Mozart. Bach. Rachmaninoff. *Those* are classical musicians," I teased. We'd had this conversation before. Eric loved classic rock.

He was silent for a moment. "And this school where Matt-chew's mother teaches . . . what would you learn there? Would it be like a high school with music classes?"

"I've heard of the university *conservatoire*, but I didn't know it had a *lycée* program."

He gave me a blank look.

"High school. I only found out when he told me about the *lycée* program last week, but I didn't give it serious consideration until his mother actually invited me to audition."

"Would she let you in if he asked her to?"

"I doubt it. They both said it was a very competitive program. The audition is invitation only." I sighed. "But even if I did want to go, there's little hope of me getting chosen. Mathieu's mother might have gotten me the audition, but I would have to really bring it to win the spot."

He kept his gaze on me. "But you want it."

"I don't know." I shifted in my seat and leaned forward. "I mean, it's a huge honor to be invited to audition, and it's a pres-tigious university, but it's *Paris*—"

"Which you no longer hate."

"True. I've started having fun with Thomas and Sarah . . . when she thinks Camille's not looking. And the city is beautiful. But when Jenna gets here on Sunday, I want to spend time with her. If I audition, I'll have to beef up my practice time to more than four hours a day. I might have to learn some new pieces, which is *insane*. I won't have as much time to spend with her." I shook my head. "What am I thinking? This is crazy."

"Maybe. Maybe not. I guess it depends on why you're doing it." He gave me a pointed look.

"I don't know. I don't even know if I want to audition at all. Maybe I should call it off."

"Liar."

My eyes flew open wide.

"You want to audition, otherwise we wouldn't be having this conversation. The question is, do you want to spend your last two years of high school in Paris, France?"

"You know I don't."

"I don't know that at all. Dad's here."

The hair on the back of my neck stood on end. "So?"

"So? If he'd asked you to come with him to Paris a year ago, you would have thrown all your clothes into a couple of suitcases and taken off without a good-bye."

I twisted my mouth into a grimace. "No way."

"You would have. I think part of why you're still so pissed at Dad is that he didn't take you with him. He went on this adventure and left you behind. If you saw him all the time, you would have a better chance of fixing you guys. I don't think this summer is enough."

"I hate you right now," I mumbled, taking a sip of my water. What I really hated was that he was probably right. About all of it. "When did you get so smart?"

"I've always been smart. You were just too stupid to notice."

I grinned. "Whatever."

"Look," he said, leaning forward and turning serious. "If you decide you really want to go to school here, do it for you, not Dad. Not Mathieu. Do it because it's your dream. Mom gave up her dream to make Dad happy, and I'm pretty sure that's a part of the reason they're divorced."

"What are you talking about?"

"Mom wanted to go to medical school, remember?"

"Yeah, so?"

"She got accepted, but then gave it up so Dad could do a fellowship in Paris."

"Why didn't they just have a long-distance relationship?"

234

"She was pregnant with me."

"Oh . . ." How had I never put this together before? "Thanks, Eric." He'd helped me more than I could have ever expected.

We walked around a bit after finishing lunch, and on a whim we ended up racing remote control sailboats against each other at the Luxembourg Gardens. Ever competitive, Eric ended up racing a group of little kids, but one of them handed him his butt on a platter. I died laughing when Eric realized the kid was eight years old.

"The look on your face!" I said as we stopped to buy ice cream cones on the way to the Metro station. "I wish I'd taken a picture so I could blow it up. I'd post it on the bathroom wall so I could see it every time I sit down to pee."

"Yeah, yeah," he grumbled. "Yuck it up. But I still say I had a crap boat. I mean, come on. *You* almost beat me. How else can you explain that?"

I burst out laughing. We got our cones and started walking, and I looked up at him as he took a bite. "Eric . . . thanks for today. You've been . . ." I paused. "I haven't had this much fun all summer."

"Not even with Math-Eww?"

I laughed and shook my head. "It's a very close second."

He pumped his fist into the air. "I'm the champion at something."

My smile softened. "Yeah. You're the champion of something, all right."

And I was pretty sure my brother had helped me make a decision I hadn't planned to make.

Which meant I really *was* crazy.

CHAPTER *Twenty-Six*

"OKAY," JENNA SAID. "Whoa, whoa, whoa! Slow down. What do you mean you're breaking up with Mathieu?"

I was pacing outside the apartment building while I talked on my phone, looking like the crazy person I'd apparently become. I'd spent the rest of the afternoon thinking about whether I wanted to do the audition for Mathieu or for me. I'd come to the conclusion that it *was* for me, especially since our relationship was still so clandestine. If I actually got into his mother's program, I would have to move to Paris, and there was no way our secret relationship could stay secret forever. Besides, I *really* liked him, and if we continued to see each other, I was certain I'd end up with a broken heart. He still hadn't asked Camille for her blessing, and at this point, it was obvious he wasn't going to.

"Now that I think of it," I said, "I'm not sure there's anything *to* break up. We just walk to and from his apartment and eat breakfast together. How do you define *that*? Oh crap. We're breakfast buddies," I said, horrified by the thought. "We're like that movie your mom made us watch."

Jenna laughed. "*The Breakfast Club*? No. You're not in trouble."

"Not yet. All the more reason to end it."

She turned serious. "But I can tell you really like this guy."

"I do," I said, fighting tears. "But I don't like all the lying and sneaking around. I deserve better."

"Yeah. You do," she said quietly. "You've really changed over there. You're more sure of yourself. Two months ago you wouldn't have even considered breaking up with a breakfast buddy."

It was nice to hear this confirmation of something I had already felt. I laughed, but it was a bitter sound. "That's because I never *had* a breakfast buddy before."

"Look at it this way. Maybe you'll change your mind about Thomas if Mathieu's out of the way."

"Maybe." But I doubted it.

"What will you do about practicing on his piano?"

"I don't know. I'd like to keep playing. Is that wrong?"

"No, I don't think so. That's how becoming breakfast buddies all began. But he might not be open to it."

"He's a really nice guy. He'll let me keep practicing." It was true, which made my heart ache even more.

"Tell me again why you're breaking it off? Oh, yeah. The whole sneaking around thing."

"That seems reason enough to end it."

"Yeah. You're right," she sighed. "But I really wanted to meet him. Can you wait until after I get there on Sunday?"

"No. I think I need to end it straightaway. Like a Band-Aid. But you'll probably meet him. If he lets me keep practicing at his place, maybe you can go with me. You can read or something while I practice."

"Yeah." She didn't sound too thrilled.

"He has a brother. He's fifteen and totally cute."

"I don't think we're old enough to become cougars."

"Maybe he's only a few months younger," I teased. "I think you should reserve judgment until after you meet him. Did I mention how cute he is?"

"You're terrible," she groaned.

"The worst."

She was quiet for a moment. "I'm sorry, Soph. I know you really liked this guy."

Once I had made the decision, I wasn't sure how to end it. I didn't want to wait until Wednesday to tell him. That would be agony. I needed to do it as soon as possible. But should I call him or meet him in person? If he were my boyfriend, breaking up over the phone would be wrong. But what was the rule for breakfast buddies?

I sent him a text.

> Can you meet me tonight or tomorrow morning? It won't take long.

He answered back in seconds.

> Are you in trouble?

His response ripped my heart open even more.

> No. I'm fine. But we need to talk.

I had no idea if the significance of those four words would be lost in translation, but if his slow response was any indication, he got it.

> OK
> 7:30 tonight at the patisserie where we get breakfast
> OK

I went upstairs and found Eric. Camille and Dane were back and the guys were playing a video game. I leaned into his ear. "I need to go out for about a half hour tonight. Around seven twenty-five. Will you cover for me?"

He kept his gaze on the screen, but his jaw tightened. "No."

"I think you'll approve of my reason for going. I'd like to take care of it as soon as possible."

His head jerked up and his eyes widened in question.

I sucked in my bottom lip and nodded.

He tossed down his controller and stood. "I'll be right back. I have to talk to Sophie."

"*Dude*, you just spent all afternoon with her."

"I'll just be a minute. Keep your pants on." He followed me into the kitchen. "Are you breaking up with him?" he whispered.

"Yeah."

"Do you need me to go with you?"

Where had all this sudden concern come from? I wasn't the only one being changed by Paris. "No. But I don't want anyone to know where I went."

"Just say you went down to *MonoPrix* to get tampons or something."

I laughed. "That's actually a pretty good idea."

A smug grin spread across his face. "See, I'm more than just a pretty face."

"I wouldn't go that far." I shook my head. "I don't want to make a big deal about me leaving. I'll just slip out. If anyone asks where I am, tell them the cover story."

"Fine. Now I've got to get back to the game or Dane's going to steal all my ammo."

Dad and Eva came home soon after that, and everyone went their separate ways after dinner. I caught Eric's attention and motioned toward the door. He gave me a nod and turned his attention back to the game.

When I reached the corner across the street from the *pâtisserie*, I could see Mathieu sitting at a table, his hands folded on the table and a serious look on his face. He stood to greet me as soon as he noticed me crossing the street.

"Do you want anything?" he asked.

"No." I'd been amazingly calm about this decision, but now that he was here with me, I was having second thoughts. The thought of breaking things off with him, of never seeing him again, was heart wrenching. Jenna was right—I really liked him. But we couldn't let this undefined thing between us continue.

"Would you like to sit?" He motioned to the chair across from where he was sitting.

I didn't want to sit—it seemed like it would just delay the inevitable—but it would be awkward to do this standing up. So I sat down and placed my hands on top of the table, waiting for him to take his seat.

"My mother was very impressed with your playing," he said quietly, looking down at my hands. "Are you really planning to audition?"

"I think so, but I don't know for sure yet," I said softly. "I need to talk to my parents." *Those* were going to be tricky conversations.

"*Maman* needs your email address to send you the information. You can text it to me and I'll forward it to her."

I nodded and cleared my throat. I decided to give this one last shot. "If I audition and get accepted, what does that mean for us?" He lifted his gaze to meet mine. "What happens with you and me?"

"I don't understand."

"Will we still be like this? A secret?"

He closed his eyes. "Sophie."

And there was my answer.

"We can't do this anymore, Mathieu. *I* can't do this anymore." He grabbed my hands and held them in his.

"I don't like the secrets and the lies," I said.

That got his attention. "What lies?"

I shook my head. "Mathieu, I've had to lie to cover this up. I even had to lie tonight to come here." I looked into his eyes. "That's not me."

He was silent for several seconds. "Okay."

For a split second I let myself think that meant he chose me. Then I pulled my hand from his. "Is this good-bye?"

He looked into my eyes. "I still want to be your friend, Sophie. We started out as friends."

I wasn't sure it was possible now that I was hearing him say it. "We tried that. Look where it got us."

He looked out at the street, then back at me. "If you decide to audition, you will need to practice."

"That doesn't seem fair to you."

"Sophie," he pleaded. "This is *my* fault. You shouldn't have to give up something you love because of me."

"Mathieu . . ."

He shook his head, his mouth set. "No. I'll fix it. Have Eric bring you on Wednesday and I'll leave after I let you in."

"Mathieu. I can't let you do that."

He gave me a sad smile. "It's not your decision. It's mine."

"I don't blame you," I said. "I understand why you can't let Camille know."

"I wish I understood." He got up then, and turned around and walked away.

I managed to hold back my tears until he was a block away. Maybe this was for the best. If it hurt this much to lose him now, how much worse would it have been in August?

CHAPTER *Twenty-Seven*

EVERYONE SLEPT IN the next day. The banks were closed for Bastille Day, so Eva was home from work. So was Dad, and we all went out to lunch. While we waited for our food, Eva asked Camille, "Are you going to the Eiffel Tower for the fireworks?"'

Camille cast a glance at Dane. "Yes. We're meeting my friends there."

Dad's eyes narrowed. "I don't think it's a good idea."

Eva gave him a patient smile. "William, I told you, it's perfectly safe. Camille and her friends have gone for the last two years."

Apparently this had already been a topic of conversation. One I didn't know anything about, but Eric didn't look surprised.

Eva saw my confusion, then said, "There is a big celebration at the Eiffel Tower and the *Champ de Mars*. There is a huge crowd, but many young people go."

My father frowned. "After Sophie got lost last week, I think she should stay home."

"I wasn't lost," I countered. I wasn't sure I wanted to go with Camille, but I wanted to make sure the option was open. "I just chose not to come home. Besides, I have a cell phone now. You can call me if you have a sudden panic attack that I might be dead."

"*Sophie!*"

"William," Eva said in a soft voice, "police and security are everywhere. It's only a few blocks away. They will be perfectly safe."

"Come on, Dad," Eric said. "Let us go."

He thought about it for a moment, and then nodded his head, a reluctant look in his eyes. "All right, but there will be rules."

"Yeah," Eric said. "Of course."

My phone vibrated, and I dug it out of my pocket, surprised to see I had an email.

Eric shot me a scowl. He wasn't happy that Mathieu wanted me to keep practicing at his apartment and was pushing me to ask Eva for another option. "It's a trick, Sophie." No amount of persuading had made him change his mind.

When I opened the message, I almost gasped.

"Sophie," Dad admonished. "No phones at the table."

"It's an email, Dad. And it's important. It's about my audition."

"What audition?"

With all the Mathieu drama, I hadn't told him. Part of my hesitation was my fear over his reaction. What if he didn't want me to live in Paris? I wasn't sure I could handle another rejection from him. But I needed his permission. Now was the time to tell him. "I've been invited to audition for the *lycée* program at Mathieu's mother's *conservatoire*."

"You what?"

Eva broke into a huge smile and clasped her hands together. "That's wonderful news, Sophie! *Félicitations!*"

"How is *that* wonderful news, *Maman*?" Camille asked, her eyes wide.

"Sophie can live with us and go to school here."

Dad looked like he'd swallowed a bug.

"Are you going to audition?" Eva asked.

"I think so, but I need to start preparing soon." I kept my attention focused on Dad. His reaction wasn't what I'd hoped for. "It's an invitation to audition, nothing more. It's highly competitive, so the likelihood of me being accepted is very small."

The slim chances of my acceptance didn't dampen Eva's excitement, but Dad picked at his food the rest of the meal. At least he stopped hounding us about going to the *Champ de Mars* for the Bastille Day celebration. But my heart ached at his implied rejection.

I practiced on the keyboard when we got back to the apartment. I caught Dad watching me from the living room doorway, but neither of us said anything. I didn't want to think about his reaction to the audition—or rather his *lack* of a reaction. Part of the reason I wanted to audition was so we could repair our relationship, but he seemed panicked by the idea of me staying.

Still, while both Dad and Eric had put a damper on the idea, I wasn't ready to write it off yet. Maybe I would just audition and let the school decide. In the end, all this drama was probably for nothing. But I needed to tell Mom, and an email wasn't going to cut it. I grabbed my laptop and went into the bathroom and sat on the floor, locking the door behind me so I could have some privacy for our video call.

I was halfway surprised when she answered since she was on her beach trip with her boyfriend.

"Sophie? Is everything okay?" I could see the ocean behind her. She looked worried.

"Everything's fine. In fact, I got some wonderful news." At least I hoped she saw it that way. "I'm sorry to call you on your trip, but it's kind of important."

She gave me a warm smile. "I can't wait to hear."

I took a breath. "The guy I told you about—Mathieu—his mother is an instructor at the *Conservatoire de Seine.*"

"*Really?* Have you asked her about the school?"

I was glad she remembered it was one of my dream schools, even if I'd never really given it serious consideration. "She heard me play yesterday and was impressed."

"Of course she was." Pride filled her words. "You've worked so hard this past year and it shows."

I swallowed, scared to tell her the rest, but forged on anyway. "In fact, she's in charge of a program for high school students and she invited me to audition."

She was silent for several seconds. "What did you tell her?"

"I told her I would think about it."

"What do you want to do, Sophie?" Her voice sounded tiny—thousands of miles away.

I needed to be honest. "I'd like to do it."

She was silent again.

"But the competition is stiff. I doubt I have a shot at getting in. I'd like to at least try and say I did."

She still didn't say anything, and guilt pricked my chest, making me uncomfortable. Mom may have forced Dad's hand on leaving, but it was his decision to block me out of his life. Mom had stepped in the best she could. She had already admitted she was struggling with me leaving in two years. I couldn't do this to her now.

"On second thought," I said, forcing my voice to remain even, "I think I'll just skip it. It will be a ton of work. I should just enjoy my time in Paris."

"No," she said quietly. "You should audition."

My breath caught. "Mom, no. I can wait until—"

"No." Her tone was firmer and she had a determined look in her eyes. "You need to do this. You *have* to do this." She broke out into a huge smile. "Sophie! You were invited to audition for *Conservatoire de Seine*! This is huge!"

Relief washed through me when I heard her pride and excitement. "I might not get in, Mom."

"You'll get in."

"But if I do . . . I'll have to leave you." My voice broke, and I swiped at a tear at the corner of my eye.

She sucked in her bottom lip, then smiled. "Unlike your father, I know how to use a phone. And email. And video-chats." She could have sounded bitter, but she sounded encouraging. "And I can get on a plane. I'm sure you'll have concerts. I'll want to hear you play."

"I don't know what to say." My throat burned and it hurt to push out the words.

"Say you'll audition and give it your all."

"Thank you, Mom."

"I love you, Sophie. I'll never stand in the way of your dream." I suddenly wondered if there was more to my mother pushing my father toward France last summer.

Next I called Miss Lori and told her about the invitation to audition. She nearly broke my eardrum with her squeals of excitement.

"Sophie, you *must* audition!"

"I'd like to, Miss Lori, but I don't even know what to play."

We went over my existing repertoire, and the news was better than I'd thought. She thought my Mozart Sonata K.332 would work for the sonata, and for the etude she suggested I try Chopin Etude Op. 25 No. 2.

"You'll have to work at it, Sophie. I mean push hard."

"I know." But I still worried there wouldn't be enough time.

"Why don't we schedule a time for you to video-chat me tomorrow, and I'll listen to your Rachmaninoff piece? With the time difference, why don't we try eight a.m. for me, two p.m. for you."

"Thank you, Miss Lori." That was later than I usually stayed at Mathieu's, but if I couldn't stay, I could always play on the electronic keyboard.

I hung up, realizing my next concern was finding sheet music. But I explained my dilemma to Eva, and she helped me look up the address for a music store in the Latin Quarter.

It was soon time to go to the Bastille Day celebration. Eric, Dane, Camille, and I left around five thirty with a blanket and a bag of food Eva had packed.

As we approached the *Champs de Mars*, I was shocked to see the huge crowd gathered on the lawn, listening to a band play on a temporary stage.

Dane stopped in his tracks. "I know you said the crowd would be huge, but this is insane."

"This is nothing," Camille said. "Besides, Marine and a group are already here."

Would Mathieu be there? My pulse picked up at the thought. His mother said they had plans, but did that mean he wouldn't be with his friends tonight?

Camille expertly wove her way through the bodies littered across the giant lawn. There were thousands of people on the grass, but she somehow knew exactly where to go. Military men with huge guns walked back and forth on the periphery, making me nervous as they watched for signs of trouble in the crowd. The police I usually saw in the city didn't carry weapons like that.

We were about halfway across the lawn when Camille began to wave to a group about thirty feet away.

I scanned the crowd and found Thomas waving at me. As we got closer, I could see that Marine, Julien, and Sarah were with him, along with about ten other people I didn't recognize. None of them were Mathieu. I was equally relieved and disappointed.

I needed to get over Mathieu Rousseau.

Thomas was sitting on the grass. He patted a space next to him, and I climbed around several people until I reached him and plopped down.

The new teens must have heard about *the Americans*, because they openly stared at us for a few seconds. To my surprise, Camille introduced us before proceeding to ignore me as usual.

I'd honestly expected to be bored, but once Thomas started talking to me, some of Camille's other friends began to talk to me too. Soon I started to have fun. Despite myself, though, I missed Mathieu and wondered what he was doing with his family. And I just couldn't shake the heaviness in my heart. I told myself it would take time. Part of me believed it.

The sun began to go down just before ten o'clock, and someone pulled out several bottles of wine and began to pass them around.

I started to panic. I'd had sips of my parents' drinks before, but I typically avoided parties that served alcohol. I cast a glance toward my brother, not surprised to see him take a swig from one of the bottles.

Thomas must have seen the look on my face, because he leaned in toward my ear. "You won't get in trouble for drinking."

The bottle was passed to him and he took a drink, then handed it to me. I took a little sip, trying not to grimace at the taste, and passed it to the girl next to me. They continued passing the bottle around, and when it came to me again I handed it to the next person without taking a drink.

A girl asked Thomas a question in French and he answered in English. "Mathieu is with his family." He shot a glance to me, and for a second I wondered if he'd figured out there had been something between the two of us. But then he turned back to the girl. "English, please. Sophie's French is improving, but she still doesn't understand everything."

His friends grudgingly listened. "I'm surprised he's coming around at all after what happened with Camille and Hugo," one of the girls said.

"You're his best friend, Thomas," one of the guys said. "What *did* happen?"

Thomas didn't answer, and someone handed him the bottle. He took a longer drink than before and shook his head. "He won't tell me details, but I know he found them . . . together."

I tried not to gasp in surprise. Camille had cheated on him? So how was it that *she* had something on *him*?

One of the guys leaned back on his hands. "I heard he's been hanging out with you guys since school let out. Are they back together?"

Thomas looked over his shoulder to see if she was listening. When he saw she was deep in conversation with Marine and Dane, he lowered his voice. "*Non.* We could tell he didn't want to be with us, but he came anyway. It was like she made him come."

His secret. She had been using it to order him around.

What a witch.

She'd probably kept him around in the hopes he would take her back. It explained why he wasn't around anymore now that she was hooking up with Dane.

A loud noise burst over our heads. Reminded of the men walking around with machine guns, I ducked, then cringed with embarrassment when I realized there were fireworks overhead. But thankfully no one noticed. Their attention was fixed on the show lighting up the sky.

My head whirled with the information I'd just heard. Why hadn't Mathieu told me Camille had cheated?

Thomas wrapped his arm around my shoulders and pulled me closer, grinning like a fool. "Tell me, Sophie Brooks, does your boyfriend back home take you to see fireworks?"

No more lies. No more secrets. I was sick of them. "I don't have a boyfriend back home."

His eyes widened in surprise. "You broke up?" he shouted over the booms of the fireworks.

I shook my head. "No. I never had one."

I expected him to be angry with me, which I totally deserved, so I wasn't prepared when he pulled me against him and kissed me. I tasted the wine on his lips and his tongue as he tried to deepen the kiss. For a couple of seconds I was too shocked to react. Then he lifted his face and smiled.

Oh no. What had I done?

He slipped his arm to my lower back, and while I wanted to shove his arm off me, I was still sorting out everything in my head. I only knew two things for sure. One, I was in shock, and two, I was slightly disappointed I didn't feel anything with him. It would have made things so much easier.

My mother once told me the heart wants what the heart wants, and it was just my luck my heart wanted someone I couldn't have: Mathieu Rousseau.

CHAPTER *Twenty-Eight*

IT WAS STRANGE not seeing Mathieu on my doorstep the next morning. The ache in my chest made me wish I had reconsidered, but I knew I'd made the right choice. It was living with it that sucked.

When I reached his apartment, I pressed the button and a buzzer sounded. "Come on in," a male voice said. It didn't sound like his voice, but I figured it was just speaker distortion, so I was surprised to see Etienne when I knocked on the front door.

"*Bonjour,* Sophie."

"Etienne. What are you doing home? Don't you have swimming today?"

"The pool water needs . . ." His face scrunched as he tried to figure out the right words, then gave up. "It's closed."

"Oh. Is Mathieu here?"

"*Non.*" He stepped to the side, unblocking the doorway. "But you can come in."

My heart hurt a little, but I walked in and headed for the piano, pulling out my music as I walked. I was dying to know where Mathieu was, but I reminded myself that it wasn't any of my business.

"Do you think I could stay later today? I'm supposed to play for my music teacher at two o'clock." He looked confused, so I added, "I'm going to video-chat her."

"I have to leave for a little while, but you can stay."

"Thank you!" I pulled out my laptop. "Also, can I get your Wi-Fi password?"

He nodded and gave it to me, and I typed it in so I'd have it ready for when I needed to call Miss Lori.

I started my warm up, the fingering so rote and mindless that I began to think about the night before. It had quickly turned into a nightmare.

Thomas tried to kiss me again after the first disaster kiss. I backed away from him, giving him the hint I wasn't open to his PDA, but the moment the fireworks finished, he got to his feet and hauled me up with him.

"I like you, Sophie,"

I was about to tell him I liked him too—just not the way he liked me—but Eric stepped between us.

"Keep your hands off my sister," he snarled.

Thomas backed up and started speaking in rapid-fire French to my brother.

"Eric!" I grabbed his arm and pulled him away. "What are you doing?"

"Watching out for you."

"I don't need you to watch out for me! I can take care of myself."

I turned around to apologize to Thomas, but he and Camille were now in a heated conversation. Not long after, he left without saying anything to me, and Camille berated Eric for his brutish behavior all the way home.

In a nutshell, it had been a lovely night of family bonding.

So now Camille and Eric weren't speaking to each other, and Dane thought Eric had lost his mind. I tried to think positive: at least Camille had turned her disdain on to someone else, and Dane was leaving in four days.

Which meant Jenna was coming in five.

And once she came, boys wouldn't matter. I'd spend all my free time with my friend.

I soon lost myself in my music. Mathieu's mother's suggestion had really helped, and now that my fingers had the timing worked out, it sounded awesome. Yet something was missing. I hoped Miss Lori could help me figure out what it was.

I still needed to work on the other two pieces, but for the first time I thought I might actually have a shot at winning a spot at the *conservatoire*.

Before I knew it, my alarm went off, letting me know my call was in fifteen minutes. I'd been sitting at the piano for over four hours, and I needed to get up and walk around and pee. I'd packed a sandwich, so I pulled it out and ate it as I stood and stretched my aching back muscles.

"Etienne?" I called out. "Are you home?"

He didn't answer, so I figured he was still gone.

As I finished the last bites, I wandered down the hall, feeling like a trespasser as I looked for the restroom.

Mathieu's apartment was like Eva's—the toilet was in its own closet. So after I peed, I found the bathroom and washed my hands, then dared to peek into the doorway directly across from me. Through the partially open door, I could see posters of swimmers tacked to the walls. The full-size bed was unmade, but the rest of the room was fairly clean. This was obviously Etienne's room, and I wondered if the door a few feet down led to Mathieu's room.

I knew I shouldn't snoop, but I was overcome by the desire to at least see some small part of him.

The door was almost all the way closed, but a soft nudge pushed it open enough for me to get a glimpse. The walls were a soft gunmetal gray, and a black duvet covered the full-size bed. A dark wood desk was pushed up against the wall, and a neat pile of books was stacked in a corner. I was dying to see what they were, but I'd already invaded his privacy enough without crossing the threshold.

On the wall opposite the bed was a TV attached to the wall and a dark wood console with a game system and controllers. There was a partially open window opposite the door, covered in white gauzy curtains that fluttered in the breeze.

I missed him so much my chest hurt.

That was stupid, right? I'd only known him for several weeks, yet he was such a huge part of my life here. He was the reason I'd given Paris a chance. This one summer in Paris was supposed to be nothing more than a forced trip to see my father. I hadn't expected to fall in love.

Oh no. I was falling for Mathieu Rousseau.

Tears filled my eyes. I had the absolute worst luck.

A sudden ringing in my pocket made me jump. It was my alarm giving me a five-minute warning for my call with Miss Lori. I carefully closed the door to Mathieu's world and went back out into the living room so I could open the video-call app on my laptop.

Miss Lori called me less than a minute later, and I tried to forget about Mathieu. I needed to focus on this call and on my music. Miss Lori was a middle-aged woman whose love for what she did was obvious from her bubbly, outgoing personality. She'd been my piano teacher ever since we moved to Charleston, so she greeted me warmly and congratulated me for earning the audition.

"What can you tell me about Rachmaninoff's Prelude in B Minor Op. 32?" she asked.

"I couldn't find much," I said, too ashamed to admit I hadn't spent a lot of time trying. "But I know it was Rachmaninoff's favorite piece he wrote."

"True. Did you by any chance pull up Valentina Lisitsa's performance?"

I grinned, knowing she was teasing me. Valentina Lisitsa was my idol. "Of course."

"And do you remember what she said on her YouTube posting? She called it depression in manifest form. Now play it for me, Sophie."

I moved the laptop so she could see my fingers, then held my fingers over the keys. Suddenly I knew what was missing from the piece. I hadn't attached it to my soul yet.

I closed my eyes and began the soft, haunting melody, the minor chords tugging at my aching soul. The first two minutes of the piece were a slow build to the heavier, faster movement that captured Rachmaninoff's frustration and desperation. I poured my heart into it, conveying through the music my profound sadness over my father, Mathieu, my feud with Camille, and my homesickness for my mother. It all bled through my fingertips onto the keys, so when I finished the last notes a little over five minutes later, I felt like I'd laid my soul bare.

I held my fingers over the keyboard as the last haunting notes faded with the pedal, then took a deep breath and waited for Miss Lori's feedback. But she hadn't said anything after several long seconds, so I began to wonder if I'd lost the connection with her. I turned to face the computer, surprised to see awe in her eyes.

"Oh, Sophie. You have far surpassed my expectations with this piece. No wonder Madame Rousseau invited you to audition. It was stunning."

I shook my head. "No. When she heard it, I was still working on the technical pieces. That was the first time I connected my heart to it."

"My darling, you will wow them, not only with the technicality but also the emotion. Brava."

She had me play a few portions over again and offered some fingering suggestions. "Do you have the music for the other two pieces?"

"No, I plan to get them this afternoon."

"Your technique has improved since you played the Mozart Sonata a year ago. It will help that you're familiar with the piece, but go after it like it's new. We can schedule some video lessons after you've gotten familiar with it again."

"And the Chopin etude?" I asked. "It's brand new."

"I think you'll be fine with it. It's a lesser-used piece for auditions, which is in your favor. It's the sonata that will be the make-it-or-break-it selection. You have a lot of ground to cover to make the entire nineteen minutes sound uniform. I read the information you forwarded. You're fortunate that you don't have to memorize it."

I took a deep breath, my nerves getting the better of me.

"You're going to do very well, Sophie. I must admit, while it would be quite a feather in my cap to have one of my students accepted to *Conservatoire de Seine*, I would be sad to lose you."

I shook my head with a wry grin. "Don't worry. I'll give it all I've got, but I have no expectation of getting in."

"You'll do very well. I'm very, very proud of you, Sophie, whether you make it or not." She sniffed and then smiled. "Work on filling out the packet, and ask me if you have any questions. I'll email you my letter of recommendation."

"Thank you."

Etienne still wasn't back when I finished my call, so I texted Eric and told him I was going to head to the music store before I went home. He ended up going with me. Camille and Dane were giving him the cold shoulder, so he was eager to leave the apartment and go to the Latin Quarter.

I practiced the Chopin etude on the keyboard after dinner that night, so I felt ready to tackle it with the real piano the next morning.

Etienne let me in again, but took off as soon as I entered the apartment. He'd obviously been waiting for me. While I felt bad about detaining him, I couldn't bring myself to tell him he didn't have to let me in anymore. Now that I'd decided to audition, I needed all the practice I could get, which included practicing on a real piano. I decided to text Mathieu later to work something out with him.

I divided my five hours in parts—the first two hours were devoted to the Chopin etude and the second two hours to the sonata. At the end I played the Rachmaninoff piece twice and worked on more of the etude. When I finished, I sat back on the bench and took several deep breaths, trying to reassure myself that I could do this. That this wasn't insane.

"That was beautiful, Sophie," Mathieu said from behind me.

I stood and spun around to face him. "Oh. You're here."

He sat in a leather chair, his eyes locked on mine. I had a hard time reading his expression. It seemed guarded, yet . . . hopeful.

"How long have you been there?"

"Long enough to realize you're learning something new. You've picked it up very quickly."

"No." I looked down and blushed. "I learned it last year, but I didn't learn it for any type of competition. Miss Lori told me to attack it like it was a new piece." I shrugged and gave him a grin. "So I'm trying to make the interpretation new and pretending I just happen to be good enough to know most of the fingering."

His mouth tipped up into a small smile. "So you've picked your pieces?"

"I think so."

"Would you like my mother to look them over? Give you some advice?"

I shook my head. "That feels like cheating."

He looked down at that, his cheeks red.

I stood and slung my bag over my head. "I should probably go." I wanted to talk to him. But my heart broke all over again each time I looked into his deep blue eyes. I didn't think we could be just friends. Being so close to him made me want more. I started for the door. "I've got to go."

He jumped to his feet. "Sophie."

I paused, my chest tight. It was taking everything in me to walk away. I wasn't sure I had the strength to leave if he kept me there much longer.

"My mother has tickets to a concert at *Sainte-Chapelle* tonight. A pianist is performing a Beethoven sonata at eight thirty. Would you like to go?"

I ran my hand over my head, fighting the urge to cry. The guy who had broken my heart wanted to give me tickets to attend a concert at the very place that had stolen my father from me. Was this some cosmic joke? "I don't know who would go with me."

"No," he said softly. "I want you to come *with me.*"

I refused to look at him. I couldn't do this again. "You want me to sneak out?"

"*Non*, Sophie. I want to come to Camille's apartment—not the door on the street—to collect you and take you with me."

My mouth dropped open as I turned to face him. "Is this because I've decided to audition?"

He slowly shook his head. "No, it's because I don't want to miss another minute with you." He paused, his hand twitching at his side. "Will you go to the concert with me? Please?"

This was too good to be true. "Are you asking me out on a date?"

His face scrunched in confusion. "The concert is today."

"No, a *date*. You know . . . where you go out with someone."

Understanding lit up his eyes. "Oh. We have no word for date."

"What? How can *that* be? How do you get to know someone?"

"We go out with a group of friends."

"Oh."

He moved closer and stopped a couple of feet in front of me. "And in France, once you kiss someone, they are your boyfriend or girlfriend." He leaned over and kissed me lightly. "I know you Americans date multiple people at one time, but in France you are only with one person."

The meaning of his words hit me. Exclusive.

"I'll go with you, but no more hiding, Mathieu."

He lowered his voice. "In France, this isn't so wrong. It's not unusual for a couple to see each other and keep it from their friends."

I looked up into his eyes. "Only one of us is French. The American part of us doesn't want to hide it from anyone."

A soft smile lit up his face. "The French part doesn't want to hide it either."

"Really?"

His smile spread. "Really." He looked down and shifted his weight. "Is Eric coming to get you today?"

"No. I was going to walk back alone."

"May I walk with you?"

"Uh . . . sure."

He followed me out the door and down the steps, and by the time we'd made it to the sidewalk, I felt incredibly awkward. "Did you have a good Bastille Day?" I asked.

"*Oui.*" His tone suggested it wasn't true, but he didn't offer any more information. I didn't ask.

"My friend Jenna is coming on Sunday."

"I cannot wait to meet your friend Jenna. Tell me more about her."

And just like that, the awkwardness fell away as I told him stories about my best friend of five years, several of which had him laughing. Before I knew it, we were at my door.

"What time will you pick me up?" I asked, suddenly nervous. This would be my first real date, even if Mathieu had claimed the French didn't date.

"Nineteen thirty." Then he laughed at my confused look. "Seven thirty."

"Oh." I'd forgotten the French used military time. "Okay. I'll see you then."

He nodded, but didn't move. I wondered if he was going to kiss me, and maybe he was considering it, but ultimately he took a couple of steps back. "I look forward to our evening." He gave me a little wave, then turned around. I stayed at the front door, my hand on the knob, and watched as he walked to the corner. Then he turned to look at me, and his grin was so wide and happy, it made me smile too.

CHAPTER *Twenty-Nine*

I TOLD MY family about my plans for the evening while we ate dinner.

Eric was not happy. My father even less so. And Camille . . . unhappy was not how I'd describe her reaction. More like controlled fury. Dane seemed stunned, and he kept staring at me throughout the meal.

Eva exuded pure joy.

"William, calm down," she murmured, patting my father's arm. "Mathieu is a lovely boy."

"And you've been going to his house every day?" he asked. "*For hours?* I didn't even know you liked this boy."

"He's kissed her," Eric said, glaring at me.

"Eric!" I shouted.

"You've kissed him?" Camille shouted. Her face was red and her eyes were wild.

Eva let out a long sigh and patted the air with her hands. "Everyone calm down." She turned to Camille. "You and Mathieu were friends for years before you were together for a few weeks. It was never serious. You moved on, and Sophie had no way of knowing you and Mathieu used to be together. Isn't that correct, Sophie?"

"I only recently found out."

"See?" Eva said with a warm smile. "And you have Dane."

Camille's eyes filled with tears, and she started speaking in French. I heard Dane's name, and then Camille stomped off to her room. Dane looked irritated as he scooted back his chair, then followed her.

Eva looked at the rest of us and shook her head with a sigh. "Young love."

But Camille's tirade helped calm my dad and Eric. Eva convinced them that nothing was about to happen to me on the Metro or at my father's place of employment.

My biggest problem was deciding what to wear. I had my sundress from the wedding, but Mathieu had already seen me in it. So I riffled through my suitcases, frustrated by my lack of choices. Going through the few clothes I had hanging in my brother's closet confirmed it. I steeled myself as I went into my shared room to riffle through my suitcases again.

"He was my boyfriend first," Camille said, her eyes red from crying.

I stood and turned around to face her. "I'm not trying to take him from you. He told me you two stopped seeing each other in May."

"Does he know you kissed Thomas?" There was a hateful look in her eyes. "He's very jealous, you know. He'll hate you if he finds out."

I had to admit the thought had occurred to me. But it wasn't like I had invited Thomas to kiss me—quite the opposite. Still, I planned to tell him about it tonight so it was out in the open. I didn't want to have to worry about Camille using it against me.

"Are you planning to tell Mathieu for me?" I asked. "Is that what you do? Blackmail people?" The blank look on her face made it obvious she didn't understand. "I know you have something on Mathieu and you're using it to get him to do whatever you want. Are you planning to go tell your mother now that you know we're going out? You'd really ruin his chances of getting the internship next summer out of revenge?"

A blank looked filled her eyes at first, but then she began to laugh. "Is that what he told you?"

I sucked in a breath.

She laughed again. "Poor, stupid Sophie. You can have him." She slid off her bed. "I hope the two of you are very happy together." She left the room, and I heard her call Dane's name. I was disturbed by what she'd said. Was there more to the story than what Mathieu had told me? I was going to get to the bottom of that as well.

But now I had to figure out what to wear. I pushed out a sigh as I held up a wrinkled pink blouse and a white eyelet skirt. This was the best I could do.

"Would you like to look in my closet? I have some things you might like," Eva said, leaning against the doorway.

I glanced up at her. "Could I? I only have my dress from the wedding, and he saw me in it that day."

"He did?"

I told her about how he had approached me outside of the restaurant.

"See?" she asked with a twinkle in her eyes. "*Destinée.*"

I followed her into the room she shared with Dad. It was small, and the queen-size bed and a dresser filled up most of it. Eva walked around the edge of the bed and looked in her closet. "How about this?

She held up a sleeveless navy blue fit and flare cocktail dress. It was the kind of dress that was classic, timeless, very sophisticated . . . and undoubtedly very expensive.

"It's classic but not formal," Eva said, "So you won't feel out of place, but you'll still be stunning." She held it up to my front. "Ah, yes. It brings out your eyes. Try it on."

She handed it to me and shut the door, then sat down on the bed.

I realized she wanted me to try it on in front of her. I'd already figured out the French weren't ashamed of their bodies, which wasn't such a bad thing. Besides, I was wearing underwear and a bra. It was pretty much the same as wearing a swimsuit. I stripped and tossed my clothes on the bed, then slipped on the dress.

"*Belle!*" Eva hopped off the bed and dug at the bottom of her closet. "What size shoes?"

"Seven."

Her head popped up, and she gave me a look of confusion before returning to her task. "Never mind." She pulled out a pair of nude heels. "Try these."

I sat on the bed and slipped them on and stood, thankful they fit.

Eva clasped her hands together and smiled. "Perfect. Look." She pointed to a full-length mirror next to the closet. I stepped in front of it and gasped. The girl staring back at me in the mirror looked so much more mature than little Sophie Brooks from Charleston, South Carolina. I couldn't believe it was me. The dress made my waist look smaller, and the hem hit several inches above my knee, which, paired with the heels, made my legs look longer.

Eva moved behind me. "If we put up your hair . . ." She gathered my hair and began to twist the strands, then held it up to the back of my head. "A little more makeup . . ." She looked at my reflection over my shoulder. "Would you like my help?"

"Yes!"

She finished helping me get ready, and I was amazed when I looked in the mirror. I looked so different from the lonely, crying girl Mathieu had met standing outside that restaurant.

I *was* a different girl.

There was a pounding at the door, and I jumped. "He's here," Eric barked from the hall.

Eva chuckled. "They are protective of you. Give them time."

Maybe so, but I hoped they would bring it down a notch soon.

I walked out of Eva's room, grateful that she'd loaned me her dress. Mathieu was standing just inside the front door, and there was a serious expression on his face as he talked to my father. He had on a crisp black suit and a soft blue tie, and I'd never seen him look more handsome. He saw me walking toward him and stopped talking, as if mesmerized.

Dad's gaze followed his, then his eyes narrowed. Eric didn't look much happier.

All three men watched me as my heels clicked on the wooden floor, and I suddenly felt self-conscious.

Mathieu was still speechless when I stopped in front of him, but then he blinked and seemed to gather his wits about him. "Sophie, you are the most beautiful girl I have ever seen."

My father scowled, and Eric's eyes narrowed too. "That's *my* sister, Mathieu, so keep your hands off her tonight."

"Eric," Eva murmured in a soothing tone as if my brother were a feral dog that needed to be talked out of biting someone. "Sophie is capable of making her own decisions." She turned to Mathieu. "But if I ever hear about you hurting my daughter, I will hunt you down myself."

Mathieu swallowed audibly. "I would never hurt Sophie."

"You will have her back by ten o'clock," my father said, his voice gruff.

"Dad!" I protested. "The concert doesn't even start until eight thirty."

"Then ten thirty."

I started to protest, but Eva put a hand on my father's arm. "Eleven seems more reasonable, don't you think, William?"

Dad scowled once more. "I guess."

Mathieu looked very serious as he nodded. "Yes, sir."

Eva opened the front door and gave us a huge smile. "Have a wonderful night, Sophie. Mathieu, give your mother my love."

"*Merci*," I said. As I walked toward the door, I looked back and saw Camille and Dane on a sofa in the living room, watching TV. Camille eyes widened when she saw me, then turned angry. But it was Dane's expression that worried me more. He looked . . . *interested*.

It was a good thing he was leaving on Saturday.

Mathieu was quiet as we descended the stairs. When we hit the lobby, he put his hand on my lower back and ushered me outside. Then he turned to look at me, and a grin spread across his face. "Sophie, you are so beautiful."

"You are too," I said, then blushed. "You look very nice in your suit. I'm glad Eva loaned me her dress."

"I will be the envy of everyone there."

I smiled, so full of joy I could hardly contain it. I stood on my tiptoes to kiss him, but he put his hands on my arms. "We have an audience."

Sure enough, three sets of eyes peered down from my apartment—Dad, Eric, and Dane.

If they bothered Mathieu, he didn't let on. "We have a car." He gestured to a black sedan parked at the curb and opened the back door. "*Mademoiselle*."

"Mathieu, you didn't have to pay for a car! We could have taken the Metro."

He smiled. "Not tonight."

I slid across the backseat and he climbed in after me. The driver turned around to address Mathieu in French, and I recognized the word *belle*.

Mathieu's cheeks turned pink. "Sophie, I'd like to introduce you to my father, Pierre Rousseau."

"Oh!" I gasped. His father drove a taxi, so it made sense Mathieu would get him to drive. I was excited to meet him. *"Bonsoir, Monsieur Rousseau."*

I held my hand out to shake his, but he grabbed it and kissed my knuckles. *"Enchanté."*

I blushed and pulled my hand free. Mathieu's father chuckled as he drove away from the curb.

"French men are notorious flirts," Mathieu murmured in my ear. "They flirt for the sake of flirting." He grabbed my hand and stroked the open palm.

My stomach tinkled at the contact. "Is that what you're doing now?" I asked, holding my breath.

"Mais, non," he said, turning to look more directly into my eyes. "I've wanted to hold your hand ever since I watched you play your Rachmaninoff prelude this afternoon. I wanted to hold the hand that created such beauty."

I grinned. "Trying to live up to the French reputation?"

His eyes twinkled. "Is it working?"

"Oui."

We stared into each other's eyes for a long moment, and the way he was looking at me brought a new blush to my cheeks.

"Thank you for coming with me tonight," he murmured softly, looking down at my lips for an instant.

"Thank you for inviting me," I managed to push out before I looked away. I'd liked him before, but now that he was full-on courting me, I felt myself falling under his spell. I wasn't sure if that was a bad thing or a good one.

We rode in silence the rest of the way to *Saint-Chapelle*, but we kept glancing at each other, locking gazes for several seconds and smiling. Several times I thought he was going to kiss me, but with his father in the front seat, I was glad he didn't.

Monsieur Rousseau pulled up to the curb and dropped us off. He opened the window and said something to Mathieu before driving away.

Mathieu could see I was curious about their exchange. "He told me to call him when we are ready for him to pick us up, but to give him a half-hour notice."

I nodded, suddenly feeling nosy.

He put his hand at the small of my back. "Let's go find our seats."

We stood in a line outside the church. Mathieu held my hand, his fingers laced with mine. Though this was hardly the first time we'd been alone together, tonight felt so different, so magical, I was worried I'd break the spell.

Mathieu eyes were filled with wonder whenever he looked at me. "I know I keep telling you this, but you look so beautiful tonight."

"It's Eva's dress."

"It's not just the dress."

I blushed. I definitely wasn't used to this kind of attention. The scaffolding caught my eye when I glanced at the outside of the chapel. "See that gargoyle? My father is restoring that one."

Mathieu's eyes flew open. "Are you serious?"

"Yeah. He brought us here last weekend to show us." I'd been too angry to appreciate the beauty of what he was doing, but standing here with Mathieu, it suddenly registered. "This building is literally *hundreds* of years old, and my father is giving it new life so people can continue to enjoy its true beauty."

"It's not so different from what you do," he said, studying the stone sculpture. "You take musical pieces hundreds of years old and give them new life. You play them so others can enjoy the work the way the composers intended them to be played and enjoyed."

I turned slowly to look at him. "How do you do that?"

"Do what?" His deep blue eyes were locked onto mine.

"How do you know exactly the right thing to say?"

He grinned, and a boyish gleam filled his eyes. "It's the gift of the French."

I laughed in response and he tugged me closer, staring at me like I was the only girl the world. At that moment, I almost felt like I *was*.

I had worried that Mathieu would be bored by the concert—most of my friends would have been, Jenna included—but he looked enthralled. We went to a nearby restaurant afterward and ordered dessert to share—cheesecake and *crème brûlée*.

But as magical as this was, I needed this growing thing between us to be firmly anchored to the truth. "Camille was upset I was going out with you tonight."

He licked the back of his spoon before he asked, "Does this bother you?"

"No, not really. She has Dane, and honestly, I think she's more upset that he's leaving. She seems to see you as more of a possession."

He nodded and took another bite. "Why do I have a feeling there is more?"

"Because you are very perceptive, Monsieur Rousseau." I sliced my spoon through my dessert. "I accused her of blackmailing you with your secret."

He watched me, waiting for me to continue.

"She insinuated there's more to the story."

He sighed, sounding weary. "Camille is into games."

I set my spoon on the table. "I need you to tell me the truth, Mathieu. If we can't tell each other the truth, we have nothing at all."

He looked down at his plate, and I could tell he was weighing his options.

"I know Camille cheated on you."

His gaze jerked up to mine.

"Thomas was talking to your friends at the Bastille Day celebration. They were surprised to hear you've been hanging out with her this summer. Thomas said it was like she had something on you." I leaned forward. "Other people see this too, Mathieu."

He kept his eyes down.

"Thomas said you found Camille with Hugo. That you found them *together*."

Mathieu sat back in his chair and looked out the window, chewing on his bottom lip.

"Why didn't you tell me about how things ended?" I tried hard to keep any accusation out of my voice.

"I was embarrassed."

"That she cheated on you? That's not on you, Mathieu. That speaks to her character, not yours."

"No. Embarrassed of how I reacted."

My chest tightened. What could he have done?

He looked into my eyes. "Hugo and I used to be friends when we were younger, but that changed as soon as he found another group of friends. His grades were always better than mine and he loved to shove it into my face, especially since he knew my stepfather accepted nothing less than perfection. Camille has known him since we were all in primary school. And she also knows we are enemies."

I had a really bad feeling about where this story was going.

"Yet she always liked him anyway, even though he never paid attention to her. But when he found out we were together, that changed. When I realized Camille and I would never work together, I told her we had to talk. She said she'd be home at five, but I got there earlier. I had a key to her apartment, so I let myself in. I heard noises in her room and went to investigate. That's when I found them."

"In bed?"

"*Oui*. There was no doubt about what they were doing."

I cringed.

"I think I was more upset that she would betray me by being with him of all people. I was furious. I hauled him out of bed, still naked, and punched him. I told Camille we were no longer friends and left. I'm not proud of how I handled it. I think I broke his nose."

"She's holding that over you? You could use it against her too. Besides, I think you were justified."

"That's not all I did, Sophie."

"Oh."

"You have to understand the depth of my anger toward him. He made my life hell all through *colleges*—what we call middle school. His family knew mine, so I was forced to endure him. He would tell my stepfather things that weren't true about me and I would get into trouble."

"That's terrible!"

"But now you see that this was the last thing I could take."

"What did you do?"

He crossed his arms over his chest. "I changed his grades."

"Excuse me?"

"I hacked into the school grading system and changed his grades."

"That's ingenious."

A small grin tugged at the corners of his lips. "Until I got caught."

"Oh no."

"I was going to be expelled, but my mother convinced the *proviseur* to give me a punishment instead. I started it this week, which is why I was gone."

"But Camille knows," I said, picking at the *crème brûlée*.

"And Thomas."

I nodded. Of course he would, though it made sense that he hadn't told his other friends. Something like that truly could destroy his future. "International banking. I would guess you need a squeaky clean record."

He nodded, looking grim. "The *proviseur* says she won't report me as long as I complete my work."

"What do you have to do?"

He gave me a wry grin. "Tutor students who struggle while they are on summer break. Some maintenance work around the school. I must complete one hundred hours."

"And you won't have to worry about it hurting your career?"

"Except for Camille."

"What about Hugo? Why doesn't he tell on you?"

"The *proviseur* discovered that Hugo had changed some of his own grades. Before me. She agreed to keep it from his father as long as he was quiet about my involvement."

"But Camille can still tell." The dessert in my stomach began to churn. "Oh, Mathieu. I hate to think of you risking so much for me."

His eyes flew open. "No, Sophie. I didn't just do it for you. I did it for *me*. Camille will hold this over my head for the rest of my life. I don't want to live like that. I did a bad thing, so I must pay the price if it comes out. I accept that."

"But for the rest of your life? Camille has control over your future."

He shrugged. "There is nothing I can do but wait and hope she doesn't tell."

That was so wrong. "I don't understand. Why did you defend her?"

A faraway look filled his eyes. "She used to be different. Happy. But that was before her father died. My friends and I hope that girl will come back."

Mathieu had shared his deep dark secret, so it was time to confess mine. Especially after the whole mess with Camille. My back tensed as I clutched my hands on the tabletop to steel my nerves. "There's something I need to tell you."

Worry filled his eyes. "Okay."

I looked down. "You guessed that Thomas liked me. Did he know how you felt?"

"No."

"I really like him as a friend. I told him I had a boyfriend back home because I didn't want him to think about me that way. Everyone else ignored me, so I was grateful for the company. Plus he's nice." I gave him a soft smile. "I can see why he's your best friend."

His eyes were guarded.

"I went with Camille and your friends on Bastille Day. Thomas was there, and I told him I didn't have a boyfriend back home." Would he get up and walk away from me forever? The temptation to keep quiet was almost overwhelming. It didn't matter. I *had* to tell him. "You and I had already broken up, but I didn't think he would . . ."

"I know he kissed you." He reached across the table and grabbed my hands in his. "He told me."

"What?" He already *knew*?

"He knew you were hung up on someone else. He called me and told me, so I told him about us."

"You did?" I cringed and squeezed my eyes shut. "Does he hate me?"

"*Non*, Sophie. He thinks I'm the lucky one who found you first."

"Do *you* hate me?"

His eyes lit up. "*Non*, I could never hate you."

I pushed out a huge sigh of relief.

"Now, no more talk of Camille or Thomas." He smiled and leaned forward. "What did you think about the concert?"

I started analyzing the piece, and a huge smile spread across his face. I stopped talking, then asked, "What?"

He shook his head. "You should see your face right now. I love watching you talk about music. You are so . . . full of life."

I lowered my gaze, feeling self-conscious. "Music . . . I just feel it. It's like a second language to me—a way to express what's in my soul better than words ever could." Had I really just told him that? I started to pull my hands away, but he held them in place.

"*Non*. Don't be embarrassed. It's wonderful. Your love for music is inspiring."

"What do you have that inspires you?"

His smile softened. "You."

"Mathieu," I scolded. "I'm serious."

"And so am I."

"Okay . . ." I grinned. "What about before you knew me? What excited you then?"

He let go of my hands and sat up straighter. "I'm not sure I have a real passion like you do, but I love banking and economics. I find it fascinating, especially global macroeconomics. China's market has increased at such a fast rate that—" He stopped and grinned. "See?"

I squeezed his hand. "So you *do* have something you love."

"Global economy?" he asked, sounding incredulous. "Most people would fall asleep after thirty seconds."

"But you love it. That's all that matters. My friends don't understand why I love music so much, not even Jenna." I shrugged. "But she knows it's my thing and she accepts it."

He turned serious. "Is it wrong that I hope you get into my mother's *conservatoire* so I don't lose you?" He paused. "I hope you don't misunderstand. I want you to get in anyway, but I also don't want you to go home in a few weeks."

A warm feeling filled my chest and spread throughout my body. "When I decided to audition, I wasn't sure I'd accept a position if I made it, but I'm rethinking that. I told my mother, and she wants me to try. She's excited for me."

"Will you live with your father or on the campus?"

Dad still hadn't given me his blessing. In fact, I hadn't told him anything about my practice or the pieces I was playing, although Eva had asked questions. I got the distinct impression he didn't want me to come live in Paris, but why? The only explanation I could come up with was that my continued presence would upset his new family. Camille pretty much openly hated me now, and I had been difficult since my arrival. Staying for the summer was one thing; moving in was another.

I frowned. "Living on campus might have to be an option. I don't think my dad wants me to go to school here, so I doubt he would want me to live with him, even though Eva says I'm welcome."

He shook his head. "*Non.* You didn't see him asking me questions before you came out of the bedroom. He cares about you." He grimaced. "Your brother might be the issue. He might not be willing to let you out of his sight for that long."

I chuckled. "This is an entirely new side of him. You saw the way he reacted to my adventure the day you rescued me from the platform at St. Michel. He used to find pretty much everything I did annoying."

A soft smile lit up his eyes. "I wasn't looking at your brother that day."

I blushed again.

He shook his head, grinning. "I couldn't believe it when I found you at the station that day—the girl from the restaurant. I wanted to stay and talk to you that night, but Camille . . ."

"You were there to meet her, right?"

"*Oui.*"

It totally made sense, especially since Camille had disappeared by the time I returned to the celebration. "But after you found me in the Metro station, you were so angry with me, not that I blamed you. I was so hateful."

His mouth dropped open. "I wasn't mad at you, Sophie. I was mad at *Camille.* I thought about you constantly after I met you at the restaurant, but I didn't think I would ever see you again. When I figured out you were *le diable,* I couldn't believe it. I knew she was wrong about you."

"In the park—after you found Camille—Eric was trying to translate what you were saying. He said you were talking too fast, but he was sure you were angry with me."

"*Non.* I was angry with Camille for leaving you like that. And then for stealing Dane from you when she knew you liked him, although I wasn't surprised. Not after Hugo." His eyes found mine.

I felt my cheeks flushing. "It embarrasses me that you know that about Dane. I can't believe I ever thought of him that way."

"And me?"

I smiled. "You? I liked you the moment I saw you. Lucky for you, I like you even more now."

"A little?" he teased.

I held up my hand and pinched my thumb and index finger. "A wee little bit."

He grabbed my hand and kissed my knuckles. "Then I have work to do."

I was looking forward to it.

Mathieu grabbed the waiter and asked for the *addition*, then called his father. We left the restaurant and walked to the sidewalk running along the Seine. We were on the Left Bank, in the section where the sixth and seventh arrondissements met. The streets were lined with souvenir shops, but most of them were closed now, their metal garage doors pulled down and locked. And all the carts and vendors that lined the sidewalk during the day were gone.

This was a different side of Paris, the real Paris behind the tourists and the glitz.

We stood next to the low stone wall, and Mathieu put his arm around my back. He pulled me against him, my hands against his strong chest, and looked deep into my eyes. Now that all the lies and secrets had been ripped away, only we were left behind.

And it felt wonderful.

"You are unlike any girl I've ever known," he murmured, brushing a strand of hair from my forehead.

I grinned. "I bet it's because you're not forced to speak English all the time with other girls."

He laughed. "True, but that's not the reason."

"It must be because I have a brother who constantly threatens to beat you up."

"That's true as well, but it's still not the reason."

I stared into his eyes, his heartbeat quickening under my hand.

"You, Sophie Brooks, have captivated my heart, something no other girl has done." He lifted his hand to cup my cheek, then lowered his head, brushing his lips softly against mine.

My heart stuttered in response. Never in my wildest dreams had I imagined I would find a boyfriend like Mathieu Rousseau. It occurred to me that my wish on the star outside of Notre Dame had come true.

As he kissed me again, I felt a new hope for doing well in the audition and getting accepted.

Now I only had to convince my father.

CHAPTER *Thirty*

MATHIEU'S FATHER SHOWED up minutes later. He gave us a huge grin, asked us if we had fun, and then let us get lost in each other all over again. There was less traffic, so we reached my apartment sooner than I would have liked. Mathieu slid out of his seat and held his hand out to me.

I leaned over the front seat. *"Merci, Monsieur Rousseau.* I'm so happy to have met you."

He cast a glance at his son. "I have never seen Mathieu this happy." Then he grabbed my hand and squeezed. *"Merci."*

Mathieu grabbed my arm and pulled me out, cringing.

"I'm sorry about my father."

"Don't be," I said as he walked me to the front door. "I like him."

A boyish grin spread across his face. "I do too."

I turned to him and wrapped my arms around his neck. "Thank you for the most perfect evening."

His lips were warm and possessive as they claimed mine. Every kiss from Mathieu Rousseau had been special and amazing, but this one topped them all. I stared at him in amazement as he lifted his head. If this was only the beginning, how much better could it get?

He reached into his pocket. "I have a gift for you."

I gasped and dropped my hold on him. "What is it?"

He laughed. "If you get this excited over gifts, then I shall get you more. But first this one." He grabbed my hand and pressed something cold and metallic in my palm. "It's the key to your heart." He laughed at my obvious confusion. "It's a key to my apartment. And my piano."

I smirked at his joke. "Aren't you worried I only want to be with you for your piano?"

Smiling, he shook his head. "I'm willing to take the risk."

I couldn't believe he had given me a key. I closed my fist, the rough edges of the metal scraping my palm, but I held it close to my chest. "Thank you, Mathieu. This means so much to me."

"Now Etienne won't have to let you in. My mother and *beau-père* leave for work at eight thirty. You can come in whenever you like after that. They usually come home at six."

"And you . . . ? When do you leave for the school?"

He gave me a sad smile. "Seven. But I get home around three."

"Then maybe I shall see you tomorrow." I'd been skirting my dad's four hours of practice a day rule, but he would have to lift it if I had any shot at getting accepted.

He kissed me again, his lips soft and adoring. "*Bonne nuit, mon amour.*"

"What did you just say?" I whispered.

He pressed the buzzer to my apartment and then took several steps backward. "Good night, my love."

My heart pounded in my chest. Did that mean what I thought it meant?

The buzzer sounded. When I pulled the front door open, Mathieu turned around and got into his father's car, pausing to give me a little wave.

Eric was standing in the open doorway when I reached the landing. I expected some snide comment, but there was a strange look on his face when I brushed past him. It wasn't an angry look, so maybe Eva had told him to back off.

"Sophie, we're in here," Dad called out, and I found him and Eva sitting on the sofa facing the doors.

I set my new key on top of the keyboard before I walked into the room.

"Come tell us about your evening," Eva said, but I could tell something was off. Was I in trouble? If so, I couldn't understand why. It was only 10:45.

I sat on the sofa opposite them. "It was good. I loved the concert. There's a tricky movement in the sonata that he fumbled a little, but most people would never have known." I was babbling, and I knew it. Each moment I spent in here was like being in a walk-in freezer. There was something badly wrong—I wanted to ask what, but I was afraid of the answer.

Eric came in and sat next to me, perching on the arm of the sofa, but Camille and Dane were noticeably absent.

"And Mathieu was a gentleman?" Eva cast a glance to my father.

"Yes. His father drives a taxi, so he took us and brought us home. We had cheesecake and *crème brûlée* after." The tension was so thick in the room, I was choking on it. "Are we done? I want to call Jenna and tell her about the concert." Maybe I was wrong; maybe I was reading them incorrectly. There was still hope.

"Sophie," Dad said, worry tugging his mouth down. "There's something we have to tell you."

Tears sprang to my eyes, and I tried to calm my racing heart. "Is it Mom?"

"*Non, mon petit chou.*" Eva leaned forward. "Your mother is fine."

"Then what is it? What's happened?"

"It's Jenna," Dad said, clenching his jaw. "She was in a very bad accident a few hours ago."

I gasped. "Is she dead?"

"*Non!*" Eva said, rushing around the coffee table to sit beside me. Wrapping her arm around my back, she pulled me close. "But she is seriously injured."

"I don't understand," I said, trying to catch my breath. "I just talked to her this afternoon to tell her about my date. She was fine. She was going to Lauren's house to go swimming."

"She was on her way to Lauren's," Dad said, his voice breaking. "A truck broadsided her, and her car rolled over."

"Is she okay?" I started to cry, and Eva's hold tightened.

"She's in the ICU with internal injuries. They aren't . . ." Dad took a deep breath. "They aren't sure if she'll make it. She's in surgery now."

My sobs broke loose. "No!"

"I'm so sorry, Sophie." Dad's voice broke once again.

"Daddy." I walked around the coffee table, lunged for him, and wrapped my arms around his neck, heaving sobs. For fifteen years, he had been the one to make everything okay. He had been the one to hold me when I woke up in darkness, fresh from a nightmare. He had been my rock of reassurance when I was scared, and I'd never been more scared than I was right now. "She can't die, Daddy. I can't lose her too."

Dad started to cry. "I'm so sorry, Sophie. I'm so sorry." I knew he wasn't just talking about Jenna.

Once I had settled down a bit, Eva knelt in front of me. "Would you like to change your clothes? Maybe get into your pajamas? Jenna's parents said they would keep us updated. We plan to stay up and wait for their call."

"You too?" I asked surprised. "You don't even know her."

Her eyes filled with tears. "She's special to you. That makes her important." She grabbed my arm and stood. "Come. Camille has laid some pajamas out on your bed."

"She did?" I asked in surprise.

"She's worried about you."

I had serious doubts about that, but I didn't have the brain capacity to work through it.

Camille was sitting on her bed when I entered the room, looking uncertain. Sure enough, there was a pair of pajamas folded on the bed.

I changed in front of her, not caring if she saw me naked. It struck me that this was another way living here had changed me, but I was too numb to give it much thought.

After I washed my face and took down my hair, I found Dad, Eva, and Eric in the living room. Dad lifted his arm, and I started to cry all over again.

Eva threw a soft blanket over me and curled up on the opposite sofa. Eric sat beside her, on the other end, his eyes red.

"You're staying up too?" I asked.

He just nodded in answer.

Eva turned on the TV and put in a DVD—*Father of the Bride*. It had been Dad's and my favorite movie to watch together back home.

He'd bought it for me.

I snuggled against Dad, his arm around me, his hand stroking my hair. The familiarity helped soothe me, and I was actually dozing a bit when Dad's phone rang.

He jerked upright, pulling his arm free so he could grab his phone off the side table. "Ron, how is she?"

He leaned forward, resting his elbow on his knee and his forehead on his palm. "I see." My heart leapt into my throat as he listened intently. "Uh huh . . . Okay . . . Keep me updated . . . Yeah, I'll tell Sophie. Let me know if we can do anything."

"Is she okay?" I asked, trying to hold back my tears.

Eric was leaning forward, waiting with an anxious look on his face. Eva had grabbed his hand, and he was holding it tight.

"She's out of surgery. They had to remove her ruptured spleen and she had some other injuries, like a punctured lung, but she's going to be okay."

My tears broke free, and Dad pulled me close and kissed the top of my head. "She's going to be okay."

Eva spoke softly in French, and Dad nodded before she said in English, "We should all try to get some sleep."

Dad and Eric stood, but I lay down on the sofa. "I want to stay out here."

Eva nodded her approval, then straightened the blanket over me. "Try to get some sleep, *mon petit chou*."

She started to walk away but I called after her. "Eva."

She squatted next to me, and tears of gratitude filled my eyes. Had she gone through a vigil like this after her husband's accident? Had she been forced to relive the trauma? It made my heart hurt to think about it.

"Thank you . . . for everything. I'm sorry I was so awful when I first came."

A soft smile lifted her mouth. "Shh . . ." She smoothed back my hair and wiped a tear rolling down my cheek. "I understood."

I sat up and sniffed. "If my dad had to remarry, I'm so glad it was you." I gave her a smile. "I love you."

Her chin quivered and she sucked in her bottom lip as she sat down next to me, then wrapped her arms around me. "Sophie, *ma cocotte*. I love you too." She kissed my cheek and then stood. "Go to sleep without worry. Jenna will be fine."

I lay back down and closed my eyes, but there were so many emotions washing through me I had trouble sleeping. I was dozing when I heard murmurs in the doorway.

"What if it was her, Eva?" my dad said. He was leaning into the doorframe. "I don't know what I'd do."

Eva was standing next to him, rubbing his arm. "Sophie is fine, but she needs you, William. Being away from you is different for her than it is for Eric. Let her audition. She might make the program, and then you can see her all the time."

"We don't even know if she'll get in. I would hate to see her put herself out there only to get hurt. This is Paris, Eva. The center of culture. The best of the best go to music school here."

She laughed softly. "I am aware this is *Paris*"—she said it the French way, leaving off the *S*—"but she is very good. Have you heard her play since she's come?"

"She might be good, but is she Paris good?"

"Madeline says she's close. But she needs more practice time. You have to give it to her."

He released a sigh. "I don't know."

"William." She sounded insistent. "You can't hold her back because of your regrets. She has to make her own choices."

"She's a kid, Eva. She's too young to make this kind of decision."

"She's no longer a child. And if you keep her from her dream, she will resent you for it. If nothing else, give her the freedom to practice as much as she needs."

"Fine. She can practice, but I still don't think she should audition." He walked away, but Eva watched me for several seconds before going to bed.

I'd already guessed that my father didn't want me to audition, so why was it so hard to hear him say it?

Maybe because I worried he didn't want me here at all.

CHAPTER *Thirty-One*

I HAD A massive headache the next morning, but an ibuprofen and a quick shower helped me feel better. When I went to gather my music, I was surprised to find a note from my father.

Practice for as long as you want.

It was what I wanted, yet his words from the night before still hurt. I stuffed the music and my laptop into my bag, then picked up the key Mathieu had given me.

The key to my heart.

Mathieu had been right. I had my music. I didn't need my father's approval. But as I walked to Mathieu's apartment half an hour earlier than usual, I realized something else was more important right now. I needed to go home to Charleston. Jenna was lying in a hospital bed on the other side of the world, and she needed me.

I sent Dad a text saying I needed to go home to Jenna, and he texted back to say we'd talk about it later that night. Ten hours wasn't going to make a difference. Mom and her boy-friend were on a weekend ocean cruise and inaccessible until Sunday night. There was no way Dad would let me go home to an empty house.

In the meantime, I planned to play my heart out on the piano.

I worried I might have problems getting inside the building, but all the doors opened without a hitch. I felt like a trespasser going into the empty apartment, but I sat down at the piano and began to play straightaway.

I was lost in the music, as always, but forced myself to concentrate on the technical side of the sonata. Anything less than perfection would be unacceptable if I wanted to succeed.

If I was even still here to audition.

I wasn't sure how long I'd been playing when my phone rang, but I was in the middle of my Rachmaninoff piece. My stomach clenched when I saw it was Jenna's mother's phone.

"Mrs. D, how is she?"

"It's me," Jenna said, her voice sounding weak and far away.

"Oh! Jenna! Are you okay?" I shook my head. "Of course you're not okay. How are you?" I stood and began to pace.

"Calm down, Soph. Breathe."

"How can I calm down when you almost died?"

"I didn't almost die . . . Mom, stop. She's already freaked out. Okay, I get it," she said, sounding frustrated. She sounded loopy too, and I wondered how much pain medication she was hopped up on. "Everyone's freaking out about how I almost died, but how do you think I feel? No more talk about me almost dying, got it?"

"Got it," I said, and Jenna's mother's answer echoed mine on the other end of the line.

"I'm calling to let you know I'm okay, although I hear I look like a patchwork quilt, which totally sucks since I got this really cute bikini on sale last week . . . Yes, Mom, it covers my butt . . . Mom! I almost died. I think saying the word *butt* is the least of my worries. Especially since I'll never wear it or any other bikini again."

"Why? Because of your scar?" I asked. "It's a war wound. Wear it proudly."

"Yeah," she said, but her voice was weaker.

"You need some rest, Jenna. Why don't you call me later, and you can tell me about all of the cute doctors in the hospital."

"I have to tell you something first."

"Okay."

"I don't think I can come on Sunday."

My heart sank. I had guessed as much, of course. "I had a feeling you might have to cancel. I think they frown on bringing IV poles on planes. It's hard to get them through the metal detectors in security. Which is why I think I should come home."

"What? Why?"

"Because you need me."

"But what about the cute French boy? What about your audition?"

"Who cares about the audition? Who would want to go to school with a bunch of fussy French people?"

"You," she said softly. "Music is your dream."

Oh, she knew me so well. "Jenna, I can't stay here knowing you're in a hospital bed, hooked up to all kinds of tubes and wires, coming in and out of consciousness with no one there to give you a fair and accurate assessment of the hotness of all the doctors, interns, male nurses, and other hospital personnel that come in and out of your room."

"Ow!" she shouted. "Stop making me laugh. It hurts. And like you would ever do such a thing. That's what *I* would do."

"Exactly. So being a good friend, I need to cover for you."

"You can't come home, Soph. You have to stay there and audition. You have to stay with your cute French boy and fall in love and one day make beautiful French-American babies."

A big part of me hoped to do exactly that. But I couldn't. "You need me, Jen."

"Please, please, please don't come home for me. I want you to stay. Especially since I can't come on Sunday. If you get into your fancy school, then I can come and stay the entire summer next year and find my own French boy."

"Jenna . . ."

"Stay where you are for now, Sophie. We'll talk about this later when my head's not so fuzzy."

The front door to the apartment opened, and Mathieu walked in, worry on his face.

"Get some rest and get well, okay? We'll go shopping for some midriff tops to show off your scars."

"Only if you get one too . . ." Her voice drifted off.

Mathieu walked up behind me and wrapped his arms around my front, pulling me against his chest.

"Jenna?" I asked after a couple of seconds.

"She fell asleep," her mother said in a hushed tone. "She insisted on calling you even though she's as high as a kite on drugs. But I thought you'd like to hear her voice and know she's really okay." Her voice broke.

"She really did almost die, didn't she?" I asked, my tears returning.

"Let's just say it was very close." She promised to keep me updated and then hung up.

I snuggled my head against Mathieu's chest. His arms cinched tighter around my waist.

"I heard about your friend."

I craned my neck to look back at him. "How did you find out?"

"Thomas. Since Jenna can't come, Camille wants Dane to stay."

"What? No!" I spun around to face him. "He *has* to go home." He studied me. "Why?"

"Because he's the world's biggest jerk and I want him gone."

He brushed several strands of hair from my forehead. "Then you better talk to your father, because Camille is pressuring her mother, and I think she's winning."

Something on his face caught my attention. "You want him gone too."

"Yes. I don't like how he looks at you."

I leaned back. "What are you talking about?"

"Do you not see it? When you walked out last night, he couldn't take his eyes off you. And it wasn't the first time."

I shuddered. "All the more reason for him to go. Camille will flip her lid if she sees him doing that. I'm already on her bad side."

He glanced at the music spread all over the piano and my laptop arranged on a chair I'd pulled over from the kitchen. "I'm surprised you're still here. I didn't think I'd get to see you."

"Why? What time is it?"

"It's after four."

"It's *that* late?" But I guessed it didn't matter now that Dad had lifted my practice restrictions. Besides, I needed all the practice time I could get. "I better go. I haven't even had lunch."

"Gather your things, and I'll walk you home. And I'll get you something to eat. I can't let you starve."

As we walked back to my apartment, Mathieu told me about his day, tutoring some younger kids with math and reading, then helping to paint a classroom. We stopped for savory *crêpes* and finished eating them by the time we got to my apartment.

"Would you like to come up?" I asked. "Now that we are out in the open? Or would it be too awkward for you with Camille?"

He paused to consider it, then shook his head. "My friends are going to hang out by the river tonight. We could go with them."

"Okay. Sure." According to him, this was how teens dated here, and besides, I wanted to get to know his friends. It would be especially important if I ended up moving here. And I had to make sure there wouldn't be any awkwardness with Thomas since he was Mathieu's best friend.

"I know Camille and Dane are coming, but I can pick you up and take you with me."

I smiled. "Okay."

He gave me a soft kiss, then smiled. "See you tonight."

Camille and the boys were in the living room when I walked in. They gave me a cursory glance before returning to their game. I went into the kitchen to get a glass of water and looked up to see Camille in the doorway.

"I heard your friend is going to be okay. That's good."

"Yeah, thanks." I took a drink, keeping an eye on her. Camille was trying her best to look sympathetic, but she had a wary look in her eyes.

"Since she can't come, that means Dane can stay."

And there it was. I was thankful that Mathieu had warned me. I shrugged.

"His parents said he could stay and my mother says he can stay. It's your father who's saying no."

"That's too bad. I hope it works out for you." I started for the door, but she blocked my exit.

"You need to convince your father to let him stay."

"Me? Why don't you ask Eric?"

"He says he already tried."

That sounded like a lie. He hadn't come out and said it, but I was sure he was counting the hours until Dane got on the plane tomorrow. "Well, if Eric couldn't convince him . . ."

"You can."

I shook my head. "Why do you think I can?"

"Because you have your father under your spell. He'll do whatever you want."

I released a harsh laugh. "Have you *seen* my father and me? We may have been like that once, but not anymore."

Her eyes narrowed with hate. "Do you know how lucky you are? You should be grateful you have a father. Mine is gone."

My resolve to defy her weakened, but then again, that's probably exactly what she wanted. Mathieu said she loved to play games. That's exactly what she was doing now. "I'll talk to him, but I can't promise anything."

I tried to move around her, but she continued to block my path.

"What do you want, Camille?"

"Either convince your father to let him stay or I'll tell my mother Mathieu's secret." Then she sneered. "Did he tell you what he did?"

I put my hands on my hips. "Yeah, I know he broke Hugo's nose after he found you in bed together in your room. Maybe I should tell your mother that."

She shrugged, but her face paled. "Go ahead."

"Call it a draw and let it go, Camille."

Her expression told me that my wording confused her, which only pissed me off more. "I have something to use against you. You have something to use against Mathieu. No one wins. Let it go."

"I can destroy Mathieu. He did something far worse than break Hugo's nose."

I had no doubt she could. And would. "I know he altered school records. I know it could destroy the career he wants more than anything. For what? Why would you hurt someone like that? No, let's back up. Why did you hurt him by intention-ally sleeping with the one guy who made his life horrible?" I shook my head. "Never mind. You probably did it just because you could. You are truly a despicable human being."

I knew part of what I said was lost on her.

"You're wrong about one thing," she said with a hard edge in her voice. "His career isn't the thing he wants more than anything right now." A smile lifted her lips. "Are you willing to let him throw away his precious future for you?"

I hated her. Truly hated her in that moment.

"You have until Dane is about to get on the plane tomorrow to change your father's mind, or I'm telling my mother everything."

"You do that, and I'm telling her everything too. And I mean everything—leaving me at the Metro, convincing your friends to be mean to me. As sweet as Eva is, I'm sure she'll have a thing or two to say about that."

Camille lifted her shoulder in a nonchalant shrug. "Mathieu has much more to lose than I do." Then she turned and walked out of the kitchen.

I was in a whole lot of trouble.

I really wished Mom wasn't on her cruise. I needed someone to talk to about this, and Jenna wasn't available. Of course, if Jenna had been available, I wouldn't be in this situation at all.

In the end, it didn't matter if I had someone to talk to or not. I couldn't let Camille destroy Mathieu.

My stomach was such a mess of nerves that I could barely take a bite of my slice of takeout pizza at dinner. Camille lifted her eyebrows and leaned her head toward my father.

I took a deep breath, then turned to my dad. "Since Jenna can't come, why don't we let Dane stay?"

Eric's eyes nearly popped out of his head.

Dad gave me a look that said *don't press it*. Too bad I had no choice.

"I mean, we were going to have Jenna here, so it's just another body." I hoped both Dane and Camille got the full impact of that insult, but it would probably go over their heads. "Camille has gotten so close to Dane that it's the least we can do to let them stay together for a few more weeks."

Dad gave me a strange look. "And let me guess . . . you want his ticket home so *you* can go home?"

"What?" I'd nearly forgotten about our text conversation from this morning. "No. I talked to Jenna this morning, and she wants me to stay and audition."

Dad gave Eva a look, but she shook her head. "Not now, William."

"Look, I know you don't want me to audition, and that's a conversation for another time. Right now we need to talk about Dane. I really want him to stay." I had to bite the inside of my lip to keep from taking it back. "And Jenna does too. She wants me to take lots of photos of Camille and Dane in Paris. I don't have any."

"Sophie." My dad was using his irritated tone, which meant I was pushing him to the limit. He wasn't budging.

Camille's expression turned ugly.

The food in my stomach churned and a cold sweat broke out on the back of my neck. I couldn't fail Mathieu. I had to pull out the big guns.

I started to cry.

It wasn't hard to muster the tears. All I had to do was think about what was at stake. "Daddy, please. I'm so upset about Jenna, and Dane has been so awesome today. If my friend can't join us, I'd like to have another familiar face around. It's comforting."

God love him, Dad looked like he was softening. My stomach was rebelling over the blatant, disgusting lie, and I swallowed the bile in the back of my throat.

Eric looked at me like I'd totally lost my mind.

And Dane . . . Dane looked at me like I was a big bucket of fried chicken at a church picnic.

Now I started to cry for real, fat tears that fell down my cheeks. I didn't want that jerk to stay. I didn't want him to be anywhere near me, either here or back home, and yet Camille had put me in this terrible position.

"Okay . . ." Dad shook his head, then looked at Dane. "But you better go call your parents right now to get the ticket changed."

Dane jumped out of his seat and left the table with Camille, but not before he gave me an appraising look.

Eric continued to stare at me, so I gave him a slight shake of my head.

Eva and Dad were subdued for the rest of the meal, and I barely ate my food, still nauseated from my performance. Dane's newfound appreciation meant I was going to have to be careful around him.

I planned to stay far, far away.

CHAPTER *Thirty-Two*

I APPRECIATED MANY things about the fact that Mathieu had "outed" us. The freedom to touch him was liberating. But as far as secrets went, I'd just dug myself into a huge hole.

Eric kept trying to corner me after dinner, but I managed to elude him. I couldn't blame him. If it were the other way around, I'd be trying to get answers too, but I wasn't sure how much I could tell him. For all I knew, he'd run to Eva with the information if I shared it with him.

Mathieu met us outside the apartment and snagged my hand, pulling me close, which effectively kept my brother away. But I had a new problem: how much did I tell Mathieu? He wasn't a fool, so he'd soon figure it out. Much better for him to hear it from me.

But that idea was shot out of the water within an hour.

We'd met Camille and Mathieu's friends on the Left Bank of the Seine, about halfway between the Eiffel Tower and Notre Dame. About thirty teens had gathered on the concrete path that ran along the river, below the road. While I was excited to spend more time with Mathieu's friends, I also wanted some time alone with him to warn him about Dane's change of travel plans.

Mathieu's friends had brought multiple bottles of wine, which they passed around. Everyone but me took drinks. Dane drank more than everyone else, getting loud and boisterous. I was thankful when he and Camille moved to the opposite side of the path.

Eric walked over to me, shaking his head in disgust. "I hope you're happy, Sophie. You get four more weeks with the jerk. Who cares what I want?"

Mathieu's arm tightened around my back as he gave my brother a wary stare. "What's he talking about?"

"Your new girlfriend didn't tell you?" Eric sneered, then stumbled on his feet. So he'd been hitting the bottles hard too.

"Eric," I pleaded. "Stop. Let me take you home."

"Home?" he asked. "Where is that? Dad's apartment in Paris or our real home in Charleston?"

"Eric. Please."

"You always were his favorite." His words were slurred, and he listed to the side a little and then righted himself. "That's why he let Dane stay even after I told him I wanted him to go home."

The blood rushed from my face. "What?"

"He promised me he wouldn't cave to Camille's whining, but all it took was for you to pour on the tears and he let him stay." He clapped his hands, each strike hitting slightly off-center. "Bravo."

"Sophie. What is he talking about?" Mathieu's voice lowered.

I looked up at him, fear clogging my throat. "I asked Dad to let Dane stay."

"Why?" But understanding filled his eyes before they darkened and turned toward my stepsister.

I grabbed his arm. "Mathieu. Don't."

"Why did you do it?" he pleaded. "I told you I wanted it out in the open."

"I couldn't let her destroy you," I said, my voice shaking. "I couldn't live with myself, knowing I could have stopped her."

"What are you talking about?" Eric asked a little too loudly.

I needed to get him home. While teenage drinking was tolerated here, public drunkenness was not.

Eric leaned forward, leering at me. "He's screwing her, you know."

"Eric!"

He laughed and pointed his finger at me. "He only wants one thing from you, Sophie, and I told him I'd kill him if he came near you."

Mathieu tensed next to me. "If he comes near her, I will kill him myself."

Eric saluted him, the gesture sloppy. "Finally, we have something in common, Matt-Pew."

This entire situation felt like it had turned into a powder keg.

"Nobody's killing anyone." I forced a smile even though my hands were shaking. "You know what? I'm hungry. Why don't we get some ice cream? Or some French bread. Let's go."

"I know you like him," Eric spat out. "I know you've liked him for two years. You thought you were hiding it, but I could see. So could he."

Mathieu froze.

I was about to die from mortification. "Eric. Enough. Let's go." I was surprised at the authority in my voice.

He must have been too, because his demeanor changed and he said, "Okay."

"Mathieu, will you help me with him?"

I could see the hesitation in his eyes, and my heart sank. "I'll explain all of it, I promise. But you have to help me get him home. *Please*."

He nodded. "Okay. I'll tell Camille we're going."

"Like she cares," Eric sneered.

Finally, something *he and I* agreed on tonight.

I watched Mathieu approach Camille and Dane, then gesture toward us. Camille literally turned her back. Seemed she was done with me now that she'd gotten what she wanted.

Good riddance.

Mathieu helped me guide Eric to the street, but we had to stop halfway toward the stairs to let Eric barf on the cobblestones.

"I didn't see him drink that much," I murmured, feeling guilty as I watched him bracing himself on his legs. He might have been my older brother, but I still felt responsible for him.

Mathieu didn't answer, but he seemed guarded, watching my brother instead of looking at me.

"Mathieu." When he refused to look at me, I was more blunt. "*Mathieu.*"

The pain in his eyes ripped my heart to shreds. "*You* are the one I want. I had a stupid little girl crush on the guy, but he turned out to be a complete jerk. Then I met a guy with more maturity and compassion than that idiot has in his little toe. Please don't turn this into something it's not."

"But you begged your father to let him stay."

"And you know why." My tone was harsh, but I had to get the message across.

"I wish you hadn't done it."

"Why?"

"Because I don't trust him. He's your brother's friend, yet your brother hates his guts. That guy is nothing but trouble, and we're all going to pay for this before the summer is over."

The memory of Dane grabbing my wrists popped into my head, and I had a feeling Mathieu might be right. But I couldn't undo it now. Besides, I'd do it all over again if it protected Mathieu, even though it stung to know I was hurting my brother in the process.

"Are you two going to talk all night or help me up?" Eric asked, on his knees.

I rolled my eyes. Leave it to me to have a serious conversation with my boyfriend while my brother was puking five feet away.

Mathieu and I each grabbed one of his arms and hauled him to his feet. "Do you think we can get a taxi?" I asked as we started walking again.

"*Non.* Even if we could get a taxi to take him, which is doubtful, he needs to walk it off."

I had serious doubts he would make it all the way home, but we didn't have a choice. "Not how you pictured our second date, huh?" I asked.

"I told you, we French don't date." Mathieu gave me his boyish grin, and some of my tension eased.

"But we Americans *do*, so this disaster is our second date."

"If you are tallying dates, why don't any of our breakfasts count?"

"Because we weren't boyfriend and girlfriend then."

"Sophie," he said softly. "I was officially your boyfriend when I kissed you on the Eiffel Tower."

"I can't help it if no one explained the rules to French dating."

"Will you two stop bickering?" Eric moaned. "You're giving me a headache. And if you keep talking about kissing, it's going to make me barf again."

"No," Mathieu said. "The bottle of wine you drank is giving you a headache and is about to make you barf again." He turned to me. "Okay, so I watched him."

I smiled, though I felt a bit guilty for feeling so happy while Eric was obviously suffering. Despite Eric's protests, we continued to talk about other differences between the French and Americans.

"Americans are loud," Mathieu said. "We French are more subdued."

Eric snorted. "Most of you French smoke. Most American's don't."

"We French find most Americans to be prudes with nudity."

"You French sleep around," Eric said.

"*Non*," Mathieu said, turning to look at me behind my brother's back. "While we aren't so strict with sex, we usually have sex only when we are in love."

"Stop talking about sex around my sister!"

I could tell my cheeks were beet red, but I forced a laugh. What was Mathieu telling me? That he hadn't slept around? I'd never suspected him of it, but it was nice to know anyway.

It took us over a half hour, but we finally reached our building's front door. Only then did I realize we had another dilemma on our hands.

"How do we get him in?" I asked.

Mathieu dropped his hold on my brother's arm and leaned against the building. "Will your father believe it if he says he has a stomachache?"

I cringed. "I don't know. Maybe."

"I don't have any other ideas. Let's try it."

We half dragged Eric up the stairs and opened the apartment door. I peered inside, surprised that it was quiet and dark. One lamp was on in the living room.

"We're lucky," I said. "They must be out."

"Let's get him to his bed."

Mathieu led him down the hall while I got a glass of water from the kitchen. He was helping lower Eric to the bed as I reached the doorway. When Mathieu started to rise, Eric grabbed his arm and pulled him back down until they were nearly nose to nose. "I might have been wrong about you."

Mathieu grinned as he stood, waving a hand in front of his face. "*Merci.*"

Eric rolled onto his back, closing his eyes. "But if you hurt my sister, I'll have to beat the crap out of you."

"Fair enough."

I set the water on the nightstand and started to pull Eric's shoes off, but he jerked upright and pointed at me. "I'm still mad at you. Dane Wallace is a prick."

"I know, and I'm *really* sorry."

He laid back down. "I'll make you pay for it later."

I was sure he would.

We left him in bed and wandered out into the hall. Mathieu glanced at the front door. "I guess this is the end of our night."

"Not necessarily." I leaned my head toward the living room. "We can sit in here and watch TV."

"Are you sure your father will be okay with it?"

I shrugged and grinned. "We're making sure Eric's all right."

"Okay."

We sat on the sofa, and he put his arm around me as we watched a French sitcom. Mathieu told me what they were saying and made me repeat the phrases.

Something warm and cozy filled my heart, bringing me a sense of peace. I looked back at him to reassure myself this wasn't a dream.

He caught my gaze and narrowed his eyes. "What?"

I stretched my neck and gave him a gentle kiss. "So many things are wrong in my life right now, but all I can see are the things that are right. Thank you for encouraging me with my piano when my dad seems intent on making me quit. Thank you for tolerating the craziness that seems to follow me around."

His smile lit up his face. "I will put up with any kind of crazy if I get to spend time with you."

I was counting on it. At least for the four weeks I had left.

CHAPTER *Thirty-Three*

THE NEXT THREE weeks flew by. I spent most of my days alone in Mathieu's apartment, practicing. Once Etienne realized I had amped up my practice schedule, he started going to a friend's house after swim practice. One advantage to being gone all day was that I had limited contact with Dane, and when we were at the apartment together, Dad and Eva were usually around too. Eric had begun hanging out with Thomas, but he'd taken to ignoring Marine, to the poor girl's disappointment. He barely spoke to me, which made me feel increasingly guilty for my betrayal.

Mathieu and I grew closer and closer. We spent part of almost every night together, whether it was a walk to the Eiffel Tower or Seine and back or watching TV with Dad and Eva.

Jenna had gotten out of the hospital, and she called me every day for updates on Mathieu.

"I can't believe I won't get to meet him!" she exclaimed.

"I can't believe I'm going to leave him."

She was quiet, then said, "I can't believe you're going to leave *me*."

"I'm probably not going to get accepted. The chances are slim. Mathieu says they're auditioning twenty students for two slots."

"You'll get in," she said, sounding sad. "I don't know what I'll do without you."

Anxiety made my skin prickly. I wanted to be with Jenna and I wanted to be with Mathieu. I wished I could have both.

But I couldn't get in if I didn't audition.

My audition was a couple of days away, and my dad hadn't given me permission. Mom had become frustrated and threatened to call him.

"No, Mom. Don't," I said. "Maybe he doesn't want me here. I mean, it could get complicated if I live here all the time with Camille." I'd told her that my stepsister and I didn't get along, although I hadn't shared many details.

"No," she said softly. "That's not it. I have a feeling this has more to do with us than you."

"You and Dad?" I asked in surprise.

"Let me call him, Sophie. I promise not to yell."

I finally relented, mostly because of the wistfulness in her voice.

Thankfully, I was feeling really confident about my pieces, especially since I was having twice-weekly video-chats with Miss Lori. I continued practicing, living in denial that I might not get to audition after all my work.

And also ignoring the fact that my plane home took off in three days.

I couldn't face leaving Mathieu. Even if Dad *did* let me audition, the *conservatoire* wouldn't announce the chosen students until a week after I left. So if I did make it, I'd see him again in a matter of weeks. If I didn't . . . I had no idea when I'd be back. Whenever I asked Dad, he changed the subject.

So I was about to get on a plane with no idea when I'd ever see Mathieu again.

Consequently, Mathieu and I had begun spending every possible minute together. He was still doing his community service work at his school, so he was gone all day, which meant we made sure every minute together in the evenings counted.

On Monday I was still at his apartment when he got home, although as usual, I hadn't heard him come in. I found him sitting in the leather chair, watching me with a sweet smile. He was wearing jeans and a T-shirt that fit him tight against the chest. His hair was slightly ruffled, and I felt a sudden urge to run my hands through it.

"You know," I said, turning on the bench to take in the sight of him. "I still haven't heard you play. You promised to play for me if I auditioned."

His eyes lit up with mischievousness as he stood and slowly walked toward me. He grabbed my hand, tugged me off the bench and into his arms, pressing my chest against his.

I sucked in a breath as the now familiar wave of belonging washed over me even as my stomach fluttered with his touch.

He bent down to kiss me, and I suddenly realized what he was doing—what he'd done every time I asked him to fulfill his promise: distracting me.

I leaned back, giving him a pointed stare. "I'm on to you. You're not getting out of it this time."

He laughed, then kissed me anyway, although I didn't protest. When he lifted his head, he grinned. "Okay. But only for you."

He maneuvered to sit on the bench, making me sit next to him, then he made a show of flexing and curling his fingers.

I lifted my eyebrows.

He grinned. "I'm warming up."

"*Joue.*" Play.

He laughed at my French, which was probably wrong. Verb conjugations tripped me up so that I was sure I sounded like a toddler. Usually he corrected me—which I wanted—but instead he rested his fingers on the keys. He took a deep breath, then plunked out a simple tune I recognized.

"Twinkle, Twinkle, Little Star."

I smacked his arm. "I don't want to hear the song that ended your promising piano career. Play something you loved. What made your heart sing?"

With anyone else, I would have felt embarrassed with that question, but not Mathieu. He understood me like no one before him.

His playfulness fell away, and he leaned over and kissed me, a lingering kiss that sent tingles through my body. When he lifted his head, he was still serious. "You make my heart sing."

Then he turned and put his hands on the keys again. "I haven't played for years. This will sound very bad."

"*Joue*," I repeated.

"*Joué*," he corrected, adding the "e" sound at the end. Then to my surprise he started to play a more complicated piece than I'd expected. It was a short allegretto—a piece played fairly quickly—and I was impressed that he made very few mistakes. But then I wasn't. Mathieu never did anything halfway.

When he finished a couple of minutes later, he turned to me with a grin. "The third movement of Bach's Sonata in F major. I suppose I should have announced that first."

"You're very good, Mathieu. You shouldn't have stopped."

He shook his head, softness filling his eyes. "*Non*. It's not my love. I hated practicing, which only frustrated my mother." Then he stood. "I'll walk you home."

That night, Dad came home early, looking haggard and older than usual. I was curled up and reading on the sofa, alone in the apartment since Camille and the boys were still out.

"Where is everyone?" he asked, sitting down next to me.

"Still out, I guess. I've been home for about a half hour." I put the book on the table next to me. "I had a video-call with Miss Lori today. We worked out the order of my pieces. She thinks I should start off with the Chopin etude, play my Mozart sonata next, and save the Rachmaninoff piece for last. She says it will impress the panel if I finish with such a strong piece. It will also help that I have it memorized."

"Sophie. We need to talk about the audition."

I sat up, my heart pounding. "Daddy, I'm begging you. Please let me do this."

He took my hand in his, his rough, calloused hand against my smooth hand with calloused fingertips. We both lived to create beauty with our hands. So why did he want to take this from me?

"Sophie, I was in your shoes years ago. Not with the piano, of course, but with my restoration work. I loved it. Still do." He sighed and put my hand in my lap. "I had to make a choice—a career I loved or the woman I loved. I chose the career, but I thanked God the woman I loved chose to follow me. And then she kept following me. Only later did I realize it ruined us. We became strangers living in the same house."

It felt odd listening to him talk about Mom like that, but I now knew about their problems. It wasn't a surprise.

"I screwed up when I left last August. I know that now. And I keep screwing up. And it all boils down to that one decision I made long ago—picking restoration over my family. I chose a profession I loved even though I couldn't offer financial stability or long-term security."

"Daddy, I never saw it as you choosing your job over me, at least not until you moved to Paris."

"Your mother did." He swallowed. "I don't want that for you, Sophie. I don't want you to make the same mistakes I did."

"But Daddy, you're not even giving me a choice at all. You're forcing one on me, and it wasn't even the choice you made. Besides, you love what you do. Despite everything."

"Yes." He sighed, looking distraught. "I love it, despite everything." He was silent for a moment. "Sophie, you have to understand. I love you. I want to protect you."

"You have to let me grow up, Dad. You have to let me make my own choices, and if I screw up, I will be the one to live with the mistakes." I shook my head. "You haven't even heard me play since last summer. Why won't you listen to me play?"

"Because your mother told me how much you began to play after I left. Now every time I see you play, it reminds me of the pain I've put you through."

"Daddy." My heart ached.

"You need more than the piano, Sophie. You need to live."

"I am! I've conquered my fears and I've been seeing Paris."

"With Mathieu."

"No. Not just with him. With Camille and her friends and sometimes just me and Eric. The point is I've changed while I've been here, but piano is still a huge part of me." He remained quiet, so I said, "At least listen to me play."

He sat there for several seconds, then got up. "Is Mathieu coming over tonight?"

He was changing the subject. "Yes."

He nodded and left the room, breaking my heart all over again.

But the next morning when I got up to leave for Mathieu's apartment—the day before the audition—I found Dad sitting at the kitchen table, sipping on a cup of coffee.

"Dad," I said in surprise. "What are you doing still home?"

"I thought I'd go to work late and come hear you play."

My eyes widened. "Really?"

"Yeah. Is that okay?"

A smile spread across my face. "Yeah."

I took him to my favorite *pâtisserie*. I greeted the woman behind the counter and ordered breakfast and coffee for Dad and me. When I handed him his food, he looked at me in amazement. "When did you learn to speak French?"

"Mathieu's been teaching me."

Dad told me more about what he was restoring. His work at *Sainte-Chapelle* would be done in six months.

"What will you do then?"

He gave me an apologetic smile. "I'll probably move on to the *Opéra*. That's how I met Eva. I had a lunch interview at a restaurant by the *Opéra*, and Eva walked into the restaurant. My coworker, Nathan, knew her, so he introduced us. I took one look at her and knew she was the one." He gave me a sad smile. "I'm sorry. That's probably hard to hear."

I shook my head. "No, I love Eva."

When we got to Mathieu's apartment, I pulled a dining room chair over to the piano. I sat down on the bench and looked over at him. "What do you want to hear?"

"Whatever you want to play."

I held my hands over the keys, mentally running through my catalogue of songs. "First I'll play *Dido's Lament*. It's meant to be sung, so it will sound overly simple, but this is the piece that changed the way I played. Miss Lori gave it to me last fall." Then I started to play, letting all my emotions pour through my fingers.

When I finished, Dad cleared his throat. "Sophie. That was beautiful."

"That was nothing, really. I just thought you should hear it. She gave it to me because of you." He started to ask me to explain, but I said, "Next I'll play you my Rachmaninoff Prelude in B Minor. I've been working on it all summer, and it's the finishing piece for my audition."

"So it's difficult?"

I gave him a small nod. "Yes."

"Let me hear it."

I closed my eyes, then began to play, my sadness over leaving Mathieu and even my father pouring into the music. When I played the last note, I turned to look at my father.

Tears were streaming down his face now, and he grinned at me as he wiped them with the back of his hand. "You've gotten better since I left."

I grinned back. "Maybe a little."

"Because of me."

I didn't answer.

"You love this"—he waved to the piano—"the music."

"Yes, Dad. I do. It's part of me. I couldn't stop if I wanted to."

He watched me for several seconds. "Thank you for playing for me." Then he stood. "I need to get to work. I'll see you tonight. Is Mathieu coming to dinner tonight?"

"Yeah."

He nodded, then turned.

My mouth dropped as I watched him walk out the door. Was he giving me his permission or not?

Miss Lori told me I was ready to practice playing through my pieces a few times, but we split it up with some of my other songs. I left after only a couple of hours and headed back to Dad's apartment. Eric was still there, and he, Dane, and Camille were getting ready to leave for an outing.

"Back already, little Sophie?" Dane asked, giving me a sleazy smile. Camille had gone into the living room, so thankfully she didn't notice.

I set my bag on the keyboard bench and began to pull out my music. "Yeah, my piano teacher told me to make it a light day."

"Then you can come with us to *Montmartre*," Camille said, emerging from the living room. "It's your last day to enjoy Paris before you leave on Thursday."

Camille had been nicer to me lately. Maybe she was capable of gratitude. Or maybe she was excited I was about to leave. Whatever the reason, I still didn't trust her.

I shrugged. "I think I'll stay here."

"Don't you want to take gifts to your friends and your mother? I know you've been too busy to buy them. Maybe you want to get a picture from an artist in the square." She looked over at Dane. "But we're going to *Sacré-Cœur* first."

I glanced at Eric. My brother had paid the price for my decision to cave to Camille's demands. Did he want me to come? One glance confirmed that he did. "Okay."

Eric's look of relief made me feel good about my decision.

We met Marine, Julien, and Thomas on the steps outside the church. From the look on his face, Thomas hadn't expected to see me.

"*Bonjour*, Thomas." I gave him a little wave.

"*Bonjour*, Sophie. How is the piano practice coming?"

"Good . . . Thomas, I'm sorry about lying to you about my fake boyfriend back home."

He shrugged. "I should have figured it out. Mathieu always got jumpy whenever I talked about you. I'm happy for you two."

"Thanks. I'd still like to be friends."

He grinned. "You're leaving in two days."

"But I'll be back," I said in my best Terminator voice.

He burst out laughing. "If you ever dump Mathieu, I hope you'll give me a chance."

I smiled, relieved he wasn't mad at me. "You're first on my list."

Thomas and Camille went into the church to see where to get tickets to climb to the top. I was trying to work up the nerve to join the group, hoping to avoid a repeat of Notre Dame. Marine, Julien, and Eric walked over to check out three men playing drums on the side of the church. I stayed at the top of the massive stairway that led to the front of the church. The building was built at the top of a hill, and the view of Paris was mesmerizing.

"I thought I'd be first on that list," Dane said in a low voice behind me.

He laughed when I jumped, and I tried to control the new rush of anxiety. I glanced around frantically. "It's okay. Eric's not around," he said, chuckling. "Jeez, he's like a guard dog with you."

I shot him my sternest glare. "Which is why you better get away from me if you don't want him to beat the crap out of you."

"You wouldn't let him hurt me, would you, Soph?"

I clenched my jaw. "Try me."

He leaned back and held out his hands. "Come on. I know you're only dating that French guy because I hooked up with Camille. But we'll be home in a few days, and I'll be all yours."

I shook my head in disgust. "Are you *kidding* me?"

"I know Eric is an issue, but we can sneak around like you did with Mathieu. I know a great place to park my truck after school. No one will have to know."

I gasped. "Wow. That offer is so tempting, but I think I'm gonna take a pass."

He leaned close to me, shooting me an ugly sneer. "You had two guys interested in you this summer, and you suddenly think all the guys are gonna fall all over you. It ain't gonna happen, Soph. Not at our school. I'll make sure of it."

"You think you can intimidate me into sleeping with you? You're disgusting." I started to walk away, but he grabbed my arm and pulled me back.

His eyes narrowed and his voice came out in a low growl. "I'm not done talking to you."

I was scared, but I wasn't about to back down. "Get your hand off me, *now*."

"Or what? What are you going to do, Sophie?"

I stomped my heel down on the inside of his ankle, letting my foot answer for me.

He dropped his hold on me and yelped.

"If you ever touch me again, I'll do a whole lot more than that. And I can't even imagine what Eric will do."

I turned to walk away, but he called after me. "You can play hard to get all you want, Sophie, but I know you want me."

I fought tears as I walked up the remaining steps, trying to get as much distance between us as possible. A few minutes later, Eric and the others had joined Camille and Thomas as they headed to the landing at the bottom of the church entrance. Eric was scanning the crowd for me.

I offered him a tight smile. I wanted to leave, but I decided to just stick close to my brother. Dane wouldn't be stupid enough to try anything with Eric around.

We had to go down to the basement to get tickets. I assured Eric multiple times I could climb the steps without freaking out. I was worried that if I stayed outside on the steps, Dane would want to stay with me, which offered plenty of motivation to face my fears.

There were a million and a half steps to the top, but I made it with only a few near panic attacks. The view from the dome was incredible, making me glad I had made the climb. I dug out my cell phone and took a selfie with the Eiffel Tower behind me. I sent it to Mathieu in a text with *missing you*.

We went shopping next, but I couldn't stop thinking about Dane and my dad. Dane for obvious reasons, and Dad because he had me totally confused. I was scheduled to audition tomorrow at noon, and I still didn't know if it was happening.

If Dad didn't let me audition, I wasn't sure I could ever forgive him.

CHAPTER *Thirty-Four*

BY THE TIME we got back to the apartment, I'd gotten souvenirs for everyone back home. Mathieu was waiting outside the building. I ran to him, squealing as I wrapped my arms around his neck. He swung me around, then set me down and kissed me. "I understand you went to *Sacré-Cœur*."

I grinned up at him. "*Oui*. I wish you had been with me."

"Me too." He gave me another kiss, slow and lingering.

"You're early," I said.

"I got off early to see you."

"And tomorrow?" Mathieu wanted to go with me to the audition. He was trying to get out of his community service for a few hours.

His smile fell. "I haven't gotten an answer yet."

"Okay."

"I'll take her," Eric said.

I glanced over at him, surprised he was still there. The others had gone upstairs, but Dane had given me a dirty look when he saw me in Mathieu's arms. "Nobody's going if Dad doesn't sign that paper."

Eric's eyes narrowed. "He better."

Dad and Eva came home soon after we did. Eva made pasta, and we all sat at the dining room table. Both of them were more subdued than usual, maybe because the full, boisterous family dinners were about to go back to only three people.

Halfway through the meal, Dad cleared his throat, looking nervous. "Sophie, I've given this some thought, and I have decided it *is* your decision, not mine. If you want to audition, I'll sign the paper."

"Really? Thank you!"

Mathieu grabbed my hand under the table and squeezed.

Dad scowled. "But we need to discuss some logistics."

"Okay."

"When you're accepted to the school, do you plan on living at the school or here? Because Eva and I would prefer for you to live here. You're comfortable riding the Metro now, right?"

"Yeah."

"Living here with us will save money, and I'll get to see you more."

"I'd like that."

Eva smiled.

"The *conservatoire* is expensive. We'll have to figure out how to pay for it. I'll need to talk to your mother about using part of your college fund."

"And I would like to help as well," Eva said.

"Not only do you want her to live *here*," Camille shouted, "but you want to help *pay for it*?" Then she began to curse a blue streak in French.

Eva lost her usual cool and shouted in French for her to stop being a baby.

I nearly gasped when I realized I understood her.

"Camille," Eva said in the harshest tone I'd ever heard her use. "That is enough. We would be thrilled to have Sophie live with us." Then she gave me a warm smile.

I was beginning to believe this could actually happen. I only hoped I'd get Eric's room if I got accepted.

Camille and Dane left the apartment soon after dinner, and Eva suggested that Mathieu and I go for a walk.

"Are you nervous?" Mathieu asked, holding my hand as we walked toward the Seine.

"Yes. No. I'm trying not to think about it. This audition could determine my entire future. I can't screw it up. I usually don't have bad nerves before competitions, but this is so much bigger than anything I've ever done."

"Don't think about it that way. Just go in there and pretend you are playing for me."

I smiled up at him. "That should be easy enough."

We walked down to the river, holding hands. When we were next to the water, Mathieu pulled me to his chest as he kissed me.

"Sophie," he whispered against my lips. "I love you."

My heart burst with happiness. "I love you too."

Je t'aime." He kissed me again. "I hope you don't mind me if I tell you in French more than English. It feels closer to my heart in French."

"Je t'aime," I repeated, not surprised that the French translation felt closer to my heart too.

♪

The next morning I spent more time than usual on my hair and makeup. I needed to leave for the audition at around 11:00 to make it to the school with twenty minutes to spare, which meant I had time to stop by Mathieu's apartment to practice. I wanted to run through everything a few more times to ease my nerves. Since Mathieu wasn't sure if he could go with me, Eric planned to meet me at Mathieu's apartment to take me to the audition.

As I gathered my music off the keyboard, I noticed Camille standing in the kitchen doorway, holding a cup of coffee. "Why are you doing this?"

"Practicing?" I asked, thumbing through the music for the fifth time to make sure I had everything.

"No. Ruining my life."

I rolled my eyes. "Drama much?"

"Go home, Sophie. Go home to where you belong and leave me and my life alone."

I stood up straight and spun around to face her. "I know you find this difficult to believe, but the entire world doesn't revolve around you. I'm sorry your dad died, but the fact is *my* dad married *your* mom. I'm part of this no matter where I live."

"I know you're doing this for *him*."

I shook my head. "You mean Mathieu?"

"It's your desperate attempt to stay with him."

I lifted my eyebrows. "If that's not the pot calling the kettle black . . . What about your desperate attempt to have Dane stay by blackmailing me?"

She had the good sense not to say anything.

My phone buzzed in my bag, and I pulled it out, breathing a sigh of relief when I saw the text from Mathieu.

I can leave early. I'll see you right at 11:00.

I texted back:

Yay! See you then!

"Tell Eric he doesn't have to take me." I stuffed the phone in my bag. "Mathieu's principal is letting him leave early, and he'll meet me right at eleven o'clock." Then I looked up at her stunned face. What was I thinking? "Never mind. I'll just text him myself."

I looked through my bag one more time. Music. My paperwork. I was already wearing a dress Eva had loaned me for the audition. It was a simple black cotton dress—sleeveless, with a scoop neck, cinched waist, and a full skirt. I looked professional and sophisticated, but not too old.

I headed for the door, and Camille called after me. "If you are set on doing this, then I wish you luck, Sophie." She gave me a smile so sweet it had to be fake.

"Thanks," I said as I let the door close behind me.

As usual, no one was home at Mathieu's apartment. I pulled out my music and set my alarm for 10:45 so I'd be ready to go when Mathieu showed up. Then I remembered I hadn't told Eric, so I sent him a quick text, to which he replied:

Camille already told me.

I was nervous. More nervous than I usually got before a competition, but there'd never been so much at stake. I shook out my hands and started with scales, my fingers playing by muscle memory before I went through my repertoire.

The alarm went off, and I packed up my music, then went to the bathroom. When I washed my hands, I checked my reflection in the mirror. My makeup and hair still looked good—I'd left my hair down, but pulled back at the sides. Miss Lori had suggested I do that so the judges could see my face.

I was ready.

The front door buzzer went off and I checked the time—10:55. Had Eric decided to come anyway? I pushed a button by the door. *"Allô?"* But no one answered.

About a minute later, I heard a knock at the door, and I cringed when I realized I must have pushed the door button instead of the call button. I hesitantly opened the front door, completely unprepared for the person I found standing there.

Dane.

"What are *you* doing here?" I demanded.

A smug smile spread across his face. "I wanted to wish you luck." He pushed past me and into the living room.

I gaped at him for a few seconds before coming to my senses. "Where's Camille? Shouldn't you be with her?"

He wandered around the room, looking at the furniture and the paintings on the wall. "No. I told her about us."

"*Us?* What are you talking about?"

He stopped and turned around, wearing a sly grin. "I told Camille that she and I are over. I told her I want to be with you."

I shook my head in disbelief. "Have you lost your mind? I thought I made it perfectly clear yesterday that there *is no* you and me. There never will be."

"Come on, Soph." He took several steps toward me and slid his hand down my bare arm. "It's okay. You don't have to hide it anymore."

I took a step backward. "Your timing absolutely sucks. You need to leave. *Now.*"

"Not yet." He turned and moved into the kitchen. "Nice apartment. Mathieu's parents must be loaded. How big is this place?" Then he headed down the hall.

My heart began to race. What was he doing? "Dane! Get back out here!"

He poked his head into the open bathroom door. "Not until I see Mathieu's room. I'm curious."

"Take your curiosity somewhere else." He was up to something, but darned if I knew what it was. I grabbed my phone and texted Eric.

> **Dane has shown up at Mathieu's apartment and won't leave. Help!**

Dane continued down the hall and stood in front of Etienne's room. "Is this it?"

"Dane, you have to leave."

He chuckled. "No, Mathieu's a lot of things, but gay's not one of them. And only someone batting for the other team would have posters of guys in Speedos on his bedroom walls." Then he moved on to the next room.

Mathieu's room.

My heart was racing. "Dane, please. My audition is in an hour. You have to leave!"

He gave me a leering wink. "You spend a lot of time in here, Soph?"

"What? No!"

I was close to tears as he barged through the door. Mathieu was going to show up at any minute.

He was *not* going to be happy to find Dane in his room.

Dane sat down on the neatly made bed and patted the spot next to him. "Come sit with me."

"No! Get out of this room!"

I heard the front door open and Mathieu call out, "Sophie? Are you ready?"

I gasped, panic flooding my head. How was I going to explain this? I started to turn around and run out to the living room, but Dane bolted off the bed and grabbed my wrist. I released a little yelp as he pulled me to his chest.

"Come on, Soph. I know you want me."

I pushed my free hand against his chest and tried to push him away, but he wrapped his arm around my back and pinned me against him, pressing his mouth to mine, wet and sloppy.

"Sophie?" I heard Camille's voice down the hall. "Are you here?"

What was *she* doing here? I heard the clack of heels moving quickly down the hall.

"*Oh, la vache!*" Camille shouted in the open doorway. "Sophie! Dane?"

I kicked Dane in the shin with my pointed shoe, and he finally dropped his hands. I stumbled back a couple of steps and spun around to see Mathieu in the doorway, his face ashen. Camille stood behind him, barely managing to contain her glee.

"Mathieu," I pleaded, my voice breaking. "He just showed up and—"

"You don't have to hide it, Soph." A lazy grin slid across Dane's face. "We should confess to Mathieu that we've been sleeping together in his bed. Every day."

I gasped in horror. What was he *doing*? "Mathieu! I swear it's not—"

But I didn't get to finish. Mathieu shot across the room, his fist flying into Dane's face.

"Mathieu!"

Dane came back swinging, his knuckles connecting with Mathieu's jaw.

"Stop!" I shouted, reaching for Mathieu and trying to pull him away from Dane.

Mathieu turned his fury on me. "I trusted you, Sophie!"

I shook my head, trying to wrap my head around what was going on. "I swear to you, Mathieu. He just showed up!"

His chest rose and fell as he struggled to catch his breath. He pointed to the door. "Get out."

I shook my head, starting to cry. "No. You have to listen to me! I haven't done anything wrong!"

"You're in my bedroom! With him! Is this why you really begged your father to let him stay in Paris?"

"It was too perfect," Dane said with a grin. "We could screw every day without worrying about anyone finding us." He tilted his head. "Sorry, Camille."

She released a gasp of outrage, but Mathieu didn't see the smile on her lips.

His eyes grew wild. "Get out!"

I cried harder, trying to catch my breath. "Mathieu, you have to believe me! I would never do that with him! Especially not in your room!"

"Then why is he in *here*, Sophie? How did he get in my *room*?"

"He just showed up!"

Disgust covered Mathieu's face. "He just showed up . . ." His jaw clenched. "I want my key back."

He didn't believe me. "What? No!"

He stomped out of the room and down the hall, then snatched my bag off the piano bench and started to dig through it.

"Mathieu! *Stop!* Don't do this, *please!*"

He pulled the silver key out of the side pocket where I kept it, then shoved the bag at me. "Get. Out."

I caught the bag before it hit the floor, but raw anger rose up inside me, pushing aside my hurt. How could he do this to us? How could he just throw me away like this? "I have never *once* given you reason to doubt or mistrust me."

He sucked in several breaths, trying to get control. "You've admitted to me multiple times that you liked him."

"*Liked.* Past tense. I've told you that part too."

But his eyes were filled with rage. He was never going to believe me, no matter how much I tried.

A sob broke loose. "Go ahead, Mathieu. Take the easy way out. You and I have never even done more than kiss, so why would I sleep with *him*?" I shuddered in disgust. "For some reason it's easier for you to believe that I would cheat on you with that jerk than to see what's really going on—Camille set us up. She wants to make sure I don't move to Paris, so she set this up to make sure that didn't happen." I turned to face her. She had followed us into the living room to see the fallout of her little arrangement. "Good job, Camille. I am *truly* impressed. You are far more devious than I ever gave you credit for."

She tried to look outraged, but acting was not her calling. "What? I'm just as much a victim here as poor Mathieu. You were with my boyfriend! You're my sister!"

"You really believe this?" I asked Mathieu, waving my hand toward Camille.

Camille turned to Mathieu. "I'm just as shocked as you are. We both saw them in your room."

The look in Mathieu's eyes made it perfectly clear he didn't believe me.

I'd never felt so betrayed. "I can't believe you would ever believe her over me. After everything."

He just stared at me.

"Last night you told me you loved me, Mathieu, but if you did, you'd fight for me. Fight for *us*." I spun around and ran out of the apartment. When I reached the sidewalk, I leaned over my legs and sobbed.

What in the world had just happened? How could we have gone from insanely happy and hopeful to completely over in less than five minutes? Especially over something so stupid.

What was I going to do? I had to go home. I had to find Eric.

I ran into him a block away. He took one look at me and his body tensed. "What did he do?"

I told him the whole, torrid story, the words getting harder to understand through my tears.

"I'm going to kill him," he growled.

"Which one?"

"Both of them."

"No. I just want to go home." But Dane and Camille would eventually go back there, and they were the very last people I ever wanted to see. I started to cry harder.

"What about the audition?"

How could I go through with it? "I don't think I can do it."

"Yes, you can. You *have* to do it, Soph."

I shook my head. "I can't! Look at me! I'm a mess."

"You were a mess when Dad left, and the piano was what got you through it. You can't give up now."

"This is different. I don't think I can."

"Sophie, listen to me." He grabbed my arms and looked into my eyes. "If you don't, Camille will win. You have to at least *try.*"

"Yeah." I nodded, wiping my face with the back of my hand. "You're right."

"I'm gonna try not to gloat over that statement." He gave me a grim smile. "You can do this."

We walked to the nearest Metro station and boarded the train. Many of the passengers gave me odd glances, but I tried my best to ignore them. Just like I tried to block out the memory of Mathieu's look of disgust and betrayal.

He hated me, and I hadn't even done anything to deserve it.

We arrived at the school ten minutes before my audition time. A young woman at the information desk gave me a horrified look and told me in French to go to the second floor.

Eric seemed surprised that I understood her, but he wisely decided not to ask any questions. I found the staircase and started up the stairs. He followed behind me.

I made a quick stop in the bathroom and confirmed my appearance warranted the funny looks I'd gotten. My mascara was smeared and most of my makeup had been cried off. My nose was red and my eyes were swollen. Touching up my face was hopeless, so I scrubbed it clean.

I was going into this audition emotionally naked. No amount of makeup would change that, so I might as well not try to hide what I was feeling.

When I got to the waiting room, Eric was pacing. His eyes were wide with worry. "Are you ready?"

I stopped in front of him, tears burning my eyes again. "Why am I here?"

"You tell me, Sophie," he said gently. "Why *are* you here?"

"Eric . . . I'm too exhausted to play mind games. Our stepsister's got the market cornered on that."

His voice softened. "When you first told me about the audition, you weren't even with Mathieu. You told me you weren't doing it for him. Has that changed?"

"I don't know. Maybe." I ran my hand over my hair. "I'd be lying if I said that staying in Paris so I could be with him wasn't a huge motivation."

"And staying with Dad too?"

I shrugged. "Maybe."

"But before all that, you were doing it for *you.*"

I nodded. "Yeah."

"Then do this for *you*, Sophie. Show them that you're better than any of them. And as soon as you're done, we're going to Eva's bank to tell her everything. She has a right to know."

I nodded. "Yeah. Okay."

A door opened, and a woman stood in the opening. "Sophie Brooks."

I sucked in a deep breath, terror washing through my body and making my arms numb. "I'm not ready."

Eric pulled my bag from over my head and opened the flap. "Yes, you are." He pulled out the music and handed it to me.

I took a deep breath and pulled back my shoulders. I could do this.

"Who cares if you get into this snobby school?" Eric whispered. "Do this for you. Play for *you.*"

He was right. Mathieu had told me to pretend I was playing for him, but I needed to play for *me*. No pretending needed.

I followed the woman into a room with a grand piano in the center. Two men and three women—one of whom was Mathieu's mother—sat at a long table. Their expressions were uniformly serious. If I'd walked in here with any hope of getting into the school, I would have been worried. But this audition was hopeless. My nerves were too shot. I was too unfocused. At this point, I was only here so I could one day tell my grandkids that Grandma had auditioned for the *Conservatoire de Seine*.

I stopped in front of them and took a breath. *"Bonjour.* I am Sophie Brooks, and I am from Charleston, South Carolina. I will be playing Chopin Etude Op. 25 No. 2, Mozart Sonata K.332, and finishing with Rachmaninoff Prelude in B Minor Op. 32 No. 10."

One of the men nodded. "You may begin."

Now I wished that I'd spent less time crying and more time limbering my fingers, but it couldn't be helped. I shuffled the sheets of music to the sonata, my second song, and set it on the stand. The first piece was short. I would play it from memory.

The Chopin etude started off fast and furious. It was barely over a minute long, but it was a minute packed with triplets played extremely fast. In fact, the piece was aptly nicknamed "the bees." I worried my fingers would stumble, but they flew across the keys, fueled by the anxiety of the morning, until the piece slowed down during the last few measures.

Next came the Mozart sonata. There was no real story to latch onto it. Mozart wrote K.332 in Vienna while on his way to Salzburg to introduce his new wife to his father. I imagined the lighter, more playful notes to be Mozart flaunting propriety. Constance had been known to spend the night at Mozart's apartment, and Mozart had been forced to marry her to save her reputation. Before today's disaster, I'd imagined the piece might be about Mathieu and me—our multiple false starts. My sadness leeched into the third movement, adding a haunting tone that didn't belong with the whimsically written notes.

And finally, I finished with my familiar Rachmaninoff. I'd played it so many times, I should have been sick of it—yet each time it dragged a new interpretation from my soul. Today, the haunting notes forced me to confront my sorrow over Mathieu's accusations and the realization that we were probably done. The section about two minutes after the opening was like a brewing storm, and it allowed me to express my own feelings of betrayal, anger, and pain. My fingers and the keys were a direct extension of my soul, laying me bare to the five judges at that table, Mathieu's mother included.

It was only when I finished that I realized tears were streaming down my face. I knew I was really done. There was no way they'd pick some emotional girl whose neck and dress were soaked with tears.

I gathered my music and stood. *"Je vous remercie de m'avoir invitée à venir auditionner aujourd'hui."*

The night before, I'd asked Mathieu to teach me how to thank the panel for giving me the opportunity to audition in French. Today my voice broke at the end.

It would be the last thing he'd ever teach me in French.

I bolted from the room.

Eric was sitting in the waiting area. His gaze lifted to me, worry filling his eyes when he saw my tears, and he jumped to his feet. "How did you do?"

"I don't know. I didn't play part of the sonata as it was meant to be played and I cried through the last piece, which I'm sure didn't come across well. Technically, I think it was perfect, but it has to be at this level." I wiped my face. "I did the best I could. It's up to them."

"I heard you play, Sophie. You were really good. Leave it to you to spend one summer in Paris and get even better on the piano."

"Yeah." It was definitely bittersweet.

I texted Dad and then Mom to tell them the audition had gone well, then Eric and I took the Metro to the *Opéra* station, which was close to Eva's bank. Eric was determined to get to her before her daughter did.

Eva was excited to hear we'd come to visit her, but the looks on our faces quickly dampened her mood. Eric asked if she had time for a quick lunch, and before we knew it, she was ushering us out the door. We spent the next half hour telling her everything Camille had done over the course of the summer. I even told her about Mathieu finding Camille and Hugo in Camille's bed.

Eva was horrified and apologized profusely. "I would hate for either of you to resent me for Camille's behavior."

"No," I assured you. "You are totally different than she is."

"Camille hasn't been the same since her father's death and then my fast engagement to your father . . . I saw she wasn't handling it well, but I chose to think she would get over it." Her eyes were glassy. "Not only is she not over it, but she's much worse than I thought. She won't get away with this. I promise."

If Camille thought she'd gained another victory this morning, I'd just claimed the war. I took small pleasure from the fact that she was about to be blindsided by her mother that evening.

Dane had the good sense to spend most of the evening alone in his room, especially after my father came home and threatened him with bodily harm if he ever came near me again. He had also assured Dane that he was going to call his parents and fill them in on his behavior in Paris.

The next morning, I woke up early, my stomach in knots. Mathieu hadn't called or texted, which meant we really were done. I understood his reaction, especially after everything that had happened with Camille, but his lack of faith in me was devastating.

Still, I couldn't leave it like this. I was leaving in a matter of hours. I had to see him.

I left a note on the kitchen table that said I'd be back in twenty minutes and raced out the door so I could catch Mathieu before he left for his community service work.

Etienne buzzed me up and stood in the doorway, blocking my view of the living room. "Is Mathieu here?"

He glanced over his shoulder before looking back at me and shaking his head. "I'm sorry, Sophie. He doesn't want to see you."

My throat burned, but I forced myself to nod. "Then will you take a message?" I asked, my voice breaking. I kept my gaze on the spot over Etienne's shoulder. I suspected Mathieu was behind the door, listening.

"*Oui.*" He looked over his shoulder again.

"Tell Mathieu this has been the most amazing summer I've ever had. I wouldn't change a thing. Our time together was worth everything, even the pain and misery." I swallowed. "And would you tell him I love him?" I choked back a sob. "Tell him I would never hurt or betray him, and it breaks my heart that he thinks I would."

I fell silent, hoping he'd heard it all and would come out so I could hug him one last time. Feel his lips on mine one last time. At least say a proper good-bye.

I leaned my forearm against the doorframe, then rested my forehead on my arm, trying not to sob.

"Sophie?" Etienne asked. "Are you okay?"

I shook my head and straightened up, my tears flowing openly now. "I can't believe it's ending this way."

"I'm sorry," he murmured.

I took a deep breath, then raised my voice. "So I guess this is good-bye, Mathieu. But if you thought I was capable of this, then it's better that it's over, because you never really knew me at all."

Then I turned and headed for the stairs, and Etienne broke out into rapid, angry French, calling Mathieu's name. I descended the steps, hoping Etienne would get through to his brother, hoping Mathieu loved me enough to come after me. I was almost to the bottom when I heard footsteps tromping after me, racing down the stairs. I slowed down, waiting for Mathieu to catch up. Wondering what I'd say.

But it was Etienne's face that appeared.

I pushed out a sigh of anguish.

"Sophie, I'm sorry."

The tears started flowing again. "He still blames me?"

"He's confused, but I told him he doesn't have time to be confused."

"Thanks for trying."

He scowled. "He may be my brother, but he's a fool."

I didn't answer. My heart was too broken. I had hoped he'd realize the truth after having a night to think things over. But he still believed the worst of me.

I went back home and finished packing. Dad hired a car, and Eva rode with all of us to the airport. Camille stayed behind, packing her own bag. Eva had taken a leave from work. She was taking Camille to a family country house in Provence while she made arrangements to assess Camille's behavior. It was obvious she had deeper issues than Eva could address on her own.

No one talked to Dane while we checked in, and he had the good sense to look embarrassed. We walked to security, where

Dad and Eva said good-bye and assured us we could come back for Thanksgiving. Dad had tried to talk about the logistics of me moving to Paris if I was accepted to the conservatoire, but I refused to discuss it. I didn't see the point. There was no way I would get in.

Two hours later I was strapped into an airline seat next to Eric, waiting for the plane to take off. I was thankful Dane was ten rows behind us. I stared at the cell phone Eva had given me, willing Mathieu to call or text me. I decided to try one last time, so I sent him a text.

Je t'aime, Mathieu.

I waited for a minute, fighting new tears. How could he just throw us away?

The airline attendant's voice sounded overhead, announcing it was time to turn off cell phones. I started to cry harder.

"He's an idiot," Eric said softly. "He doesn't deserve another chance with you, Sophie."

In the end, did it matter? I still had a broken heart. Then I realized I had to stop hanging on, no matter how much it hurt. I had to let him go.

So I typed a final message and sent it. Then I turned off the phone and sobbed into Eric's shoulder.

All I knew was that I'd lost Mathieu forever. My text said it all.

Au revoir, mon coeur.

Good-bye, my heart.

CHAPTER *Thirty-Five*

"SOPHIE, YOU HAVE to go to Paris," Jenna said as we walked out to the student parking lot after school.

I pulled my sweater tighter around me. November in Charleston didn't get that cold, but the wind had a bite today. "I'm having déjà vu."

"You protested last time and you went anyway."

"Last time I was forced. This time I have a choice."

I unlocked my car and slid behind the wheel while Jenna got into the passenger seat. Her parents still hadn't replaced her car after her accident. They only let her ride with me because I never drove over the speed limit and I'd never gotten a ticket.

I started the engine and put my hand on the gear shift, but Jenna put her hand over mine. "Sophie, stop."

I sank back in the seat. "What?" Of course, I already knew what she was going to say.

"It was bad enough that you turned down the offer from that school in Paris. But you can't shut your dad out again. And what about Eva?"

I shook my head. "Camille will be there. I can't face her."

"I thought she sent you a letter apologizing."

Camille had been seeing a therapist since I'd left. Part of her therapy was to apologize to the people she had wronged. While her letter seemed genuine, I still had a hard time believing her. "She did, but you know she probably only did it because she had to."

"So you're never going to visit your dad again?"

I didn't answer, watching the other students drive out of the parking lot.

"You ended up loving Paris."

I did, but I wasn't ready to go back. The thought of being there hurt too much. But I'd go back eventually. The fact that I'd rearranged my schedule to take French this year was proof of that.

"Do you ever wish you hadn't turned it down?"

"The school?" I asked. I considered lying, but why hide it from her? Besides, she'd see right through it. "Yes. Every day."

"Sophie!"

I shook my head. "It doesn't matter. It's too late. Besides, I won the piano competition last month. Now I have a ten thousand dollar scholarship to apply to a more practical school."

Jenna held her hands out palms up, then lifted and lowered them as if they were a scale. "State school. Parisian school. I wonder which I should choose."

I shoved her arm. "Stop. I told you, it's too late."

"But what if it's not?" When I didn't say anything, she continued. "I love you, Sophie, and I will most likely die without you—like literally wither up and die—but you need to go to that school. Even Miss Lori says you've outgrown her."

"It's too late, Jen."

She turned in her seat to face me. "What if it's not? Email the dean or whoever, and ask them to reconsider."

"I don't know . . ."

"It can't hurt to try. But you need to go see your dad. Regardless."

"But Eric can't go. He's got some basketball thing." He'd changed since we'd come home. We both had. We were closer than we'd ever been. He'd cut Dane off as a friend, and since Dane was more popular, my brother had suffered socially. I felt partially responsible for that, but he assured me he wouldn't change a thing.

Jenna was like a dog with a chew toy. She wasn't about to let this go. "Then go by yourself."

Last June, I would have freaked out at the thought. But I wasn't that girl anymore. I gave Jenna a smile. "I think you're right. About all of it."

♪

Three weeks later, my plane landed at Charles de Gaulle airport, and I couldn't help comparing this flight to the one that had first brought me there. I was a different person.

Dad was busy with a project at work, and he'd offered to get a car to take me to the apartment. I only had a carry-on bag, so I told him I could take the Metro. Once I made it past security, I pulled out the phone Eva had given me and turned it on. It was set up for France, so it had been worthless in Charleston. But I'd promised Dad I would text him from the airport. I sent the text as soon as the screen lit up and then bought several Metro tickets with euros Eric had left over from the summer.

I stuffed my phone into my pocket and concentrated on the signs telling me where to go. A train was pulling up as I reached the platform. I rushed through the doors, rolling my suitcase behind me, and found a seat, proud of myself for making it this far. This was a far cry from the girl who'd gotten lost on the subway a few months ago.

I pulled my phone out of my pocket to see if Dad had texted back, and I gasped when the screen said I had twenty-seven messages.

How could Dad have sent me twenty-seven messages in less than five minutes?

I opened the app and saw the last message received was from Dad, telling me to take the Metro to *Cité*, next to *Sainte-Chapelle*, then text him when I got off so we could eat lunch together.

But the twenty-six previous messages were from Mathieu.

The last message was on top.

Au revoir, mon coeur.

It was dated at the end of September.

He'd told me good-bye.

With shaking fingers, I scrolled back to the first of the messages.

He'd sent it an hour after receiving my good-bye text.

Camille came to the school this morning
and confessed. She convinced Dane to
come to my apartment so I would find you
two together. She hoped to destroy you and
me and make you so upset you would miss
your audition. She says she feels terrible
for what she did, although I'm not sure
I believe her. I think she's more worried
about Eva.

The next message was minutes later.

Sophie, I am so sorry. I hurt you so badly,
and I'm sure you can never forgive me, but
I'm begging you to forgive me anyway.

The next message was four hours later.

I know you are probably still on the plane,
so that's why you haven't answered. Je
t'aime, Sophie. I hate that you left this way.

I started crying.

The next message was two hours after the last.

> Sophie, I don't deserve you now. I know that. But I'm begging you to at least answer so maybe we can talk about it.

His next text was a couple of hours later.

> Maman says you auditioned and that the judges were in awe of your performance. The night of your audition Maman asked me why you were upset, but I refused to tell her. After Camille talked to me, she found Maman and told her what happened and asked her to give you a new audition. Maman says she is amazed you could play so well.

> I know I have no right, but I'm proud of you, Sophie. I am so sorry that I didn't listen to you. I am sorry I sent you to your audition so upset.

Then minutes later—

> I love you, Sophie, and I am begging you to forgive me. I am begging you to give us another chance.

I was sobbing now. He hadn't thrown us away. He'd only given up after months without any word from me.

The next message was a week later.

> I miss you so much it hurts. Please text me back. PLEASE.

Then for the next week, he sent me one-sentence texts every night around the same time—based on the time stamp, probably when he went to bed.

> I miss your laugh.
> I miss your smile.
> I miss holding your hand.
> I miss seeing the passion on your face when you play the piano.
> I miss teaching you French.
> I miss your kiss.

I cried even more.
He didn't text for several days.

> Maman told me you got into her program. I am so proud of you. I know you never want to see me again, but please don't let that stop you from accepting.

Then a week later—the very end of August.

> Maman told me you have declined your position. My heart hurts that I did this to you. I can never forgive myself.

He began to send me a few random texts in the beginning of September.

> There's another piano concert at Sainte-Chapelle, and it reminded me of our date.
> Je t'aime, mon coeur, even still.

And—

> I lay awake at night wondering how you
> are doing and if you are okay. That is the
> hardest part . . . wondering if you are okay.

There were several more texts similar to the others, then in the middle of September he sent another message.

> Today marks the two-month anniversary
> of the first night I kissed you. We've been
> apart longer than we were together. So why
> does it still hurt so much?

A week later he sent a string of texts.

> I must accept that you have given up on us.
> I know my life will be filled with many
> regrets, but you will always be the biggest
> one of all. But I will finally let you go.
> Au revoir, mon coeur.

The train came to a stop at the station before *Châtelet*, and the older woman next to me gave me several napkins and stroked my cheek. She spoke to me softly in French, and I was startled to realize I understood her. "An affair of the heart?"

"*Oui.*" I nodded.

She said something else, and though the intricacies of the translation were beyond me, I thought it roughly translated to *nothing is impossible with the heart.*

I wiped my cheeks. "*Merci.*"

I only wished it was true.

I transferred trains without getting lost and got off at *Cité*, then texted my father to let him know I was there.

I stood on the corner across the street, and he came out to meet me. He pulled me into a bear hug and then leaned back to study my face. "Did you have any trouble getting here from the airport?"

"No." I gave him a soft smile. "I'm a pro at the Metro now."

"You look tired. Would you rather go home?"

"No. I really want to eat lunch with you."

He took my small suitcase, and we found a nearby café. I ordered a *croque-monsieur*, just like I had on my first day in Paris.

"How's your brother?" he asked.

"Good. He really wanted to come."

He nodded. "I understand. I'm hoping to fly back to see one of his basketball games."

"He would like that." I took a breath. "I'm not going to lie, Dad. I know Camille has supposedly seen the errors of her ways, but I don't trust her. I'm nervous about seeing her."

"We understand. Eva and I considered sending her to Eva's brother's for the weekend, and Camille agreed to go." He put both hands around his glass of water. "She seems sincere. I think the therapy sessions have made a difference. She voluntarily told Mathieu and his mother what happened. Eva also called Madeline and apologized profusely." He was quiet for a moment. "Eva feels responsible. She's still willing to send Camille away for the weekend, and she offered to go with her. Whatever makes you feel most comfortable, Sophie."

"No," I said softly. "I love Eva. I want her to stay. And I don't want to send Camille away from her home."

"Look." He dropped his hold on his glass and sat back, looking into my eyes. "I've made a lot of mistakes, Sophie. I've spent most of my life running from problems and conflict, but I've lost the things that were most important to me along the way—I want to fix that. I want to fix *us*."

"I'd like that." I took a deep breath, nervous about bringing up my next topic. "Would it be okay if I moved to Paris during Winter Break?"

He blinked. "With me?"

I nodded. "Yes. I emailed Madame Rousseau and asked her if there was any way I could start school for the spring semester. She told me yes."

He shook his head in disbelief. "I thought you didn't want to go to school there. You turned it down."

"I was too upset to change my entire life that soon after what happened with Camille and Mathieu. But I'm ready now. I'm ready for the challenge, and I want to spend more time with you."

"But your mother . . ."

"She gave me her blessing."

He stared at me for several seconds before his face broke into a huge smile. "I would love for you to move to Paris. As long as you're sure this is what you want."

"And you're okay with me going to the *conservatoire?*"

"I want you to be happy and follow your heart. Besides, Madeline told Eva and me how talented you are. She was disappointed you turned down the position." Happiness filled his eyes. "I'm glad you changed your mind. For *your* benefit *and* mine."

I leaned across the table and gave him a hug, laughing when the table got in the way.

"Have you talked to Mathieu?" Dad asked.

I looked down at my plate, my smile fading. "No."

"He says he tried to contact you multiple times, but you never responded."

Tears filled my eyes. "He texted the phone Eva gave me. It didn't work in the States. I never saw any of his messages until I turned on my phone and read them all on the train."

"Eva said he was heartbroken, but he made us swear not to try to sway you one way or another."

I nodded. "I understand." And I did, but if they'd only told me, maybe . . .

"Eva says she thinks he's finally moved past it. He got the internship at her bank next summer."

He's moved past it. I supposed people could say the same about me. Outwardly, I'd moved past it, but inside I was still dying. "That's great. It's what he really wanted."

"He told Eva about his probation at the school."

My eyes widened in surprise. "And they still gave him the internship?"

He smiled softly. "If she gave her own daughter a chance at rehabilitation, then she figures she can do the same with her other daughter's boyfriend."

I blushed. "Ex-boyfriend."

He didn't answer.

The food arrived at our table, and I told Dad how Jenna was doing. "She's sad that I'm coming to Paris, but she understands. She says she's going to look into becoming a foreign exchange student next year. Do you think we could be her host family?"

"Our luck with our kids' friends staying with us hasn't turned out so well." My heart began to sink, but then he grinned. "Good thing I know Jenna so well. We'd love to have her. Eva too."

"Thanks, Dad."

We finished lunch, and I told him I had to go by the *conservatoire* for a meeting with Mathieu's mother.

"Do you think you're up to it?"

"Because of my jet lag or because she's Mathieu's mother?"

"Both."

I gave him a sad smile. "The first isn't too bad, and the second I'll have to learn how to handle. She's the instructor of the music program. I'll see her fairly often."

"I'm just worried about you, Soph. You're my little girl, no matter how mature you are."

I kissed his cheek. "Thanks, Dad. This will probably take a few hours. Would you like to ride the Metro home together?"

His face lit up. "But I have to work until six. Can you wait that long?"

"Just text me when you're done."

I left my suitcase with him, then walked the few blocks to the Latin Quarter.

I spent several hours at the school. Madame Rousseau was kind and polite, and I was proud of myself for not asking her questions about her son.

I filled out paperwork and shadowed a music theory class. My guide brought me back to Madame Rousseau's office when my class was done. She got up from her desk. "We are eager for you to join our program, Sophie. I'm happy you changed your mind."

I swallowed, then asked, "Does Mathieu know?"

Sadness filled her eyes and she shook her head. "*Non.*"

I nodded, trying to swallow the burning lump in my throat.

"Mathieu was very distraught for several months. I thought it best not to upset him again."

"I understand." But my heart ached. The pain had started the moment I'd gotten off the plane—*before* I'd received his messages. Maybe moving here wasn't such a good idea after all.

But I knew it was. I'd just channel my heartache into my music. It was something I had learned to do all too well.

"What are your plans now, Sophie?"

I looked at the time, surprised it was close to five. "I'm meeting my dad around six to ride the Metro home with him. So I think I'll wander around Notre Dame."

She nodded. "*Très bien.* Have a good weekend with your father, and we'll see you in January."

"*Merci*."

Before I left the building, I texted Dad that I was done and not to worry about me waiting on him. I'd just tour Notre Dame.

Maybe I'd actually be brave enough to go up to the top this time.

I knew Mathieu's school was close, and I considered stopping by, especially since his dismissal time was around five. But instead, I pulled out my phone and checked my messages. The sight of his texts broke my heart all over again.

Had he moved on? Would I hurt him if I texted him? I decided to go with my gut.

> I never gave up on us. I've never stopped
> loving you.

I sent it before I could change my mind.

My stomach felt like it was in my throat as I walked out the door of the *conservatoire*. Would he text me back? I was so focused on my phone, I was startled when I heard a familiar voice call out, "Sophie."

Camille stood at the bottom of the steps with an anxious look. She was wearing her school uniform—black skirt and tights, paired with a black V-neck sweater with a logo on her left chest, and a white blouse and striped tie underneath. Her black hair was longer and hung in loose waves around her face.

I sucked in a breath and stopped in my tracks, unprepared to face her.

She saw my hesitation and seemed to shrink into herself. "I wanted to see you before we went home."

"You mean *your* apartment." The words were out of my mouth before I could stop them.

Her lips pressed together and she looked apologetic. "It's yours now too."

Camille was the one part of returning to Paris that worried me the most. Now I was second-guessing this decision.

She took a step toward me. "I wanted to tell you how sorry I am about what I did." She took a breath. "After my father died . . ." She paused. "I did some things I shouldn't before *Maman* started seeing your father, but I always knew she would love me anyway. It was only the two of us. Then you showed up . . ." Her eyes turned glassy. "You were nice and pretty and everything I thought *Maman* wanted in a daughter, and I knew she would love you." A fierceness filled her eyes. "So I had to make you leave before she loved you more."

I took a cautious step toward her. "That's crazy, Camille. Eva loves you and she would never replace you with *anyone*."

"I know that now." She paused again. "And I know I was terrible to you. I've spoken with *Maman*, and when you move here for the *conservatoire*, I will live with my uncle."

"What?" I asked, shocked. "No! I would never make you move away from Eva. If you really don't want to live with me, I'll see about moving into the school dorm." It would add to the expense, but I'd never chase Camille from her home. No matter how horrible she'd been.

She shook her head, a tear trailing down her cheek. "*Non*. You misunderstand. I would move to make you happy."

"Oh." That surprised me. I wondered if Eva had forced her to make this offer, but the look in her eyes convinced me that wasn't true. "No, I think we can live in the same apartment as long as you don't try to sabotage me anymore."

She shook her head. "*Non*. I will be on my best behavior."

I had doubts about that, but at least she planned to try. "Okay, then it's settled. But I want my own room. Whichever one you don't want."

She studied me for a moment, then stuck out her hand. "Deal." The corners of her mouth tipped up into a small grin.

I shook her hand.

Her smile spread as she dropped my clasp. "I always wanted a little sister. Or a dog." She laughed, but it wasn't malicious. "*Maman* said no to both."

I laughed too. "We'll start with trying to be friends first."

"Good idea." She glanced behind her before turning back to me. "I really am sorry. About everything."

"Thanks." I wasn't ready to be BFFs with her, but it was a start.

"I'll see you at home." She headed toward the Latin Quarter shopping area and, still in shock, I watched her until she turned a corner.

Then I remembered Mathieu and looked at my phone. Nothing.

I started to walk toward the cathedral, holding my phone in my hand and telling myself that the fact he hadn't responded didn't mean anything. Maybe he was in class. But Camille's appearance squelched that theory. I kept staring at the screen as I walked, willing him to text me back, but he still hadn't answered after ten minutes. I reminded myself that Mathieu had waited for a response from me for months. Ten minutes was nothing.

The square was crowded, but not as much as it had been during the summer. I got in line to enter the sanctuary and noticed the bronze star on the ground to my left.

I stepped out of line and moved toward it. This time there were only a few curious onlookers, but they quickly moved on. I took a deep breath and stood on the star, wondering what I should wish for this time. I could go with the obvious and wish for Mathieu, but perhaps it was time to do something selfless. According to his mother, he'd been devastated for months. If my silent phone was any indication, Mathieu Rousseau was done with me and I needed to respect that.

I closed my eyes and wished for Mathieu to be happy.

"Sophie?"

It sounded so much like his voice, I was sure I was hallucinating.

My eyes flew open, and he was standing in front of me. He was just as handsome as I remembered him. His school uniform was nearly identical to Camille's except for the black pants. His dark hair was a little shorter but was just as unruly. His clear blue eyes were full of tears.

"I wasn't ignoring you," I gushed out. "My phone didn't work in the States. I never got any of your messages. I didn't even know you texted me until I got on the Metro this morning. I'm so sorry." My voice broke.

He looked guarded. "I saw your message about twenty minutes ago. I never thought I would see you again after I treated you so badly. Can you find a way to forgive me?"

I nodded, tears streaming down my face. "I already have."

He looked worried. "Why are you crying?"

"I was scared I'd lost you forever." My chin quivered. "I'm scared I'm too late."

He shook his head and a soft smile lifted his mouth. "*Non, mon coeur.* You're just in time."

I threw myself at him, wrapping my arms around his neck, pressing my mouth to his. His arm slipped around my back and pulled me tight against him. Being in his arms was like being home. Mathieu Rousseau was where I belonged.

When he lifted his head, he grabbed my cheeks and searched my face as if he was committing me to memory. "Why are you here? Are you visiting your father?"

"*Oui.* I'm here for a short visit, then I'm moving here at the end of December. I'm going to school at the *conservatoire* here in Paris."

His eyes widened. "But *Maman* said you turned down the position."

"I changed my mind. She's admitting me to the spring semester." *

"I can't believe you are really here." He kissed me again, holding me close as though he was worried I'd disappear.

I grinned against his lips. "I'm here."

Burying my face into his chest, I tightened my hold around his neck and clung to him for several seconds before I realized how unlikely this meeting was. I looked up at him and asked in amazement, "How did you know where to find me?"

He held my gaze. "Camille."

"What?"

"I got your text, then five minutes later she called and told me you were in Paris."

"But how did you find me *here*?"

"Your father sent me a text seconds later telling me to look for you at Notre Dame. I thought it would be more difficult to find you. It was fate."

Dad got involved? I couldn't believe it.

My smile fell. "I don't think your mother wants us back together. She's worried I'll hurt you."

"My mother wants me to be happy, and you make me happy."

"That was my wish." I nodded toward the star. "The first time I was here—right before I got lost in the Metro—I wished for a boyfriend. And I got you." I looked deep into his cerulean blue eyes. "But this time I wished for something different. I just wished for you to be happy. I didn't want you to be sad anymore."

He gave me a shy smile. "And I've been here at the star at least once a week to wish you would come back to me." He cupped my cheek, his face shining with happiness. "And now you have."

He pulled me onto the star and kissed me until my knees were weak and my head was fuzzy. When he lifted his head, he smiled down at me, his eyes full of adoration. *"Je t'aime, mon amour."*

"*Je t'aime, Mathieu. Mon coeur.*" He was right. It meant so much more in French. I swiped a tear from my face.

He slid his backpack down his arm and unzipped it, then pulled out a napkin and handed it to me.

I took it and laughed, wiping my face. "I think this is how we started. Outside the restaurant."

He dug his phone out of his pants pocket and looked at the screen. "And this is a text from Camille, just like last time."

My smile fell. "She's calling you away?"

"*Non.*" He shoved the phone back in his pants pocket. "She's making sure I'm not fool enough to let you go again."

I laughed and grabbed his sweater, pulling his lips to mine and showing him how much I missed him.

"I don't remember that happening the first time," he teased.

"That's because this has a different ending."

His playfulness fell away. "*Non, mon coeur.* No more endings. Only beginnings."

I liked the sound of that.

BLINK

Want FREE books?
FIRST LOOKS at the best new fiction?
Awesome EXCLUSIVE merchandise?

We want to hear from YOU!

Give us your opinion on titles, covers, and stories.
Join the Blink Street Team today.

Visit http://blinkyabooks.com/street-team to sign up today!

Connect with us

 /BlinkYABooks   /BlinkYABooks

 /BlinkYABooks   BlinkYABooks.tumblr.com

YOUR NEXT READ IS A BLINK AWAY